THE MAN I CAN'T HAVE

SHANORA WILLIAMS

D1715677

THE
MAN
I CAN'T
HAVE

Ward Duet Book One

NEW YORK TIMES & USA BESTSELLING AUTHOR

SHANORA
WILLIAMS

PROLOGUE

MARCEL

8 YEARS AGO - CHARLESTON, SOUTH CAROLINA

IF MY MOTHER could see me now, I'm certain she'd pick up the nearest object and smack me on the back of the head with it.

Granted, the nearest object is the cold bottle of beer clutched in my hand, but sure enough, she'd have grabbed it and hit me with it, just to knock some sense into me.

She'd raised me to be better than this. I wasn't supposed to grow up and become a twenty-seven-year-old drunk, sitting on a busted-up bar stool in a dive bar named Lionel's, especially when it was well after midnight.

Unfortunately, this day called for it. My rent is late. Bills are piling up, and not one motherfucker in town will hire me since the little scandal I had with my boss's wife.

1

Hell, it isn't my fault she wanted me; I didn't even know she was married. She wasn't wearing a ring the night I met her. I was at a party at my boss's house—well, mansion, really. She came onto me, and Mr. Powell caught us in his office with *her* hand on *my* crotch.

Mr. Powell is a highly respected man—the most well-known business contractor in our state. I'm sure he's told the businessmen of Charleston to never hire a son-of-a-bitch like me.

Most of the jobs I've applied for are in construction, electrical, or mechanical. All I'm good for is my hands, really. I'm great at fixing shit, yet no one around here who has a great business (and a wife) wants to hire me. *Figures.*

I can't forget to mention that taking care of Shayla, my sister, is stressful as hell. Twenty-one years old and able to buy her own bottle of liquor, she thinks she has life all figured out. She has no idea how hard life is, considering I've piggy-backed her every step of the way.

Too bad Momma isn't here anymore. Maybe I need her to hit me upside the head with something so I can stop pouting like a whiny little bitch and get a move on. I can hear her voice now, *"You got time to mope at this bar, but no time to search for jobs?"* I'd shrug, and she'd smack me on the head or arm with a firm hand and a deep, intimidating frown. I'd frown right back, but she wouldn't give a damn. She'd give me a lecture about how I was destined to live a good life—that she named me *Marcellus Leo Ward* for a reason. To her, my name was powerful. It was a name that no man could ignore, because it was strong, and most men in this world—especially ones who want a successful business—hire men with solid names. Lately, that has proven to be untrue.

2

With a sigh, I finish off my beer and then lean forward on one elbow, pulling the slim wallet out of my back pocket. I slam a soggy five-dollar bill on the counter and focus on Lionel who is behind the counter, cleaning beer glasses. "Give me one more."

"You sho? This'll be yo' third one tonight, ain't it?" he asks. His accent is so thick that when I first met him, I had no idea what the hell he was saying. After many nights of coming here, though, I can comprehend most of what he says. You can definitely tell he's from Summerville, South Carolina. Same place I was born. We connected because of that—being born in the same city.

"I'm positive." Lionel gives me a sideways glance, like he knows I need to just take my ass home already, but I wave a hand, silently encouraging him to hurry up before I put the five he could use back in my pocket.

He uncaps my beer, slides it across the counter in my direction, and I push the five his way, putting on a smug smile.

"Know it ain't my business or anything," Lionel goes on, drying a glass with a towel, "but what you sittin' 'round here down in the pits fo'? Bringin' the whole mood down around this place."

"Been lookin' for jobs," I mutter after taking a swig of beer. "No one in Charleston will hire me. Don't have much experience. Had a good job but got fired over some bullshit. I'm in need of a *big* job. Something great."

"Big job? What you mean by that?"

"Somethin' stable that comes with health insurance or at least dental, you know? Need it for me and Shayla."

"Ah." Lionel's eyes get bigger. "I see. Why don't you just make yo' own?"

"My own business?" I scoff. "Yeah…I wouldn't even know where to start."

Lionel chuckles. "I can see you gettin' away with something like dat."

I look sideways at the small TV in the upper right corner where a basketball game is playing.

"Tell you what? I would hire ya, but my numba' one rule is to never let a man who loves drinkin' work at my bar."

I smirk. "Good rule. Better that I don't work around all this alcohol anyway."

Lionel laughs again, walking off to help someone at the end of the bar. I take a chug of beer, about to lean back in my chair and think about where the hell else to apply, but my cell phone vibrates in my pocket.

"Fuck," I grumble, fishing the phone out of my jeans.

I check the screen and, of course, it's Shayla. Always the one to ruin my buzz.

"What do you want, Shay?" I answer, exasperated.

"Marcel, I need you to come pick me up." Her voice sounds panicked.

"What the hell's wrong with you?" I sit up higher on the stool.

"Please—stop askin' questions and just come get me!" she hisses into the phone. "There was a raid at Tommy's house but I was out back and ran away before anyone could catch me. My fuckin' purse is still in there with my ID in it. They'll probably find it and call me in, so I need an alibi. If you come get me now, I'll have one, and it'll seem like you and me were together."

4

"Goddamn it, Shay!" I push out of my chair and march to the door, bursting out of Lionel's. Wasted five dollars on that damn beer. "I told you to leave that dumb motherfucker alone! Where the hell are you?"

"I'm at the gas station near the beach—uh, you know, the one Momma always took us to when we wanted snacks?" Her voice trembles as she says Momma's name. Probably 'cause she knows Momma wouldn't be proud of the shit she's gotten herself into.

"All right. I'm on my way." I hang up before I say something I regret. Unlocking my truck, I hop behind the steering wheel and drive straight to the gas station. It doesn't help that I've had three beers. I'm good driving, but I hate leaving the bar until I'm completely or mostly sobered up. I lost my mother to a drunk driver. I refuse to be *that* kind of man who thinks he's too good to sober up, but Shay needs me right now.

It takes less than ten minutes for me to get to the gas station, where I spot Shayla standing beside the ice freezers, her hands buried in the pockets of the white coat I bought her for Christmas a few weeks ago. I pull into the parking spot in front of her and her eyes widen, swirling with relief as she rushes to the passenger side. After I unlock the doors, she climbs inside.

"Let's go," she demands.

"Let's go?" I turn to face her, frowning. "You realize the shit you're in, right? You interrupted *my* fucking night for some shit that I've told you repeatedly to stay out of!"

"I know, I know, Marcel, but can we not do this here! Tommy's house is, like, right up the street, and I saw a cop drive by a minute ago!"

I grimace, putting the car in reverse and leaving the gas station. Shayla has been getting worse and worse ever since Momma died. She was sixteen, and I was twenty-two when we lost her. I took on the role of taking care of her. She had no one else but me, and I knew that, but with each passing year, I wish more and more she'd get her shit together and find her own fucking way in life.

"I'm gettin' really tired of this shit, Shayla," I mutter, turning onto a single lane road.

"And I'm tired of you chastisin' me over the shit I do. It's my life, Marcel."

"Well if it's your fuckin' life, why the hell are you stayin' in my fuckin' place, eatin' all my goddamn food then?" I glance over and she's glaring at me.

"See? This is why I never come home! Because you're always bitchin' about somethin'!"

"Oh, I'm always bitchin'? Really? I'm here bustin' my ass trying to find a stable job so we can keep a roof over our heads, and I'm bitchin'? You think I wanted this shit to happen? You think I wanted to be the one responsible for your lazy ass? No, but I am! This is life, Shay, and you need to grow the hell up already! Get a real job or somethin'!"

"Oh my God—okay, you know what? Stop the car. I wanna get out."

I shake my head. "I'm not letting you out in twenty-degree weather."

"I don't give a damn! I can walk home from here!"

"Yeah, and freeze to fuckin' death? You know what? Maybe I should let you do that, then you'll be out of my life for good!" I can't stand when she acts like she knows everything. I've done everything I can for her—have been

6

since Momma died—because I love her and vowed to always have her back. The least she can do is make my life easier, but does she do that? Fuck no. She always causes trouble—always hangs out with that stupid weed dealer, Tommy.

"Let me out! Now!" Shay demands.

"No!"

"I'm not kiddin', Marcel! I'll open this door and roll out! I don't wanna be in here with you! All you fuckin' do is judge me and complain about me being around! Why bother callin' when you're just going to be a dick about it?" She grips the door handle, glaring at me with glistening blue eyes. Without much thought, I reach across the console just as she pulls the door handle. The door flies open, and the inside of the truck fills with cold air.

"Shay! Close the goddamn door!"

"Fuck you!" she shouts, but the vehicle is going fast, and she's clinging to my arm like her life depends on it. She knows damn well she isn't going to roll out of a truck that's going over forty miles per hour. To my luck, I get the door to shut, and she gasps, almost like she wants to thank me for saving her from doing something so stupid, but my sister has too much pride to do such a thing.

"Are you out of your fuckin' mind? I swear, you do some of the dumbest shit sometimes, Shay!" She has to be drunk or high. That's the only explanation for what she's doing right now.

"Marcel!" she screams as headlights slash across her face. "Look out!"

I gasp and look through the windshield. "Shit!" Jerking the wheel, I try getting back in my lane as the car ahead of me honks the horn. I move out of the way successfully, but it's too much for my old Ford to handle.

The truck veers sideways way too quickly, and Shay screams to the top of her lungs as we start to spin out of control. I do everything in my power to gain control of it, but the roads are slick from old snow and the shower of rain that just passed, and this truck is too old, with tires that I should have replaced years ago.

I look over at Shayla, and her eyes lock on mine, her face panicked. For a moment, I swear everything around me goes absolutely still. All is quiet, and it's only me and my sister staring at each other, realizing this is the fear Momma must've felt when she got into that car accident, before dying in the hospital less than thirty minutes later.

This shouldn't be happening to us. We're supposed to live on for her, right? It's what I always tell Shay. We're here to carry on her life's work. She raised us to do good—to *be* good.

The world spins again.

I look away, holding the steering wheel tight, but the truck flips once, and then another time, right before slamming into a thick tree trunk.

When I open my eyes, shattered glass is everywhere. My mouth is numb, like I've just gotten punched in the face, and I taste blood. *Fuck*, I smell it everywhere.

I look down and see blood on the steering wheel. I must've hit my mouth there.

Something's piercing me, just below the ribs, and it hurts like hell.

"Shay?" I call.

No answer.

"Shay? You okay?"

No answer.

"Shay! Answer me!" I yell as loudly as I can, the potent, warm stench of blood stinging my nostrils. Deathly afraid to do it, I look over and see glass all over Shay's side of the car. Her window has completely busted, and from the lights in the console, I can clearly see dark-red blood on the bark of the tree that's right outside her window. Some of her brown hair is strewn over the open window, but most of it is covering her face.

Fighting whatever pain I feel, I lean over and grab Shay by the shoulder. Her head rocks back as I use as much force as I can to get her to wake up.

Her face drips with blood. It's pouring from a gash in her forehead.

"No, no, no," I cry. "No. Shay. Please." I wince as pain shoots up the right side of my body. I don't care about the pain. I grab her face between my fingers. "Shay! Wake up!"

No answer, just like before. I look down and spot a sharp piece of metal protruding from her stomach. It has ripped through her stark white coat. I try to pull on it, but it doesn't budge, and she doesn't make a sound.

"Shay! Please! Wake the fuck up!" I cry out as a blue light flashes behind me. A siren sounds, but I refuse to give up on her.

With every word, my voice breaks, the pain below my rib growing more intense.

I don't give a fuck.

I want this pain to sweep through me and swallow me whole, because it doesn't take a genius to know that my sister—the only family I have left—is gone.

And it's all my fucking fault.

ONE

GABBY

PRESENT DAY

I'VE ALWAYS FELT like something was missing from my life.

I've never been able pinpoint it, but I swear, I've only discovered a small portion of the *real* Gabrielle Lewis. Well —let me rephrase that. A small portion of who the real Gabrielle *Moore* is. I married my husband, Kyle Moore, three months ago. It's still a strange, new feeling calling him my husband, especially being so young.

Ever since I'd met him, he's always been Kyle. *My* Kyle. I never called him boyfriend, yet everyone around me did. I always used to say we were "talking," but Kyle always declared we were so much more than that.

To Kyle, I am his winning prize. He's told me that since the day we've met, and sure enough, he'd dropped to one knee and asked for my hand in marriage in front of the Empire State building on New Year's Eve a year after meeting me. There was a crowd of people around us, hearts in their eyes and big smiles on their faces as they waited for me to answer him, so of course I said yes. The last thing I wanted to do was embarrass him. As soon as that weekend was over, I ran to my parents to ask them if all of this was happening too fast. I mean, it'd only been twelve months since I'd met Kyle. He'd attended my graduation, and we hung out quite often when he was free from work, but I was still learning things about him.

Mom told me I would learn something new about the person I loved every single day, and that you never completely know someone until you're spending every day with them. Dad said he was safe, so he was all for it. Not that I could trust their opinion—they got married within six months of meeting each other, so of course twelve months was more than enough time to them.

I met Kyle in a café I used to work at, Nuni's. I was a waitress there, sporting a red apron with a smiley-faced toast logo on it, and he was a handsome businessman who visited every week, sitting at the same table to order the same meal: pulled rotisserie chicken sandwich, sliced bananas, a pickle, and a green smoothie. I always thought it was a strange meal and had even teased him a little about it during his visits. He told me not to judge it until I tried it. We joked about it so much that he finally asked me to join him after my shift to try the meal for myself. He said he had meetings, but was willing to postpone them and wait for me. I did, and I admit, it wasn't bad, even if I wasn't a fan of pickles.

We laughed, he flirted, and I blushed. We exchanged

numbers that very night, and he sent me a text every single morning and visited the restaurant for lunch several times a week. From that moment on, Kyle and I became inseparable.

Now, it's move-in day. Kyle had his own loft apartment in New York, where I had stayed with him after graduating, but I wanted to move somewhere sunny and warm after we got married. He promised we would find a home I loved before the big day, and the next thing I knew, he was handing me a silver key and informing me that we now owned a house in Hilton Head Island.

My parents live in Fredericksburg, Virginia. I grew up in that city, accustomed to cooler weather, ponchos, boots, and damp hair whenever a random shower of rain or snow happened. Weather was too unpredictable there. When I was old enough to think about a life for myself, I knew I had to get away from that state and experience something more —some place bigger. I went to college in New York, the state where I met Kyle. Not that the weather was any better there.

I carry a box into my new art studio, dropping it in the far right corner. A few of the paint brushes jostle around in the box, the wood rubbing together, the sound music to my ears.

Taking a step back, I look out of the floor-to-ceiling window ahead of me. The window is intricately designed, with crown molding that gives a braided effect. It brings the room to life. I put my focus on the large backyard. It's lovely, but it could use a little more. Some chairs, a table—even some large stones to give it life. Hell, maybe even a hot tub could work for those cooler nights. Not too far off is a stunning view of tan sand and dark, turquoise waves.

When Kyle presented this room to me, I just about died. It's bigger than any room I've ever had of my own. The ceilings are tall, with thick, brown beams running through them. The walls aren't painted—they're an eggshell-white, but I'll have fun painting them myself one day. The floors are made of hard, dark wood, which is perfect because I tend to get very messy when I work. An elegant ivory fan spins in between the beams above my head, cooling the beads of sweat that have collected on my temples and on the back of my neck due to Hilton Head's relentless humidity.

"Here we go. The last box for this room." Kyle walks in, placing the box that's in his hands on the middle of the floor with a soft grunt. He then walks my way, dropping both hands on his hips and letting out a deep sigh. "You sure you like it in here?"

"Babe, are you kidding?" I turn to face him, grinning like a goof. "I love it! Seriously. I love it so much."

"Good." He smiles, facing me, too. His hands go to my waist, and he brings me closer. "I just want you to be happy here."

"I will be."

His smile grows wider. "A few of the neighbors are already asking about us. One of them stopped by to greet me when you walked inside."

"Oh, Lord. Don't tell me they're the nosy kind," I groan.

"They might be." He winces playfully. "But don't worry. When I bought this house, I made sure we had plenty of trees and a long driveway so people couldn't see the front of our home. My wife and I will need all the privacy we can get." He plants a kiss on my lips. "I want to fuck you all over this house. Break it in properly," he murmurs on my mouth, and I curl my fingers into his shirt.

"Then do it," I challenge.

"I will…" He kisses me again. "Right after we get the last of these boxes."

With one more kiss, he pulls away, and I lift my hands in the air, groaning before letting them drop to my sides. "Remind me again why we didn't hire movers?"

"Because, as newlyweds, we have to experience it all, Gabs! This is our first house together. We'll feel much more accomplished doing it ourselves."

"Yeah, gotta tell you, Kyle…I'm not feeling so accomplished at the moment. Bringing the boxes in is one thing, but unpacking them is a whole different ball game."

He laughs on his way down the stairs.

We get the rest of the boxes from the U-Haul we took turns driving, and for the rest of the day, we unpack what we can until our bodies grow weary.

We decide to eat a delivered dinner on the only available space we have—our sofa—and chat about Kyle going back to work next week and me starting a live online seminar for young art students. I'm getting paid $15 per student for the session, and so far I have twelve students attending. Not too bad for my first online class.

"I'm nervous about it," I admit, tossing my plastic fork in the brown paper bag. "What if I don't make any sense? Or they secretly hate my artwork?"

"I highly doubt that, babe. You're extremely talented. My dad bought that painting from you, remember? He loved it."

"That's 'cause he's your *dad*, Kyle," I laugh. "Of course he's going to support me, even if deep down he may hate it."

"He has it hanging in his house—the house he lives in and takes pride in. I'm certain he at least favors it, if it's hanging where he has to look at it every day."

"Right. Oh—well, speaking of this whole *house* thing, what do you think of doing a housewarming or something? Maybe we can cater some food, some wine, everyone bring a little gift." I look around. "We could use a broom and mop, now that I think about it."

"Very true," he agrees. He looks around as well, sighing. "When, though? You know I'll be out of town a lot, catching up."

"Maybe in a few weeks? When we get everything settled? Maybe we can even have the backyard fixed up—add a hot tub, some flowers. All that stuff?"

"And you think all of that will be done in decent time? You'd have to find a landscaping business and everything. That stuff takes a while."

"I know. I'll work on it."

He sighs. "Maybe."

"Maybe I'll hire a maid to help me around the house, too." I wink at him, and he presses his lips, giving me a *yeah, right* look. "Come on. What do you say? It'll be great for us —the housewarming, that is."

His mouth twitches before a slow smile spreads across his lips. "Okay, sure. We can do it. I'll do whatever makes you happy. Find out how much landscaping the yard will be. Ask around, do some research."

"I will. Thank you, my love." I kiss his cheek before

grabbing our empty plastic plates and then standing. "I'll clean up. I'm sure you're tired, so go shower and rest. I'm going to unpack some more boxes and meet you up there."

"All right. I've gotta make a quick call too." Kyle kisses my cheek in return and then heads for the stairs, but not without giving me a charming wink over his shoulder. As he walks up, I go to the kitchen, tossing the empty plates in a trash bag we have hanging from a doorknob and putting the leftover food in the fridge with a smile.

I unpack more of the dishes in the kitchen, but I can't help taking small glances around. I never thought that by twenty-five I would be married, yet here I am. To most people, I have a normal life. I was just married, and I've moved into my dream home…but like I'd mentioned before, something feels like it's missing.

This is something I would never confess to Kyle, but in spite of all the good in my life, I yearn for something that will make me burn, in a good way. I have no idea what it is…but there has to be *something* out there like it. Maybe I need to travel more, break out of my own shell…

Don't get me wrong—Kyle has many moments when he sets my mind and body on fire. When he isn't tired, he is *incredible* in bed. But he works so much that he's often exhausted, and it also doesn't give us much time to just be with each other. When we first started dating, he was an animal, but with time—especially when he took over his father's company due to his father's mild heart attack—he became more predictable. Just a quick roll over, a few heavy moans, and it was finished. I didn't mind it so much. I knew what we had was much deeper than just sex.

Maybe it's the move and all the changes? I'm over five

hundred miles away from my parents and my best friend, Teagan. At least when I was staying in New York with him, I could drive to see them. They're a quick call away, yes, but everything changes when you can't drop everything and visit like before. I miss them like crazy, but I suppose when you're married and want a good, stable life, this is the way things have to be.

With Kyle, I don't have to work too much or worry about the bills being paid. He allows me to just live after working my ass off for years straight, so I need to do just that.

I unpack the box I'm working on and then go upstairs. I take a quick shower, change into pajamas, and then climb into bed with my husband. I curl up beside him and he stretches his arm out, welcoming me in with a tired groan. I smile, warmth coursing through me. I'm safe here with him. I have nothing to worry about.

This is my life now, being here with Kyle, and I'm going make the best of it.

TWO

GABBY

CLEARING out boxes became a habit for Kyle and me for the next four days.

Most of the items inside the boxes had been placed in their designated rooms or spots. It helped that we didn't have much stuff to begin with. We agreed to start fresh, minus Kyle's living room furniture, kitchen table, and his bed that's still in good shape, considering he'd hardly slept in it until we started dating.

When Tuesday arrives, our personal cars have been delivered, courtesy of a service Kyle hired before we moved, and Kyle is standing by the door with the handle of his suitcase in hand.

You'd think I'd be used to him coming and going, but I'm not, especially now that he will be so far away for work. For lack of better words, I consider him my other half, so there's always an empty feeling when he's gone. Not to mention this big, new house will be way too quiet without him around.

"I'll see you in three days," he says, tossing his suitcase in the trunk. He steps in front of me, planting a kiss on my lips.

"I'll be here waiting." I lean into him as he wraps a hand around my waist.

"You'll keep the bed warm for me?"

I giggle. "Sure will."

"Good." With one more swift kiss, Kyle lets me go and turns for his BMW. He sends me a wink after hopping into the car and I watch him pull out of our driveway, giving the horn a small beep before passing the palm trees along the curb of our house. When I can no longer see him, I sigh, taking a look around the front yard in detail this time.

It's immaculate. Dark gray cobblestone leads up to the roundabout driveway. Palm trees and bushes are lined up outside of it that truly do block the view for anyone to see what's going on in front of our house.

The driveway is designed on a short hill, so one would have to drive up to leave it or walk down to get to our front door. It almost represents a home in Beverly Hills or Malibu. Funny, as a little girl I used to obsess over the revamped version of 90210, wishing I could live their life. Now, in my own special way, I am living that life…minus all the drama and gossip.

I look up at the sky. It's mostly clear, blue, with hardly any clouds around. It'd be the perfect day to lounge in the backyard and sunbathe. Not too hot. The perfect temperature. Walking down the steps of the porch, I make my way up the driveway to check the mailbox. There is one piece of junk mail from a plumbing company.

"Make sure you grab the mulch too!" I hear a voice yell across the street. I glance over, noticing a black pickup truck in front of the home across the street from us. The words *Ward Landscaping & Design* are stamped on the door.

A blonde in a purple dress and black pumps walks down her driveway, meeting up with the men. She points at a few spots in her yard, and one of the men, sporting a thick beard and raven hair, nods his head, says something to her, and then meets the men in the yard to get to work.

She goes to her mailbox, taking out her mail. I start to turn, but catch her eye along the way.

"Oh! Hi, neighbor!" she yells across the street, waving wildly.

I turn back, smiling and waving. "Hi!"

"Oh—wait a minute! Let me get a good look at you!" She trots across the street with her mail in hand, swishing her hips a little too much. "Oh my goodness—look at you!" She beams at me, her teeth a stunning white. "Your husband wasn't kidding—you're gorgeous!"

"You've met my husband?" I ask, continuing a smile.

"Sure did—just yesterday." She taps me on the shoulder with her mail. "Mrs. Bertha next door was out here chatting with him when I pulled up. I jumped in to say hello to him. I heard we would be getting new neighbors soon." She looks me up and down, but not in a critical way, more like admiring what she sees. "You're so young!" she exclaims, and I just keep smiling, because not smiling is impolite. "And beautiful—flawless skin. That's naturally curly hair, I bet. Cute bust and hips and still petite—honey, you are the full package, aren't you?"

I laugh as she does. "Thank you." I point at the men

across the street, steering the subject a different direction because the way she's looking at me is slightly uncomfortable now, almost like she wants to jump right into my skin. "What are those guys working on for you over there?"

"Oh—one of my trees is dying, for some reason, so they're replacing it and also adding more mulch around the garden to make up for it." She plants a hand on her hip, turning halfway to look at the men, who are already stained with sweat. The humidity will do that to you. "Between you and me, I wanted the tree gone, but my husband insisted that I call them and get it replaced. I thought the owner would show—he normally does for these sort of mishaps—but not today. Must be busy."

"Do you know the owner well?"

"Oh." She sighs dreamily, a smile pasted on her face. "Honey, I wish I did." She giggles, and it hits me that this woman isn't dressed up to go to work or a day out. She dressed up in hopes she'd run into the owner. I'm not sure what that says about her, but she's pleasant, and I don't know what her home life is like, so who am I to judge? "Anyway, I saw your husband leaving. Is he headed to work?"

"Yeah—out of town for the next three days."

"Oh—bummer. Those days when they're gone are always the worst. Bill works out of town a lot, too. Does architectural designs for commercial places, so locations always vary." She huffs.

"Oh, that's cool. Kyle runs an investment banking company in New York." I don't know why I tell her that, but I figure since she's sharing her husband's occupation, I should share mine too.

"That's amazing!"

22

"I was actually looking into having someone do our backyard. It's nice, but I want to liven it up, make it a place I'd actually like to hang out. Not only that, but we're thinking about having a housewarming in a few months or so to break it in."

"Oh, honey, hire Ward Landscaping! I am telling you, the owner is a genius! He has a great eye, and he's efficient and quick. Everyone around here uses him—ask Mrs. Bertha and Mr. Hull. I'm sure he's made himself a pretty penny landscaping all of our houses."

"I will have to look into them. Thank you for the recommendation."

"Oh, no problem! Just let him know I sent you!"

"I didn't catch your name," I say, realizing how rude of me it is to not have asked when she first trotted over.

"Oh, I'm Meredith Aarons! And yours?"

"Gabrielle Moore, but most people call me Gabby."

"Well, Gabby, it was a pleasure meeting you."

"Same to you," I smile again, and she turns, waving goodbye as she rushes back across the street.

"Oh—no! Wait!" she yells at the landscapers. "That's not the color mulch I wanted! Do you have something darker?"

I laugh on my way back to the house, shutting the door behind me and going to the kitchen to make a cup of mint green tea.

After it's made, I walk around the corner to get to my studio, where my laptop is. I type *Ward Landscaping* into the search bar of Google and the company pops up as an ad first, and then as the first search result.

"Well, someone has good advertising skills," I mumble to

myself. I click on the website, and it pulls up a beautifully designed website. The background of the website is a wooden design, and there are several square photos of large pools, well-laid backyards, colorful gardens, decks with fire pits, and shrubbery.

I click on the "about" page next. It's been a habit of mine for as long as I can remember. I always like to know who I'm searching or looking into before getting deeper, but there's not much there. It only mentions that the owner of the company, Marcellus Ward, started Ward Landscaping & Design five and half years ago and that the company is known for both residential and commercial landscaping. The phone number and email are listed at the bottom of the page.

On his website he has several tab sections—one for outdoor living, pool and spa design, and of course landscaping. I jump to the portfolio next and scroll through, clicking on the images that catch my eye the most.

The gardens are my favorite. The array of colorful flowers lures me in so much that I'm pretty much sold on the idea of hiring them. Although Kyle makes most of the household money, I do some work from home. I teach classes online, and sell my art. I also saved most of the money Kyle gave me when we dated and he wanted me to "treat" myself. Considering all this, I think I can afford some of the remodeling on the backyard, and maybe I can surprise him with it. I'm sure he'd love it, plus he loves being outside. Not only that, but this Ward guy has a financing option.

After doing some more searching for landscape designers in the area, I only come across one, but his website is really basic, and there isn't much information about the company. Now I see why my brother, Ricky, is always insisting that having a nicely designed website is important. It only makes sense to choose the Ward company over this other one.

"Screw it," I mutter, and go back to Ward Landscaping, copying the email address and pasting it into the address bar. I send the company a short email about what I've been looking for and how I hope they have some openings. I also mention that my neighbor highly recommends him, hoping it'll give me footing in the door, and then hit the send button.

I check a few of my emails afterward. Some are from the students in the seminar, sending me shots of their works in progress. I give a few of them a proper response with a little feedback. As I'm finishing an email, my computer *dings*.

The notification reads: **Email From Marcel Ward, CEO of Ward Landscaping & Design.**

Holy shit. That was fast. This guy means business. I click the notification bubble, making a mental note to get back to the email I was working on.

Hey there Mrs. Moore,

I'm glad you reached out to me about your project. I'm certain I can accommodate whatever needs you have for your backyard. I must be frank, I'm only responding to this email so quickly because I am at the dentist, a place I really can't stand, waiting for my appointment, and saw this notif-

ication pop up. I am much better on the phone. Will you be available to speak at noon?

Thanks,

Marcel Ward
CEO of Ward Landscaping & Design

I smirk at his comment about the dentist. Witty. That's good. He's not some serious asshat I have to be awkward around. I give him a quick response.

Hello Mr. Ward,

Well, I thank you for getting back to me so quickly. A phone call would be much more convenient, that way I can really explain. Noon sounds great. You can call me at 212-907-0486, but if that time doesn't work out, I am available for the rest of the day so feel free to call at any time.

Best,

Gabrielle Moore

After I finish up the email to my student, I close my laptop, polish off my tea, and then head back to the kitchen. With a humph, I sit on the stool, looking around the empty kitchen. There's so much to do, yet I'm not motivated to do any of it right now. Without Kyle around, it is never the same. Unfortunately, for the next three days, I'm on my own.

Instead of moping, I write down a list of groceries and other things we need. I should get to know the area better anyway, so after freshening up and changing into better clothes, I stuff the list in my purse, grab my keys off the hook, and head to the garage. With GPS, I can find anything I need.

My problem with shopping? I always end up coming out with more than I'd written down on the list. I only needed the essentials, like toilet paper, water bottles, and a shower curtain, but of course I stopped by the snack aisle, the wine aisle, and many others, until my cart was full.

I stuff most of the bags in the trunk of my Challenger, but they don't all fit, so I grab the remaining bags and drop them in the passenger seat. As I shut the door, my phone buzzes and I dig in my back pocket for it.

I don't know the number, but it's a South Carolina area code, leaving no doubt it's the guy from landscaping company.

"Hello?" I answer, pushing my red cart to the nearest station.

"Hey, is this Mrs. Moore?"

Wow. His accent is not what I was expecting. I don't think I've ever heard a Southern accent so thick. "This is she," I reply, keeping the remark about his accent to myself.

"Hey, Mrs. Moore. This is Marcel of Ward Landscaping & Design. Is this a good time?"

"Hey—yes, right now is fine! Just left the store. So glad you called!" I rush back to my car, getting inside. I've already broken a sweat from the heat.

"Of course," he replies. "So, what exactly is it you're lookin' for?"

"Well—we just moved in to our new home. We have a pretty spacious backyard, but there isn't much back there for us to enjoy, so I figured I'd look into sprucing it up. The only issue is I'd prefer that it's finished before we host our house-warming in a couple of weeks."

"Describe a couple weeks?"

"I'd say within four weeks, while the idea of our move is still fresh in people's minds?" I know it's asking a lot, but I'm hopeful.

"Well, Mrs. Moore—I'd have to say that is a little too soon, considering you mentioned wanting a hot tub as well," he chuckles.

"Really?" I bite into my lower lip. "So you don't think you'll be able to do it?"

"Well, it depends on the size of your yard, for one. Also depends on all you want included. If you're lookin' to have hard landscaping, I'd have to set up a consultation with you to map out a design for the yard space and figure out which package you'd like to go along with the space. We have a variety of packages that fit many budgets."

"Well, that's good to hear. Maybe I can draw a design I have in mind, if it helps."

"That's always helpful. Go for it."

I push-start the engine. "How long does it usually take for you to design and create the actual layout?"

"To design it, no more than a day or two, as long as you have your blueprints on hand so I can plan with those. As for creating the layout, it all depends on your needs. My average time frame for a full patio with stones, concrete, and all those things is between four to six weeks. Ten max, if the homeowner is looking to add a pool, bar, or anything else."

"Okay, well, when do you think we can set up a consultation to discuss it? I really would like the hot tub."

"I checked my schedule before callin'. I'm available tomorrow mornin' from nine to eleven, then I have to leave town for a commercial job. Would 9:30 tomorrow mornin' work for you?"

"Nine-thirty sounds great, Mr. Ward. I'll text you my address."

"Okay. Sounds good, Mrs. Moore. See you tomorrow."

"Yep. Bye."

After sending him my address, I head home with a car full of groceries and a big smile on face.

THREE

MARCEL

OF COURSE she lives in Venice Heights. It's the first thing to run across my mind as I pull into the driveway of Mrs. Moore's house.

Most of my business has come from this exact neighborhood, and though they have been good to me, the demand here is off the charts.

With every new resident, it means I get an email or phone call to set something up, and oftentimes they want it done in an unreasonable time frame. While I appreciate the business, it's making it a lot harder to wind down my residential work to become more commercial based.

Ward Landscaping is growing—has been ever since I opened it in 2014, where I got my big start working solo on a home for the governor, who needed a last-minute job before a big outdoor party. His backyard was ruined due to a tropical storm, so he looked up local landscapers, called, and then booked me. He couldn't thank me enough for the work I did, and had even recommended me to all of his friends, most of whom wanted residential work. I've been on good ground ever since.

I kill the engine of my truck and step out, taking a thorough look around. The front yard isn't too bad, and the driveway is appealing. The bushes and flowers in front of the house are well-kept, which is a given for newer homes. After collecting my notebook and laptop, I walk up the steps and give the door a knock.

It doesn't take long for the door to be answered. A young lady swings it open, a big smile on her face. Her eyes are wide and green, not a trace of makeup on her face. Her curly, dark-brown hair is pulled up into a messy bun and she's wearing a long-sleeved white shirt. Her hands are covered in a bunch of chalky-looking shit, as well as her clothes. Her smile slowly falls as she focuses on me, like I'm the last person she expected to show at her doorstep.

"Uh—hi." She's mildly confused. "You're Mr. Ward?"

"Yes ma'am, I am." I take a step back. "And you're Mrs. Moore?"

"I am," she responds, a slight pep in her voice. She extends her arm to offer a hand, but obviously realizes they're dirty because she yanks it away just as quickly. "Uh—I'm sorry. I was upstairs working on a sculpture. Please, come in. I'll wash my hands and we can get started."

Nodding, I follow behind her, watching as she hustles toward the kitchen, which is in plain view from the door, due to the open layout.

"I'm sorry about the mess!" she calls out. "I think I mentioned to you that we've just moved in. My husband will break down the boxes and take them out when he gets back."

"Not a problem." I enter the kitchen, looking at the large four-top table set up by double doors. "Okay to sit here?"

"Yeah, go right ahead," she urges, scrubbing her hands in the sink. She rinses and dries them off as I place my laptop and notebook on the table.

"Wish I had more time, Mrs. Moore, but I'll have to make this a quick visit. The job I'm headed to needs me there for an early meeting."

"Oh, no problem at all." She smiles, turning for the fridge and pulling out a bottled water. "Can I get you anything to drink at least?"

"Sure. I'll take one of those bottles of water you're havin'." She hands one to me with a small smile, then pulls out the seat across from mine. "So, before we actually get into the details, can I take a look at the backyard?"

"Oh—yes, it's right this way." She rushes to the double doors to my right. I follow her lead as she unlocks them and pushes one of the doors open. She steps out of my way and I walk out, giving it a hard sweep.

"It's pretty spacious," I laugh.

"I know...but to be fair, I want a small patio space. Just enough for a few people to sit, stand, or whatever. I'd like to still keep some of my grass out there, in case I decide to get a dog or something, you know? I love dogs."

"I get you." I take another step out, studying the bushes that skirt the yard. Pulling my cellphone out, I take a few pictures to have on hand. "It's a great view, though. Beach

32

right there. I see why you'd want to have a comfortable spot out here too."

"Yeah. This would really make it the dream home we envisioned having."

"Well, let's go inside and talk it over, Mrs. Moore."

"Oh, man. You know what—Mrs. Moore sounds really weird, so just call me Gabby," she laughs, walking in behind me and shutting the door.

"Very well, Miss Gabby." She laughs at that. I smirk, sitting and opening my notebook. "Don't mind it. It's a natural habit. Everyone is Mister or Miss where I'm from."

"Where are you from exactly?" she asks. "I noticed how heavy your accent was on the phone yesterday. Caught me by surprise," she laughs. "It's obviously from somewhere around here, right?"

"Yep. Born and raised in Summerville, South Carolina. Spent most of my adulthood there before movin' to Hilton a couple years ago."

"Oh. That's nice."

"And what about you? Seems like you're from upstate. I'm hearing a slight accent from you too."

"Oh, yeah. Born in Albany, New York. Lived there until I was seven, then we moved to Fredericksburg, Virginia."

"Interesting. And now you're here?"

"Where I lived, it always rained or snowed, especially in New York. Needed a change of scenery." She smiles and shrugs. Apparently, she loves doing that—smiling, that is. Momma always told me people who are always smiling are usually the ones hiding the biggest secrets. But that's none of my business. For all I know she's just a regular woman, happy to be in her new home. Probably married to some rich, arrogant prick like all the rest of the women in this neighborhood. Either way, not my problem.

"Well, let's discuss what you're lookin' for." I open my laptop and go to my pricing sheet, then pull the pen from behind my ear, uncapping it and writing down her last name on the top of the paper. "I have a variety. Anything you have in mind that you really want back there?"

"I actually drew a quick sketch of what I wanted. Maybe this will help?" She stands and walks to the counter behind her, grabbing a white sheet of paper and sliding it across the table. I look over it as she speaks again. "A blueprint of the backyard is beneath it. I know for sure that I want a hot tub. Since we have the beach, I don't really care to have a pool. I also want a full patio with a built-in fire pit. Also, big flower beds to go around it, to give it a little life and lots of color." I place her design down to write everything she just said, nodding. She continues. "Maybe built-in seating where people can sit, in case we don't have enough chairs for everyone."

I give a little laugh at that.

"What's funny?" she inquires.

"Nothin'." I finish writing the last thing she mentioned.

"No, tell me," she says with a small laugh.

"Well, I'm tryin' to figure out who you think can create so much within a four-week time frame is all, Miss Gabby. These projects take time. I would need at least six weeks for yours alone."

"Oh." Her face falls. "So it can't be done?" She unleashes a sad sigh.

"It can. It's more of a risk for the business, if anything. In order to finish it, I'd have to have my men working overtime to get it ready in time for the housewarming you mentioned. Not only that, but I'll most likely have to work with them to give an extra hand and to make sure everything is running smoothly. I have a different crew for the spa and bar. My landscaping crew would handle the patio and ground work."

"Would you be willing to give the extra hand?"

I put on a smile. "I don't deny many jobs, Miss Gabby. Especially one like this, when it means so much to someone so…*bright-eyed*."

"Bright-eyed?" She guffaws, propping her folded arms on top of the table. "What exactly is that supposed to mean?

"Just means this is exactly what you said it is. It's your dream home. You're proud of it, and it's my job to make sure you have the backyard you've always dreamed of havin'."

"I see." She grins, looking hopeful again.

"The only issue I'm seein' with you is the time frame, and that'll determine whether I can take this project on or not. I need at least eight weeks due to this commercial job I'm runnin' at the moment. Once that's over, I can focus on your project a bit more. If you can give me just a little bit of a stretch, I can definitely squeeze it in for you."

Her lips twist. "Well, I haven't told anyone when we would be doing the housewarming, so I can work around your schedule."

"Exactly what I'd hoped to hear. We can't rush these kinds of projects. If you hadn't given me leeway, I would have had to refer you to someone else."

"I understand." Her olive eyes shimmer.

I lower my gaze to my laptop. "Well, the package I

would suggest to you is our Mover's Package. This package includes a nice twenty percent discount for recent movers, and also includes installation of the patio space, a walkway, shrubbery and trees to shade the area, two full-sized flower beds and the option of a hot tub or half-sized pool. You mentioned a built-in fire pit with seating and a wet bar, but that will cost you a little more."

"How much more? Can you give me the total for all of it?"

"Sure you'll be able to handle the number I'm about to give?"

She folds her arms. "Throw it at me."

"For all of it, you're looking anywhere between $10,000 to $20,000, depending on what appliances you want at the wet bar and whether you want built-in seating there as well.

"Holy shit." She lowers her gaze, nodding. "Well, I have about ten grand saved. If it's more, I can always ask my husband to cover the rest of it, if he likes the idea."

"Wait a minute." I hold a hand up. "You haven't spoken to your husband about this?"

She locks on my eyes. "We've talked about getting a landscaping company, but I'm really only supposed to be looking. What can I say? I like to take initiative." She smiles sheepishly. "I was hoping I could surprise him. I'm paying for some of it with money I've saved. Just want to do something nice around here, take the load off of him."

"Hmm."

A silence sweeps over the kitchen table. Her gaze stalls on mine.

"I tell you what." I shift in my chair, straightening my back. "I'll add in the fire pit and seating with the package so you can get the discount, that way all you'll really have to worry about is the wet bar and hot tub."

Her eyes light up. "Oh, Mr. Ward, you really don't have to do that. I can reconsider the fire pit and seating. It's really not a big deal. I can just get more chairs if I need to."

I hold up a hand. "No, no. My job is to make sure you're happy, Miss Gabby. You've just moved in, lookin' to be happy here, right?"

She nods and sighs.

"Okay, then. Don't think too much of it. If you really want that built-in seating and fire pit, I'm more than willin' to fit it into your budget."

She gives me a relieved smile. "Thank you. I really appreciate that. So…how much would it be total?"

"For everything, including construction costs, I estimate about eighteen grand plus tax. I offer payment plans as well, if you need them."

"Okay, great. A payment plan would be amazing."

"If everything works out, the budget shouldn't change too much," I tell her.

"Great!" she chimes as I write down the package and features she wants added. "And when do you think you can start?"

"Next week I'm full, but the week after, I'm all yours."

"Good." She stands with me. "I'm really glad to hear that."

"Yep. I'll get everything taken care of and come up with a few designs for you. When I have them ready, I'll email 'em and let you take a look at a few layouts, see which one works best for you."

"Okay, great!"

I pack up my things, tucking the laptop and notebook beneath my arm and pushing the chair in. "I suggest you fill your husband in about this upcoming project, though. Last thing a workin' man wants is to come home and hear construction noises in his backyard."

She follows me to the front door. I swing it open, walking out. "I'll let him know when he gets home."

"All right then, Miss Gabby. It was nice meetin' you. I'll email you in a few days with those designs.

"Awesome. Thank you for squeezing me in, Mr. Ward."

"Mr. Ward?" I shake my head, walking down the steps. "Call me Marcel. Formalities don't suit a man like me."

With that, I turn and walk to my truck, opening the door and hopping behind the wheel. Gabby stands on her porch, watching me go. I bring the engine to life and leave the driveway.

On my way out, I look through the rearview mirror. She's turning to go back inside, and of course I notice her ass before the door shuts. There were a lot of things I noticed about her. The freckles that dotted her umber skin. The spark in her olive-green eyes. How carefree she acted, but deep in her eyes, there was a lot of concern.

The move had obviously been too much for her, and she was coping with it by creating a backyard. That, or she was worried about doing this whole ordeal without her husband's consent.

Didn't matter. Wasn't my problem. Money was money. She was a client now, and if building this was what she was requesting, so be it.

Though my life has been a wreck, it doesn't mean I can't make someone else's a little more tolerable.

FOUR

GABBY

"I'm telling you, T, he is *not* what I was expecting!"

I still couldn't get over the man I'd just met—the chiseled, Southern god who sat at my table wearing dusty jeans and a solid white T-shirt as if he were just some average Joe. At first, I assumed he had the wrong house, or that he was a neighbor wanting to introduce himself, but then my eyes fell down to the laptop and notebook tucked beneath his arm.

It wasn't a coincidence this man had shown up around the time our appointment was set. Not only that, but when he spoke, I knew it was definitely him. His accent was so thick and smoky, it was hard to mistake him for anyone else.

"Next time, take a picture of him!" Teagan, my best friend, demands. "You're a lucky girl, you know that? First you win the heart of a man who has inherited a multi-million-dollar company, and then you get a house on the beach, and now a hot as hell man is about to be visiting your house on a regular basis, sweating, probably taking his shirt off. Lord knows I could use some eye candy around here."

"Another slow day as RN Teagan, I presume?" I tease her.

"Yes. I'm so over it, girl."

I laugh.

"Seriously, though. I need to make a trip soon and visit you, check out this landscaper with the hot Southern drawl."

"The landscaper isn't a big deal," I tell her with a soft laugh. "He's going to do his job and be done with it."

"Mm-hmm. So, is everything good with you and Kyle since the move?" she asks

"Yeah, we're fine. Just exhausted. It's taking us some time to get used to it all. The weather here is definitely better than New York, though. So much warmer, and it's only April."

"Has he been an overbearing dick lately?"

"T, he is not a dick! He only becomes one when *you* get under his skin." I giggle, sitting on the barstool at the counter.

"Yeah, yeah." I can tell, even from over five hundred miles away, my bestie is rolling her eyes and waving a dismissive hand.

"I plan to visit, though. I have the hours saved. I want to break that new house in with you, girl."

"You should come! We can have a girls' night, go out to get our nails done—all that fun stuff. I miss you so much already. It's so boring here, even more so without Kyle around. Would probably be better if you come before the housewarming, anyway."

"Well, if you want me there before that housewarming, I'm coming. I don't care what Kyle says."

I shake my head with a smile. Teagan has never been a Kyle fan. She didn't like that he'd roped me in so quickly, and she swore he was swindling me, flashing his money and buying me pretty things to win my affections. I tell her repeatedly that I don't care about his money. I'm not with Kyle for his assets. I'm with him because I truly do love him.

"Well, you just let me know, and I'll get the guest room comfortable for you."

"Okay, girl. I'll let you know! Keep me updated about the gardener!"

"He's not a gardener!" I bust out laughing. "He's a landscape architect! And there's nothing to stay updated on, crazy. It's his *job*!"

"Yeah, if you say so. You know, just 'cause you're married doesn't mean you can't look. My mom used to tell me that all the time. *Look, but don't touch.* Just saying."

Laughing, I say, "Bye, T," and hang up. I walk out of the kitchen and go upstairs to my studio. I take a look around, sweeping my gaze over the unpainted tea pots, freshly molded cups, glazed figurines, and then my random pile that has sculptures in all shapes and sizes that I call my "scrap" pile.

It would be nice to have Teagan here for a few days. It's always hard adjusting to a new home. I remember when I moved out of my parents' house and into the apartment I shared with my first roommate. It was hard to get used to. In fact, it took me nearly eight months before I became comfortable with the idea of being on my own. It didn't help that I had a party-going roommate who was hardly

41

ever there. She would leave early and come back late every single day, so the apartment was always quiet, for the most part.

My parents are naturally loud people. My mom has no problem telling people off, and my dad is somewhat of a drill sergeant. If something doesn't fly with him, he will go on and on about it until it changes. Fortunately for me, he was keen to Kyle. Mom doesn't care about Kyle's money, but Dad does, and he knew Kyle could take care of me, so when I told him we were getting married, he told me it was the smartest thing I could do.

Living with my parents was chaos. My older brother, Ricky, is practically a genius, and went to college on a full academic scholarship. He now runs his own tech business, where he mostly helps elderly people work their phones, tablets, and computers. He also teaches classes for those wanting to learn how to use a certain app or software. Trust me, it pays more than you think. We grew up confiding in one another, and at some point, we figured out that our parents married more out of convenience than passion.

Don't get me wrong, my parents love each other, but my dad had just graduated college when they met, my mom a waitress for a run-down diner in New York. My mom got knocked up by my dad with Ricky when she was only twenty years old, and my mother is a full-blooded Colombian with a family who feels strongly about marriage. Even long distance, my grandparents insisted she get married to my dad before Ricky was born. Luckily my dad really liked my mom, and my mom didn't have much to lose, so they made it happen.

I think having Ricky made them love and respect one

another a lot more, which is good. They have a balance that is hard to find with most couples. They also co-parented really well. When my mom yells, Dad is calm. Dad hardly ever yells and, somehow, he knows how to calm my mom down when she's caught a temper.

I miss her. Hell, I miss both of my parents, and Ricky too.

I grab some clay and sit at my work desk, deciding I'll give my parents a call after I've finished my project of the day and have taken some pictures of it to upload to ArtMeUp, a popular website where hobbyist artists can sell their creations.

After I've finished, I clean up and then go to the fridge, pulling out the salad I prepared this morning. It's topped with cut strawberries, walnuts, and has a raspberry dressing.

Kyle always insists that we eat clean, and after working at Nuni's for well over a year to pay for books and the two-bedroom apartment I shared with my roommate, Chelsea, it's safe to say that I crave clean foods now. I got so sick of ordering takeout from there and stuffing my face with cheesy macaroni, or thick sandwiches that had way too much meat on them.

Preparing my own food is a rewarding feeling, and when Kyle's home, I love to go above and beyond to give him a meal I think he'll love. Most times, I knock it out of the park. Then again, he enjoys everything I cook, just so long as I cook.

After eating my salad, I go to Netflix to find a movie and then grab my cellphone. The noise from the movie fills the void. I give my mom a call, and she answers after a few rings.

"Gabby! It's about time you called me!" Her shrill voice catches me off guard, and I pull the phone away from my ear with a small laugh.

"Hi, Mamá."

"I called you a few days ago! What happened?"

"We were still unpacking, and by the time I remembered to call back, it was already too late. I was exhausted."

"Well, at least I'm hearing from you now. How was the move?" I can tell she's grinning, wanting all the details. My mom is a bit of a gossiper. She grew up on Spanish soap operas and tabloid magazines. Gossip and drama is all she knows, really. I always wonder how she settled down with my dad. I guess it is true when they say opposites attract, because although my dad has his moments where he can never shut up, he is as simple as they come.

It's extremely rare for him to get truly upset. Mamá could sit next to him and spill every little detail about some crazy woman at the store who bumped into her and it would go through one of his ears and right back out of the other.

"The move was good, even though Kyle insisted we do all the moving ourselves." I tuck my legs under my butt. "He claimed that he wanted us to *take in the experience* and to *appreciate it*…whatever that means." I roll my eyes just thinking about it.

"You know, he's always been very dramatic to me," she says, and I laugh because she's the one to talk.

"What are you doing right now?"

"I just left the hair salon. I got my hair trimmed and blown out. It was getting too long. I'm on my way to the nail salon now. It's me and your dad's wedding anniversary tomorrow."

"Oh, crap! I completely forgot about that! Happy anniversary!"

"Thank you, sweetie!"

"What are you guys going to do?"

"Probably the same old thing. Grab some dinner, catch some drinks. From there we will probably wing it. There's a restaurant I've wanted to try for a while, so he's taking me there."

"Well that's nice." I glance at the TV screen. I chose some random show with Vikings in it. Again, only on to fill the void.

"You know Ricky is coming up to see us this weekend?" She says it as more of a statement than a question.

"Is he really? What for?"

"He said he bought us a gift, wants to deliver it to us himself. I pray he doesn't bring that trashy wife of his though."

"Ma!" I scold.

"What? It's true! She's so trashy! Do you see the things she wears for Thanksgiving and Christmas? It's disgusting, Gabby!"

I laugh harder, plucking at a loose string on my sweatpants. "Ricky loves her."

"But is he *in love* with her though?" she asks, even though she and I both know he isn't. Ricky lost the girl he loved to another man. Her name was Christine, and he'd never asked her to go on a date or anything. He was always afraid of rejection and assumed she was keeping him in the friend zone.

He brought her home for the holidays once because she didn't have much family around. Her mom had passed

45

away, and her father was nowhere to be found, so he invited her, and we were happy to have her. I saw the way Christine looked at Ricky, though. She was a shy girl too, but if he'd asked her for more, I'm certain things would have turned out differently for them. Unfortunately, life got in the way. Ricky graduated, and Christine got whisked away by another guy and ended up engaged to that same guy a year later, right after she'd graduated.

After Ricky found out about her engagement, he came home with Violetta—the one my mom calls trashy—for Thanksgiving, claiming she was the one. Got married to her a year and a half later. But Ricky didn't look at Violetta the way he looked at Christine. Violetta was more of a place filler than anything.

"He'll realize it sooner or later," I say, getting off the couch and walking to the kitchen. "I swear, it's so lonely in this house with Kyle gone. We have five big rooms and this huge kitchen and living room, but he'll hardly even be here!"

"Well, he's a busy man, sweetie," my mother says, and she sounds slightly out of breath. "He's given you that beautiful house, but he has to pay for it somehow."

"Yeah, I know. It's just so quiet."

"You just have to get used to, Gabrielle." A bell chimes on her end, and I hear someone greet her. "Okay, well, I'm here at the nail salon. Let me go and get my nails done. I'll call you Sunday, after this weekend settles, okay? But call me if you need anything before that!"

"I will, Mamá. Enjoy your anniversary. Sorry I can't come visit too."

"It's okay, honey. Enjoy your new house! I'm sure I'll see you soon."

We say goodbye, and I lower the phone, staring at it for a second. On the screen is a picture of me and Kyle standing in front of our new bathroom mirror. He's kissing my cheek and holding me from behind while I smile big and wide, the happiest girl on earth.

Sighing, I go back to the couch after making another cup of tea, flipping through the movies until I find one with Vanessa Hudgens having a lookalike.

I settle into the couch, but as the movie plays, I can't help letting one little thought distract me.

How am I supposed to enjoy this new home with my new husband if he's hardly ever here?

FIVE

MARCEL

"MARCEL, LOOK OUT!"

I sit up quickly, gasping and swiping the thick sheen of sweat off my forehead. "Fuck." I look sideways at the alarm clock that reads 3:00 a.m. and let out a heavier breath.

This has been happening a lot lately. Normally stress does it to me. I've taken on too many jobs, hoping the work will suppress the memories. It's clearly not working.

Pressing my back to the headboard, I run both hands over my tired face, then pick up my phone. There's a text from Lucy and an email from Gabrielle Moore. Although a rumble in the sack with Lucy would be a good distraction, Miss Gabby's email lures me in.

Hi, Mr. Ward,

I know it's really late, Mr. Ward—err, I mean, Marcel, but I thought I'd let you know that I have to cancel our landscaping plan. My husband doesn't approve. Says it's too pricey for us at the moment. Anyway, thank you for your help and for taking the time out of your schedule to sit with me and chat about it.

Best,

Gabrielle Moore

Well, shit.

I have clients fall through all the time, but something about this email seems off to me. What the hell is his problem? Does he think I'm not good at my job? And he can't beat my prices—I'm the most affordable landscape architect in Hilton, no doubt, and if there is a price that's better than what I offer, I'm always ready to match it.

At first I brush it off, shutting the screen of the phone off and tossing it aside. I try going back to sleep, but between the nightmares and this deal, it's impossible.

What's bugging me most isn't the fact that she canceled. *My husband doesn't approve?* What kind of shit is that?

I grew up in a home with an independent woman who raised me, and a father who always told me to treat women like queens, after realizing his mistakes. After my father died, my mother had no one to lean on but us, and even so, she hardly ever let her rough days show. My mother always had our backs and stayed strong for us.

That woman—Gabby? She wanted that backyard. She wanted it so badly that I could see it in her eyes.

I know for a fact her husband has shoved her ideas aside, and she's most likely crying on the inside. I've worked around enough privileged men and women to know how it works. The men like to take charge, hardly ever giving control to the woman.

Gabby had it all planned out, I'm sure. So why couldn't he let her go through with it? It's not like he's going to be home often to see it anyway.

Thinking about it gnaws at me way too much. I know it's not my business, and I should just let it go, but I can't, for some reason. She had some money saved. It's not like he'd be coming out of pocket for the entire project. And hell, judging by their house on the beach, I'm certain money isn't the issue.

I get back up again, grabbing my phone and responding, this time without the proper business etiquette:

Miss Gabby,

Not to boast, but tell your husband that he won't find anyone with better prices than me, or anyone who does the quality work I do, in the Hilton Head area. I can absolutely guarantee that. Now, I saw the glint in your eyes when you explained to me what you wanted. You want that dream yard, I'll give it to

you, and I won't make a hassle of it, either. Matter of fact, I'm willing to cut down the price a few grand, just to prove to you that I'm always ready to get a job done and make any customer happy.

Let him know if he has any questions, he is welcome to call or email me. I am more than willing to discuss it. And my word of advice to you: don't give up so easily on something you really want.

Marcel Ward
  CEO of Ward Landscaping & Design

With a satisfied smirk, I place the phone on its screen and roll back over. This time, it's much easier to fall asleep.

SIX

GABBY

"I DON'T LIKE HIM. He seems like an arrogant prick." Kyle stands in front of the mirror that hangs on our closet door, fixing his burgundy tie. I'm on the bed with my phone in hand, reading the email Mr. Ward sent back.

"He's not an asshole. It's just how people down here are. They're not afraid to speak their minds...in the kindest way possible."

"Well it's very unprofessional, so explain to me why you'd want to work with someone like that?"

"The neighbors say he's really good." I press my lips and rub the little ball on my ankle, cross-legged on the bed. I have to admit, I'm a little upset with Kyle. I was so happy to tell him about the new backyard we would have. At first, he only nodded and said his "mm-hmms", but as we sat at the dinner table, sharing a meal of baked salmon and garlic crusted asparagus, he simply said, *"Call the landscaping off. We don't need it right now, Gabby."*

"What? Why?" I asked, mid-chew.

"Because we've just moved, and the last thing I want is a mess in the backyard." He took his last bite of salmon. *"I know I said you could do some research, but I didn't say set it in stone. The pictures you showed me on his website aren't all that spectacular."* He stood from his chair, picking up his empty plate and carrying it to the sink. I felt him come behind me and he capped my shoulders with gentle hands, placing a kiss on the top of my head. *"There are much better candidatres out there, I'm sure. Plus, the price you told me is a bit much for what you're asking. We can find someone else at a more convenient time and with a way better package deal."* And then he walked off, saying, *"Dinner was good!"* on the way out.

I remained slumped in my chair. Suddenly, I'd lost my appetite. I dumped my half-eaten meal into some Tupperware, and then washed what little dishes we had. I didn't speak to Kyle much for the rest of the night, and was slightly relieved he'd fallen asleep after I'd taken a shower.

Now, I can't stop thinking about the email Mr. Ward sent back. I feel awful, knowing he's probably already started a design, and I believe him when he says we won't find anyone with better prices. I've searched, and landscapers in Hilton are pretty expensive. He's given the cheapest quote so far, compared to some of the others I've emailed.

"I really want this backyard before the housewarming," I plead with Kyle. "Can we just give him a try? Please?" I climb off the bed and walk to him, lightly swatting his hand away and straightening his tie. "He said he would have it done in plenty of time before our housewarming even happened. I'm thinking sometime in May, we could do it."

Kyle sighs, dropping his eyes to look down at me. "You waste money on things we don't need, Gabs."

"But this is different. It's *permanent.* An investment. I can't give it away or shove it aside, like a new shirt or a pair of shoes."

He knows I have a point, because one of his eyebrows shifts up.

He pulls away from me, turning to grab the jacket of his suit. As he slides his arms into it, glancing at me one more time, I give him a hopeful look.

"Please, Kyle?" I beg, because begging is so *not* beneath me. "You wouldn't even have to pay for the whole thing. I have money saved!"

He groans, mumbling beneath his breath. When he meets my eyes again, he says, "Oh—fine, Gabby! Fine. Email him back and have it built, but he better have it done in the timeframe he says, and it better look beyond spectacular."

"Oh my gosh! Thank you!" I rush to him, throwing my arms around his neck and kissing his cheek. He tries to fight a smile but ends up chuckling. "I'll make sure they finish on time. It'll be great. You'll see, babe."

"Yeah, sure." He plants a kiss on my mouth. "Well, I have to go meet Mr. Cress for lunch. Let me know what you want for dinner. I'll pick something up."

"Okay, I will." I give him one more kiss as he cups my ass in one hand. "Love you. Thank you."

With a squeeze on my butt, he smiles on his way out the door, and I watch him go. When I hear his car door shut, I pretty much dash to my studio, popping my laptop open and sending Mr. Ward an email back, telling him to disregard my last email and that he can continue with the job.

He doesn't reply right away. I'm ten-fingers deep in glazing a sculpture when I hear my laptop ding.

It takes a few moments to get my hands clean enough to type in my password and get to my emails.

Miss Gabby,

Glad your husband came around. Also glad to know there are still people out there with good taste in yard work. Let's hope I don't fail either of you.

Working on the prints. Will email proofs to you within 24 hours. Looking forward to building the dream backyard for you.

Have a great week.

Marcel Ward
　　CEO of Ward Landscaping & Design

I laugh at his email, especially the part about my good taste in yard work. I reply "sounds good," and leave it at that, but while I finish glazing my sculpture of a mama and baby elephant holding their own balloons, I can't help thinking about his email from last night.

"Don't give up so easily on something you really want." I hadn't read that part out loud to Kyle, and with good reason, because Kyle would have felt challenged by a man he didn't even know. Still, it's almost like Mr. Ward knew Kyle had shut the idea down. That one sentence pushed me, in a way, the screams inside me demanding that I don't give up on it because I really do want it.

Kyle wouldn't have found another landscape architect worth the price. I'd done my research after finding Mr. Ward, and most of the landscape architects I found do only commercial work. Not residential. The ones who do residential are way too pricey.

I really want this. I daydream about waking up in the mornings, brewing a fresh cup of tea or coffee, and sitting on a cushioned chair to watch the sun rise, or even enjoying a nice glass of wine while bathing in the sunset. I want the fresh scent of newly buried flowers and air doused in salt engulfing me. The vision is so crisp and clear I can taste it.

So yes, this is something I have to push for, and for once, I'm glad I didn't shove the idea aside all because Kyle told me to.

SEVEN

GABBY

To my luck, my backyard is going to be started on much sooner than expected.

I got a call from Mr. Ward two days ago, saying that if it was okay to get started, he could bring his crew on Thursday. Apparently, he wants to get this job done before a big one he has coming in May.

It's now seven in the morning on Thursday, and I'm standing on my porch with a mug of coffee in hand, watching as they carry tools and supplies to the backyard.

I smile as each guy passes by and they return the smiles. A familiar black Ford pickup truck pulls into the driveway moments later, stealing my attention.

Mr. Ward steps out in a plaid blue and white button-down shirt, but the buttons aren't done up, and the sleeves are pushed up to his elbows. It's wide open, revealing a white, ribbed tank. It doesn't look like he did much with his hair—almost like he rolled out of bed and ran his fingers through it. It's kind of hot. When he spots me, he puts on a small smile, then walks up the stoop.

"Mornin', Miss Gabby," he greets, stretching his arm out and giving me his hand.

I reach to shake it, catching a whiff of him. He smells like Irish Spring soap and sandalwood, a complete contrast to Kyle's *Bleu De Chanel*. "Good morning, Mr. Ward. Glad to see you here, and a few minutes earlier than you said."

"Well, I think it's safe to say my team is eager to get this job started."

I laugh. "I can't wait to see what you've got."

He smirks at me as he reaches under his arm for the clipboard that I didn't even realize was there. "I just need you to sign a few papers for me. Basically givin' me the consent to destroy your yard before makin' it look all nice and done-up again."

He pulls a pen from behind his ear, and I gladly accept it, signing on the dotted line. Once signed, he tucks it back under his arm and replaces the pen. "Thank you. It'll turn out nice. Let me know if you have any questions. My crew won't be in your hair at all, so carry on with your day."

"Thank you, Mr. Ward."

He chuckles. "You aren't gonna let that name up, are you?"

"Only if you let up on calling me *Miss Gabby*." I sip from my mug—the one that says **Mrs. Bitch**. There's a matching one that says **Mr. Asshole** that belongs to Kyle. Teagan bought them for us as a gag wedding gift. Let's just say Kyle hates his mug.

He walks down the porch steps. "Ain't happenin'…

unless you want me callin' you the name that's on that mug you got there."

A laugh bubbles out of me. "That wouldn't be very professional."

"I agree, so Miss Gabby it is." He winks over his shoulder, then heads toward his truck. I watch as he places the clipboard inside and then he walks to the bed of it, taking out a set of tools and papers.

As he walks on the path that leads to my backyard, I yell, "Wait—are you really going to be working with them?" I'm so shocked. I truly thought he was kidding about it in the emails and during the consultation we had, just to make himself seem more professional. I mean, he *owns* the company for Christ's sake, and he has plenty of men back there to work.

"I enjoy workin'. I didn't open this company just to sit on my ass all day."

I open my mouth to argue, but really I don't have much to say to that. Most owners I know come to check things out, not to do the work themselves. He seems to be in a position where he can sit and relax, yet he works. It's interesting.

"Shall I continue?" His Southern timbre is much stronger as he raises a dark, slightly bushy brow.

"Uh—yeah, sure. By all means." He hikes the strap of his tool bag higher on his shoulder and continues down the path. I watch until he disappears around the corner before going into the house.

From the double doors in the kitchen, I see the men setting up. Some have already started digging out the old flower beds, scooping the dirt out like it's sand.

I finish my tea and head up to my studio, although I

have very little inspiration today. Instead of sculpting, I hop on my laptop and visit ArtMeUp to check for any messages or notifications. There are none, so I check out the market, but mostly the sculptures. Some of them are so intricate and beautiful, selling for thousands of dollars.

I study one by an artist named Big Hands. His work is amazing, so detailed, and the way he colors and glazes his sculptures blows me away. He has to have a top notch kiln.

Shit! Speaking of kilns!

I jump out of my chair and rush out of the room, hurling myself down the stairs and out the double doors in the kitchen.

"Hey! Wait!" I yell, looking to my right. As soon as I do, I realize how much of a fool I've just made of myself.

Mr. Ward and his crew are standing in the far left corner. His papers are on a small folding table the crew brought along, and all of the men peer up at me with confused expressions.

"Oh…um, sorry." I wince, then point to the white shed that's on the left, a short walk from the door. The shed isn't very small, but it has my kiln inside, and I need it to bake my sculptures. I would have it inside, but Kyle feels like it'll cause a mess. "Please be careful around this shed."

Mr. Ward nods, glancing sideways at the oven before focusing on me. "You got it, Miss Gabby. We'll be careful."

I sigh. "Thank you. Okay—I'll leave you alone."

He bobs his head once more, and I turn on the heels of my feet, rushing back inside, completely embarrassed.

The crew works for four hours straight before taking a break. By the time they do, it's my lunch time, so I go to the kitchen and make a hot turkey sandwich the way my dad always makes it, with American and provolone cheese, Dijon mustard, mayo, bacon, and lettuce.

As I sit down to eat, I notice Mr. Ward in the backyard again. He's sitting on the short cement wall near our private beach entrance with a lunch box in hand. He digs into it, taking out a sandwich and a bottle of water. He guzzles some of the water first, then bites into his sandwich.

For a while, I watch him. His eyes are on the ground and his head is hung low. He seems so…lonely.

Suddenly all these questions start to hit me. I wonder if he has a family? A wife or a girlfriend, maybe? Not that that is any of my business or anything, but I am curious. I wonder if he has any pets, or maybe a fish that he tends to when he gets home?

His eyes veer to the left, and he focuses on the door, where I'm sitting. I look away, finishing my sandwich and then going to the fridge to take out a green tea. Walking to the double doors, I step outside, going toward Mr. Ward.

"Everything going okay so far?" I ask, because how else do you start a conversation with your landscaper?

"Everything is all good." He bobs his head, balling his sandwich bag up and stuffing it into his lunch box.

"Oh. Good." I take a look around. The flower beds are completely gone and some of the grass has been dug up. "Man, you weren't kidding about it getting ugly," I laugh.

"Think of it as an ugly duckling. Starts out lookin' real ugly, but blossoms into a pretty swan. In the next few weeks, your yard'll be a swan, Miss Gabby."

I smile.

"Tell your husband I was gettin' started today?"

"No—haven't had the chance." I sigh. "He's busy, doesn't get the chance to talk much. He'll text or call when he's free though, I'm sure."

"What does he do exactly?"

"He owns an investment banking company in New York. He's supposed to be moving his office here really soon."

Mr. Ward sits up straight, raising a brow. "Oh, really?"

"Yep."

"And he's 'bout the same age as you, ownin' a company like that?"

I laugh. "No. He's thirty-three."

"And you are?"

"Twenty-five."

"Not to sound rude, but how does an older guy end up gettin' with you if you're in college?"

"He used to come to lunch a lot at a restaurant I worked at. Mostly whenever he was in town for work. He started requesting to sit in my section. We got to know each other well through that."

"Oh, *that* kind of thing." He puts on an arrogant grin and takes a swig of water.

"What's that supposed to mean?" I can't fight my smile, probably because his accent is both intriguing and slightly attractive.

"Nothin'." He chuckles. "You're a good-looking girl. I could see why a man would want you to keep servin' him."

I laugh. "Sure. Thanks, Mr. Ward."

"You know what? That Mr. Ward thing is really blowin'

me. It's all everyone ever called my dad. I need you to start callin' me by my real name."

"Marcel?" I tease.

"Actually, my real name is *Marcellus*."

"Marcellus. You know, I saw that on your website. It's a cool name."

"It's Latin for 'young warrior.' Also means hammer, or somethin' crazy like that. My mother said it was a powerful name. The kind of name that no man would overlook or disrespect. She always told me it was a name she loved callin' because it always made her feel protected...but then that Ross character from the show *Friends* got a pet monkey and named him Marcel. For years, everyone thought my name was hilarious because of it. Guess my name doesn't sound so solid anymore."

I break out in laugh. "Oh my gosh! You know what? I remember that monkey! Wow, now every time I think of you, I'll picture a monkey on your shoulder."

He laughs at that. "Oh, you got jokes?"

I giggle, then I sip my tea. "There was actually a character named Marcel on a show I really loved called *The Originals*. His sire always called him *Marcellus*, all passionately. I always thought the name was so unique, but the kind of unique you'd only hear on a TV show or read in a book, not in real life."

"Well, I have no idea what a *sire* is, but I'm glad you like the name. I like the fact that it's rare. I've never met or heard of another man named Marcel."

"Neither have I. Does your family live close to Hilton? Your mom?" I'm trying to feel him out. I'm curious if he has any family or friends here, but as soon as I ask that, his eyes fall, and his eyebrows narrow.

"No. She doesn't. Don't have any family here."

"Oh. Okay." I shift on my feet before taking a step back. Maybe asking about his family wasn't the way to go. "Well, I should probably let you get back to work. Don't want to hold you up."

He stands up, and his height, just like the first day we met, catches me off guard. He's several inches taller than Kyle for sure. His shoulders roll back, and I'm just now realizing he took his plaid shirt off and is only wearing the ribbed tank. He looks down at me, tipping his head sideways.

"You aren't holdin' me up. Just makin' casual conversation on my lunch break, which is fine by me." He studies the side of our house. "You spend a lot of time alone, I assume?"

Me? Hell, I was just thinking the same about him. "Yeah, I do now, but it's fine. I get a lot done, plus I'm starting to get used to it." Okay, that's a lie. I'm not used to it yet. When I lived upstate, Kyle drove home to me every night he could. But now, there are flights that stand between us, and by the time he gets home now, he has to fly right back out.

He works a lot—it's been that way ever since his dad had a mild heart attack. He took on the company, and he wants to make sure it stays afloat, and I don't blame him. I almost feel bad that I wanted to move to South Carolina, but he agreed that it would be good to have a fresh start, plus he hated the rain and snow of New York, too.

"Well, if you ever wanna have a chit-chat, I won't mind it one bit," Marcel says, looking sideways at me. "It's better anyway, especially while workin'. Makes time go by faster." I hear some men talking and a few of his crew members are walking our way.

"Okay. As long as I don't bug you. I tend to ask a lot of questions. I'd hate to offend you."

"It's damn hard to offend me." He picks up a blueprint and reads over it. "But I do have one condition for you: if you're makin' conversation with me, then there won't be any more of that Mr. Ward shit. Just call me Marcel."

I laugh. "But Mr. Ward is much more formal."

"Formalities are bullshit." He looks over his blueprint at me.

"Okay. Fine. Marcel it is. And if that's the case, you can just call me Gabby. Not *Miss Gabby*."

"All right." He places the blueprint down, and his men have already picked up shovels and tools to get back to work. "Gabby it is." His Southern drawl is heavier as he says my name, and I look away, fighting the blush I feel creeping up on me out of nowhere.

I step back, going toward the doors with a grin. "Let me know if you need anything, *Marcel*."

"Sure will, *Gabby*."

I grab the door handle, but not without noticing the smirk on his face. When I close the doors, I can't help sneaking a peek as I put my tea back in the fridge.

Mr. Ward—*Marcel*—is standing with a shovel in hand. He stabs it into the ground, leaving it standing upright, and then he crosses one arm over the other, reaches down for the hem of his shirt, and pulls it up, right over his head.

With the sun beaming directly on him, of course he stands out. His tan skin is unmarked minus one long scar right below his right rib. He's sculpted but not bulky, almost like he does just as much cardio as lifting to get his lean, toned appearance. His abs lead down to a sharp vee that disappears beneath his belt buckle and jeans. A few hairs jump out from beneath the buckle as he grabs the handle of the shovel.

As he snatches the shovel out, he pauses midway. My eyes travel up to find his, and it's then I realize I've been staring. He narrows his eyes a bit, but a smug smile lightly tugs at the corners of his lips.

"Oh, shit!"

I back away, bumping into the nearest counter edge. When I hear one of the men yell something, I look again, glad Marcel has moved away from the windows of the doors to tend to the person. I hurry back upstairs, and this time I don't look back, even though a small part of me is dying to see those abs one more time.

EIGHT

GABBY

I DON'T KNOW what possesses me to make lemonade for the Ward Landscaping crew. It's their second day of hard work, but unlike the six men they had yesterday, who handled the brunt of all the work by digging a large square in the back for the stone patio I'll soon have, there are only three today.

There's Marcel, who introduced two young guys to me when he arrived this morning, Alex and Jacob. Alex is tall with a lanky build. He takes his shirt off like Marcel, but it does nothing for me.

Jacob is much shorter than Alex. He doesn't take his shirt off, but he does roll the sleeves up really high over his shoulders, revealing toned arms. He has dimples that he doesn't mind flashing and dark skin that I'm sure is constantly kissed by the South Carolina sun. I can tell he's of Latino heritage by his downward mustache and goatee.

Alex and Jacob goof around a lot, I notice. Sometimes I

catch Marcel getting annoyed with them, snapping at them to get back to work, and other times I catch him trying not to laugh as he indulges in their shenanigans. I find it interesting on Marcel's behalf, especially when he laughs or smiles, because he doesn't seem to do it much.

One thing I didn't expect was to lose my creative flow with the remodeling of the backyard. I want to watch how it transforms from this ugly duckling to a beautiful swan, like he promised. I'm sure it'll make it much more enjoyable for me in the end, too, seeing the final product and knowing the hard work that was put into it.

After I finish squeezing lemons and adding sugar, water, and a special ingredient my mom always uses, I put the glass pitcher on the tray I sculpted and glazed myself, grab a few plastic cups, and then carry it all to the backyard.

The landscaping crew has a folding table in the corner with their lunch boxes and cell phones scattered over the top of it, so I carry the lemonade there.

Marcel looks at me curiously. "What's all this?"

"Do you know it's eighty-nine degrees today?" I ask, setting the tray down. "And humidity is at eighty-four percent, so it actually feels hotter than that?"

"Nothin' I ain't used to," he says, cleaning off his hands with the towel that was previously hanging from his back pocket. He steps up beside me, and even though he's about two steps away, I can smell him very clearly. Sweat, and the last remnants of whatever soap or body wash he uses.

"I'll take some of that!" Alex calls out as I fill the empty cups.

"Yeah, me too," Jacob chimes in. They come over, and I hand them each a cup. They walk off with it, taking big gulps before setting the cups down and getting right back to work.

I hand a cup to Marcel, who nods his head once while accepting it. He takes one sip. Then another. "Good," he notes, eyebrows shifting up like he's surprised.

I smile. "Thanks. It's my mom's recipe."

"What's in it that makes it taste sweeter than usual? Can't just be lemons, sugar, and water."

I pretend to physically zip my lips. "It's a secret. Not supposed to tell."

"Well, I can guarantee you I won't be makin' lemonade, so your secret's safe with me."

"I don't see you as a lemonade-making man, so perhaps that's true." I pour myself a cup and take a sip. "Between you and me, she uses organic agave syrup."

"And just like that, I'm fuckin' clueless. Got no idea what that even is," he laughs, and I laugh with him.

"It's a natural sweetener. More of nectar. It's good and good for you."

"Well, I like it. I'll have to look into this *agave* stuff." He takes another sip, then his eyes bounce over me as he turns and looks at his men, who are now doing some deep digging with shorter hand tools. "You know you don't have to do this, right, Gabby? Not that I don't appreciate it, but you're payin' us for this job. We don't expect special treatment."

"I know, but I don't mind treating you guys every once in a while." I sip from my cup. "It's just…well, never mind."

"Just what?" he asks, looking me over.

I wave it off. "It's nothing."

"You've got my attention. May as well fill me in," he adds smoothly.

I smirk at him before turning and looking up at the arched window on the second floor. "Normally, around this time, I'm working on something. Sculpting a crazy new masterpiece. But let's just say I'm having somewhat of a block."

"A block?" He narrows his eyes and I face him again.

"Yeah, a creativity block. Ever since you guys have started on the yard, I can't concentrate, for some reason."

"Are we too loud?" he questions, and I can tell it's a serious one by the way he lowers his cup and his eyes get bigger. He's worried. "If we're causin' too much of a distraction, just let me know, Mrs. Moore. Alex and Jacob are goofs and can get pretty loud, but I can always have different crew members here, which means less noise—"

"No—God, no! It's fine. It's totally fine. And please, Marcel, don't call me Mrs. Moore like that. It's just...it's weird to hear. You don't have to be so serious." It's insane how he switched from personable to business all in the span of a few seconds.

His eyes drop down. I look with him and realize my hand is on his arm. His skin is hot beneath my palm. I pull my hand away quickly, looking into his eyes briefly before focusing on the window again. "That window up there is where my studio is," I tell him, and I don't know why. I just figure he should know. "What's funny is I was wishing there would be *more* noise around here—more commotion. This house is too big for just one person to be in. Without Kyle here, it's just so...*boring*."

He nods. "I bet it is. I'd hate to be in a home this big by myself too. It calls for company."

"Yep."

"And Kyle is your husband?" he asks, sipping from his cup.

"Yep, that's him. He's looking forward to the outcome of all of this. I sent him a picture of how torn up it was last night, and he freaked out." I snicker, just thinking about the shock-faced emoji he sent back.

"It'll be fine."

"I know." I shift sideways. "I think my block is coming from our move, too. I'm still getting used to this new work space. At first it was inspiring, but—and I hate that I'm even saying this—I miss being upstate. The weather is better here, yes, but I'm craving a cold night and a blanket right now."

"And maybe you miss your husband too," Marcel suggests. "It's tough being in a new city alone."

I meet his eyes. They're a bright tropical blue with dark-blue flecks surrounding them. "Kyle works a lot. He's always been a busy guy. I'm used to him being away."

"Right."

"But not while living here," I continue. "It was easier before, because I could just pack a bag and drive a few hours to see my friends or family, or even visit him at work. Here, I have no friends. I guess I should start making some, though, huh? Sign up for some of those book clubs that are on the posters I see in town."

"Yeah, better you make some lady friends and catch drinks and nights out with them. It's much better than servin' lemonade to hired landscapers," he teases.

I laugh again, and it feels good to do. Kyle hasn't gotten in touch with me all day. He's probably in meetings. He will usually text me if he has meetings and can't call, but he hasn't done that either, and I'm worried. Another reason why I'm too distracted to work today.

"Well, since you're distracted and bored, how about you do a small task for me?" Marcel says, placing his cup down on the table behind him and picking up the garden fork.

"Sure. What is it?"

"I was going to ask you once we got closer to laying the concrete for the patio, but we never discussed what kind of flowers you want in the gardens." I watch as he digs the fork into the ground and scoops some of the grass out of a section. "How about you look for a few, let me know which one you're leaning toward. You can choose two types if you want."

"Okay...I can do that."

"I suggest lookin' for flowers that bloom best in late spring and early summer. That'll require some research, so that should keep you occupied for a few and not so bored around here."

"Okay. I'm on it." I start to turn, but a thought hits me and I catch myself, looking at Marcel again. "Um...look, if I'm bothering you in any way, please tell me. I feel like I'm annoying you, which happens a lot, trust me. I'm too friendly sometimes—which my husband always says isn't such a great thing—but I try to do what I can to make people feel welcome and—"

"Gabby, Gabby." With a slight chuckle, Marcel cuts my ramblings off. "I already told you, I don't mind chattin' with you. You aren't botherin' me, and I appreciate your hospitality. It's rare around here, especially in Venice Heights." He takes a look around, as if he can see the whole neighborhood. "People around here aren't usually so kind. It's a nice change."

I can't fight my smile, or the blush that creeps up on me. *AGAIN? Gah!* What is up with me and blushing around this guy?

I tuck a few loose strands of my hair behind my ears, nodding. "Well, it won't happen often, promise. Besides, I'm mostly coming out to see how everything is going, making sure my little clay oven is okay back here."

He returns the sarcasm with, "Yeah, yeah. I get you." I turn for the door and open it, but I don't walk in without looking back at him. "Find those flowers, Miss Gabby. Make sure they're good ones, too." He quirks a brow at me, and I close the door, unable to get rid of the smile he sent me in with.

NINE

MARCEL

MY CREW WRAPS up on the yard work for the day, and I haul my supplies to the truck. I feel something scrape me as I collect my pliers and sheers, but I think nothing of it, lugging it all to the bed of my pickup.

As I toss my lunch box through the window, I catch a glimpse of the clipboard on my passenger seat, a clear reminder that I need to give my client the run down and prepare her for what comes next. I head toward the Moore's front door, giving it a knock. Gabby answers, smiling up at me.

"Just want to let you know we're wrappin' up for the day."

She steps outside, nodding. "Okay, cool."

"Tomorrow, we'll be stakin' the yard and framin' it, gettin' it prepped for where we'll lay the stones you chose. Most likely won't get to the stones 'til about Tuesday or

Wednesday."

She takes a long blink before looking me in the eye and laughing. "I'm not sure what any of that means, but I'll keep that in mind!"

"Landscaper talk, that's all."

She looks down, and her eyes stretch a bit as she focuses on my arm. "Oh—shit. You have a cut on your arm. Are you okay? You're bleeding." I look with her, noticing it too.

"Oh, it's nothin'." I wipe the blood away with my thumb, but more of it accumulates quickly. I guess it wasn't *just a scratch.* "Must've happened when I was grabbing my tools. My shears are pretty sharp. Happens all the time. Nothin' to worry yourself about."

"Are you sure? Looks like there's dirt on it. It might get infected. I actually have a first-aid kit in the kitchen. I can grab it—"

"No, Gabby—it's fine. I can take care of it when I get home." I hold my hands up but she shakes her head, turning away from me and rushing back inside without a word. I sigh, pressing a hand to the wall outside the door. She comes trotting back my way with a small black case in hand.

"Sit right there," she demands, pointing at one of the cushioned chairs on her porch.

"Gabby, really, it's fine—"

"Marcel, don't be such a guy. It looks like a deep cut, and it will get infected if you don't clean it out." She cringes. "Sit down. At least let me flush it out."

"Jesus," I groan, walking to the chair. I slump down in it, watching her pry the case open. "You're a demandin' little thing. This what your husband has to deal with?"

"No," she says, trying to fight a blush. "My husband isn't

as oblivious to things like this. Besides, I'm just trying to help." She pulls out a small water bottle. "Put your arm up here, please." I do as she suggests, placing my arm on the arm rest of the chair. She squats down, spraying my arm with the water, or at least I thought it was water.

"Shit!" I hiss, yanking my arm back, and she quirks a brow at me. "The hell is that?"

"Isopropyl alcohol. Nothing to worry about, my ass," she mutters with a smug smile. She grabs a folded paper towel and wipes the wound off, then digs into the kit for ointment. She smears some over the cut before taking out a large bandage that'll cover that area and more, ripping it open, and placing it over the cut. She brings my arm closer, and as she does, my eyes drift down to the V-neck of her long-sleeved shirt before lowering to her tanned thighs. I have no idea why she insists on wearing those hot-ass shirts. It must be her thing. She did just move from upstate, so I guess it's all she has in her wardrobe.

She's careful not to let my knuckles brush across her chest. For some reason, I'm wishing she weren't so tentative. I clear my throat and look away. She's my client...but she's making it damn hard *not* to look.

"It wasn't even that bad," I mumble as she finishes up. "Could've waited 'til later."

"Well, knowing you, I'm pretty sure you would have just let it dry up and get infected."

I laugh, pushing out of the chair. "Nah. I know how to take care of myself, Miss Gabby."

"Yeah, the same way most men take care of themselves. By not bothering at all." She collects her stuff, putting it all back inside the kit. "My brother never used to cover his wounds. Such a pet peeve of mine."

I step off the porch. "You think you know men well, huh?"

She folds her arms. "Never said that, but I know most men."

"What could you possibly know about most men?"

"Um, just because I'm a little younger than you, doesn't mean I don't know much," she says matter-of-factly.

"I'm ten years your senior, Gabby. And other than your husband, you probably don't know much about other men at all. *Real* men."

"What's that supposed to mean?" She narrows her eyes at me.

"Just means he's probably your one and only. He's all you know. There's nothin' wrong with that. But it proves my point. Good girls usually stick to one guy, and that one guy is all she really knows."

Her eyes are rounder. She's tongue-tied. Her arms fall to her sides, then she turns to pick up the first-aid kit, inching toward the door. "You think you know me well…huh?" She's mimicking me, looking me right in the eyes.

"Not at all." I walk to my truck, still peering over my shoulder. "But with time, I'm sure I'll figure you out."

She huffs a laugh and grabs the doorknob, pushing the front door open. "You're so full of it, Mr. Ward!"

"Yeah, yeah. See you tomorrow, Miss Gabby!" She doesn't look back, but by the way her shoulders shake, I can tell she's laughing.

When her door is shut, I hop into my truck, start the engine, and leave her driveway, but during my ride to the liquor store, I can't get our conversation or that altercation with the first-aid kit out of my head.

Her hands were on me—not once, but *twice* today. I can tell she's just being nice—trying to fulfill her Samaritan role in life—but the girl doesn't know a damn thing about personal space.

Maybe it's the way she grew up. I can tell she and I are complete opposites. I'm not the one to reveal how I feel. I repress my emotions, yet she lays it all on the table and doesn't care how awkward it might make one feel. Hearing her talk about her family was strange, but in a way, I couldn't stop listening, because at least she has a family to talk about.

TEN

MARCEL

ALL YOU FUCKIN' do is judge me and complain about me being around!

Memories are the best and the worst sometimes. Memories serve as a means for comfort, or worse, your own demise. There are days when I only remember the good, and I smile.

My heart feels full when I think of Momma and Shay in the kitchen making french toast and eggs and singing to hits by Queen. For a moment, those memories make my life seem somewhat complete. And then there are the days when the bad memories come tunneling in. No matter how hard I try to avoid them, they pop up, and they are relentless.

So, I drink, hoping it will block it out. Sometimes it helps. Tonight, it doesn't.

I have a bottle of bourbon clutched in hand. I refill my empty glass and down it, then fill it halfway again. One thing that's worse than the memories? The regrets. There's so much I wish I could change. If only I could go back to that one night when I lost Shay…

Maybe if I hadn't been so angry, things would have tuned out differently. If I'd known it would be my last night around my baby sister, I would have told her I loved her. I wouldn't have been so damn mad at her for making a mistake.

"Fuck," I grumble. I top my glass off one more time, chug it down, and then push off the sofa, stumbling toward my table. I slam the bottle and empty tumbler down on the flat piece of wood, then drag my weight to my room, flopping face-down on my bed.

I roll over a little, looking to my left. Lucy is taking her usual nap before she leaves, her skin pale from the slits of moonlight spilling through my blinds. I use her, too, when I need a distraction.

I roll onto my back and tip my head up so my chin is pointed at the ceiling. I can see the moon from here, full and round, standing out in the blank, midnight blue sky. Wisps of clouds slowly roll past it.

I close my eyes and hear my pulse in my ears, and for a second, I drown in that sound—drown in the way my heart races due to the alcohol I drank. Blood rushes to my head, and there's nothing but the thudding of my heart, the swoosh of blood.

"You okay, baby?" Lucy's voice causes me to pop my eyes open. Her hand is on my chest, her eyes lazily peeled open.

"You need to go," I mumble, pushing her hand away and sitting up.

"You look like something's botherin' you. Sure you don't want another round? You have me all night." She climbs on top of me. I move my arms behind me, planting my palms on the bed. "Whatever's bothering you, I'll take it away," she whispers on my mouth.

"I don't know what I want." My words slur, and she sighs.

"Oh, baby," she croons, then she kisses the bend of my neck. I close my eyes and picture dark, curly hair in place of Lucy's blonde. Her lips trail down my chest and then she climbs off my lap, continuing down until I feel her mouth on my pelvis. "After I take care of you, I'll let you sleep."

A ragged breath escapes me. This is why I have Lucy around. She doesn't ask many questions unless I allow it. She knows I have issues, but she absorbs them and morphs all of my worries into pleasure. Don't ask me how she does it—I don't know—but it works, and I don't complain, especially on nights like this.

But as she drops her head, taking my erect cock into her mouth, it's not her I'm imagining down there while I have my eyes closed. I imagine dark-brown hair. Pouty pink lips. Light-brown skin sprinkled with freckles, and perky tits in a damn long-sleeved shirt. Unlike Lucy, this face is bare—no makeup, not even mascara around those olive eyes. She doesn't need it. Her natural lashes are long enough. She looks good every time I see her. It's a damn shame she's married.

"Gabby," I pant as Lucy runs her tongue over my balls. Fuck. *Gabby?* Why the fuck am I saying her name? Why the hell am I even thinking about her?

I open my eyes and look down at Lucy, trying to focus

on her blonde head and the smeared red lips around my cock.

I'm so fucking hard. I palm the back of her head, forcing myself deeper down her throat, but not without noticing the bandage on my arm. The bandage *Gabby* placed there while squatting in front of me.

Lucy takes me all in, gagging around me. I don't let up. I close my eyes and thrust upward, fucking her throat, pretending she's someone I know I shouldn't even be wasting my time fantasizing about. I pump quickly and Lucy moans loudly, until a deep growl rips out of me and I spill all I have down her throat.

"Oh, fuck," I groan as she swallows every single drop of my cum, the same way she always does, never letting any of it go to waste. My eyes slowly peel open again, and Lucy is licking dribbles of cum off the head of my cock before standing up straight.

This is Lucy. Fucking Lucy, not my client. What the fuck is wrong with me?

"This Gabby chick must have made you upset. You've never been *that* rough before," she says, running her fingers through her hair. She's smiling. She clearly liked the roughness.

I don't say anything.

She walks away, picking her clothes up and getting dressed while I fall on my back, throwing an arm over my forehead. When she's fully dressed, she leans over and kisses my cheek. "You clearly don't want to talk about it, so text me when you need me again," she whispers, and then she's walking out of the room. I hear the front door of my house close, and I know she's gone.

My eyelids grow heavy. If I weren't drunk, I'd be embarrassed, but Lucy doesn't know who Gabby is, and Gabby doesn't know shit about me.

I fantasize a lot…but not about my clients. Thinking about Gabby, even for that small moment, made me forget about the troubles. It made some of the pain go away…

Well, that's what I think, until I hear the screams.

The bad memories resurface again.

"Marcel, look out!"

"No," I groan, digging the heels of my hands into my eyes.

I feel the familiar stab beneath my rib, like I'm reliving that night all over again, then turn on my stomach to suck in a breath.

I wish I would have died that night. It would have made things a hell of a lot easier.

I have no one.

No family.

No friends.

I'm alone…and it's all my fucking fault.

ELEVEN

MARCEL

I'M HAVING second thoughts about doing this backyard for Gabby.

For one, she looks at me too closely. Most of my clients usually ignore me—pretend I don't even exist—but she's not like them, and I knew that from the moment I set eyes on her.

Also, she's the youngest client I've had. Doesn't take a genius to see it. Not only that, but she likes to pry. I can tell she's only making conversation—and that she's clearly bored out of her mind at home—but when she asked about Momma yesterday, it rubbed me the wrong way, and it made me think about my family way too much afterward. Thinking about Momma always leads me to thinking about Shay and even my father. It's a given.

Working helps me avoid thinking about family. I don't need Gabby fishing around, asking about them...because

I'm not talking about it. Not only that, but after remembering what I did to Lucy because I was thinking about Gabby has me feeling a little jolted. I can't stop stealing glances of her, just to make sure the vision I had in my head matches what I see now.

Dark and curly hair. Pouty, rosy lips. A full rack and hips that I see clearly due to the fact she's wearing a yellow tank top today. Her ass is round and plump enough to grab and squeeze with both of my hands. She's exactly what I envisioned last night—if not better. I'm so glad she can't read my mind right now.

"So, I think I finally figured out what kind of flowers I want planted," Gabby announces as she walks my way with her phone in hand.

I stand up straight after dropping my shovel. "Yeah? What kind?"

She practically shoves her phone in my face. My eyebrows rise as I take a step back, fighting a smile. I take the phone from her, studying the picture on the screen.

"Ah. Begonias. That's a good choice."

"Yeah? You think so?"

"Yeah. One of my favorite flowers to order and plant. Mainly 'cause they're low maintenance, take well to shaded areas, and can pretty much grow anywhere. Good for people who live in neighborhoods like these, who don't have much time to tend to their flowers, too. If they don't have the time, I usually come back or send someone to come and tend to the yard."

"Oh good!" She looks at her phone again. "I was thinking begonias and dahlias. Is that a weird combination?"

"Hmm...no. But you're the first client who has wanted dahlias. They're beautiful flowers, but also kind of expensive."

"I know, but I'm sure they'll be worth the money. I want them so I can think about home whenever I see them." She shuts the screen of her phone off and tucks it into the back pocket of her jean shorts. "My mom used to buy dahlias from her favorite flower shop. Granted, they never lasted for long, with our crazy weather, but they always soothed me when she bought them. She puts them in vases around the house. She would put some in a square vase on top of my dresser every week. Seeing them always put a smile on my face, especially in the mornings."

"Your mother sounds like a real nice woman."

"She is. She loves flowers. I have a love for them, too."

"Well, if those are a must-have for you, I'll be sure to order some of the best and have them planted when it's time. Dahlias take a few weeks to bloom. I believe eight weeks or so. Should be enough time before your house-warmin', though, if I get the order in now."

"Well good. That's perfect."

I pick up my clipboard and write the dahlias and begonias down on the sheet. She turns to look at the ocean in the distance, where it's slightly hidden behind green shrubbery and trunks of the palm trees. I look her up and down sideways, even though I've told myself a thousand times to stop fucking looking.

She's barefoot on the plush, green grass. Her legs are toned and bronze, like she's tanned and also like she enjoys doing squats.

She's definitely unlike my other clients, who always wear

dresses or suits. Her hair is damp and curlier than usual, like she's showered recently. She folds her arms over her chest, pushing her tits together, which isn't helping me one damn bit.

After what happened last night, my only wish is for her to go away so I can work in silence and without a distraction. I'm not really in the mood for much conversation today, but when she shifts on her feet and looks at me, almost like she's expecting me to carry on the conversation, I can't help it.

There is something about a bored, rich housewife. They're lonely creatures. All they want to do is talk and feel human, since their life partner is never fucking home, and if their partner is home, they're probably making any excuse to go out and sleep around. Why not indulge her?

"So," I start, placing my clipboard down, "other than that housewarming' you're hostin', what is it about the backyard you're most lookin' forward to?"

Her eyes light up as soon as I ask my question, and her arms fall rapidly, a simple gesture that means she's eager to chat and express herself.

"Oh—a lot of things." She sighs, taking a look around with wide eyes. "I've always wanted a space where I can go out and have a cup of coffee in the backyard before the sun rises, you know? Just seems so peaceful and a great way to wake up and kickstart the day." She drops her head and laughs.

"What?" I ask, laughing with her.

"Nothing. It's just...before you asked me that, I was thinking about this thing me and my brother used to do the first day of summer with my mom. She'd make me and my brother a big pitcher of lemonade, turn on the sprinklers for us in the backyard, and we'd play for hours. I always wanted one of those big pools, but knew my parents couldn't really afford it. My mom was always upset that she couldn't get it, so on my tenth birthday, when my dad got a promotion and a good bonus, they surprised me and my brother with one. I was happy, swam in it all summer long. Never got tired of it."

"Sounds like a good childhood. Lovin' parents."

"They are very loving. Very good people."

"They live close?" I squint my eyes a little when I look up at her, the sun nearly blinding me.

She shakes her head, and I watch her eyes sadden. "No, but I wish they did. Would make some of my days a lot more fun."

"You miss 'em so much, why don't you go and visit?"

"I don't know. Feels too soon for a visit after our recent move, you know? They'll be here for the housewarming, I'm sure. I can wait for that."

"Well, it's never too soon to see a loved one, Miss Gabby." I grab the garden fork from the corner and walk a few steps away from her, pitching it into the ground. I'm trying to bite my tongue but it's damn near impossible. This girl is definitely lonely. "How long have you and your husband been together? If you don't mind me askin'…"

"No, I don't mind. We've been together for two years. Married for three months now."

"Three months is still fresh. It's March now, so when did it happen—back in December?"

"Yep. We had a Christmas Eve wedding," she states proudly.

I almost start to say he shouldn't be able to stay away from her for so long, but who am I to say it? Also, a Christmas wedding? What a cop-out, picking a date that's easy to remember. "Well, congrats on gettin' married. I'm sure he's a great guy. Lucky to have you, definitely."

I don't know if it's just me, but it's almost like she hesitates before saying, "Yeah, he is a great guy."

She steps away, looking toward the double doors of the kitchen. "Well, I'll leave you to it, but can I get you anything? I can make a snack or whatever to get you through the day? I have lots of veggies and peanut butter."

"Sure. Make whatever you want. I don't turn down food." I don't usually eat while I work, either, but like I said before, I grew up with manners grounded into me by my mother and father, and it's common courtesy for us to accept what's offered…unless it's from strangers or people who can't cook, of course.

"Okay. I'll see what I can whip up for you." She rushes back into her house, and I get back to work. I can't help thinking how she should be making snacks for her *husband*, who should be at home with her, not for me, but I won't complain.

It appears she needs something to do—that she wants to be useful to someone. I won't deny her hospitality, but it does concern me that a girl like her—so friendly and vulnerable—is in this brand-new home and alone for days, especially with random men working right at her back door.

Sooner or later, a quiet home starts to drive people up a wall. And trust me, I know all about that from experience.

≈

"Hey, Ward—Miguel just texted me. Said he'll be here Monday with the stones and paver sand," Jacob informs me as he walks around the corner with an extra gardening hoe. It's almost time for my crew to wrap up, and I'm ready. I could use a hot shower and a good meal right now.

"Good. That means we need to have the base done and get ready to put the frame around the perimeter today. Won't be workin' this weekend. Got meetings."

"Got you." Jacob uses the hoe to remove more of the grass and weeds from the soon-to-be patio area.

"Hey, not even kidding though, the girl we're working for is fucking *hot*," Alex says, smirking at me as he saws a piece of wood for the frame. "I see you flirting with her too, boss."

"No one's flirtin'," I mutter.

"Yeah right," Jacob laughs. "She's got her eyes all over you!"

"She's married," I inform them.

"So what!" Jacob laughs. "Women who live in houses like *these* are always looking for their next lawn boy to bone. Shit, if you don't do it, I will."

I put the clipboard down and head to the patio area, grabbing the mallet and stakes. I hammer one of the stakes into the grass before looking up at him and raising a stern brow.

"I'm just saying," he laughs, throwing his hands in the air. "She's bringing us snacks and drinks. She *wants* us to see her."

"She's bein' nice. Leave her alone." I move over, pounding the next stake into the ground.

Jacob and Alex look at each other and then snicker. I

ignore them both. They're my youngest employees, but good at what they do. I'd much rather work with Mauricio and Rob, though. Less goofing off with those two.

"You two go get the gravel so we can start on the base," I order, and they drop their tools, walking around the house to get to the company truck. I add another stake into the ground, and as I do, I can't help looking up at the second floor.

Gabby is in front of the arched window that she'd told me belonged to her studio. Her cellphone is pressed to her ear. I frown a bit as she closes her eyes for a second and then says something, almost in defeat. Then she hangs up and turns away from the window quickly.

I don't think much of it as Alex and Jacob come back with the gravel and dump it into the wheelbarrow. They dump and spread it in the rectangular cutout we shoveled before, and while they do, I go for my bottle of water on the cement steps. I hear a car door shut a short distance away and then the car lock alarm gives a short beep.

I get back to work, but I notice a tall Asian man walking into the kitchen of Gabby's home. He's wearing a blue button-down shirt and gray dress pants. He's saying something—assumedly to Gabby—and then he moves out of sight, and she walks through the kitchen to follow him.

When they're back in plain sight, he says something to her that makes her smile, then cups her face in his hands, kissing her on the mouth. It's not a delicate or passionate kiss, like most married couples' are. He holds her face like he *owns* it, kissing her way too hard. She stumbles a little, but gains her footing as he kisses her again.

By the third kiss, I look away and get back to work.

Maybe that's what she likes, and maybe she was right about what she said to me yesterday. Maybe I don't know shit about girls like her.

Of course, not even a minute later, the double doors swing open. Gabby walks out with the man trailing behind her. She smiles at me, but it's not warm like the others she'd given me before. This one is forced.

The man steps beside her and takes a look around the backyard. From where he stands, I realize he's almost the same height as I am, and I'm six-foot-two. He's wearing dress shoes, though, so maybe he's around six feet even with them off. Gabby is about five inches shorter. She's slightly shorter than Shay, who was about five feet and five inches.

"Man, this is a mess!" the man says to no one in particular, eyes widening. "Think I liked it better the way it was."

"It's not done yet, Kyle," Gabby says to him, her voice soft. So this is the infamous Kyle. I can see why she's with him. He's a decent-looking gentleman. Clean, crisp clothes that are clearly tailored to fit him. Gabby's eyes swoop over to meet mine, and this time her smile is warmer. "This is Mr. Marcel Ward, the owner of the landscaping company. They're doing a great job so far. Fast workers. Marcel, this is my husband, Kyle Moore."

Kyle takes a small step forward as I extend my arm to shake his hand. "Nice to meet you, Mr. Moore."

"Likewise, Mr. Ward." He steps back, reclaiming his spot next to Gabby. His hand goes around her waist and he reels her in just a bit, tightening his hold around her. I briefly focus on the hand he has locked around her waist before peering up at her, but her smile doesn't change. She smiles even harder. Clearly, she's used to this motherfucker's ways.

I put my eyes on his again. "I appreciate you letting us take on this project, Mr. Moore. We won't disappoint you."

"I sure hope not," he replies way too smugly. "Then I'd have to hire someone to rip it up and start all over."

I avoid saying something slick. I've met men like him. Small dicks and big egos, as I like to call it. I know how to handle him.

"That won't be the case with my crew workin' on it." I really want to pick up a shovel and hit him square in the face with it. I don't know what it is about him, but I know for a fact that this guy's an asshole. How did someone as caring as Gabby end up with an arrogant fucker like him?

"Right." Kyle grabs his wife's hand and turns for the house. "Well, it was nice meeting you, Mr. Ward. Gabby, let's go before we're late for our reservation, hmm?"

"Yeah, come on." She nods at Kyle before glancing over her shoulder at me. He's escorting her into the house, his hand on the small of her back.

"Have a good weekend, Miss Gabby."

She turns and looks at me in full this time, putting on a real smile. "Thank you, Mr. Ward. Have a great weekend."

The doors close quickly, courtesy of Mr. Kyle Moore himself, who gives me a slight frown beforehand, and for the first time since I've visited this house, the blinds of the double doors slide shut too.

"Well damn," Jacob says, resting most of his weight on the handle of a shovel. "That guy's a fucking prick."

"A prick with a smokin' hot wife," Alex eggs on, then he goes back to compacting the gravel. "It's always a fucking shame when girls like that choose money over happiness. Did you see her eyes? She's trying to be all go-lucky happy around him, but that chick is probably miserable as fuck on the inside. I bet he doesn't satisfy her. She needs a real man, you know what I mean, boss?"

"Not my problem," I mutter, as I get back to the stakes. "We'll finish stakin' and compactin' and get back to this on Monday mornin'." I side-eye the double doors and can't help wondering what they might be doing on the other side of them.

It shouldn't bug me that they could possibly be fucking on the table I once sat at, but it does, and only because that motherfucker doesn't deserve a girl like her. I've only met him once, and I'm already not a fan.

I'm hoping that come Monday, that prick is back on a plane and over eight hundred miles away, not here, shifting everyone's mood, including his wife's.

That wasn't the Gabby I'd been talking to for the past three days. That was someone else, and whoever that was she was trying to be, I don't fucking like her one bit.

TWELVE

GABBY

Kᴍᴇ ᴡᴏᴜʟᴅɴ'ᴛ ᴛᴇʟʟ me where we were eating while I got dressed, but an hour later, I find myself seated on the second floor of *Ellie's L'Etoile Verte*. In front of me is a freshly tossed house salad and to the right of me is a bottle of champagne on ice.

"Kyle," I say, laughing a little. "What is all this?"

"Just a little way to warm ourselves up to the area," he says, smiling wide at me. "We haven't had the chance to celebrate our move. I've been busy working, and we were unpacking for the past two weeks. We deserve this time to relax, escape." He reaches across the table for my hands and squeezes them.

"Aww. This is really sweet."

"Had a table reserved since last week." He motions to one of the waiters, and as if he'd told her the plan before, she takes the champagne off the ice and opens it, causing a loud *pop* to ring around us.

I giggle as the champagne slowly spills over, but the waitress is skilled. She already has two glasses in her right hand, allowing the champagne to serve itself as the frothy, gold bubbles fill the glass. "Enjoy," she murmurs, placing the glasses down in front of us. Kyle gives her a simple bob of the head, and she walks off.

"Let's make a toast to this new beginning." Kyle lifts his flute up and I do the same. "This is to our happiness, a brighter future, and to our love. Nothing will ever break us, babe."

I nod in agreement. "Nothing, babe."

Our glasses clink, and we sip while classical music softly plays from the speakers around us.

"So," Kyle starts, sitting back in his chair. "The men doing the backyard aren't giving you any trouble, are they?"

His question catches me off guard. "Why would they be giving me trouble?"

"Well, just that you're home alone a lot, and there are a lot of them compared to you. I know how those men like to catcall and stare and whatever else they do."

"They're fine, Kyle." I sit up straight. "They're actually really nice. The boss answers all of my questions and gives me the rundown on what's next, so I'm not confused about what they're doing."

"Hmm." He sips his champagne. "I still think my instincts were right about him, though. Seems like an incompetent jerk. Knew it from that email he sent you when he got you to make me change my mind."

I laugh. "He's not an asshole. He's a good guy—his whole crew is great."

"Well, I'll be glad when they're done. The yard is a disaster," he scoffs. "Are you sure they're going to be able to get it done within the next few weeks? The plan is to have it done by May, correct?"

"He guaranteed it. I'm sure they will finish before then."

"All right." Kyle sits forward, resting his elbows on the table. "Look, Gabs. I feel like shit for working so much. I'm trying really hard to have the office relocated to South Carolina, or at least someplace that's within reasonable driving distance."

"Oh my gosh, Kyle. I told you it's fine, babe! Stuff like that takes time."

"Yeah I know. It's just a tricky situation. If I move the company, we'll have to find new employees around the area. I'm sure most of them won't want to relocate. They have families, all of that stuff. I have to work out the kinks."

"I understand." I place my hand on top of his, rubbing it. "Is everything okay with your dad? Did you see him?"

"Yeah, he's better," he sighs. "Mum says he's been stubborn, probably mad he's stuck in the house for most of his days now. No more golf trips or hiking. None of that extreme stuff he liked to do."

"Poor Pops."

"Yeah. But, he'll be okay. It's good that he gets to stay home. He needs to relax, for once in his damn life."

"I agree." I look him over and feel a rush of warmth run through my chest. My husband is truly, truly handsome.

When I first met him, I fell in love with his almond-shaped eyes and the thick lashes that surround his dark-brown irises. His beige skin is several shades lighter than mine, his black hair always combed with gel. His muscles are solid beneath his white dress shirt, and I want so badly to run my fingers over his chest, just to feel how rock hard and solid he is. Kyle loves to keep himself in shape. He's the reason I started taking my health more seriously.

I found out on our second date that he's biracial—mixed with British and Malaysian blood. He was born in Malaysia, was brought to Great Britain as a baby, and then his family moved to the United States when he was thirteen. He claims his accent isn't as strong as it once was, but to me it's still defined, and the sound of it is to die for.

Sometimes I love when he leaves because when he returns, I always find more things to love about him that I hadn't noticed before. For instance, his smile. When he's worried, it becomes lopsided, but it makes him appear so sweet. So innocent. I can tell he's concerned about his father, but he wants to keep the mood positive, so I let it go…for now.

"What?" he asks, smiling at me, revealing one of his dimples.

"Nothing. I just missed you. That's all."

His eyes light up. "I missed you too, babe." As if we've read each other's minds, we both lean over the table just enough to give a peck on each other's lips.

The waitress returns several minutes later, this time with the food we ordered. She places my crab salad down in front of me, and Kyle's grilled tuna in front of him. Kyle thanks her, and she leaves us to our meals.

The food is simply amazing, and for the rest of our dinner, Kyle and I talk about some of the changes he's making to the company as well as the lunch he shared with his parents yesterday.

By the time we walk to the car, I'm satisfied, filled with good food, and even greater champagne.

Kyle drives home with the sunroof of the BMW open, laughing at me as one of my favorite songs by Rihanna comes on. I sing about diamonds in the sky while he cruises home, and we both take in the beach air and our new surroundings.

Palm trees are on every corner, and the AC is on, mixing with the natural beach air spilling through the sunroof. I try to get him to sing with me, but he's so modest, waving a hand, telling me I've got it. Nights like this with him are always the best. When he comes home, I have all of his attention.

When we get out of the car, Kyle wraps an arm around my waist, then lowers his hand to cup my ass as we walk up the stoop. I grin up at him as he leads the way to our front door, but as soon as we're inside the house and the door is locked behind us, I can't hold back anymore.

I turn in his arms and jump up. He catches me, cupping my ass in his hands as I kiss him. "I missed you," I moan between kisses.

"Mmm, I missed you too, babe."

We don't even make it to the bedroom. He's stumbling to the kitchen with me in his hands, bumping into the island counter. I tear at his creaseless buttoned shirt, yanking it apart. The buttons fly across the kitchen floor, but I don't care. I've waited long enough. I need him.

"Mmm…babe. What's going on?" he asks as I suck on his bottom lip.

I have no idea what's going on, and I don't want to think about it or make sense of it. For once, I want us to chase our instincts.

Kyle likes to take the lead. He's always been that way, but I want him to sense my urgency. I want him to stop asking questions, stop treating me so delicately, and just *take* me.

But, of course, he doesn't. His hands carefully roam down, drifting over my waist. He moves between my legs, his strained cock on my lower belly. I press on his chest, trying to push him back so I can climb down and get on my knees, but he resists. I groan in protest. He pretends he doesn't hear it.

"Unfasten my belt," he mumbles on my mouth, and I do so without hesitation. I unzip his pants too, even though he didn't ask me to. When he lowers his pants, he brings my bottom closer to the edge of the counter. His hand runs up my thigh and goes beneath my skirt.

"Shit, Gabs," he breathes on my mouth. "Why aren't you wearing any panties?"

"I've been waiting for this since you called and told me you were on the way," I pant.

He studies my eyes very briefly, then he goes back to it, cupping one of my cheeks and using his other hand to grip his cock and point it at my entrance. When he tilts his hips and thrusts inside me, I gasp, throwing my arms around his neck. I want him to go slow, torture me just a little, but he doesn't.

Kyle is tired. I can always tell by the way he starts thrusting quickly, not even giving me a chance to adjust around him. It's been a week since we last had sex, and he hates when I play with myself while he's away, so I don't tease or taunt my own body. I just wait for him.

I'm so impatient right now that I beg him to take it slow, to take his time, but he's so lost in the moment—so lost inside me.

He brings the hand on my cheek up to the back of my neck and holds it, gluing his chest to mine, trying to get deeper. He succeeds, and I moan while his body stiffens. By the way his other arm locks around me, I can tell he's about to come.

"Oh, God. Oh, yes, Gabby." He's holding me close, coming hard. He remains still for a split second, then sluggishly pulls himself away.

I press my lips, tucking my hair behind my ears.

"Damn, you're so good," he says, then drops a kiss on my lips. I force a smile as he helps me off the counter. "Come on," he murmurs. "Let's hit the shower. Get some sleep."

I nod, but deep inside my heart plummets. I hate the thoughts that take over, because I know Kyle is exhausted. I know he's had a long week and now that he's home all he wants to do is rest.

Our sex sessions are never long, and if he doesn't take care of me the same night we have sex, he definitely will the next morning. I try not to stress over it.

Once we've showered, I rub some lotion on while Kyle puts on his pajamas. He drags himself to bed, curling up on his side of the mattress. I finish putting on lotion and then toss on a silky, pearly-white gown. It's his favorite one—the one that reveals a lot of bosom. Shutting off the lights, I climb in bed and rest my head on his chest.

"Kyle?" I call.

"Hmm?"

"Let's go again," I plead.

He's quiet a beat. His breathing levels out. "I'm tired, Gabs. It's been such a long day. I'll make it up to you tomorrow, I promise."

The disappointment I feel stings, but only because I don't want to wait until tomorrow. I want—no, I *need* it —right now.

"Kyle," I whine, but he doesn't respond, and I'm annoyed that he made me sound like a whiny little bitch. I pick my head up to look at him, and he's asleep.

Gah! I swear he's narcoleptic, falling asleep at the drop of a hat!

"Ugh." I roll away from him, lying flat on my back. I feel a fire between my legs—its raging and needs to be put out immediately. I cross my ankles and stare up at the ceiling, trying to block the urgency and fall asleep, but it's impossible.

I sit up and peer around the dark room. *I need wine.*

Rolling out of bed, I walk downstairs to get to the kitchen, pouring myself a glass of white wine. Afterward, I walk to the living room and sit on my favorite spot on the L-shaped sofa.

From where I sit, I can see the backyard. The lights reveal the stakes that are in the ground, as well as a wheelbarrow with the words *Ward Landscaping* printed on the side of it.

Seeing it instantly reminds me of Mr. Ward. I sip my wine, ignoring the thought that rapidly crosses me. Then I take another sip. And then comes a big gulp. Before I know it, I've finished my wine, but I don't let myself sit for too long. I go back to the kitchen and refill my glass, then head back to my spot on the sofa.

I take several sips of the fruity wine, staring at that damn wheelbarrow, remembering Marcel that first day, without his shirt.

"No," I mutter. *No, I'm not doing it. I'm not about to put images in my head of my landscaper.* That's what I tell myself, but the longer I focus on that black wheelbarrow with white letters, the more I think about his voice. His smoky, Southern accent, that I find way too damn appealing.

I place my glass down and then sit back, sinking into the cushion of the sofa. My hands slide over my belly, then across my inner thighs. The silky material of my gown is pushed up to my hips, and I'm not wearing panties, due to the anticipation of having Kyle again.

I know he doesn't like it when I do this. He hates when I play with myself. He believes that since we're together, I should only need him. Normally, I respect that, but for some reason—in this very moment—I can't help it.

I keep picturing Mr. Ward standing outside, watching me as I run my fingers over my thighs and across my bare pussy.

My breath hitches as I slide a finger between the damp slit and press on my clit. I suck in another breath, running circles around it, causing it to swell rapidly. I can't stop. I picture Mr. Ward telling me to keep going while he watches, then I picture him working all day, shirtless, but still having the energy at night to carry me into the kitchen and place his mouth between my legs.

It's so fucked up, but I hear his deep groans as he tastes

my pussy, calling me a *demandin' little thing*, all because I know what I want.

I know what I *need*.

And what I need is to come. *Right now.*

"Oh my God." A ragged breath slips out of me. Before I know it, I'm completely unraveling, and I can't hold back on the shrill yelp that escapes my parted lips. My legs shake violently as my fingers slow in pace, dragging in slow, torturous circles, and I come hard—way too hard—all over a fantasy.

A fantasy that involves my damn *landscaper*.

When I'm done, I look around, as if Kyle can see me, but no one is around. Nothing but that damn wheelbarrow. I swear the letters on it are taunting me.

I hurry to sit up, grabbing my glass and taking it to the kitchen sink, shutting the lights off, and then tip-toeing back up to my bedroom.

I climb back in the bed, but I feel so guilty about my fantasy and the powerful orgasm that followed that I don't even bother cuddling with Kyle. I'm afraid he'll sense that I've pleasured myself behind his back, so I roll over with my back to him instead.

My body is satisfied, the fire between my legs no longer blazing like a furnace, but there's still a slight yearning for more. After a while, it becomes harder for me to keep my eyes open, so I fall asleep.

It's the best sleep I've had since moving into this house.

THIRTEEN

GABBY

I SPEND the entire weekend with Kyle, and it's definitely needed. We wake up early Saturday morning, catch breakfast, and then go to the nearest outlet for new clothes. He purchases new dress pants and shirts, while I hunt for jean shorts and tops I can wear around the house.

When we come across an art store, I gasp, releasing my hold around Kyle's arm to run inside. Of course, I don't leave empty handed. I find clay, paint brushes, and modeling tools. I start to pull my wallet out of my tote bag, but Kyle stops me, smiling down at me with his wallet already in hand.

"I've got it," he says to both me and the cashier.

I shake my head and grin up at him, but I don't stop him. I do, however, blush like a dazed idiot.

After we leave, we catch lunch and then a movie before heading home. At home, we curl up in bed, and this time he doesn't hesitate to satisfy me first. He uses his fingers, sliding them between my legs and thrusting two of them inside me, just the way I like, while his lips hover over mine, feathery light. Teasing.

"You're so beautiful," he murmurs on my mouth. "My gorgeous wife."

I come around his fingers, clutching his arm tight, and after my body has died down, he shifts his way between my thighs, his boxers already shoved below his waist. He grabs my waist to tilt my hips up and enters me with a deep grunt, holding me tight.

This time his thrusts aren't quick. They're fluid and easy-going, and the longer he goes, the more I feel myself reaching the highest of heights. But I need more to truly get there.

There are times when I wish Kyle would talk to me more while we have sex. Now is one of those times. It's more of a fantasy, but then again, he's not much of a talker during our romps. We just watch each other's eyes and let our bodies conjure whatever noises they naturally make.

I told him what I wanted once, in a very overly-sexual manner, and he stopped while we were doing it to question it. He seemed confused, but went back to it, pretending it never even happened.

Ever since I saw that look in his eyes, one of shock and displeasure, I don't tell him what I want much. I don't like ruining the moment, so I just take him as he is, even more so now because he leaves town a lot to work.

I watch Kyle come, squeezing his eyes tight, his muscles glistening with sweat as they lock. He drops his forehead to my chest, resting it in the gap between my breasts, panting raggedly as he pulls out of me.

"I love you so much," he breathes.

"Love you more," I whisper back.

Kyle falls asleep first, but I don't drift off without realizing there's a fire again—an insatiable hunger that aches for so much more. If only my husband would realize this too.

Then again, how can he, when I'm too nervous to mention it?

Before I know it, it's Monday morning. Kyle has to catch a flight for work and won't return until Thursday.

"I can't believe it's already time for you to go." I pout a little, helping him carry his briefcase downstairs. I follow him to the door, and he presses his lips. As I place it down, I think I move a little too quickly, because I feel a pain on my shoulder and wince.

"You okay?" he asks, touching my shoulder. I nod, smiling up at him. "Yeah, I'm fine. Think I just moved too fast."

He looks me over, mildly concerned, before sighing. "Stretch it a bit. It should help. This week's important, otherwise I'd just work here. So much is in transition with my father being out of work, you know? I want to make sure it's all handled properly."

He cups my face, and I nod with understanding. "I get it. Trust me."

He focuses on my eyes. "You don't like being here alone." It's a statement. And it's true.

I shrug. "It gets a little boring."

"I'll call more—twice a day. That way it'll feel like I'm still here with you."

I smile up at him. "Once is fine, as long as it's for more than ten minutes," I laugh.

He chuckles. "Okay. I'll be sure to give you a call tonight. I won't let work get in the way this time."

It's interesting that he says that. Work does come in the way a lot. Kyle wakes up early to work and goes to bed after 2 a.m. most nights, which leaves little time to talk on the phone. He does text me when he can, which is fine. He has never really been big on phone calls. We started getting serious through text messages and face-to-face meets, but now we're married, and there's distance between us the majority of the week, so phone calls are a must.

Kyle kisses me with my face still in his hands. I kiss him back, sighing as he releases me to grab his suitcase. I follow him to his car with the briefcase, where he pops the trunk and tosses his suitcase inside. Before he can close the trunk, I see Alex and Jacob getting out of a car and collecting their tools, then a familiar black Ford pickup appears, rolling into our driveway and parking close to the grass and out of Kyle's way.

"Oh, boy," Kyle groans as Marcel climbs out of his truck. "They're a little early, aren't they?" he asks, tossing a wave at Marcel as Marcel gives him a quick nod of the head.

"No, they're always here this early."

"Hmm." Kyle looks away from him and focuses on me. I hand the briefcase to him and he takes it, then holds one side of my face, kissing my cheek and then my lips. "I'll text you as soon as I land."

I nod. "Okay."

He pulls away and goes to the driver's side, climbing in and starting the car. I watch him leave the driveway, but not before giving me a wave goodbye, his arm out of the open window. I wave back, and then he's gone.

Sighing, I turn to look at Marcel. He's already got his tool bag hitched on his shoulder. There's a dip in his brow as he looks from where Kyle just drove off, to me, and if I'm not mistaken, his head shakes only slightly, and then he gives me his back, walking around the house to get to the backyard.

I huff a laugh, staring off at where he disappeared. *What the hell was that about?*

"Morning, Mrs. Moore!" Alex yells as he takes the path that leads to the back.

"Morning!" I yell back, waving. I still haven't gotten used to that name.

"What will you be treating us with today?" he asks, and I notice the way he smirks at Jacob before giving me a lazy grin.

"Sorry, guys. Nothing today." I walk to my porch and up the stoop. "I have lots of catching up to do today, unfortunately."

"Aw, that sucks." I hear them chuckle, but I don't pay it any mind. They remind me of my brother and his friends, when we still lived with our parents. He and his friends constantly goofed around. It's nothing new, and nothing I can't handle.

They probably don't realize that I've noticed the way

they look at me, as if I'm a piece of meat. They don't do it blatantly, and for that they get my respect, but I can tell when they've been looking because when I catch them, their eyes always swoop up fast, like they hadn't done anything at all.

Same goes for Marcel, although he doesn't look at me like meat. He looks at me more like I'm a puzzle he's trying to figure out. I wonder if he realizes he's just as much a puzzle to me as I am to him.

Either way, I shouldn't care so much. He's just the landscape architect. Nothing more.

FOURTEEN

GABBY

My Monday is occupied with the tools and clay Kyle bought for me at the outlet. I don't know why, but something inside me tells me to sculpt a flower—a dahlia, to be exact.

I've been working on it all morning, using my fingers and hands to mold the clay, and then my cutter to get the detail of it in production. I normally work with music, but it's quiet today, minus the sounds of the men in my back-yard working…which I try to ignore.

I don't realize it's lunch time until the alarm on my phone goes off. I set alarms for lunch or a snack, especially if I'm sculpting, otherwise I will lose track of time and forget to eat, especially without Kyle around. The other day I had a really bad headache and couldn't figure out where it'd come from. I'd complained on the phone with Kyle, and the first thing he asked me was, "Did you eat, Gabs?" It hit me

111

in that moment that no, I hadn't eaten all day. I'd had some tea, but no actual food.

Sighing, I place my tools down and go to the bathroom in the hallway to wash my hands. When I make it to the kitchen, I pull out the ingredients to make a Caesar salad and start preparing it at the island counter.

From where I stand, I can hear one of the men grunting. I look over and see one of them carrying what looks like a bag of sand or dirt. I'm curious by nature, so of course I want to know what they're doing. Not only that, but Marcel mentioned they're going to start laying the stones today, and I want to see how it looks…then again, I'm a little too nervous to go out there today. After what I did Friday night, I don't know if I can look at Marcel the same without thinking about it.

Instead, I finish making my salad, pour myself a cup of watermelon juice, and sit at my table. I look out of the window, noticing Marcel standing a few steps away from some of the men who are organizing the stones and laying them down. Both hands are resting on his hips and of course—*of course!*—he's shirtless.

I know I shouldn't, but this time I really study his chest. It's not bare like Kyle's. Marcel has light traces of hair on the middle of his chest and on his lower belly, but not so much to make him look like a grizzly bear. His dark hair is damp with sweat, clinging to his forehead. He drops his hands to walk to a table behind him, where water bottles are lined up. He cracks one open and chugs half of it down.

Then his eyes shift over, right to my door. He is not the least bit surprised to see me gawking. His eyes narrow, lips pushing together. By the mischievousness that begins to swirl in his eyes, I'm pretty sure he was hoping I'd catch him with his shirt off...which is stupid to think and can't be true, because he's not interested in me.

I clear my throat and finish my salad, ignoring him as much as possible. As I sip my juice, there's a knock at the patio door. Marcel is standing behind it, peering through the blinds. I set my glass down, pushing out of my chair to get the door.

"Yes?" I ask when the door is open. I purposely avoid looking down, but the mixture of his sweet-smelling sweat and deodorant that runs past my nose is hard to ignore.

"If I weren't mistaken, I'd say you've been avoidin' me today, Miss Gabby! And here I am, thinkin' we're friends!"

I laugh, but his statement couldn't be truer. I have to avoid him, to avoid thinking about the fantasy I had of him. "We *are* friends. I've just been busy sculpting. Came down for some lunch."

"Oh, okay. Yeah, we'll be having lunch in a minute. Anyway, just wanted to know if you'd like to check out the stones so far," he says, and he's talking just like before. Friendly. Casual.

"Uh...I'll probably take a look later. I don't want to get in the way, plus it's really hot today." I force a smile.

"Yeah, it is." He steps backs and gives me a sideways glance. "All right then, just checkin'."

He starts to walk back to where his crew is bending down and aligning the stones.

"Mr. Ward?" I call, and he halts, peering over his shoulder.

"Are we resortin' to formalities again, Mrs. Moore?"

I frown. "No—I'm sorry. Marcel," I correct myself.

"Yes ma'am?" He turns to fully face me, hands at his waist again.

"Earlier you gave me a look when Kyle left…" I start my sentence, but can't finish. That look has been bothering me all day.

"Oh, you mean the look I give to all the people who I think are full of shit?" His eyes have lit up, like he's been looking forward to having this conversation, or at least glad to get that statement off his chest.

"Are you talking about my husband or me?" I ask, folding my arms defensively.

"Of course it isn't you, Gabby. You're much nicer than he is."

"So…my husband then?"

He shrugs, but his eyes tell it all.

"You hardly know him. How could you possibly assume he's full of shit?"

"I know he doesn't approve of me and my crew. Still thinks he'll find someone better, which he won't. Also, I have no doubt he's the kind of person who'll find someone to rip all of this up, just to prove how much of an arrogant, rich asshole he is."

"Wow." My eyes stretch, brows nearly touching my fore-head. "You do realize that he's my *husband*, and I tell him pretty much everything, right?"

"No, you don't." He drops his hands and my barely-there smile collapses. He sounds so sure of himself. "Wanna know how I know?"

I don't say anything. He fills me in anyway.

"Because after you introduced us, and when I called you *Miss Gabby*, he looked at me sideways, like he didn't understand the name, probably wonderin' why I didn't call you Mrs. Moore instead. If you tell your husband everything, then you would have told him that I made up some silly, harmless nickname for you as a little inside joke after I'd said it, but you didn't, and probably never will."

I narrow my eyes at him, taking a step forward. "It's just a name. Doesn't mean anything more than me calling you Mr. Ward or you calling my husband Mr. Moore. And like you said, it's a habit of yours. I'm sure you call all of your clients Mister or Miss."

"Actually, you're the first one who has gotten the M-I-S-S tag, despite the fact you're married. Most are called by the M-R-S tag along with their husband's last names...just to keep it all business."

I scoff and look away. "Either way, it's still harmless. No, I didn't tell him about the name, but it's only because when I do get the chance to talk to him, the last thing on my mind is the *landscape guy.*"

Marcel's eyes stretch wide. He looks taken aback, and by the dip in his brows, I can tell I've just ruined his whole mood. I clamp my mouth shut, immediately regretting the words that slipped out. *Why did I say that? Oh my gosh, I'm such a bitch!*

"Oh, I see." He backs away, nodding as he looks off.

"Wait—Marcel, I didn't mean it that way. There's nothing wrong with you being the landscape guy. It's perfectly fine, and you're great at it!"

"No, Mrs. Moore. You know what? This is my fault. I've clearly gotten a little too comfortable around here the past few days, and it shouldn't be that way. After all, this is busi-ness, and I'm here to work. I stepped out of line the moment I shared my first personal conversation with you. That was a mistake on my part. It won't happen again."

"Marcel, I—"

He turns away from me, heading back to his crew without looking back. He doesn't hesitate to help Rob with lining the stones evenly. I go back inside, but take one more look at him along the way. His jaw is clenched tight, brows furrowed.

I've really upset him.

God, why would I say something so ignorant?

FIFTEEN

MARCEL

How can one little comment ruin my whole fuckin' day?

It's what I keep asking myself, but it doesn't make any sense.

She's my client and, trust me, I've had people say worse shit than that to me, but when it comes from *her*, that shit stings for some reason.

There I was, thinking we were on the same page. I guess I was wrong, and maybe she's built for that asshole husband of hers more than I assumed.

By the time the sun has set, half of the patio has been laid with stone. It's good for our first day, so I call it quits until tomorrow and have my crew pack up.

As I collect my lunch box and tools, I hear one of the patio doors open and roll my eyes.

"Mr. Ward? May I have a word?" I hear Gabby ask

meekly. I glance over my shoulder. Most of my men are gone. Only Rob remains, but as soon as he picks up his bag, he walks around the house and tosses a wave goodbye at me.

Only person left is me.

With a sigh, I turn to face Gabby. It's then I notice the plate of cookies in her hands. She gives me an innocent smile as I walk closer. "I, uh, I made these for you. I had to call my mom for the recipe. I even went to the store to get vanilla extract and baking soda."

I glance down at the plate. Chocolate chip.

"Thanks, but I'll have to pass," I mutter, hiking the strap of my bag on my shoulder.

"Oh, come on, Marcel! It took me two hours to make and bake these! Take them with you, eat them at home."

"I'm not goin' straight home."

"Well I can wrap them in foil and put them in a container."

"No. Busy tonight."

"Oh." She seems disappointed. "What is it? A guy's night out kind of thing? Work related?" She puts on a smile, trying to lighten the mood. It's too fucking late for that.

"How is that your business, Gabby?" I wasn't kidding about what I said earlier—this is business and nothing more. No more accepting lemonade and cookies and shit.

She frowns, shifting on her feet nervously. "I'm just asking."

I sigh and turn, walking toward the path that'll lead me around the house.

"Wait—Marcel! Are you really not going to take these? I made them just for you."

I swing around. She's still standing in the same spot,

watching me. "You ever think that maybe makin' shit and givin' it to people isn't the way to solve your problems? Nothin' is ever solved that way."

"W-what do you mean?"

"Not once have you apologized, Gabby—not that I'm expectin' you to. I could give a shit about an apology. They don't mean anything to me. But my thing is, if you're feelin' like you have to do all of this just to talk to me—bakin' cookies and shit—well, clearly you aren't pleased with what you said, which warrants an apology from most people." I narrow my eyes at her as she looks at me absently. "But I've known since the day I met you that you aren't like most people, and, frankly, it isn't my job to figure you out or want to know what kind of person you really are, whether that's a happy woman who loves her husband, or a bored wife who is playing a charade and pretending this is the life she wants, just to get by. I'm only here to clock in, do my job as the *landscape guy*, and go home, so let me do that."

She opens her mouth, but it clamps shut instantly. Her eyes are glistening, but she blinks right away, getting rid of the sheen in her eyes.

I look her over once more before walking away, and I don't bother looking back, even though I feel her watching me go—even though I'm tempted to see the look on her face one last time.

It shouldn't bother her. She's got a good life. Most housewives brush it off, rant about it with their friends, and chase it away with a glass of wine.

But Gabby is complicated as fuck, blurring the lines between business and being personable, and I don't like it.

The best thing I can do is keep my distance before I end

up in the same position I was in eight years ago: jobless because of a rumor about me and a rich man's wife.

SIXTEEN

GABBY

"He did not say that!" Teagan yells into the phone.

I pull the phone back a little, wincing as her shrillness seeps through the receiver. "He really did," I say, then bite into a cookie. "Now I feel like shit, and I'm eating these cookies to make myself feel better."

"Girl, if I was there, I'd eat them with you. I can't believe your gardener said that!"

"T, he's a landscape architect," I correct her. "I think that's why he got so offended. Because I called him *the landscape guy*, like it was a bad thing or something. I'm sure he makes great money and makes a great living. The stuff he does isn't cheap."

Teagan laughs. "Yeah, but he knows it's an occupation that's severely underrated, and men have so much pride when it comes to their careers. He has to work for people that make *great* money, so hearing it from the wife of a man who makes *great* money is like rubbing salt in a wound. Not only that, but if he gives Kyle dirty looks, you know it has to bother him. And you said you guys are friends?"

"We chat when he's around. He's a nice guy, talks about real-life stuff."

"Sounds like he got a little too attached to chatting it up with his client," she replies sarcastically. "You sure they're harmless chats?"

"Harmless—T, what are you trying to say?"

"Well, you're not an ugly chick, Gabby! You're beautiful, but you underestimate yourself way too much. There's a reason Kyle locked it down with you, and it's probably the same reason that designer is interested, too."

I sigh, finishing my cookie. "No, it's really just casual chats," I respond, mouth full. "But he doesn't like Kyle. Like at all. He's made that clear."

"That makes two of us then," she mumbles lowly.

"Heard that."

"You were supposed to. Look, he's right about not mixing business with friendship, Gabby. But you also have every right to defend yourself and your husband if he's being disrespectful. Doesn't matter how much I dislike Kyle sometimes, he's still your guy, and I respect that enough to keep most of my shit-talk to myself."

I laugh. "You're insane." My phone beeps and I pull it from my ear to check the screen. "Wow. Speaking of the devil, Kyle's calling."

"Well, that's my cue. I'm heading back to work anyway. Had to grab some lunch for this night shift. Call me if you need me. Love you, bye!"

"Love ya!" When she ends the call, I switch over to answer Kyle. "Hey, babe."

"Hey, what's going on? His voice is calm, and somehow it instantly relaxes me. I sink into the couch.

"Nothing. Munching on cookies I baked."

"Oh, really?" he chuckles. "What's the occasion?"

"Nothing. I just felt like making them. Called my mom for the recipe." God, I hate lying to him. But it's more of a white lie than anything. I refuse to tell my husband I made cookies for Marcel out of sheer guilt. I shouldn't even be in a position with Marcel where I feel guilty for saying anything about him to my husband. It should be strictly business between us, so why isn't it? When did it become *this*?

"Your mom's cookies are pretty great. Wish I could share some with you."

"Don't worry. You're not missing anything. They're not as soft as hers." I get off the couch and pick up the plate of cookies, carrying it to the kitchen and placing it on counter before I end up eating them all. "What are you up to?"

"Just got back from the last meeting of the night. It went well. I'm about to eat my salmon with broccoli and do some work before going to bed. I am unbelievably exhausted."

"I bet."

"What all did you do today?"

"I started a sculpture of a dahlia," I inform him.

"A dahlia? That's interesting."

"Yeah, I'm working on getting the detail right. Also have to figure out what color I want it to be. It has to be the right color, you know? I want it to be an amazing 3-D dahlia that's hard to look past if someone sees it."

He laughs uncertainly, like he has no idea what I'm talking about, but wants to support the idea. "Yeah, babe. I get it," he says, even though he totally doesn't.

I walk back to the couch, but before I can sit, there's a knock at my door. Frowning, I look toward it. There's a small window at the top of our door and sidelight windows on either side. All I see are sprouts of dark hair behind the window at the top of it.

"Did you get anything else done today?" Kyle asks as I get up and head for the door. I look out of one of the sidelight windows, and when I see Marcel, my frown grows even deeper.

"What the hell?" I whisper away from the phone.

"Gabs? What's wrong?"

"Uh—nothing. Yeah, I went out earlier for some vanilla extract and baking soda for the cookies. I'll probably go out tomorrow for more groceries."

"Good. And you ate today?"

"I did." I look out of the window again. Marcel is still standing there with a white T-shirt on and jeans, his hands buried in his front pockets. He's looking at the details of our porch, waiting for me to answer. When his eyes shift over to the window I'm looking out of, I hold up an open hand and mouth the words, "What do you want?"

He points to the door. "Open the door and I can tell you."

I sigh and back away.

"Well, are you gonna tell me what you ate?" Kyle asks, bringing me back to our conversation.

"Huh?"

"A friend of mine always used to say 'if you can "huh,"

you can hear.'" He does a corny chuckle. That silly saying. My dad said it to him once, and he's been using it ever since. I've always been glad he considers my dad a friend, though.

I force a laugh. "Oh, yeah. I had a Caesar salad for lunch and for dinner I ate a bowl of cereal before diving into the cookies."

"Cereal and cookies? You couldn't find anything a little more nutritious, babe?"

Kyle's words go through one ear and right back out the other as Marcel rings the doorbell this time.

"Is someone there?" he asks.

"No, that's the TV," I lie, then I close my eyes helplessly.

"Oh okay. Well, it seems like you're pretty occupied, so I'm going to let you enjoy your night of TV and homemade cookies."

I'm so relieved. I walk to the sidelight window again. Marcel is glaring right through it. I hold one finger up rather impatiently, giving him a death stare, and then turn my back to the window.

"Okay, babe. Call me whenever you're free tomorrow."

"Sure will. I love you."

"I love you too."

When he hangs up, I step in front of the door and swing it open. "Why are you here?" I hiss at him.

"One of my guys left his cellphone out back. I told him I'd come check, and I didn't want you to think some random creep is walkin' through your backyard."

"Oh. Well, go. It's fine. You can check."

He nods and turns back around, walking down the stoop. I watch him walk around the house, and then I close and lock the front door, going back to my spot on the sofa.

From where I'm seated, I see him pass by the windows, looking around the tables and wheelbarrows his crew left out there. He bends down to pick something up, and I watch him slide it into his back pocket. I assume it's the phone. He then turns and walks past the windows again.

I release a steady breath, waiting for him to ring the doorbell and make the announcement that he found the phone, but a minute passes and there is no knock or doorbell ringing. I get up to unlock and open the door again, taking a look outside.

Marcel is standing by his truck in my driveway, talking on his cellphone. He looks my way when the door is open, brows dipping.

"Everything okay?" I call.

He holds up a finger, says something else into the phone, and then hangs up.

"No," he mutters, walking to the stoop again. "He claims he took his wedding band off too, when he was levelin' the sand. Idiot, he is. He said he left it on the table back there. Mind if I check again?"

"No, I don't mind. Go ahead."

Marcel takes off again. I shut the door and walk to the kitchen, opening the patio door.

"I apologize for stopping by so late, Mrs. Moore." Marcel grunts as he looks beneath the table, using the flashlight of his phone. "My men don't think straight sometimes." I flip a light switch and the exterior floodlights turn on, giving more leeway. "Appreciate that."

"No problem." I watch as he looks near the sand bags. "Do you need some help?"

He shrugs. Nothing more. I fetch my house slippers and

go back outside. I look near the wheelbarrow. Nothing. I use my phone to check between the stones they've laid. Nothing around there either.

"I don't know what he did with it. He normally puts it in his lunch box when he takes it off." Marcel stands straight, running a hand over his head. I can't help noticing the way his biceps flex and his shirt lifts at the hem, revealing a silver of his tanned skin and wisps of dark hair.

"Well, it shouldn't be too far, right?"

"Who knows. I'll just have him come early in the morning to look for it. I don't have time for this tonight."

"Sheesh. What's the hurry?" I ask in a mocking tone.

He gives me a once over. "As I stated before, it's none of your concern, Mrs. Moore."

"Oh, please with the *Mrs. Moore* thing! I know what you're trying to do, and it's not working."

He narrows his eyes at me, looking me hard in the eyes. "And what am I tryin' to do exactly, *Mrs. Moore?*"

"You're trying to act like this is all business-like, but it isn't. You can't go from having conversations about life-stuff to *this*."

"This? Sorry, but I'm not so sure what *this* is," he laughs dryly.

"This—you know! Pretending I'm just the lady who lives here, and you're the guy who's fixing her yard!"

"Isn't that exactly what this is?" His eyes narrow, head cocking sideways.

"You're being an asshole."

He scoffs. "Trust me, Gabby, I've been called worse."

He starts to turn, but for some reason my blood is boiling. "Why won't you let it go? I'm sorry for what I said to you! I swear I didn't mean it that way! I didn't grow up with that mindset. All jobs are important—hell, my dad owns a docking and boat rental business!"

He laughs at that. "You think that's gonna save your ass? Layin' facts on me about your dad's work?"

I shake my head. He's impossible.

"If you're so proud of your daddy who rents out boats, then why on earth are you with a rich prick like your husband?"

"You can't control fate," I mutter with a shrug.

"Fate? Is that what people call it now? Rich guy comes into what most would assume is a college-oriented restaurant and sniffs on you, and you assume that's fate? He knew what he was lookin' for. Hell, I'm sure he wasn't the first man to do it, either. You're an attractive girl, probably got hit on all the time. What was it about him that made you consider it *fate*?"

I challenge his glare, folding my arms. "Because, unlike you, he was being nice."

"Oh, please! That man doesn't have one nice bone in his body!" He takes a step toward me. "See, I know men like him. They play the nice, wealthy guy who donates to a charity or two—not because he wants to, but because he *has* to. Why? Because he makes way too much money and doesn't know what to do with it. The world, and women like you, think he's good, but deep down, you know he's so full of shit."

"My God, Marcel!" I drop my arms. "What is it that you have against my husband? You met him once and assume he's the antichrist!"

"Okay…hold on. Back up a minute." He throws both

hands in the air, almost as a surrender. "Before I start havin' you think I'm some crazy, over-the-top man, let me ask you this…"

I brace myself for his question, standing taller.

"Has your husband ever brought me up in a conversation with you? Maybe mentioned an email he sent to me recently?"

I frown. "No. I handle all the emails with the landscaping."

"So you think."

"What is that supposed to mean?"

"It means that just like you don't tell your husband every little thing that goes on in your life, he doesn't tell his wife every little thing either."

"Oh my gosh, stop running circles around me. What are you getting at?"

Marcel inches closer, and this time his chest is almost bumping into mine. He's breathing as evenly as possible through his nostrils, but I can tell by the fire in his eyes that he's pissed about something, and I want to know what it is.

"The night that I met your husband, I got a little email from him while we were packing up."

I blink quickly. "What did it say?"

"He asked me not to show up today."

"What?" My heart skips a beat. "Why would he tell you to do that?"

"He claimed that you aren't very good at choosing the right companies for jobs like this. He stated that he wanted to look for other possibilities." Marcel smirks. "I replied and told him that you signed a contract and that he could kindly fuck off."

I swallow thickly. "You're lying."

"I'm so serious, little thing."

I take a step back. Between the bomb he just dropped and our proximity, I can hardly breathe. Why would Kyle do something like that behind my back? Does he really think I'm that incapable?

"I held off on that cold, hard fact all day for your sake, Mrs. Moore. Even after you said that havin' me, the *landscape guy*, around was the last thing on your mind, I kept it in… but I thought you should know why I'm not a fan of your husband." He looks me over beneath hooded eyelids. "He has no respect for you. He treats you like a child, and it's fucked up because I've gotten to know a little about you over the past few days—enough to realize you're a smart woman. Naive sometimes? Yes. But you're smart…and you deserve better than what he gives you."

My throat feels dry as I look him over. I study his eyes the most, the dark-blue flecks in his irises, then I look away, down at my feet. I don't even know what to say to him. I almost wish he'd told me sooner.

"Again, I apologize for interruptin'. See you in the mornin', Gabby." When he says my name, I swing my gaze up, but he's already turning away. He walks off, peering over his shoulder once before disappearing around the corner. I walk back inside when I hear his engine come to life, then I slump down on the couch.

I can't believe Kyle sent an email like that. I almost don't want to believe it, but why would Marcel, a man I hardly even know, lie about something like that? I look over my shoulder, toward the staircase. It's not like me to check

Kyle's things, but I have to this time. I need to know the truth.

I hop off the couch and rush up the stairs, going to his office. I log into his computer with the same password he always uses, KMan3322, and go to the little mailbox on the screen.

I scroll through his sent box but don't see anything, so I automatically assume Marcel is lying…but then I see that his trash inbox is full. I click on it, and sure enough, there are a string of emails between Kyle and Ward Landscaping & Design.

Hello Mr. Ward,

This is Kyle Moore. I'm emailing you in regard to my backyard, which you are currently working on.

I assume you won't read this email until you are in the comfort of your own home, which I prefer so that we don't cause a scene with my wife around. I just want to let you know that what I'm seeing in my yard is not how I would have liked it carried out. I love my wife, but sometimes she's not so great when it comes to choosing companies to carry out big projects such as these.

I looked through your website thoroughly and even tried to find you on Facebook, but I don't see you anywhere. Frankly, I am not

comfortable with your crew working on my yard and would like to find someone else to finish the job.

It would be best if you don't show up Monday morning, for mine and my wife's sake.

Regards,

Kyle Moore

I release a tattered breath and scroll down to the next email.

Mr. Moore,

I'm glad I waited to read this email when I got home because it is quite shocking, though it would have been better to talk about this in person, don't you think? But you're a busy man, I get it.

Seeing as your wife, who is perfectly capable of making her own choices, signed a contract to have the yard finished, I'm afraid I'll have to ignore your request and continue with the project. I don't believe in breaking contracts, nor do I think your wife made a poor choice. What you're seeing in your yard is just the ground work, but I assure you when it's done, you will be satisfied with it.

I suggest you have a little talk with your wife if there are truly any concerns. Otherwise, I'll see you Monday.

Best,

Marcel Ward
    CEO of Ward Landscaping & Design

Mr. Ward,

There is no need to chat with my wife when I am the owner of the house, and if I don't want your company in my backyard, I suggest you take yourself and your crew elsewhere. Please don't let me take this to court.

Kyle Moore

Court? Now, that's a funny one, seeing as I'm not doing anything but my job and keeping my word with the contract. Like I said, have that talk with your wife. Maybe it'll do you some good. Communication is key after all.

Marcel Ward

CEO of Ward Landscaping & Design

Do not tell me what to do with my wife.
Cancel the damn work. Break the contract if
you have to. I'll pay for whatever fees come
in the way.

Kyle Moore

Mr. Moore

Look, I'm saying this in the most respectful way I possibly can. May not make me a professional, but for my own personal gain, I'm just going to tell you right now to talk to your wife and to kindly fuck off.

If your wife ends up taking your side and wants to break contract, well I guess I'll see you both in court then, huh?

Marcel Ward

CEO of Ward Landscaping & Design

"Oh my gosh." I place a hand over my mouth, reading the emails all over again. I thought Marcel was kidding about telling him to fuck off. Why didn't Kyle tell me about this?

I dig into my back pocket and pull my iPhone out. My finger hovers over Kyle's name. I'm desperate to call him and figure out what's going on, but a tug in my chest stops me.

I know if I call him, this will change things for us. Our trust will break or bend, and I can't have that. Not after just moving into our own place and living our new life. If Kyle didn't say anything, it's because he knew telling me would hurt me.

I place my phone on the desk, then rake my fingers through my hair. The only thing I can think about is Kyle's betrayal. Why marry me if he feels I'm not smart enough to make my own decisions?

What kind of husband does shit like this?

SEVENTEEN

MARCEL

I SHOULDN'T HAVE TOLD her. She's a nice girl, and despite how badly her words stung me earlier, I still knew I couldn't tell her, but seeing the shocked look on her face as I got riled up about her husband only told me one thing: she thought I was crazy.

She assumed I had no reason to dislike her husband, but after the emails he sent me, I have every reason not to like him. The guy is a fucking dick, through and through. The way he spoke about Gabby blew my mind. Does he think she's some dumb trophy wife? Because trust me, I've seen the bimbos, and she isn't one of them.

I knew I shouldn't have come back for Rob's phone. I wanted to leave what happened in the dust, go back to square one when it was just business, but then shit got heated in the yard. I have no idea how she can bring so much out of me. It blows my mind.

I'm back at home, sitting on my recliner, watching a baseball game. My legs are spread apart, my arms resting on the arms of the chair as sucking noises surround me.

"Oh, fuck." I close my eyes, tossing my head back as full lips seal around the base of my dick. Her tongue moves over my shaft and then caresses my balls. "Shit, that feels good."

She brings her mouth back up to wrap it around the head of my cock. I look down at her wet lips around me. I'm so goddamn hard in Lucy's mouth, wishing this was someone else's.

Gabby's chest brushed across mine earlier. I could tell she wasn't wearing a bra. She was so damn close, and after watching the hurt in her eyes, all I wanted to do was hold her face and steal a kiss—let her know there are better men out there than her husband. But who am I to do that? She's made her choice. Now she's stuck with the asshole.

"I had a shitty day at work," I mumble.

"Yeah?" Lucy pauses, but pumps my cock up and down in one hand. "Tell me about it."

"My client is...she's confusing the hell out of me."

"How?" She keeps pumping.

"I don't know. She's a good girl. Smart. Nice. *Young.* I can tell she does a lot of stuff from the heart, but her husband is an asshole, and I wish she could...see it." I stiffen in my chair as she jacks me off faster.

"So, you like her?" Lucy asks, her voice still steady, seductive.

"I don't know what the hell it is. It almost feels like I need to protect her or something like that." I clench my fists, closing my eyes. "She deserves better."

"How do you know? Maybe she feels that's what she

needs." Lucy's mouth seals around my cock, and this time she swallows me down inch by inch.

"Oh, shit." I can't hold back any longer. She gags around my dick, and I bring a hand down to the back of her head, thrusting upwards and shooting my cum down her throat. "Oh, fuck, Luce. *Fuck*."

She gags once more before moaning. When I know she's swallowed it all, I relax my grip and she leans back, glancing down at my sated cock before meeting my eyes. "That was a lot of cum," she says, smirking as she wipes the corners of her mouth with the pad of her manicured thumb.

I grunt in response, shoving my dick back in my pants. Lucy gets up to grab her water bottle from the table and then sits on the love seat that's next to my recliner, taking a large gulp from it.

"You've always been complicated, Marcel. Ever since the day I met you. You know that?" She sips her water.

I look her over in her leather skirt and suede crop top. "What are you talkin' about?"

"I mean…you always seem to enjoy being around people you know you shouldn't have. Take me, for example. I work for a company where I'm paid to suck your cock or fuck you. You know you can't have me, probably feel like a fuck with me is an illicit one, and that excites you."

"Not true," I mumble, getting out of my chair and walking to the fridge. I pull out a beer, crack it open with the bottle opener, and take a deep chug.

"It's so true!" she laughs. "You want your life to be this complicated mess because it's a form of distraction for you. You're runnin' away from somethin'. I can see it. I *feel* it."

All right. She's going a little too far with this. I sit back in my chair, focused on the TV. "You can leave now."

She's quiet a beat, then she sighs and stands up, pulling her skirt down and grabbing her purse. She stops in front of me, blocking the TV.

"Luce, move," I demand, but she doesn't budge. I swing my gaze up.

"Marcel, whatever you do, don't ruin that poor girl's life."

"What the hell are you talkin' about? How can I possibly ruin her life? Shit's already ruined by being with him. What other damage can be done?"

She laughs softly. "You're charmin' and irresistible when you want to be, Marcel. You play this role of tough guy, but deep down you're a big softy. Fortunately, this information will always stay between you and me—terms of our agreement and all."

"Yeah, yeah."

I expect her to move, but she stands in place, still in front of the TV. I look up at her eyes again, but they're glossy this time. They're also sad, but strangely a smile lingers on her lips. "Before I go, I just want to let you know this will be my last night doin' this with you."

I sit up higher in my chair. "What? Why?"

She bends down in front of me, holding my hands. "I got engaged last weekend. He's a great guy. Sweet. He knows about what I do for a livin', but he wants me out now that we're makin' it official, and honestly, I don't blame him. He promises he's going to take care of me."

"Shit, Luce. I didn't even know you were seein' someone. That's fuckin' weird that you're out here suckin' my cock but have a man waitin' at home, isn't it?"

"No. He's older. Much, much older," she sighs. "He likes to watch me do stuff with other people sometimes."

"Fuckin' perv."

She laughs, and a tear skids down her cheek.

"Well you seem glad about this. What are you cryin' for?"

"Because…you've been the best client I've had. Not only that, but I bonded with you when I wasn't supposed to. I should have ended it the moment I felt like I was gettin' in too deep, but…I couldn't. You needed someone. *I* needed someone."

"Damn, Luce, don't tell me you fell for me," I tease, and she sputters another laugh.

"No. I just understand you. That's all. Unlike the others, you treat me like a human. Remember the first night we did this? When you ordered food and even offered me a beer? I know it's my job to be confident and all, but no one has ever made me feel so at ease. I will never forget that."

"Hmm." Yeah, I remember that night all too well. The first night a hired escort arrived at my house, I had no idea what to do. I knew exactly what she looked like. The head-shot they had of her was gorgeous, and I didn't want her to think I was some brute, so I ordered food and bought some beer to break the ice.

I'm glad I did, because when she showed up, there was a bruise around her wrist. I finally got her to tell me where it came from and she said one of the last guys ended up grabbing her too roughly when she told him his time was up.

I knew hiring an escort was wrong, and swore I would

only do it once, but Lucy is different. She's good at what she does, yes, but she's also great company. We're good friends…even if our arrangement is a little strange.

She releases my hands to wipe the tears from her face, then she stands up straight, holding her arms out. "Well, don't just sit there! Give me a hug before I go!"

I stand, wrapping her up in my arms. "I'll miss those lips around my cock."

"Always the jokester. It's okay to show a little emotion, you know," she laughs again, but the emotion is thick in her voice. Pulling away, she smiles up at me, then she turns, tucking her hair behind her ears and opening the door. "Bye, Marcel," she sniffles.

"Bye, Luce."

The door shuts, and I sit back down in my seat, releasing a breath and staring absently at the TV screen, sipping the rest of my beer.

The thing is, Lucy and I do share a bond. It's hard to fully explain, but I've never wanted her as anything more than a woman who can give me as many blowjobs as I want, for fifteen-hundred bucks a week.

She is right about one thing, though. I do want things I know I can't have.

I know that deep down, I want to *fuck the shit* out of Gabby, just to prove to her that I'm a much better man than her husband, but she's such a good girl that I know she'd never even consider it, and knowing it pisses me off.

Is that selfish of me? Yes, but I can't deny it anymore, no matter how hard I try. I also can't act on it. What Lucy said sticks with me—the part about not ruining her life. I'm like a virus—a deadly one. Everyone around me always seems to

141

either disappear or die, and I'd hate for any of those things to happen to Gabby.

I shut the TV off and go to my room. It's late, and I'm tired, so I take a quick shower and climb into bed.

I wish it were easy for me to fall asleep, but it isn't, because the worst part about Lucy leaving for good is that, just like Momma and Shay, I'll never see her again.

I'm still waiting for the day my losses make me numb, but this is not the day.

EIGHTEEN

GABBY

THE CREW PULLS into my driveway around seven in the morning, taking their tools out. An hour passes, and there isn't a single sign of Marcel.

I head downstairs and pop my head out the door, looking at Rob and Alex, who are reading over a sheet of paper. Rob is the guy I saw in Meredith's yard the day I met her—the one with the black beard and hair. Something tells me he's a big teddy bear.

"Hey, guys!" I call, and they both look up at me. "Where's Marcel?"

"Oh, I don't think he's coming here to work today," Rob says. "He said he has work to do at the office."

"Oh." I sigh, somewhat disappointed. "Okay, then. Well, let me know if you guys need anything."

"Will do," Rob says. "By the way, I found my ring!

Thanks for letting the boss look for my phone last night. Really appreciate it."

"Oh, no problem!" I smile at him, but it disappears rapidly as I turn for the door.

I close it behind me and brew a fresh cup of coffee. A part of me thinks Marcel is avoiding me after what he told me about Kyle, but another part of me thinks maybe he does have work to do at his office. He is the owner, after all.

I assume that is the case, until he doesn't show the next day either. I don't even waste my breath or time going outside to ask what's up. I let his men work in peace while I do some yoga in my living room. It's hard to truly relax, though, when something is bugging you.

For one, I have my backstabbing husband, who apparently thinks I'm an idiot, and then there's my landscape architect, who has probably lost all respect for me and never wants to see my or my husband's face again. Can I blame him for not wanting to come around? We've made his life a living hell, when all he wanted to do was work and give us something great.

I give up on my usual breathing technique and roll my yoga mat back up, tossing it in the closet. I head upstairs to shower and then go to my studio, reading a few emails on my laptop.

The hopeless part of me wishes Marcel's name would pop up in one of the unopened emails, but it doesn't. As I read over one from a student, my phone dances on the desk, buzzing loudly. *Kyle.*

"Ugh." I was hoping he wouldn't call today, seeing as he didn't call yesterday. He sent me a text yesterday, though, and mentioned he was working out kinks with one of his clients, which meant he wouldn't have much time to call.

But he's my husband, and even though I'm annoyed with him, I still answer.

"Hello?"

"Hey, babe. What are you doing?"

"Checking a few emails."

"Oh. Anything good?"

Not in my inbox, but in yours? Yeah, there's a lot of juicy shit. "No, just some questions from some students." I sit back in the rolling chair and spin around to look out of the window.

"Well, I wanted to call to let you know that Mr. Tran wants me to fly to Seattle to see him Friday. I told him I would. He's interested in working with our company, and we could use him right now."

"What?" I sit up again, frowning. "So when will you be coming back home?"

"I don't know. He wants to golf, have dinner. Maybe Sunday night?" I can tell he's doing that wincing thing he always does when he knows I'm disappointed and am about to serve him some backlash.

But I have no backlash for him. I'm still upset and seeing him tomorrow wouldn't be pretty. He needs more time away and I need more time to figure out how to talk to him about what I discovered without blowing up on him. "Well if it's important to you, go for it. I'll be fine here."

He sighs, relieved. "Are you sure? I can fly you out there with me. Maybe we can make a weekend of it?"

"No. It's fine. Besides, the backyard is still being worked on. *One of us* has to be around while they fix it, right?"

He's quiet, and my hands start to shake. It's a brief

silence but I notice his hesitation. "They'll be working on it over the weekend?"

"Yes, I think so. They're trying to get it done as quickly as they can."

"Good." He clears his throat. "Well, I just had a deposit go through our account. If you need groceries, want to shop, or anything, go for it. Money's there." At the change of subject, I roll my eyes but keep my tone even.

"Okay, sure."

"*Okay, sure?* Gabby, what is going on with you? If you don't want to be on the phone right now or you're busy, just tell me."

"What? Kyle—Jesus!" I groan, pinching the bridge of my nose. I'm just like my mom sometimes, during moments where I feel like he should be able to read my mind, and then getting upset when he doesn't catch the hint. Then again, isn't that all women? But I know now not to get too upset with Kyle, so I breathe evenly through my nostrils and say, "Look, I got on your computer to pay a bill, and I saw something that really bothered me."

Silence. Only for a short moment. "What did you see, Gabs?"

"An email between you and Mr. Ward. A string of emails, actually."

Kyle is quiet again.

I continue, and my hands are really shaking now. I hate confronting him with stuff like this. Absolutely hate it. "If you were really that unhappy with having the yard done, maybe I should have just left it alone like you said. I mean, if you really think I'm that much of an *idiot*—"

"Gabrielle. Stop it." His voice is firm. I seal my lips, my

heartbeat picking up in speed. I hate arguing with him, mainly because I never win. "The yard is already being landscaped. I was hoping Mr. Ward would stop before he started laying the stones, or at least be coherent, but he wasn't. I wanted to do something better for you. Surprise you."

"Then why couldn't you just tell me that? Why go behind my back to the owner and say that stuff about me?"

"Gabby, you're blowing this out of proportion. It was more of a ploy—a man-to-man thing."

I scoff. "Am I really blowing it out of proportion?" I shoot out of my chair. "I am your *wife*, Kyle. You can't go around telling people stuff like that, like I'm some dumbass who doesn't know anything! When he told me what you said to him, I felt like an idiot! I was so embarrassed that I didn't even know what to say!"

"Calm down," he sighs. "I've told you to watch your temper. Think about what you're saying first before letting it out."

"No—just stop. D-don't tell me to calm down! You told me one thing, but went behind my back and said another. Where is the trust, Kyle?"

"Gabby, just relax, okay? We'll have this discussion when I'm back home on Sunday. You're getting your backyard anyway, so let it go."

No, I won't let this go, but I won't tell him that. "You know what? I think it's best if you stick in Seattle for the whole weekend, like you wanted. Apparently, we need the space."

"Gabby, come on. I—"

I end the call before listening to what he has to say next

then slam my phone down on the desk, sitting on the edge of the chair and burying my face in my hands. My hands are still shaking, so I wait for them to stop, and for my heartbeat to go back to a steady rhythm, before dropping them in my lap.

For a while, all I hear is the landscaping crew working, but then I hear a familiar, deep voice that pulls me out of my funk. I pick my head up and listen harder.

I stand up and walk to the arched window. Sure enough, Marcel Ward is standing in the backyard. He's not wearing work clothes, though. Just the usual attire—jeans and a plaid shirt with a ribbed tank beneath. Normally he's rocking a pair of dusty jeans and a T-shirt with work boots. He points at something to his right, then walks to the table set up in the corner, picking up a clipboard and reading over it.

My heart is racing now, and I have no idea why. Why am I so excited that he's here? Why do I care so much about this man's presence?

I leave the office and walk downstairs to the kitchen. I watch him from the door as he checks things off on a clipboard. Then he turns around, looking at the double doors, as if he senses someone watching him.

I wave from where I stand. He cocks a brow and gives me a quick nod. Before I know it, he's crossing the workspace to get to the double doors.

I open it, looking up at him as he gets closer. "Surprised you're here," I say, crossing my arms.

"Rob phoned me, needed me to look into something. Several broken stones out there."

"Oh. They told me you had work to do at the office?"

"I did. Working on a few prints for a commercial job."

"Oh. Well that's cool."

I look past him at Rob, Jacob, and Miguel who are digging a jagged line outside of the stones. There is an empty circular space where I assume they're going to build the hot tub. My eyes swing back over to Marcel. He has his arms folded as well. I drop mine and shift on my feet.

"Do you want to come inside? I'll make some tea or something. I want to talk about what Kyle said to you in those emails."

"So you read 'em?" he asks, quirking a brow.

"I did."

"Not a pleasant guy, your husband."

"He's not always like that. He has control issues sometimes."

Marcel looks me over and a small dip forms between his brows. After clearing his throat, he says, "I don't drink tea, but if you have more of that lemonade I tried last time, I'll gladly take a glass."

I smile up at him. "Yeah, I actually made a fresh batch the other day." I walk inside, and he follows behind me, closing the door along the way. I walk to the fridge while he stands by the island counter, looking around.

"I take it you've talked to him about it?"

"Not really. More like argued about his lack of respect," I mutter, taking out the half-full jug of lemonade. "I just…I can't believe he said that to you." I meet his eyes. "I know I shouldn't be the one apologizing for his actions, but I'm sorry he sent that. He was trying to put you in a tough spot. I'm glad you didn't cave."

"It's fine. No need to apologize for somethin' you had no control over."

I grab a glass from the cabinet, rinse the dust out of it, and then fill it with lemonade. I hand it to him, and he accepts it appreciatively. After taking a sip, he places the glass on the counter.

"Can I ask you somethin'?" he asks as I rest my lower back against the edge of the counter.

"Depends on what it is."

"It's kind of personal."

"Hmm...you can ask, but I may or may not answer."

He plants both hands on the edge of the island counter in front of him, focused on my eyes. "Are you in love with your husband?"

His question is way more personal than expected.

"Wow. That's *very* personal," I scoff, looking him over.

He shrugs, his demeanor way too calm. "Just a question."

"I have a feeling that's a loaded question."

Smirking, he says, "Might be."

I let out a slow breath. "Honestly, I don't think right now is the best time to answer that question after knowing what he did."

"You're handling it too well. This must not be his first time doing something so stupid."

I meet his aqua eyes, keeping my lips sealed.

"Hmm. I see," he murmurs, picking his lemonade up. He stands tall with it, and it's now that I notice how out of place he is in my kitchen. He's such a big guy, rugged and dark in comparison to the gray counters and white backsplash.

Marcel finishes off his lemonade and then walks around the counter, placing the glass in the sink. He's standing right beside me now, and I draw in a breath when he turns my way. I smell the soap that lingers on his body—the Irish Spring that he probably uses religiously. My eyes slide up to his. He's already looking down at me.

"I've been thinkin', and somethin' tells me this life you're livin' isn't really you." His voice is low, gruff.

"It's a good life," I tell him.

"That is obviously built on stupidity and bullshit."

I narrow my eyes, peering up at him. My heart is racing all over again, my mouth going dry.

"Answer my question," he demands, voice still low.

"Why does it matter to you?"

"Because if you aren't in love with him, then maybe I won't feel so bad about the things I wish I could do to you."

I swallow hard, staring into his eyes. "I love my husband," I say, but the statement is feeble, even to my own ears.

"Do you?"

"I do."

Marcel smirks. "But are you *in* love? Answer that for me." He's taken the final stride, standing right in front of me. He closes me in, planting his hands on the edge of the counter on either side of my waist, getting face-to-face with me. I look away, avoiding his eyes now, but I can't avoid the giant in front of me or the heat radiating from his body.

"Maybe you should go back to work," I whisper.

"I will once you answer me. And I want a *real* answer, not anymore of your bullshit."

I shake my head. It's hard to think with his body this close, his scent wrapped up around me. It's much more primitive than Kyle's. All man. "I love him a lot, and I would do anything for him."

"Would he do anything for you?"

That question catches me off guard. My brows draw together. I don't know how to answer that.

My silence lingers for only a second before Marcel makes a throaty noise. "Hmm." He lowers his head, lightly running the tip of his nose across my jawline. "Damn shame," he rumbles, then he inhales and groans, like he's always wanted to know what I smell like this close. "If you were mine, I'd drop everything for you. Give you the whole goddamn world, little thing."

His mouth hovers over my cheek, his warm breath running over my skin that's now sticky with sweat. I close my eyes, hating myself for indulging in the sensations, but I can't help myself. It's...*different*. And wrong. So very wrong.

Doesn't matter how upset I am with Kyle, having another man this close to me in *our* kitchen is wrong. A fantasy is one thing, but actually *doing* it is a whole other ballgame. Though I'm sure it's an amazing feeling for a woman to have Marcel Ward between her legs, or pushed up against her body, that woman can't be me, so I raise my arms and push him back.

He's solid, so he hardly budges, but I make do, sliding sideways to get further away from him.

Fortunately, Marcel backs away with an arrogant smile. He heads for the double doors and pushes one of them open, still smiling as he looks back at me one more time. "See you soon, Gabby," he says before walking out and shutting the door behind him.

I let the breath in my lungs escape, pushing off the

counter and looking all around me, like I'm in trouble. What in the hell was that? What was he thinking! Maybe I was wrong about what I thought of the landscaper. Maybe he does see me in other ways…and deep down, I want to know what they are.

"Fuck my life," I mutter and leave the kitchen before I can replay that whole scene in my head all over again.

NINETEEN

GABBY

THE NEXT DAY, I'm still fed up with what Kyle did.

He called several times last night, but after that little altercation with Marcel in the kitchen, I couldn't answer. Not only that, but I was still pissed at him. He can stay in Seattle for the next week. I don't care right now. My temper gets bad sometimes, but I know how to manage it. If I don't answer the phone, I won't spit fire at him. Simple.

After pouring myself a mug of coffee and dumping some almond milk creamer into it, I slide into my slippers by the door and walk outside, going up the driveway to get to the mailbox.

None of Marcel's men are at the house today. It's St. Patrick's Day, which usually doesn't call for a day off work, but seeing as I overheard all of the men talking about their favorite beers last night, it's safe to assume they're probably drinking their day away.

Yesterday, after that interesting conversation I had with Marcel in the kitchen, I overheard Miguel saying he was glad they had a half day at the commercial job, because he couldn't wait to go to the bar with his buddies.

As I take the mail out of the mailbox—more junk and takeout menus—I notice Meredith getting out of her red Tesla with various shopping bags. She spots me, and I wave. She waves back, grinning.

"Hey, neighbor!" she practically squeals.

"Hi! How are you?"

She trots across the street in her white open-toed heels and maroon sundress. She has a white sunhat on her head and her hair is sleek beneath it, pulled back into a low honey-blonde bun.

"I'm wonderful! I haven't seen you in a while! How are you?" she asks, and she opens her free arm, leaning in for a hug.

We don't know each other all that well, but I return the hug, glad my coffee doesn't spill down her back as I do."I'm great!"

"Good! I couldn't help noticing you took my advice and hired Ward Landscaping." She's giving me a devious smirk, like she knows my darkest secrets but isn't going to say a thing.

"I did," I laugh, and just hearing Marcel's last name sends a sweep of goosebumps over my arms, despite the heat. I sip my coffee to get rid of the feeling.

"What's he doing for you, anyway?"

"They're installing a patio with a wet bar and hot tub. I'm looking forward to when it's finished."

"Oh, that sounds lovely. You know, I don't have a wet

bar, but I have been thinking about adding one. Do you mind if I take a peek?"

"Oh—sure! Come on back." I turn, and she meets up to my side as we walk along the path that leads to my back-yard. "It's not the nicest looking place right now," I admit as she stops beside me, taking in the view of my backyard. There are piles of dirt in almost every corner. Most of the stones have been laid, but there is now a deep hole across the yard, surrounded by caution tape, in preparation for the hot tub.

"Oh, that's quite all right. All part of the process. You'll have to let me know when you break that hot tub in! We can celebrate with wine and a warm dip!"

"That would be amazing. I'll be sure to let you know."

We turn and go back up the path. She looks down, focusing on the pathway so she doesn't step on the grass in her spiked heels. "Is your husband home?" she asks.

"No. He's out of town for work."

"These dang men of ours. My husband works constantly. Plans on going into early retirement. I can't wait for him to do it. Then we can travel more, and it won't be so boring at home." I almost start to ask if she has kids but realize it's none of my business. Some people get offended by that question. I'm one of those people.

Kyle and I just got married, and his mom started hounding me several days after our wedding day, asking when I was going to give her a grandchild. All I can ever think when she asks is, *woman, I'm only twenty-five. Let me live a little first.* My mother is the exact same way, but in her mind, she's giving me a year before we decide to conceive. *Moms.*

Meredith looks up at me when we reach the cobblestone.

"I know how lonely it gets, you know? That's why I occupy myself with shopping, catching drinks with friends, getting the yard done, all that little stuff."

"Yeah, it does get lonely. I just have to get used to it."

"It took me seven months to get used to him being away so much when he got his promotion, and even still, I really miss him. Don't get me wrong—when he's home, he's a pain in the ass most of the time, but I love him. He's my life partner."

I only smile at her as she studies my eyes. I sip my coffee and look away as we walk toward the end of my driveway again.

"Funny question, but do you like dancing?"

I fight a smile. "I enjoy it from time to time."

"And what about drinking?"

"Who doesn't love a good drink?"

"I only ask because one of my girls rented a table out at this really nice club in town. We'll be having drinks and doing a lot of girl-talk and dancing. We call them our Sassy Nights, because we dress up, get pretty, and act sassy. They only happen when our schedules coincide and all of our husbands are away for work. You should join us!" She stops beside the mailbox.

"Aww, Meredith, that sounds amazing, but I'd hate to interrupt your night or be a burden. You don't have to invite me out of pity."

"Are you kidding me? You wouldn't be a burden at all to me and pity, shmitty! No such thing. Anyone who loves dancing is going to be a good addition to our group. Plus, they all go to these things with a buddy, and I'm always the third wheel. It would be nice to have a buddy of my own."

I think it over as her smile grows wider. I can't even remember the last time I've been to a club. "I don't know…"

"It'll be a harmless night. Just a bunch of girls letting their hair down, getting a few drinks, and listening to great music. You'll love it, I promise."

Honestly, I don't have much to think about. I do need more friends in this new state of mine. I don't have any, and quite frankly, it would be nice to go out and let my hair down, especially after all the shit that has happened within the last forty-eight hours. I could use a real drink, not just wine. Wine isn't going to spare the anger I have toward Kyle, because with wine, I still think about that and other negative shit, but if I have a few shots of rum or vodka, that will certainly do the trick.

Meredith bats her eyelashes at me, waiting for an answer.

I sigh and nod. "Okay, sure. I'll go."

"Yes!" She squeals. "You have no idea how happy I am to hear that! I'll drive us there, and drinks are on me, so you don't have to worry about a thing but what to wear!"

"Okay, let's do it! I'll have to go shop for something to wear, though—I haven't gone out to a club since my college days!"

"Go right ahead!" She can't contain her excitement. I swear if she were a pot of boiling water, the water would bubble right over. "I would go shopping with you, but I have an appointment to get my nails done at one."

"That sounds fun."

"I should be back by three. We won't be heading out

until around seven tonight. Just come knock on my door when you're ready."

"Okay. Sounds good."

She beams at me again before turning and walking across the street. I walk back down my driveway but I can't help wondering what the hell I've just signed up for. Meredith seems fun to hang around, but she also looks like she loves a good party. And also like she's easily distracted. Hopefully she doesn't leave my side to busy herself doing something else.

I enter the walk-in closet I share with Kyle and rummage through the dresses and skirts on hangers. I didn't party much in college. I worked more than anything, so there's really nothing here. I have my graduation dress, that's black with silver sequins, a couple fancy dinner dresses, and sundresses. The graduation and dinner dresses are too fancy, and my sundresses are too simple. I check my shoes, and I only have two pairs of heels, one of which I wore at—you guessed it—graduation. The other pair is a plain black heel I wear for a fancier occasion.

I huff when I realize I have absolutely nothing good enough to wear to a bar or club or wherever the hell we're going, so I get dressed in a pair of leggings, a pink T-shirt, Nike shoes, throw my hair up into a neater bun, freshen up, and then trot down the stairs. I warm my coffee back up in the microwave, dump it into an insulated tumbler, and then I'm out the garage, climbing into my Dodge Challenger.

Kyle can't stand my car. He told me it was too manly and constantly asked why this was the car I wanted at the dealership the day I bought it. A white Challenger with yellow stripes. For starters, yellow is my favorite color. But he had me twisted if he thought I was going to be driving a BMW every day like he did.

Ever since I was can remember, I have loved cars like this—the types with rumbles in their engines. The type of cars that make their presence known before you can even see it. When my dad wasn't working at the dock or renting out boats, he would work on old cars that sounded loud, and I remember being mesmerized by them.

He used to take me for a spin in an old 1970s Hellcat Challenger he fixed up, until one day he sold it to pay for three months of late mortgage payments.

I could tell selling that Hellcat hurt him a lot. He loved that car—hell, I loved that car. He'd take me and my brother out for ice cream in it on the warmer days, or even to the park. To this day, he still collects old cars, fixes them up, and sells them. It's a hobby he does at one of his friend's garages. When I got my car and named her Lady Monster, I took a picture of her and sent it to my dad first, and he was so proud. His exact words were, "You better not make the mistake I did by getting rid of the damn thing."

When my Challenger comes to life and growls, it makes me feel powerful, because *I'm* in control of this beautiful machine.

I make it back home around four in the afternoon, much later than anticipated, but I got distracted. I found an outfit for tonight, a sleeveless navy-blue dress made of velvet material that fits like a glove, as well as a pair of black open-toed heels. On top of that, there was a hair salon near the mall. I decided to pop in, and luckily, one of the ladies had an opening. I was nervous to have a woman I'd never met do my hair, but she did a great job. She washed and blew my hair out. Now it's board straight and sleek, resting on my shoulders and my upper back.

I check the time on my cell again, and as I do, a call comes through from Kyle. I ignore it. I'll talk to him when he's home. Phone calls are just a waste of my breath at this point. I put on a shower cap and jump into the shower, making sure to shave my legs and under my arms.

I haven't gotten prepared for a night out like this in a long time. I used to go out every blue moon with Teagan whenever she came to visit me, and I remember the process was always tedious, so I despised it. I feel like that girl all over again, but this time I'm enjoying the process. Deep down, after all the moving and the stress of it, I know I need this.

I have three hours to get ready, so I take my time doing my makeup. I've always been good at that part. Call it the artist in me. By the time I'm finished with my makeup it's now six o' clock. I have one hour to get dressed, but I'm finished getting ready within the next thirty-five minutes.

I check the floor-to-ceiling mirror in my room, looking myself over way too many times to count. I don't know who that woman is looking back at me. I'm so used to seeing myself in jeans and a paint-splattered T-shirt, but this is another version of myself. She looks sassy and sexy, perfect for tonight's little shindig with Meredith and her friends.

I walk downstairs and shut off the lights, then grab my keys and wallet and tuck them into the clutch I also bought.

My phone buzzes again as I get closer to the front door, but this time it's a call from Dad.

"Hey, Dad!" I answer excitedly, and I really am excited. He hardly ever calls. He's more of a one-sentence text kind of man. When I texted him to let him know I'd moved in, his exact words were, "Good. Love you. Be safe."

"Gabby, I'm a little upset with you. Hope you know that."

"What? Why?" I ask, but I can't fight my smile. This is a thing he does, and he's been doing it ever since I was a kid. He'll tell me he's mad at me, but he'll have a smile on his face. Right now, I hear the smile in his voice.

"You haven't called me since the move, monster!" When he laughs, I do, too.

"Oh my gosh, Dad!" I tuck a loose piece of hair behind my ears. "I sent you a text letting you know we made it safely."

"A text isn't the same as a call."

"Well, my bad. I should have called. I'm sure Mamá filled you in though."

"She did, but I missed your voice. It's weird not having you around here every weekend."

"Aw. I know. I miss you guys a lot."

"Miss you too. Listen, I'm really calling because your mother wants to do a big Easter dinner. Wants the whole family here. Your brother will be here, and your Aunt Carolina and her husband are coming with the twins. You should come up, bring Kyle."

"That sounds really fun, Dad. I'll let him know."

"Good. I miss my princess."

"Keep me updated on the details." I open the door and

walk out of the house. "Kyle has been working a lot, but I'm sure he won't be that weekend since it's a holiday weekend."

"Sure thing. Everything okay there? Sounds like you're busy."

I lock the door and walk down the stoop. "Everything is good. I'm actually going out for a few drinks with my neighbor."

"Your *neighbor?*" He laughs at that. "How old is this neighbor?"

"Umm...I'm not sure, actually. But she looks like she's in her late thirties."

"That's funny."

"How is that funny?" I laugh.

"Because you're going out, for starters. Isn't like you. Two, because you've never really cared to hang out with your neighbors or make friends with them. Remember the little girl who stayed next door? You couldn't stand her. I guess this new life of yours is changing you."

"No, this neighbor of mine is actually really nice, unlike the girl who stayed next door. She invited me out, and since I've been cooped up in the house for the past two weeks unpacking and sculpting, I figured this will do me some good."

"Kyle hasn't been home as much, I bet. Is that why you're going out?"

I slow my pace as I walk up Meredith's driveway. "You know he works a lot, Dad. He's not in town with me anymore, so I don't get to see him as much as before."

"Gotta make adjustments." He sighs. "I've been trying to get a hold of him, too. Haven't been able to reach him yet."

"He's probably busy."

"Most likely. That kid is always working." There's a brief silence. "Well, can you tell him to give me a call when he's around? Gotta catch up with the kid."

"Sure dad. Is everything okay?"

"Everything is fine. I'm glad you're doing other things besides staying trapped in the house with your art. It's good to take a breather."

The front door of Meredith's house swings open, and she waves at me, then rolls her hand, gesturing for me to come inside. I hold up a finger and she nods, rushing back inside but leaving the door wide open.

"You know if I could live with only my art, I would." I smile.

"Oh, I know it. Trust me. Well, have fun and be safe. And call me more! You're not here, so I need to know you're okay."

"I will. Love you, Dad."

"Love you too, monster."

"Everything okay?" Meredith asks as I meet up to her at the door.

"Yeah, that was just my dad calling to check in."

"Oh, how sweet." She closes the door behind me and steps to the side, grabbing her heels off the coffee table and sitting down to slide into them.

As she does, I take a thorough look around. There are book cases in some of the walls, full of random books that I'm sure are for show. Picture frames hang on the walls, photos of Meredith and a much older man in each of them. I'm assuming he's Mr. Aarons. He's shorter than Meredith. I smile at it. The height is somewhat comical. Since all of the

THE MAN I CAN'T HAVE

photos are of just the two of them, it answers my question about whether she has kids or not.

There is white furniture in the living room that looks like it's hardly been used and furry gray rugs on the hardwood floor. A chandelier hangs in the hallway, elegant, shimmering like it's made of diamonds. I'm dying to know what the kitchen looks like, but I'm sure I'll get the chance to see it soon enough. This house screams *Meredith*.

"Wow. Your house is beautiful. Totally puts mine to shame," I tell her with a laugh.

"Oh, please. It needs redesigning," she says, waving a dismissive hand. "Haven't had the time to update things with my interior designer, but hopefully soon." She's back at the door after grabbing her keys and purse, twisting the doorknob. "You ready?"

"Yeah."

"Good, because tonight is about to be one of the best nights of your life!"

I smile on the way out the door, but deep down I can't help wondering if I should be excited or worried about her statement.

TWENTY

MARCEL

I DON'T KNOW what made me think it was okay to let a client of mine convince me to come to a club, but here I am.

I'm working on a new clubhouse for him in the next few weeks, and we just closed the deal. He insisted that we celebrate over a drink, but he didn't tell me he had an entire section reserved for himself, nor did he mention there would be a train of women, barely dressed, perched on his lap. He's a smart business man, but judging by that ring on his finger, he's a sleazy husband.

I finish off my beer, looking sideways as he cups the ass of the girl on his lap. I shake my head. Good thing I drove. Thirty more minutes, and I'm getting the fuck out of here.

I push to a stand, glancing at Oliver, my client.

"Where you going, man?" he calls after me as I walk past the velvet ropes.

"Grab another drink."

"Oh, just ask the waitress!" He starts to flag the waitress down, but I hold a hand up.

"It's all good. I need to stretch my legs a bit."

"Suit yourself." He looks away, his eyes dropping down to the rack of the girl on top of his right thigh. She giggles as he places a kiss on her cleavage. I roll my eyes and walk down the stairs.

The music is loud as I reach the dance floor, the bass pulsing through my boots. I have no idea what the song is that's playing, but it's clearly a favorite, because there are way more people on the dance floor now than there were ten minutes ago.

I spot the bar and notice an empty space in the middle. I don't mind standing there for twenty minutes or so. I'm sure Oliver won't notice that I'm gone. He's occupied, after all. Not just with one woman on his lap, but two.

I reach the empty space, planting my elbows on the counter and waiting for the bartender to come my way.

Glass shatters behind me, and I hear someone yell, "Fuck my life!" The voice is way too familiar. I turn back and look down at the woman behind me. She's in heels and a blue dress. Her head is down as she looks at the shattered cup she just dropped, with liquid all around it.

"I am so sorry!" a guy says, holding his hands in the air in front of her.

"Watch where you're going next time!"

The guy shrugs and disappears within the crowd on the dance floor. The woman looks up toward the bar, in search of help, but when I see her eyes, I'm surprised.

Holy fucking shit. "Gabby?" I call, standing taller.

Her eyes stretch wide when they shift over to me. She

blinks twice, like she doesn't believe the person she's seeing either

"Marcel? What the hell are you doing here?" she asks with a smile.

"Here with a client, supposedly celebratin'. I'm sure the question is more what the hell are you doin' here? This isn't your kind of scene."

"No, it's not. I'm sure you can tell by the glass I just dropped on the floor that was full of fresh rum and coke." She lets out an exasperated breath. I turn toward the bar and whistle for the bartender who is at the end of the counter, flirting with three girls. He hears me, and although he seems pretty annoyed, he comes rushing my way.

"Spilled drink over here, man, and there's glass. Unless you want your boss gettin' a lawsuit and havin' him blame you for it, I suggest you call someone to clean it."

The bartender gulps and nods, taking his job a little more seriously. He picks up a two-way radio behind him and says something. I grab several of the napkins on top of the counter and hand them to Gabby.

"Thanks." She wipes her hands off.

When she's done with them, she moves in the spot where a woman just left and dumps the crumpled towels on the counter.

"Who are you here with?" I look around, thinking maybe her asshole of a husband is going to pop up. *Shit, I hope not.*

"I came with my neighbor, Meredith. They have a table reserved over there." She turns and points to an area behind her. I see several women at a large booth, drinking and laughing.

"Oh, so you're makin' friends? I knew you'd take my advice sooner rather than later."

"Your advice sucks, okay? I don't think they like me very much, hence the reason I'm at the bar getting my own drinks and not there right now."

"How do you know they don't like you?"

She shrugs, pretending not to care, but I can tell it's bothering her. Her eyes drop down to a wet spot on her dress and she wipes it away. Her dress is way too fucking short. All I see are thighs and legs and, fuck me, if she doesn't look fuck-able right now. "They're older than me. Mid-to-late thirties. I think some of them are jealous, and it shows. It's like some of them think I'd be a threat to them."

"Hmm." I turn around again, and this time the bartender is replacing glasses and doing his job. A cleanup guy comes and sweeps the glass and Gabby apologizes repeatedly to the man. He shrugs it off as just doing his job. While she explains what happened like she's under interrogation, I request a rum and coke and a *Modelo* beer from the bartender. He whips them up and then slides them across the counter.

"How much have you had to drink?" I ask, picking up the rum and coke and handing it to her. She starts to reach for it, but I pull back a little, raising a brow.

She laughs. "What? Are you babysitting me now?"

"Not at all."

"I've only had two." She gives me a shit-eating grin. "Would be three if that dickhead hadn't made me drop it."

I chuckle, then hand her the drink. "Three is a good number."

She wraps her glossed lips around the skinny straw. I

look away before she can catch me staring at them, taking several gulps of beer.

"And speaking of the group I came with, they were doing *coke* in the parking lot before we came in. That's not really my thing. I think they hate me even more because I didn't want to try it."

"So just stay where you are then."

"Here? With you? Why are you even here? This doesn't seem like your kind of scene either."

"It's not. I came with a client, but he's a dick."

She giggles. "Look at us. The pity party duo." Placing her glass down on the counter, she climbs onto the stool in front of her to sit.

"I wouldn't necessarily call it that. You just don't like sniffin' coke, and I don't like watchin' a married man act like a teenage boy with two girls on his dick."

"Whoa." She bursts out laughing. "That's who you're stuck with? But shouldn't you love that? The girls, I mean? You aren't married, are you?" She looks down at my hands. "No ring."

"No, I'm not married. But that doesn't mean I want two random girls on my dick either."

She fights a smile, picking her drink up and sipping again. "That's bullshit. It's pretty much every man's dream."

"Okay...maybe. But not here at a club that reeks of sweat and horniness."

She cracks another smile.

I smirk before taking a chug of my beer, and then look at the dance floor. It's jam-packed now. Everyone is wearing green for St. Patrick's Day. Some of them are even drinking green beer and paying seven bucks extra for it, just so they can post it on social media. *Morons.*

"Why aren't you married, Mr. Ward?" Gabby asks, stealing my attention away again.

"Just haven't found the one, I guess."

"Have you ever been in a long-term relationship?"

"Nope. Not since I went back to school, and that only lasted a month."

"Seriously?" Her eyes nearly pop out of her head.

I shrug and sip again. She sips too.

"Do you not like commitment?"

"I wouldn't say that I don't like it. Just doesn't fit me."

"So, if you found this perfect woman, and she seemed like a match made in heaven, you wouldn't try to make it work?"

"I would try, but nine times out of ten she'd be too good to be true. Nobody's perfect, and people come and go."

"Well, of course nobody's perfect, but you learn to love the person for who they are, imperfections and all."

"Is that how you love your husband?"

She narrows her eyes at me and her whole mood changes. Fuck. I couldn't help myself. Why did I have to go there?

"Wow." She grabs her drink and pulls her clutch from beneath her armpit. "You're even more of a dick when you drink," she snaps, hopping off the stool.

She flags the bartender down, but he's hardly paying attention again.

"What are you doin', Gabby?"

"Leaving this pity party." She has her debit card out and yells for the bartender.

"Come on, I didn't mean to offend you. I'm just giving you hell."

"Yeah, when *don't* you give me hell?" She glares up at me.

I don't smile, even though I really want to. She's cute when she's upset. A damn firecracker.

"I ordered that drink for you, so let me pay for it."

"Thanks, but I don't need you to." The bartender finally comes to where she's standing. I have a feeling that if she weren't so attractive, he'd have rolled his eyes before coming her way, but he did a double take and rushed right over.

"I got a rum and coke," she says, sliding her card across the counter. I place my hand on top of her card and fish my wallet out with my free hand.

"Marcel, what are you doing?"

I ignore her, slapping a twenty on the counter. The bartender doesn't hesitate to take it. I pick Gabby's card up and hand it back to her. "I'm sure you don't want your husband seein' the charges from a bar on your card, do you? I've got a feelin' he doesn't even know you're here."

Her eyes are wide now. A deeper dip forms between her brows. "Actually, I've bought two drinks with his card, so it doesn't matter, and if he asked, I'd tell him where I went. I swear you are the biggest fucking asshole I have ever met!"

She snatches up her drink and tries to elbow herself away from me, but I catch her arm, fighting a smile.

"Get the hell off of me," she snaps.

"I'm just teasin' you, little thing! Calm down!"

She's standing in front of me now, her drink clutched in hand. "What's so funny about sharing money with my husband?" she demands.

"I never said anything about it bein' funny. I just like how riled up you get when I say somethin' about him to you."

"Yeah, because my marriage is *such* a joke." She rolls her eyes, and the sarcasm is heavy in her tone.

I hold my hands up innocently. "Never said that."

"You're lucky I'm pissed at him, otherwise I'd throw my drink in your face."

"Would you now?" I fight a grin.

She's fighting one too. "Hell no. I wouldn't waste a good drink on you. You're insane." She looks back at the booth where her friends are. "I should get back before Meredith starts wondering what's taking me so long." She starts to turn, but I catch her by the arm. She clashes into me, gasping.

"What are you—"

"Those women will do their best to convince you to do coke one way or another. Trust me. I know women like that. I've attended several events with women like them. They'll make you out as the new girl and tell you that's the way to fit in. Don't be like them."

"I'm not," she breathes.

"Weed is better. Still illegal here, but better."

She narrows her eyes. "Wait…you have *weed*?"

"Do you smoke it?"

"I used to—a lot, actually. In college. Made the whole college experience more fun."

"I only smoke it on the weekends." I look at the exit. "You've had a shit week. I have a joint in my truck. Wouldn't mind sharin' it with you."

She's debating with herself. Her eyes shift back over to

the booth. I look with her and see the ladies she came with taking shots now. They aren't even thinking twice about her, and as if she realizes it too, she nods.

"Okay. Fine. We share it, and then you can take me home. I'll text Meredith and let her know." She plucks the straw out of her drink and chugs it down before slamming the empty glass on the counter.

"Give you one better. We smoke the joint on the way to your house. Get a ride and a buzz at the same time."

She grins, like this is nothing new to her, yet it still excites her. "Even better."

TWENTY-ONE

GABBY

I'M sure it isn't the greatest idea to have Marcel drop me off. What he said to me in the kitchen is proof enough that he's interested in me and that I should stay far away, and at the club, he was definitely flirting. I should have walked away when I said I was going to.

I'm a married woman. I shouldn't even be entertaining the idea of this man, yet when his eyes drop to my legs or my chest, I can't ignore the heat that builds up inside me. I secretly love that it's hard for him to look away.

The thing I like about Marcel is that even though he may be interested, he knows his limits. He's been close all night, but not as close as he got to me in my kitchen. Maybe he, too, realized that it was wrong—wrong for him to even admit that to me—and he's making up for it by staying in the friend zone.

Because that's all he can be. A *friend.*

Before we left the parking lot, Marcel already had the joint lit, like he'd been waiting to leave that club and smoke it all night long. When he passed it to me, I got that old feeling back—the one I used to get in college when I'd spark a joint with my roommate, Chelsea, before a study session.

People make weed seem like a such bad thing, but it helped me in more ways than I can count. For one, when I first got to college, I was lonely and missed my family terribly. I missed them so much it hurt sometimes. When I started smoking weed, it eased the troubles. It calmed my mind, soothed my anxiety. It settled me in a way a Xanax never could.

After I met Kyle and he found out I did it habitually, he wanted me to stop. He found it unattractive, and at the time, all I wanted to do was please him, make him happy since we'd first started dating. It was a struggle giving it up, I admit. Some days I miss it.

If I had a joint to smoke at home before sculpting, my artwork would better. In fact, I know it would be better, because I wouldn't doubt myself. Let's just say when I'm high, I don't think too much. I just let things happen…but now that I'm alone with Marcel in his truck, I'm starting to think getting high with him is a terrible decision.

"You don't look like the kind of man to buy pot," I say as a song by Eminem streams out of the speakers. It's playing on the radio, and Marcel is tapping his thumb to it on the steering wheel.

"It's an occasional buy. Hope this doesn't interfere with business."

"Not at all." I take one more hit and then hand it back

to him. "Believe it or not, I smoked almost every day in college."

"Really? Let me guess, with your husband?"

I spit out a laugh. "Hell no. You'd never see him touch a joint. It was with my roommate."

"Your husband has never smoked weed before?"

I shake my head.

"Not surprised when it's comin' from a tight-ass like him."

I shouldn't laugh, but I do. "You really don't like him, huh?"

"No, I don't. Straight up."

"I honestly can't blame you." Marcel is pulling into Venice Heights. He goes past several houses before stopping in front of mine. "What he did to you was wrong. I still can't wrap my head around it. All he had to do was tell me he didn't really want it, and I would have canceled it. I mean, he said so before, but I thought he'd genuinely changed his mind. Wasn't expecting him to go behind my back."

Marcel sighs, parking the truck and shutting the lights off. He slouches in the seat, peering through the windshield. "It's my fault. I shouldn't have told you. Might've saved you the argument."

"No, I'm glad you told me." I sit up in my seat, looking at him. "And deep down, I'm glad you told him to fuck off."

He chuckles. I smile.

"Oh, man." I press the back of my head on the head-rest. "I haven't felt this good in ages. Who knew all I needed was a few drinks and a joint?"

"Well, whenever you need a joint, just let me know. I'll have one ready for you." His eyes find mine. His smile is complacent, eyelids heavy. He's definitely stoned. He lowers his gaze to my dress. "When I first saw you, I didn't even know it was you. You clean up well."

"Are you saying I looked like shit before?"

"Nah. I actually prefer the natural look of a woman over all the glitz and glam. If anything, it suits you much better."

I feel a blush creeping up and drop my head so he can't see. Interestingly enough, Kyle loves it more when I get dolled up and fancy.

We're quiet a really long time. I start to tell him that I should get inside, but he speaks again.

"I was serious about what I said the other day. You deserve better, Gabby."

I meet his eyes and his are dead serious now. They shimmer from the blue lights in his dashboard. "Even if I felt like I did, it's too late, Marcel. He's my husband. I can't just back out like it's a starter-level relationship."

"Yeah, but I can see how scripted you are with him. That first day I met him, when you introduced us? I knew you enough to know that side of you wasn't you. And when he got home, you looked worried about it."

"Worried?" My heart pounds, but I continue acting nonchalant. "How?"

"I saw you in your studio. It's like you knew he was comin' and that you were wishin' he hadn't arrived so soon."

"What?" My voice is hoarse. "That is—that is insane, Marcel. I was probably annoyed about something I needed to do before he got there."

He doesn't say anything, just looks at me. He knows I'm lying.

"What?" I ask, and I can't pretend to be nonchalant anymore.

"How long has this been going on?"

"Has *what* been going on?"

"You pretendin' you're happy with him." It's a statement.

Cut and dry.

No questions about it.

A cold, hard fact.

I don't even know what to say. I feel my mouth working, but no words are forming. "I—" I clamp my mouth shut. *What the fuck?* Who is he to question my marriage? "I need to go." I open the door and climb out. Marcel calls after me, but I refuse to look back. I rush down my driveway, damning the cobblestone for making it harder to walk in these stupid heels.

"Wait—Gabby!" Marcel calls, but I keep going until I'm stomping up the stoop.

"Damn it, where is my key!" I hiss as I dig through my clutch. I finally feel the cold metal and shove it into the lock, but before I can turn it and get inside, a hand is on my shoulder, gripping and whirling me around.

"Gabby," he says, breathlessly.

"What, Marcel?" I snap. "What more could you possibly have to say about my marriage?"

"I just…I don't get it. I see women like you, and you're so fuckin' miserable, and I just want to know why. Why do women like you do this to yourselves?"

"Women like *me*?"

His throat bobs, but his eyes are intense. He really wants an answer.

"Because women like me don't have *shit*, Marcel! That's why!"

"What do you mean, you don't have shit? You told me you had your parents—a brother. You went to college, so you obviously had *somethin'*."

"I went to college on a partial scholarship and even still, I had to get a job to pay for my own books and supplies, and for my rent, so I could stay in an apartment close to campus. Every day was hard. I was always tired, and I still came out with debt. I now have a break from it all and get to do what I love, and you mock everything about it. I don't even know why I care about what you think!"

"That's not true." His voice is deeper.

"Yes it is! You mock everything I say! Every time I mention Kyle or he comes up in a conversation, you're scoffing, or rolling your eyes, or telling me that I can do better. But you're wrong, Marcel. I can't do better, because he's what I need right now."

"No." Marcel's head shakes. "That's not what I was talkin' about. You *do* know why you care so much about what I think."

Why?" I challenge, glaring up at him. "If you're so smart, then tell me. Why do I care?"

"Because you can relate to me much more than you can to him, and you know it. Because when he isn't around, you look to me for comfort. You like havin' me around, Gabby. You think I don't see the way you look at me? I know that whenever I'm around, it's a relief for you."

I shake my head and look away. My words are lodged in my throat.

"He makes you feel lonely, even when he's here. I don't. And you know it."

He's so close to me now. My skin is humming, knowing that he could easily reach down and touch me. Kiss me, even.

My eyes travel over his mouth. I stare at how plump and full his lips are, then the stubble surrounding his mouth and his jawline and bottom half of his cheeks. I take in the way he smells, like the mint I saw him pop into his mouth when he put the joint out. I can't stand him. I hate that he knows all of this about me. I hate that he's so close—way too close.

"I'm going inside," I mutter and turn away. I twist the doorknob, but before I can enter, the heat of his body is on my backside.

"You don't have to pretend with me," he rumbles with his lips on the shell of my ear. A shiver wracks through my body, my hand freezing on the doorknob. "I'm not your husband. I don't want you to be anything else but who you really are."

"Don't." It's supposed to be a demand, but it comes out as more of a plea.

"Why are you livin' a lie?"

"Marcel." My voice is weak and so is my resolve. I feel his breath run across my cheek, down my neck. I close my eyes, swaying on the heels that I now hate.

"I could do so much to you right now, and he wouldn't even know it."

My head shakes again. He's pressed fully against me now, and I feel something hard digging into my backside.

He's hard? Oh, God. What is going on?

"Turn and look at me." It's a soft command, spilling from his lips.

"I can't."

"Turn, Gabby."

A sigh escapes me. "If I turn, we both know something will happen that I'll only end up regretting."

"Think so?"

"I know so."

"So you *do* want me?" There's a trace of laughter in his voice now.

"I never said that—"

My argument is invalid. Marcel turns me around himself, then he lowers a hand, pulling the door shut. My back bumps against it, keeping me steady as he looks down into my eyes.

He presses his palms flat on the door, just above my head, his chest almost touching mine. His head hangs low as he looks me over.

"I'd never force anything with you, but you wouldn't regret it if somethin' were to happen between us," he murmurs. "You can count on that."

"You can't do anything…"

"Oh, I can," he assures me, revealing a sure smile. "But for your sake, I won't." He looks me over again, sweeping his eyes up and down the length of me, like he's trying to figure out where he'd kiss me first if given the opportunity.

Finally, he pushes away, and his chest is no longer on mine. His scent has faded.

"I think you need a reality check, Miss Gabby. You don't know what the hell you want."

I'm breathing erratically, watching him look off at

anything but me. He looks at me again, and I can't stop the words that leave my mouth.

"What I have with my husband is my business," I state. "And if you have a problem with it, then maybe you shouldn't come around so much."

He blinks once.

Twice.

His parted lips seal together, and he leans back, studying every single feature of my face as if he'll find a trace of a humor on it.

What he doesn't realize is that since I'm so good at *pretending*, I'm also good with my poker face.

I don't flinch.

I don't smile.

I just stare at him.

"Damn." He sucks in a breath and takes a step back. "And here I was thinkin' you were different."

I want to cry. I really do. But only because his words are so heartbreaking—only because I know my words were cruel, and they'll change things.

But we can't be, and we can't act on whatever impulses or desires we're feeling. We simply can't, and he knows this.

Marcel walks down the stoop, and with each step he takes, I feel like someone is stepping on my heart, wearing the heels I'm standing in right now—the ones I hate.

"Goodnight, Mrs. Moore," he says when he's reached the last step, and without a moment's hesitation, he turns away and walks up the driveway.

I watch him until he disappears between the shadows of the palm trees. I hear the engine of his truck come to life and can even hear him driving away. I go inside before the threatening tears can fall.

I don't allow myself to think as I trudge upstairs to my bedroom and strip out of the club clothes. I chuck the shoes in my closet, put on a nightgown, and climb into bed. I don't even care that I'm about to crash with makeup on my face—a pet peeve of my mom's. I let the buzz I'm still riding rock me to sleep…and then I dream.

It's me and Marcel at the club again, but it's empty. The dance floor is vacant, and we're laughing by the bar. I drag him to the dance floor and beg him to dance with me. He refuses at first, so I turn around and shove my ass onto his groin. "Will you dance with me like this?" I can hear myself ask it, and my voice is way too sultry and seductive. I don't even recognize it. I don't have the same dress on. I'm wearing a red one.

Marcel doesn't say anything. He pulls me closer to his body, and I feel his erection digging into my ass.

"I love that you know me," I tell him in my dream. "I love that you get me."

Still, he doesn't say anything. I feel his hand come up to the strap of my dress. He's pulling the straps down, his erection growing harder. My breasts fall out of the dress and then his hands are at the hem of it, shoving it up to my waist. I don't know how I end up standing in front of the bar, but I'm there the next second, almost like we teleported. I still feel his erection on my back. I turn around with a smile, but when I look up, Marcel isn't smiling anymore.

He spreads my legs apart, still quiet, and then picks me up. I don't have panties on in this dream, and his cock is already out, so he slides me down on top of him. He's stiff and thick. I can feel everything.

I'm moaning just as loud as the music, but he's not thrusting. He's just watching me with his cock inside me. Gauging my reactions. Realizing how much I'm enjoying having him inside me.

"I knew it," he rumbles, and a slow smile spreads across his lips. "I knew you wanted me to fuck your married pussy." I should hate his words, but they turn me on even more, making me moan even louder.

He's still not thrusting, and I'm writhing and need movement, so I bounce on his cock. I keep bouncing, up and down, riding him like a maniac, crying out his name as he holds my waist. He's groaning, on the brink of orgasm, and just as I'm about to come, I hear a door slam into a wall.

I gasp and look over Marcel's shoulder to the back door of the club. Kyle stalks across the dance floor.

"You fucking bitch!" he roars. That vein is visible on his forehead —the one he gets when he's upset. His eyes are like balls of fire.

He's standing there, yelling, and Marcel doesn't care. He doesn't look back once. He takes the lead and turns me, placing me on a stool and thrusting hard into my pussy. I don't know why I haven't told him to stop. Why haven't I pushed Marcel away? I just got caught!

"Your pussy is mine," Marcel growls, as if Kyle isn't even there. I'm looking Kyle right in the eyes, and I'm mortified. But I'm still wet for Marcel. "Gonna come inside you." Marcel's voice is gruff. "Gonna make your pussy all mine."

And he does.

He comes with a groan and kisses the back of my neck. Kyle is still yelling.

After Marcel fills me with his cum, Kyle rushes toward him and tackles him over the bar, shattering liquor bottles and glasses.

TWENTY-TWO

GABBY

"WHAT THE HELL!" I gasp and sit up straight in bed, pressing a hand to my chest and using the other hand to wipe the cold sweat from my forehead.

I sit against the headboard, staring out the window to my left. It's still dark outside. I lower my hand, and my nipples are rock hard. I'm throbbing between my legs. "Oh my God. What is wrong with me?" I push out of bed and rush to the bathroom, staring into the mirror. My makeup is a mess. My mascara has run and is smeared around my eyes, making me look like a raccoon. My once-sleek hair is matted and all over the place. My lip gloss is completely gone.

I go to the shower and turn it on, trying to forget about the dream, but it's impossible with the fire between my legs. Should I even call it that? How did it feel so real? It truly felt like Marcel was *inside* me. And judging by how wet I am…I *liked* it. A lucid dream is what that was, and an intense one at that.

"Oh, God." I groan and get into the shower, letting the water pour over me. It runs through my hair, down my back. I remain this way for a while, hoping to rid myself of this intense fire, but it won't budge. It needs to be settled somehow. *I could play with myself,* I think, but as I come to settling with that idea, I feel a draft of cool air run over my legs and then fingers are on my shoulders.

I scream bloody murder as I spin around.

"Hey—hey, it's me!" Kyle says, holding my shoulders.

"What the hell, Kyle! You scared the shit out of me!"

"I'm sorry," he murmurs. I look down and he's naked. I wonder if I'm still dreaming. I pinch my own cheek to make sure and it hurts a little, so no, I'm not.

"Why are you pinching yourself?" he asks, laughter in his voice. "And why are you in the shower at four in the morning?"

"I woke up sweaty," I murmur. I swallow but it's hard to do. My mouth is dryer than a desert. I look him over, and I feel a flash of anger strike me. "I don't want to shower with you, Kyle. Nothing has changed. I'm still upset."

"I came home early for you," he tells me, like that's going to solve everything.

"You still went behind my back and didn't apologize."

"That's why I'm here now. To apologize." He grabs my hands and I watch droplets from the showerhead fall on his lips. "I'm sorry about what I did. I really am. I swear I didn't do it to degrade you or to make you feel insignificant. I did it because he seemed like the kind of man who would take to that kind of bait. Degrading women, making them feel lesser than. I'm so sorry, babe."

Oh, how wrong he is. If he'd had one conversation with Marcel beforehand, he would have known that was far from the truth. Marcel is respectful. I could never see him saying something like that about a woman he cared about, even if it were a joke.

I lightly pull away and turn my back to him. "How long did you practice that apology on your flight home?"

"Not long enough, obviously." I can hear the irritation in his voice, so I ease up and let it go for now. I grab my body wash and sponge to wash myself up. Kyle is standing there, but I don't know what he's thinking. Most likely trying to find better words to use. It's what he usually does.

I feel a hand wrap around my waist. He pulls me toward him and I can feel his erection on my ass.

"Are you kidding me?" I try to pull away, but he doesn't let up. "Kyle, seriously. I'm not in the mood." But that would be a lie. I'm desperate for sex, but not with him. Not right now.

"Do you realize how sexy you look right now with all that soap on your body? It's been days, babe. Let's forgive and forget."

"Screw that," I mutter, but his lips are already on the back of my neck, the same place Marcel kissed me in my dream. He kisses me there repeatedly, tall enough to move his lips to the crook of my neck next. Damn it. Why? Why did I have to have that stupid dream? I wanted to stay mad at Kyle for a little longer. I wanted him to work for my forgiveness, but my body is on fire right now. I can't even think straight because that dream is crowding my headspace.

Kyle spins me around, forcing my hands on the marble wall. He wastes no time entering me from behind, and I'm so slick with need that I take him right in.

"Shit, Gabs," he pants, pressing his forehead to the base of my head. "You're so fucking wet for me." But he's wrong. I'm not wet for him. This wetness was created by someone else—well, a fantasy version of him anyway.

Kyle thrusts slowly, and I'm glad because I don't want it to end quickly. His hands roam my body, palming my breasts. He's kissing the top of my shoulder and my neck again, and I'm moaning way too loudly.

"You're so tight," he breathes over my shoulder. "Is that what you want? For me to talk to you while we fuck?"

I nod. "Oh, God, yes."

"I can do that. I'll do whatever you want me to do."

I moan again.

"Tell me you missed me."

"I missed you."

"Tell me you love me."

"I love you," I breathe.

"Say you forgive me."

I don't even hesitate. The words just slip right out. "I forgive you." I do a small cry, my forehead on the shower wall, and he thrusts harder. "I forgive you, I forgive you." I repeat the words, feeling my climax brewing. I'm desperate. So desperate.

"That's my Gabby." Kyle drops his head and sucks on

my neck from behind. His thrusts become rigid, a hand sliding down to my pussy. He spreads the lips apart and uses a finger to rub circles on my clit. I swear I almost die. I'm pent up from that dream, needing release, and with his cock swelling up inside me and his finger right there—I can't take it.

"Oh, yes!" I squeeze my eyes shut and come around his cock. "Yes, please! Fuck me, Kyle! I need it!"

He loses all sense of control. He thrusts rapidly and water splashes. Smacking sounds fill the air, and a deep groan rips right through him.

"Oh, fuck, babe." His voice is thick, drizzled with desire as he comes. "Oh, fuck. Oh, fuck," he repeats. I press a hand to the wall weakly, my cheek now flush against it.

He pulls out of me, breathing rapidly, then he grabs me and turns me in his arms to hug me.

"I'm sorry, Gabby. I'll never do it again. You were right before. You are my wife, and I should respect your decisions."

I close my eyes, even though the water is a little cooler now.

After we get out of the shower, we climb into bed and fuck one more time. I tell him to take me from behind again, because I don't want to see him, and I hate myself for thinking that way.

I know he won't let me take over—not after that shower fuck—so I make do. I come again, but this time with my own hand. And as Kyle comes this second time, I'm imagining Marcel coming inside me, just like I did in the shower. Just like he did in my *dream*.

I've never had to fantasize this much to get off before

moving to this house, but Marcel does it to me every time, and since I can't act on it, all I have is this. A made-up fantasy. A lie. My husband's cock to take care of what will never happen.

But I don't care, because when I fantasize about Marcel, I have the best orgasms of my life.

TWENTY-THREE

GABBY

It's no shocker Marcel doesn't show up in my backyard with his crew on Saturday. To be honest, I'm glad.

Kyle will be home for the next four days. I need to settle my mind and body. Marcel's presence only confuses me. I don't know what I want when he's around, and I don't like that feeling. I don't like to be unsure, or to feel like I've lost control of myself.

When it was just me and Kyle, I was positive that I loved him, positive that he was the man I needed. But lately, he's been feeling like anything but.

On Sunday morning, I'm preparing Kyle's favorite breakfast, an omelet with cheese, red peppers, and red onions, as well as toast with peanut butter and banana slices. As I finish up cracking the eggs for the omelet, I hear him coming downstairs.

"I'm making your favorite," I call out before he can get to me. "Coffee's brewing."

"What is this?" His tone is sharp, and I spin around. He's standing in the kitchen with the dress I wore to the club, holding it by the strap like it's a disgusting piece of left-over spaghetti.

"Just a dress," I breathe. "I wore it Friday night when I went to a club with our neighbor, Meredith."

Kyle scoffs, his face less tense, as he places the dress on top of the barstool. "I had no idea you were going to a club."

"I didn't tell you," I say. "I was still upset about what you did with the emails. Meredith saw me at the mailbox and invited me to come out with her and a group of friends. It was a fun night."

"Was it?" His tone is condescending.

"Yes, it was. You think I can't have fun without you?" I smile over my shoulder to lighten the mood.

"I didn't say that. I just wish you'd have told me. What if something had happened, and I had no idea where you were?"

"Oh my goodness. Please, Kyle. Nothing happened. I'm here; you're here. Everything's fine."

I carry the bowl of scrambled eggs to the stove and dump them in the pan. I glance over my shoulder as Kyle sighs, making his way toward the coffee that has just brewed in the Keurig. He pours a cup and sips it black. "Meredith, huh?"

"Yep. The woman across the street. She's nice." I grab the spatula and start fiddling with the eggs, ready to flip it to make the omelet.

"I met her the first day we moved in," he continues, and I wish he would stop. "She's not the kind of person you'd normally hang out with. Did you drive there, to meet her at the club?"

"No, she drove us there."

"And she brought you back home in one piece?"

I avoid his eyes then, but I don't hesitate. "Yep, I'm fine. You saw me that night. I had a little too much to drink and felt a little queasy. That's why I was in the shower when you got home." Another lie for the books.

"Mm-hmm." It's the only noise he makes. A curious sound. Nothing more, nothing less. One of the chairs at the table scrapes across the floor as Kyle pulls it back. He sits, and I sprinkle some shredded cheese in his omelet, finish it up, and then bring it to him on a plate. I kiss his cheek before going back and making one for myself, minus the peppers and onions.

When I've poured my coffee and am sitting across from him, I notice he's looking at me. His eyes are narrowed, and he works his jaw, like he's trying to assess me.

"What? Is the omelet not good?" I ask quickly.

"It's fine."

"Then what is it?"

"I don't know. You just seem…*different*."

I purse my lips.

"I think I'm spending too much time away from home."

"We've talked about this, Kyle. You have to do what you have to do, and it's only been a few weeks. I just have to get used to it."

"You should come with me to Rhode Island."

I take a bite of my omelet, scrunching my nose. "Rhode Island? What's there?"

"I have a meeting there. New client, but it's only one meeting. We can sightsee, do something nice for ourselves afterward."

I clear my throat, picking up my coffee. Would it be wrong to say I don't want to go on that kind of trip with him right now? He's my husband; I should be jumping at the chance to be around him. I decide to change the subject instead.

"Maybe. Speaking of traveling, my dad called the other day. He said he's been trying to get a hold of you. Wants us to come up for Easter dinner."

Kyle slows down on his chewing for a moment but then he finishes the bite of egg, breathing in deep before exhaling. "Why Easter?" He waves his fork, like the thought of going to my parents' house annoys him.

"He just wants us to come up. My mom is cooking a big meal and my brother and aunt will be there. I told him you usually don't work holiday weekends."

"I don't, but I'm not so sure I want to spend it there."

"In Fredericksburg?"

"Where it always seems to rain," he says, deadpan. "There's literally nothing there but gray clouds and water, Gabs."

"I don't know." I shrug and smile. "I kind of miss the weather. I miss getting cozy and wearing rain boots. Never had to look stylish in shoes because they'd only get messed up with all the mud and puddles."

"You can go," he responds curtly, and then finishes his omelet. He stands with his plate, carrying it to the sink.

When he comes back, he picks up his coffee and then leans against the edge of the counter. The same edge Marcel planted his hands on when he closed me in several days ago. I let that thought slip my mind.

"You don't want to?"

"It's not that I don't want to—I just don't see an Easter dinner being a solid reason to book a flight and fly up there. But if you miss them, you should go. It'll be good for you to get away."

I frown. "Kyle, we are *married* now, you realize that, right? If neither of us are working or occupied, they'll expect us to show up *together*."

"Every marriage isn't the same," he mumbles.

"Seriously?"

"What—come on, Gabby! You can't be serious right now!" He sounds like he wants to laugh. He's mocking the entire situation.

I place my fork down and push out of my chair. "You know what? I can't. I really can't with you right now." I leave my omelet and coffee on the table and rush around the corner to get upstairs.

"Oh—Gabby, come on!" Kyle yells.

I ignore him and go to our room, heading into the closet to take down some jogging pants and a T-shirt.

"What are you doing, Gabs?" Kyle asks at the door of the closet, arms folding across his chest. He's still carrying that condescending tone.

I hike my pants over my legs then tug my shirt over my head. As I pull my hair up into a bun, I meet his eyes, one of my brows tilted, and say, "Going to walk some steam off before I end up stabbing you with my fork."

"Oh, really. Your fork?"

I ignore his remark, grabbing my shoes. I start to walk around him, but he catches me by the arm, and I come to a halt.

"Let's walk together then."

I look down at his hand before pulling away. I sit on the bench at the end of the bed and shove my feet into my running shoes. "I'm not doing anything with you right now."

"You have been so feral lately; I hope you realize that."

"When am I not?"

"You aren't usually *this* feral."

"Yeah, well, maybe I'm just tired of some of the things you say and do, Kyle." I pause, looking sideways at him. "You're a little selfish sometimes."

"Selfish? Gabby, I work my ass off almost every day. Forgive me for not wanting to travel for once in my life just to attend a *dinner*."

I push to a stand. "I get that, Kyle, but that's my family, and I miss them! I haven't seen them in weeks. I used to see them every day. Think about how that makes me feel. You should understand why I'd like to go up there—or even why my dad invited us. They miss us."

"No, they miss *you*," he corrects.

"Whatever." I wave a hand and leave the bedroom. I don't expect Kyle to stop me again. He's not a two-time man. He'll come after me once, but if I'm still upset over something he considers trivial, he drops it and lets me go to cool off.

The whole emailing Marcel thing was big, and he knew it, that's why he came home and apologized. But even so, that was his first and only apology. I forgave him through a heated fuck and he hasn't brought it up again.

Sometimes I wish he would come after me twice, try and cheer me up any way he can, but that's not who my husband is.

Sadly, that will never be who he is.

Marcel doesn't show for the entire week, and I'm worried. It's now Thursday, and he has yet to make an appearance.

Kyle left this morning. I let the whole Easter dinner thing go after my walk. He was right. He traveled a lot, and he had a right to stay or go. I wasn't going to make him, but I knew I was going for sure. I figured eventually he'd come around and want to tag along.

I try to pry with Marcel's crew as they work on installing the hot tub. The man who's designing my wet bar, Albert, tells me that Marcel has been at a commercial job finalizing paperwork and working on the overall layout. He told me the new client Marcel has is picky, so he's been redesigning it a lot and waiting for approvals.

I almost start to buy into it, until I remember the conversation we had the night he dropped me off. I was drunk and high and so mean to him. I've thought about it every night since it has happened, and I feel like a true bitch for telling him off.

By Saturday, I can't deal with the guilt weighing on my chest anymore. The guys are out back, close to wrapping up on the built-in seating and gardens. The hot tub has been completely installed and the cement has dried. They'll be working on the control system soon. It has only been two and a half weeks. Fortunately, the wet bar will take a few more weeks.

Marcel still hasn't come around, and of course it bothers me, so I go upstairs and fetch my laptop. When I'm back on the sofa, I send him an email.

Mr. Ward,

I realize you called me Mrs. Moore before you left the night you dropped me off. That was a week ago, and I haven't heard from you since. I realize that it was your way of saying you'll keep your distance after what I told you. I hate that you actually stuck to your word, then again you are a man who does only that.

Truth is, it's not the same around here without you, and I'm sorry for hurting you. I do enjoy being around you, but not in the way you're thinking. I simply enjoy your company and your presence. You have a good energy, and I could use more of that in my life.

I also know you're thinking that I'm just emailing you because my husband isn't around, but you're wrong. I've been tempted to email you all week, but waited because I didn't want to look like I was overreacting.

Your guys say you've been working on a big commercial job, but I know you've been avoiding me, which is totally understandable, and I can't blame you for it.

Please let me make it up to you. I'll cook tacos and make Jell-O tequila shots, if that'll help. You can even choose the flavor. I'd hate to ruin our friendship over my stupid, drunk words.

Talk soon…I hope.

Miss Gabby

I wait all night for an email back. I even make dinner and some skinny banana pudding to distract myself, but nothing comes through.

By eleven p.m., I know he isn't going to respond so I give it up, putting my laptop back where it belongs in my studio and going to bed.

TWENTY FOUR

MARCEL

I STARE at the email on my screen, my elbow on the arm of my chair and my chin resting on my knuckles.

I read over it repeatedly—four times to be exact—and then I close the lid of my laptop.

"Fuck that." I push out of my desk chair, collecting some paperwork and designs to look over at home. It's late now, nearing one in the morning. I need to get home.

During the drive, of course I can't stop thinking about the email she sent. Shit, at least she's noticed that I'm not around. After what she told me, that if I had a problem then I shouldn't come around so much, I realized she was right. I shouldn't have been coming around. My men could handle the rest of the job.

She had just gotten married and was obviously living the life she always wanted. Who was I to interfere with that?

Some fucked up part of me still wants her, even while

knowing she's tied to another man. That part of me can shut the hell up, because I'm not doing it. I'm not torturing myself by being around her, craving her even more than the day before, and I damn sure am not about to end up with my hands stuck in my pants with all of her fucking teasing.

I admit, when she turned me down, I was pissed, but I went home, got in the shower, and realized my dick was getting hard. I showered and ignored the rock between my legs as much as I could, but my cock was throbbing. I couldn't stop thinking about her. That short dress and her legs. Her perfect tits. Hell, even watching her smoke the joint turned me on.

I couldn't fight it anymore. I stroked my hard cock back and forth, slow at first, and then sped it up, and came right on the shower wall. It was a powerful orgasm.

I park in front of my house, shutting the headlights off and killing the engine. After I collect my paperwork from the passenger seat, I get out, my keys jingling as I walk to the door. All I want to do is have a stiff drink and go to sleep. This week has been hell.

A whimpering noise comes from my right, and I frown, looking toward the wired fence. I hear a scraping noise and then another whimper.

"What the hell is that?" I place the paperwork down on my porch chair, then walk over to the fence. The motion light by the garage turns on and shines right on a puppy. Judging by its long, floppy ears, I think it's a beagle.

The puppy whimpers even louder when it sees me. One of its legs is caught under the fence. That leg is bleeding badly, there's a small hole beneath the puppy, like it dug its way under the fence.

"Oh, man. How'd this happen, pup?" I crouch down in front of the puppy and pull the wire of the fence up. The puppy shrieks, but it rushes out and limps its way to my boot. It's still whimpering. Whining, now. I pick the puppy up—he or she can't weigh more than about five or six pounds. I check its leg, glad it's no more than a small gash. Nothing too bad.

"Poor pup. How long you been trapped there?" I rub some of the blood away with the pad of my thumb. "Runnin' from somebody? Did they try and hurt you?" The puppy whines again and looks up at me. Those damn eyes kill me. "Come on. Let's clean you up and find you some food." I pick the puppy up and carry it inside. When I'm in the kitchen, I place the puppy on the floor but not before checking its belly area.

"You're a girl. Good to know." I grab the first-aid kit on the counter and then pick her up. I don't have any alcohol so I grab a bottle of vodka, dab it on a paper towel, and wipe it over her leg. She does a cry-whine, and I shush her. "Sorry. Gotta clean all that dirt out." I place her on the counter. She's shaking now. Poor thing probably thinks I'm going to hurt her. I clean her leg really good, smear it with ointment, then wrap it with some gauze. She tries to bite at it. "No, no. Keep it there. You remove it, and it might get infected." I pick her up from the counter, tucking her beneath my arm, and then open the fridge. I search but don't have a damn thing for a puppy to eat. There's more beer and old takeout than anything.

I sigh and look down at her. She runs her tongue over her muzzle. I grab an empty bowl from the cupboard and fill it with water, then place her and the bowl down on the floor.

"Go on. Drink up."

She sniffs around it, then she starts sipping. She's so thirsty she practically drinks the whole bowl.

Sighing, I look down at her as she peers up at me. "Stop lookin' at me like that. I can't keep you," I mumble. "Everything around me always ends up destroyed or worse…" I pretend I'm cutting my own throat with my thumb. She cocks her head, clearly confused.

I huff a laugh. "Let's get you some food, figure out where the hell you came from." I pick her up and go back outside, locking my door and then hopping into my truck. I place her on the passenger seat and head to the nearest store to find some dog food.

When we're back home, she demolishes the food, and after she's eaten, she walks to me, sniffing my boot and then laying on top it. Right on top of my boot. Her head is still up, eyes wide. For a puppy, she's calm. Or maybe she's tired after fighting that fence all day.

With another sigh, I pick her up and carry her to the couch. I don't even get the chance to go over any of the paperwork. I rub her head as she rests on my chest. I have no idea when I fall asleep, but it's peaceful.

However, I wake to the sound of liquid spilling.

I sit up straight and look around, and the puppy is pissing right on the middle of my floor.

"Aw, hell! You serious? I thought we were friends!"

She looks at me then dashes away from the spot, running to the kitchen and sniffing around her bowl. "Jesus." I grab paper towels from the kitchen and clean up the mess. "Yeah, I gotta figure out where you came from. Pissin' all over my floors is not cool." After I feed her, I pick her up and decide to make my way around the neighborhood before heading to work. She's a beautiful puppy. I'm sure someone is looking for her.

TWENTY-FIVE

GABBY

STILL NOTHING FROM MARCEL. It's ten in the morning and his crew arrived three hours ago. I'm in my studio, watching them work. It's coming together nicely, and all the piles of dirt that were around before, are mostly gone now. My chest feels tighter as I watch some of the men carrying dahlias to one of the bigger flower beds.

Turning away from the window and going to my laptop, I check my emails one more time. Nothing. My phone buzzes, and there's a text from Kyle.

Kyle: I want to make you happy, any way that I can. Let's go see your family for Easter. I know how badly you want to.

His text makes me smile. I'm glad he thought about it. I text him back, saying thank you with a heart emoji, then I

206

place my phone down. I look at the dahlia I was working on. I need to paint and glaze it then stick it in the kiln out back.

To distract myself from my thoughts, I get right to it, putting on my apron, tossing my hair up in a bun, and glazing the flower.

When I'm done, I place it on the tray I always use and carry it downstairs. When I get outside, the men are louder. They're so used to me coming out that they simply wave or ignore me.

I smile since I can't wave, making my way to the shed. I slide the flower into the kiln carefully after covering it with aluminum pans, then sit on the yoga mat in front of it after setting the timer.

As I wait for the flower bake, I hear a rapid panting noise, followed by a tiny bark.

I look to my left and see a puppy dashing through the backyard. It's tiny, with sandy-blonde ears and a spot on its bottom and tail to match. The rest of its body is a pure white. It's clearly a beagle, but I've never seen one like it. They're usually covered with more black and brown, than white.

"What the hell!" Alex yells as the puppy dashes around with a limp, like it's having the time of its life. I laugh as it runs past some of the workers. It zooms back in the direction it came from, and I stand. As if it notices me for the first time, it comes my way and stops right in front of me. It sniffs and sniffs, and I laugh, bending down to pick it up.

"What are you doing here?" I giggle, rubbing its head and then scratching behind its ears. I lift the puppy above my head to check it out. "A girl? You've got so much energy, girl! Who do you belong to?" I check the black collar around her neck, but there is no tag.

"She's yours if you want her," a familiar voice says, and I look up quickly. The puppy wriggles in my hands, and I place her down. She dashes for Marcel, who scoops her up in his large hands. One of his hands is big enough to hold her.

"Marcel," I say, and I don't know why I can't process the fact that he's here right now. I shake my head, pulling myself together. "Where did she come from?" I ask.

"No idea. She was stuck in my fence last night. She got cut up pretty bad, but I think she's much better now. Wound wasn't too deep." He points to her leg, at a little cut that I hadn't even noticed before. "I went around my neighborhood all morning and asked if anyone owned her or knew who did, but none of my neighbors had a clue. She's been with me since."

"So why don't you keep her?" I ask. I reach for her again, and she finally settles down. I cradle her in one arm, stroking her head and back with my hand.

"I work too much. I leave early and don't get back home till late at night. Wouldn't have anyone to watch or look after her."

I scratch behind her ears again and she turns her head. She really likes that. "I'm not sure if I can keep her, either. Kyle isn't a big fan of dogs. He loves them, but doesn't like the idea of owning one."

Marcel almost looks like he wants to say something, but instead, he clamps his mouth shut and shakes his head. "The last thing I want to do is put her in a shelter. She seems like a good puppy. Playful. Sweet. Not only that, but she clearly likes you."

I smile, placing her down. She rolls onto her back by accident, and I rub her belly. She loves that too, because she stays there with her tongue halfway out. "I don't know...I'll have to check first."

"Well, in the meantime, you think you can keep her here? Just 'til I can find her a good home? I'll keep askin' around and if nothin' comes up, I'll take pictures, put her up for sale if I have to. I refuse to put her in a shelter."

"Yeah." I nod. "Sure, I'll keep her until then."

Marcel nods. "Good." He bends down, and the puppy jumps up, rushing for him. She starts nibbling on his hand. "Think she's teethin'," he laughs, letting her chew on his fingers.

"Have you named her?"

"No. Don't want to get too attached."

I nod and look away. "I'm already getting attached to her," I admit with a small laugh.

"You like dogs." It's a statement not a question, but I answer as if he asked.

"I used to have a chocolate lab when I lived with my parents, but she got really sick. She was a sweet dog. Her name was Cammie."

"Cammy?" He looks up, squinting a little when the sun hits his eyes.

"C-A-M-M-I-E."

"Ahh."

We're quiet a beat. His crew is talking, and the puppy is snarling adorably, trying to bite his finger harder.

"I'll just keep her," I finally blurt out. "I wanted another dog so bad after Cammie died. This one doesn't have a home. I'm sure Kyle will understand why I took her in."

"You sure? I don't want to cause any trouble."

I shrug. "It'll be fine. She'll be my responsibility." Marcel pulls his hand away from the puppy and stands tall. She comes my way, and I bend down again to pick her up. "Cammie had a sister named Callie when we adopted her. I always loved that name. I think I'll name her that."

"Callie." He smirks. "Hmm. I like it. It fits her."

Callie yawns.

"Well, I have to get some work done. Came by because they told me the hot tub is finished." Marcel looks around. "Backyard will be all yours pretty soon, give or take another two weeks or so."

"Yeah." I don't know why hearing that makes my heart drop. "Your guys will be finished early."

He winks at me. "Best crew around."

I shift on my feet, rubbing Callie out of nervousness now. "I, um…I emailed you last night."

"I know." He looks into my eyes, unwavering.

"Did you read it?"

"Yep. Didn't know what to say."

"Just say yes," I murmur. "To dinner, I mean."

"I don't think that's a good idea. You tend to freak out whenever we're alone."

"Well, after what happened last time, I'm sure my freak outs are within reason. This time will be different. It will be cordial."

"You'd freak regardless, but it's fine. You don't have to apologize. I've already let it go. I'm just here to check a few things out and then head to my office."

"Marcel." My frown has grown deeper. "Weren't you the one who told me to stop pretending?"

He shrugs.

"Stop pretending you *aren't* interested in eating tacos with me. You and I both know it would be a lie if you say you aren't."

"I'm not pretendin'," he mumbles, stepping back.

"Sure. Okay." I roll my eyes and turn for my kiln. The timer for it has gone off. I place Callie down and open the oven door. Heat escapes, but I use the oven mitt hanging on the wall of the shed to take it out.

"I'll go home, get the dog food I bought if you want it," Marcel says.

"Nah. That's okay. I'll go grab some stuff for her. I don't mind."

"You sure keeping her is okay?"

I force a laugh. "It's fine."

He looks me over with a nod before going to meet with Alex and Jacob by the bed of flowers. They start filling him in about work, so I take my dahlia sculpture inside and tell Callie to follow me. I think she follows me more out of curiosity than obedience.

I place the hot tray on two pot holders on the island counter and watch as Callie prances around. She stops by the table and I hear a pitter-patter noise, like liquid has spilled.

"Are you peeing?" I shriek, and she kicks her leg before running away.

I rush to the double doors. "Marcel! Are you kidding? She just peed on my kitchen floor!" I yell.

Marcel looks up at me, and when he takes in my shocked

expression, he breaks out in a smooth laugh. "I think that's her way of saying she likes it there!"

I laugh then shut the door. I grab some cleaner wipes and paper towels and use them to wipe it up as she trots into the kitchen again. "You're going to give me hell, aren't you?" I ask, dumping the towels in the trash bin, then drumming my fingers on the counter. I need to get her some supplies and a dog bed, at least, but first I have to break the ice with Kyle.

I rush upstairs and grab my phone. Callie is waiting at the bottom of the staircase, her head tilted, like she's been waiting for me to come back the entire time. I snap a picture of her and send it straight to Kyle with the message *"We have a puppy now!"*

That'll break the ice for sure.

I pick Callie up and go to the door, sliding into a pair of flip-flops. I leave the house, but not without locking up, and go to the maps app in my phone to search for the nearest pet store. There are three around.

I go to the closest one and fill my cart with dog food, a dog bed, chewing toys, puppy pads, and even little treats. By the time I check out, my buggy is full.

"You're spoiled already," I tell Callie on the way to the car. She's on the seated section of the buggy, loving her surroundings.

When we make it back home, I'm surprised to see Marcel is still in the backyard. He's standing close to the door, hands planted on the folded table in front of him as he reads over a blueprint. I watch him while pulling out Callie's dog bowl and toys.

Like he feels my gaze, he looks up, but I look away,

handing a squeaky ball to Callie. There's a knock on one of the double doors and I look at it again. Of course, it's Marcel. I go to open it.

"Can I come in?" he asks. "Just want to go over the final layout for the wet bar again."

"Yeah, come in."

He steps inside and looks at Callie, smiling as she does her little growl while biting the ball. It's too big to fit in her mouth, and she's clearly upset about that.

"What's going on?" I ask.

"I'm looking over the prints for the bar. Just wanted to know if you wanted shelves built into it or to keep it counter-like?"

"Will the shelves cost me more?"

"Shouldn't, if I include it as a note with the prints."

"I'll take the shelves then."

He nods. "All right. Good to know." He turns for the door, twisting the knob and opening it. Before he walks out, he says, "I've had time to think about your email and what you offered. For your sake, I won't be able to take you up on those tacos." He runs a hand over the top of his head. "Not only that, but work has me busy. Plus I'm taking your advice. Keepin' my distance." He pauses, looking into my eyes. "I'm sure you understand."

My heart feels like it's fallen right into the pit of my stomach. I blink quickly but to act as if I don't care, I say, "Oh, okay. No worries."

He nods once, then shuts the door behind him.

I slouch down in a chair at the table, dragging my palms over my face. "Fuck my life," I mutter.

Well, I guess that's the end of whatever friendship we

had. I have to admit, I'm bummed. But he's right. Distance is best. After seeing how he acted with beer and weed in his system, there's no telling how far he'd go if he ends up with tequila in his bloodstream while around me.

Something tells me my life would become even more of a mess than it already is...and I'm pretty sure I don't need that right now.

TWENTY-SIX

GABBY

Two weeks and three days later, and the landscaping job is complete.

I'm upset.

Don't get me wrong, my backyard is stunning in every way, and you'd think I'd be a little happier about it being finished, considering I was really looking forward to the outcome.

The stones are identical to the cobblestone in our driveway, and the hot tub is big enough to fit at least ten people. There's built-in seating by the fire pit, as requested, and the lush magenta and yellow begonias and dahlias that surround the patio are too beautiful not to stare at through my studio window. I can't wait to break the patio in and make use of it. Now that it's done, though, I'll probably never see Marcel again.

For the past two weeks, he hasn't come around much.

He visited three times out of the past two weeks, and each time was very brief. No longer than fifteen to twenty minutes each visit, and that was only to check on the yard and to make sure his crew was making progress.

I spotted him from my studio during those three visits, while Callie would either gnaw on her toys or sleep. Every time he left, he would look up at the arched window of my studio, like he was looking for me, and every time he did, I would back away, getting out of sight.

Things haven't been so great at home with Kyle either. He never responded to my text about Callie the day I agreed to take her from Marcel. Instead, he showed up several days later from work and asked me a million questions.

Where did it come from? Why would you keep it? Are there any shelters you can give it to?

His questions irritated me. Not only that, but it pissed me off that he kept calling her an *it*. I didn't tell him the truth about where I got her. I told him I'd found her without a dog tag and that she was hurt. I refused to mention that she came from Marcel. He really would have hated having her around then.

She's going to ruin the furniture, Gabs.
The house will smell like a dog now.
You realize she's going to get bigger, right?
She better not be sleeping on our bed.

Despite saying all of that, he's gotten over trying to get rid of her. I told him I like having her around when he isn't home—mentioned that she keeps me company during the days he's away—and ever since I've said that, he's backed off, but he refuses to do anything for her. Won't feed her, walk her, or play with her. He acts as if she doesn't even exist. Doesn't matter. He doesn't have to. I love taking care of her.

Now, it's one week shy of Easter. I got a call from my best friend Teagan yesterday, saying she'd booked a flight to come see me. She claimed she wanted to surprise me, but couldn't hold it in. Now, I'm waiting for her at the airport, standing on my toes, hunting for any sign of her.

As soon as I see her coming my way, she opens her arms and I run right into them. We both squeal and jump, and I'm sure to everyone else we look like two absolutely ridiculous grown-ass women, but I don't care. I've missed my friend and the hugs and squealing are much needed.

"Oh my gosh! Look at you!" I scream. "I missed you so much, T!" I hug her around the neck again as she laughs. When I pull away, I grab her upper arms and squeeze them lightly. "You look so good!"

"Thank you, honey! I've lost some weight since you last saw me!"

"I see that! You look amazing!" And she really does. Teagan is gorgeous. Her long chocolate hair is in loose curls, parted at the crown of her head and long enough to reach the middle of her back. She's wearing a white belly shirt with jeans and sandals. Her red lipstick matches the script on her shirt.

"Where's that husband of yours?" she asks, dragging her suitcase on the wheels behind her as we exit the airport.

"He's home, clearing some of the boxes out of the guest room."

"Was he too good to come with you to the airport and get me?" she jokes.

I laugh. "No, T. I drove my car, and it's only a two door. You better not start that! You came here to have a good time with me. You and Kyle better not be bickering the whole time."

She holds a hand up. "Can't make any promises there, but I'll try."

I shake my head, fighting a smile as we reach the parking deck. She tosses her bags and suitcase in the trunk and we buckle in and take off. We grab lunch first, then manicures and pedicures next—apparently Teagan *really* needed one. When we're all set, we head to my house.

"Kyle?" I call as we walk through the door leading in from the garage. I hear little paws pitter-pattering on the floor and a jingling noise. Callie runs for the door as I walk in, jumping up and down, begging me to pick her up. "Hey, girl!" I pick her up in my arms and Teagan walks around me.

"Aww! You have a puppy now?" Teagan exclaims, closing the door behind her.

"Yeah, her name is Callie."

"Hi Callie!" she sings, and Callie gets even more excited to meet her friendly stranger. "Look at you! You're adorable!" Teagan rubs Callie's head and lightly scratches beneath her chin. She then looks at me as I place Callie down. "Kyle approves?"

I shrug and roll my eyes at the same time. "He's dealt with it."

Footsteps drift down the stairs and I see Kyle before he makes it down to the main floor. "We have a guest, I see!" Kyle exclaims, being way too sarcastic about it.

"Don't act like you didn't know I was coming." Teagan props a hand on her waist.

"It was pretty last minute, but at least we have the space to accommodate." All right. He's being a smart ass and judging by Teagan's *oh-hell-to-the-no* expression, I intervene.

I meet up to him. "Babe, she has a few bags in the trunk. Can you grab them?"

He looks sideways at Teagan before focusing on me. "For you? Anything." He plants a kiss on my cheek, and I force a smile as he walks around me, going out the door in his house slippers.

Teagan scoffs. "You would think he'd be less of an asshole after not seeing me for a few months."

I ignore her comment. I really don't want her upset already. She just got here. "Let me show you the room you'll be staying in. I fixed the bed up just for you."

She follows me up the stairs and I go to the room across from my studio, pushing the door open with the tips of my fingers.

We had several boxes in this room but ended up putting them in our office in the meantime. A full-sized bed is in place, swathed with a navy-blue comforter along with pillows in white and navy-blue pillow cases. Teagan sighs and goes straight for the bed, laying down on it.

"Ahh, laying down feels so good," she sighs.

"There's a TV with cable, so you can watch whatever you want. The bathroom is down the hallway—it's all yours."

"Thanks, G." She sits up, and I take the spot beside her. I can feel her watching me. "Everything okay?"

"Yeah, everything is fine."

"You look…down," she murmurs. "On the ride here, I was talking, and it seemed like your mind was somewhere else."

"Really?" I press my lips. "I don't know. I've been thinking about the class I'll teach next for my sculpture course. And whether or not to keep Callie." Just as I say that, Callie comes running into the room. She's finally mastered the stairs, even though they take her a while to climb. She sniffs around the room, seeing as she's never been in it before. I swear if she pees here too, Kyle will really end up making me get rid of her.

"So, he *doesn't* approve then." I look over and Teagan's lips are pursed.

I meet her eyes briefly before looking away. "I told him she keeps me company when he's working so many days away. When I said that, he didn't push on getting rid of her anymore, but I know he doesn't want her here."

"Is that what's bothering you so much?"

I laugh, but it's dry. In all honesty, Callie is the least of my worries. "Nothing is bothering me. This is just a minor blip. He'll grow to like her. She's a sweet girl."

"She really is." We watch Callie walk to the nightstand. She sniffs and then starts to squat.

"Callie! No!"

She tries to give me puppy-dog eyes, but I get off the bed and pick her up. "You pee outside or on your pads. You know that, right?" I walk to the door but not without looking back at Teagan. "The patio is amazing, T. Come check it out!" She hops up and follows me back down the stairs, just as Kyle is going up with her bags.

"Thank you, good man," Teagan says in her formal,

British-man voice. She always does it to Kyle. He can't stand it. I can only see the back of his head at this point but I'm sure he's just rolled his eyes. He hates being mocked.

I place Callie down when we're outside and Teagan takes in a breath. "Oh my goodness. This is stunning!" Teagan walks past me, looking at the entire patio, zoning in on the hot tub. "You didn't tell me about the hot tub!" she shrieks.

"I wanted to surprise you! We haven't used it yet. Maybe you and I can tonight?"

"Hell yeah!" She turns toward the gate that leads out to the beach. "And look at that view! Girl, no wonder you love this house so much!" I look with her. The ocean water is rushing up to shore. From here, you can hear the waves crashing.

"Gorgeous, right?" Kyle asks behind us. We both look over our shoulders at him. He stands next to me, wrapping an arm around my waist and reeling me closer to him.

"You finally did something right," Teagan teases.

Kyle doesn't find it humorous, I'm sure, but a small smile traces his lips. "What would you like for dinner, Teagan?" he asks. "Neither one of us could figure out what to order or make."

"Whatever you guys want is fine with me."

"I was thinking since it's your first night here, we could try this restaurant in town," Kyle suggests, looking between us. "They serve great Mexican food with big bowl-like margaritas. Everyone I've talked to in the neighborhood has suggested it."

"Margarita is my middle name. I'm cool with that, but since you have all the moohlah, you're paying, right?"

"Of course, Teagan," he chuckles. "It's my treat."

"Mexican food sounds good, babe." I pat his back.

Kyle nods, pulling away from me. "Good. I'll call, make a reservation."

I smile up at him, watching him leave. When he shuts the door behind him, I walk to the built-in seating area to sit. Teagan walks over too, sitting with me. "It's lovely here, but I can see how it could get lonely."

"It does sometimes. Still getting used to it."

She's quiet for a long time. "G, are you guys okay?"

"Yeah." I wave a dismissive hand. "We're fine."

"I bet he hates that I'm here," she snickers. "He'll have to deal with me laughing at him or cracking a joke on him every second. He's way too serious."

I laugh. "You purposely try to get under his skin, and he knows it."

"Yeah, I do." She huffs and shrugs

"So, anyway! Who is Miss Teagan talking to lately? Any new guys?"

"Actually…there is one," she confides, and her smile gets so big. I'm glad I could change the subject. If there is one thing Teagan loves most, it's talking about herself. Not in a self-centered way, but she doesn't talk much about herself to anyone but me, so when she gets the chance, she tells me *everything*.

"Holy shit, T! This is the biggest you've smiled over a guy!"

"Well, he's worth it, okay? So, I met him at work. I was doing a late shift in the emergency room, and he came in with a sprained thumb. He was worried, thought it was broken. I checked him out, ran his vitals, all that good stuff.

The doctor told him he'd be fine and gave him a brace, but before he left, he asked to speak to me. He said he just wanted me to know that I was the prettiest girl he'd ever laid eyes on and was glad I was assigned as his nurse."

"Aww!" I clasp my hands together. "That is the sappiest, sweetest thing ever!"

"Yeah, it was! And totally random. I was having a bad night that night too. He asked for my number, I gave it to him, and he said he'd text me. It took him three days to text me. I told him I hated waiting and got nervous. He apologized and asked me out for lunch. Since then we've been kind of kickin' it. He doesn't take things too seriously and neither do I. We talk every day, but don't really get to see each other all that often because of our schedules, which is fine for both of us. We fit."

"What does he do?"

"He's a part-time personal trainer and a part-time private tutor for college students."

"That's amazing, T! I bet his body is hot!"

"Yeah, I guess."

"You guess?"

"Yeah, I don't want to get too attached. When things go wrong, it hurts, you know?"

"Oh, yeah." I blow a breath. "Trust me, I know. But don't think about it that way. Just live in the moment. It can't hurt to live, right?"

She nods in agreement. She starts talking about more things about her new guy, whose name is Josh. I'm glad she talks about him, because I don't want her prying for more about me.

If she keeps asking what's going on with me, eventually

I'll crack. I tell her everything, even the bad shit. But when it comes to how I'm feeling right now, I'm ashamed to admit it to anyone, even my best friend.

Easter is coming in a week, and I need something to wear for the dinner my parents are having. Teagan has been a great distraction for the past two days. Kyle went back to work yesterday, much to Teagan's relief, so we've been hanging out at the beach while catching up, watching movies, and going out for breakfast, lunch, and dinner. Teagan used to be the outgoing one, but to my surprise she hasn't mentioned going to a club or lounge once, and I'm so glad. My last club night didn't turn out so great.

Just thinking about it—how it all led to being *alone* with Marcel—gets to me. For some reason, I've been thinking about him more often, and I don't understand why. What's worse is I'm thinking about him more than my own *husband*. It's not right, and I need to stop it, but I can't help wondering what he's been up to. I'm sure he's working, but I wonder if he's found another resident to talk to who is friendlier than I am. God, I hope not. I don't want to be a replaceable client.

I guess with time this feeling will fade, but right now, it's stuck on me, and I can't shake it…and I'm starting to think everyone can tell.

"What color are you looking to wear?" Teagan asks, holding up a pink blouse in one hand, a yellow one in the other.

"Doesn't really matter." I rustle through the clothes on the rack, the metal of the hangers scraping by.

"O-kay." Her tone is slightly frustrated, and I look over my shoulder to see she's frowning.

"What's wrong?" I ask.

"*What's wrong?* Gabby, ever since I've gotten here, you've been acting weird. You sure you're okay?"

I force a laugh. "T, I'm fine!"

"No, you're not *fine*. I can always tell because when something is wrong you always say you're *fine*. If you were great, you'd tell me you're great." She takes a step toward me and I sigh, rubbing my elbow and looking away with a huff. "You know you can talk to me about anything, G. That's what I'm here for."

I meet her sincere eyes. "I know but...it's really not a big deal. I'll get over it.

"If it's bothering you this much—to the point that I can *see* something is wrong with you—then yeah, it is a big deal." Her brown eyes study my face. "You know what? Forget about the outfit for now. Let's hit the food court, grab a pretzel from Auntie Anne's or a Cinnabon."

I smile as she grabs my hand and drags me out of the store. A Cinnabon does sound delicious right now. Then again, for the past several days, all I've wanted is carbs. Emotional eating. I always do it.

After we've ordered our Cinnabon, Teagan finds a two-top table and sits. I take the seat across from her and dig into my cinnamon roll, biting the edge and getting a good amount of the cream cheese icing with it. "So good," I moan.

"Remember when we used to go to the mall and talk

about everything while eating these?" She sighs and smiles, looking down at her cinnamon roll. "We'd sit at the table for, like, an hour straight. I miss those days." She looks me over. "So tell me what's going on."

I take another bite, filling my mouth so I don't have to speak right away. She waits, her expression screaming the words, *I've got all day and you know it, so talk!*

"Okay…you have to promise you won't judge me about it."

"Bitch, like I ever would." She waves a hand. "Spill it."

"Okay…" I sigh, placing my fork down. "Remember when I was telling you about the landscape architect?"

"Yeah…I remember. What about him?"

"Well, there was one night I went to a club with a neighbor and he was there. We were at the bar a while, he bought a drink for me, and we left together."

Her eyes stretch as wide as saucers. "You *left* with him?"

"Not like that!" I hiss. "The neighbor I went with was doing coke and stuff with these other ladies, and I just wasn't feeling it, so he offered to take me home."

She looks relieved. "Oh. Okay." She takes a bite of her roll. "Go on."

"We smoked a joint on the way to my house, but when I got home, things got all weird. I went to the door, and he chased after me and said all these things about me and him. About me and Kyle, too."

"Things like what?"

"Like how I deserved better than Kyle. How I wouldn't regret doing something with him if something were to happen. Or how Kyle would never know about it."

She's wide-eyed again. "That's one bold motherfucker."

"But I got *mean*, T. I told him what me and Kyle had was our business and that if he didn't like it, he could stop coming around."

"Wow! Cold-hearted as fuck!" she exclaims.

I shake my head, picking my fork up and scraping it over the icing before bringing it to my mouth to lick it away. "It's not cold-hearted when my marriage is none of his business—or anyone else's outside of it, for that matter."

"So…it's bothering you because you said that to him, or because he actually listened?"

"It's because he listened. I won't lie, I enjoyed his company. He made things around the house less…boring. Not to mention he was nice to look at." I blush, just thinking about his shirtless days. "But I shouldn't care, right? I'm married, and he was just doing his job for the most part. He was high that night and not thinking clearly, so I turned him away before he did something he wasn't supposed to."

"You mean before *you* did something you weren't supposed to." I meet Teagan's eyes. "Don't kid yourself, Gabby. You wanted that man."

"*What?*" The word comes out winded. I'm stunned by her accusation and my heart races.

Teagan gives me a matter-of-fact smile. "You wanted him. But you're married, and you felt guilty for wanting him, so you hurt him to try and downplay your emotions." She sips her drink. "Now I really want to see what this landscape architect looks like."

"Teagan, this isn't a joke, okay? I mean he was *this* close to kissing me that night!" I hold a hand up, showing her how close with my fingers. "If I hadn't said what I did, he would have."

She shrugs. Nothing more.

"You are not taking this seriously."

"You know how I feel about Kyle. I honestly don't give a shit about him, but you're my friend, and I support you. It's the only reason why I tolerate him."

"So, you're saying you wouldn't be surprised that I ended up *cheating* on my husband?" I narrow my eyes at her.

"Not at all. He would deserve it. He treats you like shit sometimes, Gabby."

I shake my head, dropping my fork to fold my arms. "That's ridiculous. Cheating is never okay."

"Is it *that* ridiculous? Because you damn sure aren't denying it. All you do is defend him whenever he does treat you like dirt on the bottom of his shoe. If your landscaper could see that your own husband doesn't deserve you, then what does that prove?"

I swallow thickly to get rid of the dryness in my throat. I hate that she has a point.

"Kyle has been good to me."

"Yeah...lately. And that's only because everything is still so fresh and new for the two of you right now, but as soon as you do something he isn't happy about, he'll be back to treating you like shit and saying whatever he wants to you. And you know why? Because you allow it to happen. He has no respect for you—"

"Kyle does respect me, Teagan. He's done so much for me and my family. How can you say that?"

She shakes her head and holds her hands up. She doesn't want to get into the argument. We've had it before, and it didn't turn out so pretty. Luckily, we forgave each other within a couple days. We never hold grudges with one another.

"Letting my landscaper kiss me would have been wrong, that's why I turned him away."

"And now you miss him. Go figure." She rolls her eyes.

"I don't miss him," I spit out.

"He's gotten a hold of you somehow, otherwise you wouldn't be so upset right now." She's doing that cocky smirk again. I sit back in my chair, but not before grabbing my lemonade and taking a hard sip.

"I'm supposed to be happily married, appreciating my life, and enjoying my husband," I mutter.

"Yeah, you are supposed to be," she agrees. "But is any of that happening?" Her question is blunt. A punch right in the gut. I focus on my best friend, watching as her brown eyes shimmer with the truth that I so badly want to ignore.

I look away before I let her truth shroud my mind, then push out of my chair, closing the container of my Cinnabon and putting it in the bag.

"Let's finish shopping," I mutter, and she rises too, but doesn't say anything else about Marcel or Kyle. But with that smug smile she's wearing as we walk to the next store, I'm certain she's still thinking about it.

TWENTY SEVEN

GABBY

TWO DAYS LATER, I'm walking with Teagan inside the airport so she can catch her flight back home.

"God, I'm going to miss you," I sigh over her shoulder, hugging her tight. "I'm so glad you came. I really needed this time with you."

"I'll miss you too, G. So much."

I pull away and look her over. "Remember, I'm thinking about doing our housewarming next month on Cinco de Mayo weekend, so make sure you take those days off and come back. It'll be fun."

"Oh, trust me, I will. Like I told you, margarita is my middle name."

I laugh and give her another hug.

"Let me get out of here before I miss my flight. Call me if you need anything, okay? I'm here to talk about *whatever* you need. No judgments from me!"

"I know, and I will." I give an appreciative smile.

She turns, hiking the strap of her purse higher on her shoulder. "Okay—gotta go! Love you!"

"Love you, too!" I watch her go, rising on the escalator. She waves once more and then she's out of sight, I sigh and leave the airport, walking back to my car.

I check my phone when I'm inside, escaping the humid air, and there's a missed call and voicemail. My heart jumps to my throat when I see who both notifications are from.

"Marcel?" I whisper.

I'm so confused. The yard is done, and I paid it in full—with Kyle's help, of course. Luckily, he loved the patio, saying it was a good investment for the house and would increase its resale value if we ever had to sell it.

I lift the phone, pressing the receiver to my ear to listen to the voicemail.

"Hey, Mrs. Moore. I have your finalized contract on hand. I've had a busy few days, but since I have a moment free, I figured I'd let you know. I give this to all of my clients who may need it for tax purposes or things of that nature. Let me know when you're free, and I can bring it by, or if you'd prefer, I can mail it to you. If you can, just give me a call back. Let me know."

I don't even think about the option of having him mail it, though it would make things less complicated. I need to see Marcel and I hate that growing, aching need. I call back right away. He answers.

"Marcel? Hi, this is Gabby. Just returning your call." My voice is formal, and I'm relieved because right now it really wants to waver. But I won't sound weak for him.

"Hey, Mrs. Moore. Glad you returned my call. Should I

go ahead and mail the information to you? Figured it would be less of a hassle to deliver it myself since I'm already in the area."

"You can bring it by, Marcel. It's fine."

"You sure?"

"Positive. I'll be home all night so it's no rush."

"Okay. I'll swing by shortly."

"Sounds good."

I hang up and place my phone on the passenger seat, but on my way home, I figure this is the chance to really give him a solid apology.

I make a pit stop at the grocery store, picking up everything I need to make tacos, and even grab some Jell-O packs. I even stop by the liquor store to grab a bottle of tequila.

This is all so unnecessary, but I refuse to give myself the chance to think about what I'm doing. Instead, I get home, lugging the groceries into the kitchen. After I take Callie out back to potty and get some air, I feed her, wash my hands, and go straight to making dinner.

Around six, the doorbell rings. The food is done and set on the countertop of the island, covered with aluminum foil. The Jell-O shots are in the freezer. I've even had time to shower and give Callie a short walk on the beach.

With a pounding heart, I walk to the door, checking one of the sidelight windows before unlocking it and pulling it open.

It shouldn't come as a surprise that Marcel is standing on the other side of the door. He's wearing a pair of dark-blue jeans and a black T-shirt that hugs his upper body, showing off strong biceps and a firm chest. His hair is all over the place, like he's been running his fingers through it anxiously on the way here. Anxious is sexy on him.

He starts to say something, holding up a white envelope in hand, but when he lowers his gaze, he pauses.

"Uh…hey." He's gawking. As if he realizes, he snaps out of it and looks me in the eyes. "You look…" He starts to speak but doesn't finish. "You goin' somewhere?"

I look down at my gray sundress that stops mid-thigh. I saw no point in wearing a bra since I was staying home, plus the dress gives my breasts enough support, but it's windy today. As the warm, beachy breeze brushes over my skin, I see my nipples growing taut.

I bring one arm up to cover them. "No. Not going anywhere. Took Callie for a walk." *Ugh. I bet I look really fucking desperate right now. Why did I choose this dress of all dresses?*

"Oh, okay. Well here is the contract," he says, clearing his throat afterwards. He hands me the envelope.

"Thanks. Hope this saved you some postage," I laugh.

"It did. Good thing you were home. Didn't wanna have to do all that lickin' and diggin' around for a stamp."

I shift on my feet, sinking my teeth into my bottom lip before glancing over my shoulder. I need him to come inside so we can chat the right way, but I don't want to force it.

Luckily, he breaks the ice. "What smells so good?"

"Oh." I smile way too hard. "I made tacos."

"Really?" He quirks a brow.

"Yeah. With lime Jell-O shots."

"Interesting."

"Have you eaten dinner yet?"

"No, but was on my way to the store to pick somethin' up before headin' back to the office."

"You have a lot of work to do, I assume?"

"I do. Big job that requires a lot of attention."

"Well, do you want tacos? I can pack some up for you and you can take them back to your office, that way you don't have to stop? I made a lot so I could have leftovers." I really did make a lot. I like planning my lunches ahead of time. Not only that, but Marcel is a big guy. I'm sure he'd eat an entire plate of tacos.

He thinks on it, looking past me, at my kitchen area. You can see the kitchen clearly from the door. "Sure that's a good idea?"

"It'll be fine. I have plenty. Let me find a container for you." I turn and walk away before letting him get another word in. "You can come in."

I get to the kitchen and it takes a while for me to hear the door shut. He's hesitant, which is understandable, but hearing it calls for a sigh of relief.

I take a container down from the cabinet and place several tacos inside it, soft and crunchy ones. I hear a small yelp and it's my cue that Callie is awake.

"Hey there," Marcel says, laughter in his voice as she trots down the stairs. I look over and Callie is running to him. She's on her hind legs, her forepaws clinging to his pants leg. He picks her up and rubs her head and chin. "This lady treatin' you well?" he asks, and I laugh, shaking my head.

"She's a good dog."

"I know she is." He's responding to me, but still looking at Callie as she licks at his chin. "I hope you're doin' what I told you to do," he croons to her, stroking her back. "Givin' her and her husband hell?"

Callie does a tiny bark, and Marcel chuckles. If I thought he was hot before, seeing him with a puppy is a game changer. I can't even imagine what he'd be like with a baby? Wait—why am I even thinking about him with a baby! I force myself to stop thinking about it, shaking my head and closing the lid of the container.

He places Callie down and she rushes to the kitchen, sniffing around, hoping to find food on the floor. She's too late. I've already swept.

Marcel follows after her, stopping on the other side of the island counter, opposite of me. "Haven't had the chance to ask how you like your backyard."

"Isn't that standard protocol for most?" My question is drizzled with sarcasm. "To follow up, make sure the client likes it?"

"Usually...but, well, you can see how protocol doesn't work when it comes to you."

I scoff. "Oh, really? And why doesn't it?"

His brows draw together, lips going into a flat line. He already knows that I know the answer to my own question.

I go to the fridge, taking out the Jell-O shots. "Want to take any of these with you?"

"Where's your husband?" he asks quickly, ignoring my question.

"Work, like always."

"So, you invite men into your home at night when he's away?" He's smirking, walking around the counter and picking up one of the tacos from the platter. He bites into it, chews, and nods. "Damn. This is good. Really good."

"Being half Colombian has its perks. You should try my street tacos. My mom taught me how to make them with corn tortillas. You'll never want to go back to the American version after eating them. They're so good."

"If they're even remotely as good as these, I'm sure they're amazin'." He picks up another and bites into it.

"Why don't you sit? Eat with me?" I insist.

He looks me over before looking back at the dining table by the double doors.

"Not there," I say. I point to the doors. "Outside. We have new patio furniture. Just had the table delivered over the weekend."

He finishes chewing his second taco, then says, "Fine. But I'm only stayin' to have a few more tacos."

But a few more tacos turns into five more for him and three for me. He downs three Jell-O shots as well, and I've had two so far. I pick up my third one and pop it into my mouth, letting the citrusy jelly wiggle around on my tongue before sliding down my throat.

"You used to be a party girl," Marcel points out, looking at me across the table.

"Not really, but I shared an apartment with a girl who loved to party. That's how I learned how to make these." I lift the empty cup.

"You never went out with her?"

"I did a few times, but not much. There were times when she liked to smoke joints and watch movies too. Those were my favorite times."

He chuckles, then reaches for the tequila I brought out not too long ago. We've been so busy taking Jell-O shots that we haven't touched it. He grabs two of the empty cups that had the Jell-O inside them, pouring tequila into both.

"Let's play a game." He slides one across the table, and I lean forward, grabbing it.

I cross one leg over the other, meeting his eyes. I can already feel a buzz from the shots. "What kind of game?"

"It's a drinkin' game."

"Okay…and what are the rules?"

"I ask you a question, and you have to answer it honestly. If you don't want to answer the question or it's too personal, you have to take a shot. Same goes for me."

I sit up higher in my chair. "Well, this will be interesting. There's a lot I want to ask you."

"All right, well, let's see if you can get the answers. Go ahead. You start."

"Okay." I clear my throat and place the plastic shot cup down. "Do you really not have a girlfriend?"

"Nope. Don't have one." He smirks.

"Why not?"

"We get one question each round, Miss Gabby. Look at you. Already not playin' fair."

I can't help but giggle. "Okay, fine. You go."

"Why did you want to make tacos for me so badly?" He narrows his eyes, like he's challenging me, daring me not to answer and take the shot instead.

I answer.

"Because I owed them to you. And I feel guilty about what I said to you while I was under the influence the night you dropped me off. I'm sorry for that."

"Under the influence? Hmm. Okay." He fights a laugh then tips his cup toward me, giving me the mic. "Only reason I'm acceptin' your apology is because of those damn good tacos. Your turn."

"Okay. Why are you such a dick sometimes?"

"Oh, man!" He breaks out in a laugh, sitting back in his chair. "You think I'm a dick?"

"Yeah, you are!" I laugh with him. "Now answer it honestly!"

He laughs a few seconds longer. "All right. Well, maybe because the world can be a shitty place, and I've been dealt a lot of bad shit in life." He lowers his gaze to his shot cup, his smile slowly fading. "Life has never been easy for me, so when I see that some people are wastin' their time, I say it. No point in holdin' my tongue, 'cause I may not get the chance to tell that person the truth again later. Sometimes tellin' the truth hurts. And sometimes knowin' the truth saves a few lives."

His gaze latches with mine. We look into each other's eyes before he looks away, toward the ocean. "All right. Since you wanted to ask such a serious question—my turn."

I wait for him to ask, and judging by the devious smile that sweeps over his lips, I know he's about to ask something that I won't want to answer.

"Why did you marry Kyle?"

He's staring right at me, folding his fingers together on top of the table, gauging my reaction. I look down at my shot. He's challenging me again, but I don't like to lose. "Because I love him," I say matter-of-factly.

"Okay...but that's not really answering the *why*. Lots of people love someone, but there has to be enough reason behind it to marry them."

I look away, then pick my cup up to chug it down. The burn takes over, and I wince.

Marcel lets out a belly-deep chuckle. "Wimp."

"Okay. Game on." I reach for the tequila and refill my cup. "Were you about to kiss me the night you dropped me off at home? After the club?"

"Sure was." He doesn't even hesitate.

I roll my eyes and fold my arms.

"Did you want me to kiss you the night I dropped you off?" His smile is faint but smug. I want to slap it off his beautiful face.

I down my next shot. He laughs so loudly that I want to hit him upside the head. I don't like him very much right now, but I'm not loving myself too much either. By taking the shot, I pretty much told him that yes, I did want him to kiss me that night.

"Any woman would think you were probably just horny after smoking and drinking. When's the last time you had sex?"

"Couple weeks ago."

"With who?" I ask, and I don't know why I feel a tingle of jealous flare up inside me when he says that.

"One question at a time, little thing." He puts on an arrogant smile.

My face is hot now, my mind searing with curiosity.

His turn. "When's the last time you had sex?"

"A few nights ago." I smirk at him. His smile collapses.

"Who did you have sex with?" I ask.

He glares at me, his blue eyes swirling with frustration now. If I weren't mistaken, I'd also say there was a hint jealousy in there too. Assuming he can't answer it truthfully, he picks up his cup and chugs the vodka down without so much as a blink. He's still looking at me.

"Do you enjoy fucking him?" His tone is no longer playful. It's dead serious.

"Sometimes," I admit, folding my arms.

"Only sometimes?"

"One question at a time, remember?"

He sits back, breathing hard through his nostrils, jaw tight now. Why is he so upset about that? Does he not expect me to do anything with the man I married? "Why are you so mad?"

"Because, I—" He stops talking just as abruptly as he started. He shakes his head, then grabs the tequila for a refill, drinking it right away. "You asked your question. My turn again. Why do you only enjoy fucking him *sometimes* instead of all the time?"

"Because there are things I want to happen while we have sex that he isn't comfortable doing."

"But you knew that before marrying him, yet you stuck with lame sex and now you have to settle with it." He scoffs, shaking his head and looking at the ocean again. "Blows my mind."

"What does?" I demand.

"The fact that you settled with *that* motherfucker."

"Why does it matter to you, Marcel? I'm just the client, remember? You don't even give a damn!" We're both staring at each other, no longer playing the drinking game. He's fuming, and I'm annoyed now. "You know what, this game is over." I grab the half-empty bottle of tequila, tuck it under my arm, and then collect the empty plates.

I take it all into the house, abandoning the plates in the sink and putting the tequila bottle on the counter, letting out a frustrated huff.

I hear his heavy footsteps, and he comes inside without knocking, which is a first. He shuts the door behind him and runs his fingers through his thick, dark hair. But he's coming my way quickly, his boots crunching on the marble, his eyes locked right on my mouth.

"What are you—"

"None of this shit is over until I say it is," he growls, and then his hands are on my waist. He picks me up and drops my bottom on the counter, sliding his large hands down my hips and over the cotton fabric of my dress.

"Marcel, are you crazy?" I breathe out, but he ignores me, watching my eyes for just a second.

"Stop actin' like you don't want me, Gabby. I'm tired of playin' games."

I start to protest, but he lowers his head and plants his mouth right on top of mine, not even giving me the chance to try.

TWENTY EIGHT

GABBY

MARCEL PULLS me closer toward the edge of the counter and cups my ass in both hands.

I moan, my palm pressing on his chest, but I don't have the strength in me to push him away. Every single muscle in my body feels like it's melting, turning into the same Jell-O I'd prepared for him.

My body is buzzing, swimming with tequila and lust. My nerves are a frenzy, all of them screaming ecstatically, pleased this is happening.

When he realizes that I'm not going to push him away, he deepens the kiss, moving deeper between my legs, and forcing me to spread them wider. It's instinct to wrap my legs around his waist, and he groans as he drinks me all in.

I moan, clutching a handful of his black T-shirt. He tastes like a mix of silver tequila and lime flavor, and I'm drinking it from his lips too. His erection is growing, anxious as it rests on my lower belly. He feels so big; I'm dying to know what he looks like.

One of his hands comes up to cup one side of my face, and he keeps kissing me like he can't get enough—like I'm filling him up with so much desire that it hurts, but also feels too good to pull away.

This is crazy—so, so crazy—but I can't stop.

I don't want to stop it.

God, what is wrong with me?

I moan as he picks me up off the counter, like I weigh nothing more than a pound of sugar, and carries me away. I don't even know where he's taking me to. My eyes are closed as I kiss him back, then my back lands on a hard, cool surface and I open my eyes. I spot the chandelier above me, knowing exactly where I am. Right on the dining table. *He wouldn't.*

Marcel pulls his mouth away and then stands tall, running his palms up the insides of my thighs. "You wore this dress, hoping I'd rip it off you, didn't you?"

I shake my head.

"Stop lyin' to me." He pushes the hem of the dress up, revealing my panties. They're white lace, and he hisses. "Goddamn it, Gabby." A guttural groan fills his throat. "How do you expect me to resist you?"

"We can't," I breathe as he works his way between my legs again, like he belongs there.

"You mean we *shouldn't*," he mumbles, lowering his chest and stealing another kiss from me. Every single one of these kisses are stolen, because I don't belong to him. I belong to someone else—a man who would *lose his mind* if he ever found out.

"Tell me to leave, and this time I will." His voice is thick, like he's using every ounce of willpower to hold back. I'm sure if he acted on impulse alone, he'd rip my panties aside and shove his aching cock right into me, "I'll leave you to it —let you live happily with a man who doesn't even satisfy you. You can do whatever you wanna do."

I bring my hands up and drag them over my face. "You can't make me do that. It was hell when you weren't around."

"Hell? Really?" His eyes slide down to my chest. "You missed me that much while I was away?"

"Yes," I breathe, and I don't even fight it. I did miss him. I missed the bickering, the heated stares, the stolen glances. I missed his sultry, Southern voice and how he made me feel so damn beautiful. He made me feel good—still makes me feel good.

"Go on, then. If you tell me to leave, I'll stop this and I'll go. But if you don't say anything, I'll take that as a sign to stick around, and if that's the case, it'll be my absolute pleasure to fuck you right on this table."

He would.

There's a clench between my thighs, and my entire body pumps with way too much desire. I'm insane, not telling him to leave, but the longer I watch his intense, liquid eyes, the more I want him to stay. The lust is pouring out of both of us like fiery lava, and I'm wound up. I want him, more than I'd ever admit to him or even myself.

I grab his arm and reel him down. His erection slides over me, landing heavily on my lower belly. "I'm not telling you to leave," I breathe on his mouth.

He studies my eyes, and as if that's his cue, he kisses me

hard on the mouth. I moan beneath him, and I soon hear the rapid *zip* of his jeans. When he pulls away, he's stepping out of them, lowering his boxers next, and pulling his shirt over his head.

He yanks my panties off too, then pulls me to the edge of the table, positioning the head of his cock at my entrance.

"Should I get a condom?" he asks as I sit up and wrap an arm around the back of his neck.

"I'm protected," I breathe on his mouth.

The head of his cock breaks through my entrance, but only that. I look down and hold onto him tighter. He's much thicker than Kyle. Even the head of his cock is large and round. Veins are throbbing along the length of him, like he's about to explode, but it's a beautiful, mean cock. Nothing like Kyle's at all, and I want it.

I want it more than anything right now.

He's exactly like I imagined.

Marcel cups one of my ass cheeks, using his other hand to grip the base of his cock. He pushes the head of it into me completely, and I gasp.

"Holy shit," I breathe. He's bigger. So much bigger. I'm so used to what I had that I wasn't expecting this one bit, but he keeps going, stretching me more and more to fit around him. Every inch takes my breath away.

"Fuck," he rasps, squeezing my ass tighter. "You're so fuckin' tight and wet." When all that's left is the base of his cock, he pulls his hand away and thrusts his hips forward, working his way deep inside me.

"Oh, God!" I cry out, locking both arms around the back of his neck. "God, what am I doing?"

"You're about to be fucked by another man," he says on the crook of my neck. "And you'll love every fuckin' second of it."

I hate that his words set my blood on fire, when in turn they should make me feel like a guilty bitch. My conscience is trying to scream at me to end this, but my buzz is louder. I'm on the borderline of being drunk after those Jell-O shots and the tequila. It's no excuse, but I feel too good to stop. I can't stop. It's already done.

I expect him to start thrusting right away, but he doesn't. Instead he removes my arms from around his neck and forces me to lie back down on the table. The wood surface is cool on my back, and he's still fully inside me.

He bends over and his breath runs between the valley of my breasts. "How does it feel having me inside you?"

"Stop stalling and fuck me already."

"I'll fuck you when you beg me for it."

"Beg you?" He's tormenting me, moving his hips in light strokes back and forth, but they're so slow that it's torture.

"Yes. Beg me. You've wanted my cock since the day you met me. I could see it in your eyes. It was written all over you."

I sigh when I feel his cock pulse inside me. It feels so good that I ignore the rational part of my brain that's screaming for me to stop this before it's too late.

But it's already too late. It was too late weeks ago.

"Did you picture me like this, with my whole dick inside you?"

"Yes," I confess.

"Did you think you'd be this wet for me, creamin' all over me like you are now?" He looks down where our bodies have connected. "You're so damn wet, Gabby." He pulls out of me, and I whimper. The absence is too much, I'm aching all over, and my body can't stand it. "I bet you taste just as good as you look," he groans, and I watch as he lowers to a squat. His head is between my legs, and I gasp as he runs his tongue through my slit, so feathery light that I clench and then quiver, *everywhere.*

"Oh, God," I pant, my hips bucking, silently begging for more.

"Yeah," he mumbles. "I can tell he doesn't eat this pussy. Does he?"

I don't respond.

"Answer me."

"No," I confess. And Kyle doesn't. He thinks his cock or hands is enough. He's gone down on me once, and it was the night we got married...and he was *really* drunk. He hates it when I bring it up.

Marcel stands back up and leans forward, placing a kiss on my pussy, right above my clit. Still teasing. I quiver again.

"Your pussy deserves to be worshiped, Gabby. Kissed. Licked. *Fucked.*" He meets my eyes. "And I'm going to do every single one of those things to you tonight."

In an instant, his tongue has pushed though the lips of my pussy and has slid over my swollen, needy clit. He groans, and that groan vibrates up and down my thighs as he sucks and licks the bundle of nerves.

It's all a shock, the way he grunts and growls like the true savage he is. I have no idea how he knows this is my spot, but he keeps going, circling his tongue in torturously slow circles, still groaning like the taste of me is unbelievable.

I'm writhing on the table, unable to hold back with everything that is brewing inside me. I squirm and buck so much that Marcel has to plant a palm on my stomach to keep me still. That palm is pretty much telling me that I'm not going anywhere. He has me, and he's not letting me go until he's finished with me.

"Oh, I'm close," I breathe out, jerking my hips, but I shouldn't have said that, because Marcel pulls away just as I'm about to reach my climax.

"What the fu—"

I can't even finish. He's inside me again, feeling even bigger than before. A sharp gasp shoots out of me as he picks up my legs and wraps them around his waist himself. His eyes are on mine as he thrusts. Hard—slow, but hard—and with each one, I'm building up all over again, gripping the edge of the wooden table. He reaches up to yank the top of my dress down, revealing my C-cup breasts. I can hear the fabric tear, but I don't care.

"Fuck, you're perfect." His eyes are like fiery ice, boring into mine. He wants me to know that we are doing this—wants me to see what he does to my body. And he's doing so much right now. I hear the sticky sounds our bodies make together, feel him touching my cervix. The table is scraping on the floor with each stroke his powerful thighs provide. Those same thighs are clapping against mine, going at a steady pace. His muscles jump and tense on his chest, his abs constricting, like this is too much for him, just like it is for me, but he doesn't stop. He holds my gaze.

"I knew you wanted me," he says. Another thrust. "From now on you won't be his." Another thrust. "You'll be *mine*."

His words. I hate them. I love them. I don't know how to feel about them, I just know I want to come. I need it so bad from him. When he drops a hand, rubbing my clit with the pad of his thumb, it takes no time. None whatsoever.

"Come on my dick, baby," he demands, and the demand in his deep, smoky voice sends me right over the edge. I cry out on the table, back arching, eyes rolling to the base of my skull.

Marcel picks me up off the table and holds my ass in his hands as I come all over him, bouncing me up and down the length of his cock. I've never heard myself scream so loudly before during sex. Ever. I'm almost afraid the neighbors will hear us.

"There it is," he groans, still sliding me up and down the length of him. "This is what you wanted." I hold onto him for dear life as he stands tall, listening to my moans fill his ear. "I'm not pullin' out," he growls, and something about that both terrifies and excites me. Before I can even say anything, though, a noise fills his throat—the kind of noise only a man can make—and he lowers his hands, clutching me tightly, completely buried inside me.

I moan again as he hits a tender spot, then look down into his eyes. His pupils have dilated, his lips spread, forming a wide O. "Your pussy," he groans, shifting me up and back down again on his thick, throbbing cock. "So good. Fuck, you're so good." And as if he can't hold it anymore, a loud moan rushes out of his mouth, and he drops me back down on the table. It's a rough drop, but he holds me close, as if he's making up for it.

My ass is hanging off the edge of the table, and he's still buried inside me, his cock throbbing, and another moan leaving him this time as he fills my pussy with his warm cum.

He moaned. *Moaned.* It was a beautiful sound, one I never thought I'd hear him make.

"Shit." He's panting, thrusting upward, still filling me up. I breathe raggedly as he looks me in the eyes, then he focuses on my mouth again. "Fuck, Gabby."

"What?" I whisper.

"Best fuck I've ever had."

I blush, but no doubt, the guilt is setting in already. *What the hell have I done?*

Sensing my sudden change of mood, Marcel pushes up on his elbow and pulls out of me. I get off the table and it shakes a bit. I look down and one of the legs is split at the base.

"Fuck my life," I mutter, pressing a hand to my forehead.

"I can fix that for you if you want me to," he says, picking up his boxers.

"No, it's fine." My response comes off curt. He notices my tension but doesn't speak on it. I try to fix myself up, adjusting my dress, but it doesn't help that I feel his cum leaking down the insides of my thighs, or that the neck of my dress is torn. "I, um…need to go to the bathroom. Be right back." I leave the kitchen before he can respond, rushing around the corner and going up the stairs.

My heart is about to burst right out of my chest. I hear Callie whimpering from the guest room, where her dog bed is. I left her a few toys and closed the door so she wouldn't interrupt the night I was about to have with Marcel. How indecent of me. Maybe I should have kept her out so she *could* interrupt us, make me realize what I was feeling for him was wrong. She looks happy to see me when I let her out.

I go to the bathroom and turn on the water, cleaning myself up. I refuse to look into the mirror. I'm afraid of the woman that'll look back at me.

Why did I let him come *inside* me? I'm not his. He doesn't have that right. Why would I let him do that? And in my own house? The house I share with *Kyle*? The man I should love with my whole heart and never want to cheat on? I'm so fucked up!

After rinsing my face with cold water, I leave the bathroom to go to my closet. I change clothes—sweatpants and baggy shirt—and then walk back downstairs with Callie on my heels.

Marcel sees me coming down. He's fully dressed, standing in the kitchen, leaning against the counter edge. Callie rushes over to him again, going straight for his foot and sitting on his boot.

"She did that the first night I found her," he chuckles, and I'm glad he's broken the ice. He looks up to meet my eyes. His hair is so messy, and there's still a small sheen of sweat on his forehead.

"Marcel, I—"

"No, Gabby." He holds a hand up, moving forward. Callie hops off his foot and scurries to the corner where more of her toys are. "Don't even say anything. It happened. It's done. It's clear you're full of regret right now, so I'll leave you alone for the night."

I'm both relieved and sad. I don't want him to leave… but I know it's best. Kyle comes back home tomorrow afternoon. I have to wash the smell of Marcel off of me stat.

He goes to the counter, picking up the container of tacos and lifting it in the air. "You won't mind if I take these with me?"

"No—not at all." I fold my arms as he walks back my way. He walks past me to get to the door and when he unlocks it and twists it open, he peers over his shoulder.

"For the record, I wasn't lyin'. Best fuck I've ever had."

I shouldn't blush, but I do.

"I don't know if I should take that as a compliment or something else." I'm trying to be playful, still flirty, but it's not working. Guilt has gobsmacked me.

"It's a compliment. Trust me." He turns around, fully facing me. Taking a step forward, he brings up a hand, cupping the back of my head. "You are everything."

Heat bubbles in my chest. I lower my line of sight.

"Hey. Look at me." His command is soft. Gentle. I look up, and his eyes are serious, focused on mine. "Nothin' changes here with you and me. I'm not judgin' you one bit, because I wanted it just as much—probably even more."

"Are you sure you're not judging me?"

"Gabby." It's all he can say. He sighs, then reels me toward him, planting a kiss on my forehead. The bubbling heat is stronger now, sweeping through my entire body. "Sleep well."

I nod. He pulls away, but not having his hands on me feels like a loss. I want his touch—I'm craving it all over again—but for now I let him go.

He walks down the stoop, looking back at me once before going to his truck and climbing inside. I watch him crank it up, and headlights flash across my face, spotlighting my betrayal. He puts the truck in reverse and backs out of the driveway, and when he's gone, I shut and lock the door, then flop face first on the sofa.

I don't even want to sleep in the bed I share with Kyle. That will really cause the guilt to eat me alive. To distract myself, I reach for the remote control on the coffee table and turn on the TV, flipping to *HGTV*, but not even the redesigning of homes is distraction enough.

Marcel's words replay in my head over and over again.

From now on you won't be his. You'll be mine.

I can't get the words out of my head, but only because no words spoken have been truer.

I became his tonight, on a dining room table that doesn't even belong to him.

He has a hold on me—a tight lasso wrapped around me that I can't break free from—and he knows it.

We both know it.

TWENTY-NINE

MARCEL

GABBY IS HAVING regrets about what we did. It was clear to me the moment I finished. After what we did, I noticed the way she looked at me.

Helpless.

Guilty.

Confused.

But while I fucked her, she loved it. Every single second of it. I relish in that fact, knowing I made her come with my tongue and cock.

I'm not ashamed to admit that I've been waiting for that to happen. It's fucked up on so many levels, but I've wanted her for so long now—since the moment our eyes connected. For weeks I'd been trying to deny whatever connection I had to her, but I couldn't anymore.

After she told me she'd recently had sex with that shit-head husband of hers, I didn't know how to take it. How could I be mad about her sleeping with her husband? That was a given in any marriage, yet the jealousy pumped through my veins like gasoline, and her confirmation was a lit match. She burned me up, pissed me off, but with the way she milked the hell out of my dick, her body begging for more with every thrust I provided, I knew her husband was nothing in comparison to me. *Nothing.*

It isn't like me to smile this much after a fuck, but I do, all the way home. It's faint, but it's there.

When I get home, I shower and then crack open a beer, sitting at my table to read over the final layout for my client. I'm too distracted to study it, though. I'm here, but my mind is still there, back in Gabby's kitchen.

I took her on a table that I'm sure she's shared with her husband more times than she can count, and I don't give a damn about it.

But she does.

It's a whisper that crosses my mind—a small voice in my head that's telling me this is all wrong. What will she do now? Is that it for us? Will she bother contacting me again now that her patio is finished, and I've dropped her contract off? I admit I was holding onto it for a while, just to have an excuse to see her again. Now that I've finally given her and myself what we both have wanted for weeks, what happens now?

She has no reason to get in touch with me unless something goes wrong in the yard. And even so, she could always request that someone else take a look at it, just to avoid seeing me.

You fucked a married woman. A young, sexy-as-hell, confused, married woman.

I rest my back on the back of the chair and drag my palm over my face.

Once wasn't enough. I need more. I don't give a fuck that she's taken, but I'm sure the sin she's just committed is eating her alive.

I'm left wondering when she'll get in touch with me—when she'll beg me to come around to take her again.

She deserves better, and I can give her that, at least in bed…then again, I know she wants to be a good person. She has morals, and I have a feeling that I won't be hearing from her for quite some time.

THIRTY

GABBY

BARKING IS the first thing I hear in the morning. I roll over on the sofa, peeling my eyes open. Callie is on the sofa, too, barking at me. She climbs onto my side and looks toward the kitchen, and I frown as she barks again.

"What are you barking at?" I groan.

"That would be me." Kyle's voice catches me completely off guard, and I spring up without hesitation, looking over the sofa and at him. He's standing by the fridge with one of the bottles of freshly pressed juice I bought from the store yesterday.

"Hey!" I breathe, pushing off the couch and walking to the kitchen. I can hardly hear my own thoughts over the sound of my banging heart. "What are you doing home so early?" I check the time on the microwave. It's nearing eight in the morning.

Kyle sips the juice and then places it down on the

counter. "We pushed the meeting to last night. Caught an earlier flight back home to see my lovely wife." He walks up to me, reeling me in with an arm around my waist. He kisses my cheek, and I want to vomit. Not because of him, but because I fell asleep without showering. I wasn't expecting him to be back until later, which would have given me plenty of time to freshen up.

"What's going on?" he asks. "Why'd you fall asleep on the couch? And what's with the tacos and Jell-O shots? Did you have a party while I was away?" He's smiling, looking sideways at the empty platter on the counter. There are three tacos left.

"Oh—I was just up. Watching a movie. Decided to have my own little *fiesta*."

"Oh. Can it be a fiesta if you're all alone?" he jokes.

I shrug.

"Well, anyway, how about you go upstairs and change clothes. I want to take you out for some breakfast."

"Okay. Sure." I force a smile at him as he rubs the small of my back. "Let me just take a quick shower."

"Okay—oh, and what the hell happened to the table?" When he asks that, my heart drops to my stomach. I'm close to the staircase, but I try not to freeze before looking his way. Kyle is by the dining table, fiddling with the splintered leg. The one Marcel broke while *fucking* me. *Oh, God.*

"I'm not sure, actually," I lie. "It was pretty wobbly for a while, and I think the move made it worse." I'm making shit up now. I'm a genius at that…and luckily, he falls for it.

"That is true. This table is old. It was my mum's." He stands tall, sliding his hands into the pockets of his dress pants. "It was handcrafted in Malaysia, and my mum

258

brought it with her when she moved. She passed it down to me as my first piece of furniture." He takes another look at it, and the guilt nearly shreds me. I fucked Marcel on a table that my husband's mother gave to him as a gift? Wow. What kind of wife am I? "I'll see if I can get it fixed."

"Okay." It's all I can say, really. "Do you think you can let Callie out for a second? She probably has to pee."

He looks sideways at Callie, then rolls his eyes and sighs. "Fine."

When he goes to the doors that lead out to our patio and commands her to come with him, I rush up the stairs and don't look back.

I'm in the shower first thing, washing thoroughly. Once I feel like my betrayal has flushed its way down the drain, I'm out and getting dressed. As I put on my makeup, though, I'm left with no choice but to face the girl in the mirror.

Since this move, she's changed. I don't know who she is anymore and that terrifies me. I no longer trust myself. I have no idea what I was thinking last night. What I did with Marcel didn't make me feel any better, and now I have to live with that guilt. I pick up my powdered highlighter and apply it, then slam the case closed, stuffing it back in my makeup bag. I leave the bathroom, forgetting about my reflection.

Downstairs, Kyle is sitting at a chair at the table, scrolling through his phone with one leg resting on top of the other. Why does he have to sit there? It's like he's purposely migrating to the place I can't bear to look at right now.

"You ready?" I ask, adding some pep to my voice.

"Yeah." He stands, going for his keys on the counter. "Let's go."

∾

"So, our flights are all booked for the trip to see your parents this weekend," Kyle informs me. I'm running the prongs of my fork over my scrambled egg whites. I hear him, but I'm not exactly listening. "Gabs? Did you hear me?"

I look up and he's smiling, but there's concern etching at his brows. "Oh—uh, yeah. That's good. I can't wait to see them."

Placing his fork down, he reaches across the table to grab my hand. "Everything okay with you?"

"Yeah, babe. I'm fine. I swear." I squeeze his hand back and smile, but the smile hurts.

"You seem a little off." He pulls away and picks up his coffee mug. "Anything I can do to cheer you up?" His smile is devious, and I know exactly what it means. The thought of sleeping with my own husband right now nauseates me, but I keep smiling, powering through it.

"I'm fine. Promise."

When we're back home, Kyle tries to come onto me in the kitchen. He's laying kisses on the back of my neck, whispering how much he's missed me. His arms are wrapped around my middle and he sighs in my hair after his final kiss. I close my eyes, swallowing hard as he brings his hands up to my breasts and cups them in hand.

"These," he growls on my ear. "These always make me happy."

Oh God. Normally his voice—that growl—sets my blood on fire, but not today. Today I just can't.

"Kyle—I'm sorry. I just—I can't today." I pull out of his embrace, turning to face him. His eyes widen, so I back myself up with an explanation. "I don't feel too good. I think it was the tacos I had last night—too much grease and cheese."

"Do you need to lie down?" He's concerned. Good. He's falling for it. His hands are on my arms, still holding me close.

"I'm okay. I think lying down for a minute will help."

"Yeah, sure, babe. Go ahead."

"Thanks." I stand on my toes, kissing his cheek. "I love you."

"I love you too," he says, but there's too much uncertainty in his voice. His phone rings, and for once, I'm glad that it poses a distraction. I hear him answer it as I walk up the stairs and into our bedroom.

I lay in bed, tossing and turning for a while, but I can't sleep. It's impossible when my mind is so crowded with thoughts I've never had before.

My husband is downstairs, expecting all of my love, and I can't even give it to him right now. I want to cry, but tears will only make him interrogate me even more.

The worst part of all of this, though, is that even with all of this guilt in my heart, there is still room to think about Marcel. I wonder what he's doing, how he's feeling. I don't know when I started to care about him so much, but things have changed...and I'm not sure if I like it or not.

THIRTY-ONE

GABBY

IT'S A RELIEF, going back to Virginia.

As soon as our flight lands and Kyle has us in the rental car, I breathe a sigh of relief, taking in the tall trees that seem to never end. I roll my window down, inhaling the fresh scent of rain and pine trees.

"I missed this," I breathe as we travel over a short bridge. From here, I spot a body of water that leads to Lake Anna. It's muggy today, but the lake is always so beautiful to me. It soothed me during my adolescent years and does so, even now.

"I know you did," Kyle murmurs. I sit back in my seat, and he reaches for my hand, squeezing it. I smile up at him briefly before looking away.

I love my husband. He's always there for me, even if he's sometimes a jerk about certain things. After I told him I wasn't feeling well in the kitchen that day, he hasn't touched me too much. I've been faking a stomach bug and started to magically feel better last night, but only because he insisted he would cancel the flights if I wasn't feeling well.

I watch him as he drives with concentrated brows, his lips pressing together. My heart hurts when I look at him, the betrayal weighing heavily on my chest.

I look back out of the window again, glad when Kyle flips the turning signal and makes a right into my parent's neighborhood. My childhood dwells here. He passes Mr. and Mrs. Weston's house. They used to give me and Ricky lemonade ice cups over the summer. Next is the playground Ricky and I played on, though it is really run down these days. They had mentioned tearing it down to rebuild, but it still hasn't happened yet.

Kyle parks in front of my parents' house, where there are two cars parked in the driveway, Mom's and Dad's. As soon as I get out, I hear a door slam shut, and then there's a loud squeal.

I laugh, watching my mom run down the cement driveway, coming straight for me with her arms wide open. It doesn't help that she's wearing heels that are clicking rapidly with every step she takes.

"Oh! My baby! I missed you so much!" If there's one word I could use to describe my mom's voice, I'd say smoky. But not in a manly way. More like Scarlett Johansson's voice, mixed with a sprinkle of Sofia Vergara's Colombian accent. I have no idea how my mom hasn't grown out of her accent yet, seeing as she's been here since she was seventeen and is well in her forties now, but it's unique, and it fits her. She rocks me side to side with the hug, like she always does, drowning me in her flowery perfume.

"I missed you too!" I laugh over her shoulder.

"Look at you!" She holds the tops of my shoulders, looking me all over. "You've put on weight, yeah?"

"Ma! Really?" I tuck my hair behind my ears, rolling my eyes.

"What? It's good, Gabby! You were too skinny, trying to fit into that wedding dress months ago!"

I laugh. She has a point. I lost twenty pounds to fit into the dress that I considered *The One*. I've slowly gained most of it back, but the weight I am now is a healthy weight. I'm comfortable here. Luckily, I'm not like her. I don't cry about every pound added on the scale. I love my body, even during the times it decides to be stubborn.

"I think she looks fantastic." Kyle comes up beside us, and Mom releases me to face him.

"Get over here!" She reels him in for a hug and he hugs her back.

"How are you, Mrs. Lewis?"

"I'm great, I'm great. So much happier now that you two are here. Come on, let's get inside! I'm sure your dad wants to see you!"

Mamá trots ahead in her strapped blue heels and blue dress that comes down past her knees.

I remember Teagan finding it so funny that I called her Mom in Spanish. She couldn't understand why me and Ricky did it, but it's what we always called my mother. When we finally asked, she'd told us she wanted me and Ricky to have something from her only that could never change, and had even insisted that she'd always wanted to be called Mamá one day. Not Mom, not Mother, but Mamá.

"Your mother is a thrill," Kyle laughs.

"She's like fireworks, you know? So loud, but so colorful and bright. You can't help but be in awe."

"Wow." He puts on a boyish smile, reaching for my hand. "That is the perfect description."

We make it inside, where aromas of freshly cooked food wrap all around us. I love when my mom cooks. She cooks for every single holiday, and every meal is delicious.

My parents' house isn't huge. It's a four-bedroom home, with a quaint kitchen and a cozy living room. The furniture is new, though, and I'm glad to see it, because I swear my dad was trying to hold onto the previous furniture for life.

"Will! Honey, Gabby is here!" Mamá yells as she trots to the kitchen.

Kyle shuts the door behind us, and we follow her there. The dining table is off to the left of the kitchen in an open area. The table seats eight, and it's freshly set with pastel purple and yellow plates and glasses, because it wouldn't be like my mother to *not* decorate the table for a holiday.

"Can I get you guys anything to drink?" she offers, standing by the fridge.

"No, I'm quite all right," Kyle says. "You, Gabs?"

"I'm good, Mamá." I smile at her. "Thank you."

"Suit yourself." She goes to the stove and lifts the lid from one of the pots. Kyle pulls out his cell when it rings and answers it. I walk over to Mamá and see she's stirring her famous French onion soup.

"That smells so good!" I lean over the pot to breathe in the smells.

"I knew you'd want some when you got here. I even bought a few loaves of the French bread you like."

"You're the best." I kiss her cheek, then turn for the counter to pick up a piece of sliced mango. It feels so good to be home. My favorite part is the fresh fruit. Mamá will drive thirty minutes just to get to the closest farmer's market and grab some. "When will Ricky be here?"

"He said he was coming tonight with Violetta." She rolls her eyes and grabs a ladle.

"Ma, be nice," I giggle, taking another bite of mango.

"It's hard to be nice! Do you know she asked for a fork when eating my *fritanga*? Who eats fritanga with a fork?"

I bust out laughing. "She didn't grow up on it like we did! I think you're just finding reasons not to like her now."

"She's trashy. Don't care what anyone thinks. She's only with Ricky because he has a good job and bought her a house. She's a user." She picks up a fork and points it at me sternly, like I'm the one in trouble. "You know that your father asked her if she was thinking about having kids, and she said no. No, Gabby! I just...I can't stand it. We all know Ricky wants babies, and she doesn't want to have them. They're not a good match. At least you are considering it!"

"Oh, boy." I move away, grabbing another piece of mango. She's upsetting herself, per the norm, and I am not about to get into the discussion of having kids right now.

"Monster, is that you?" A voice booms from the hallway. I look over, and Dad is walking into the kitchen with a big smile and a pair of square-framed glasses on his face. His beard is gone, but he's kept his peppery mustache. He stands tall—tall enough to touch the ceiling of this house without trying. He opens his arms and I rush right into them.

"Hi Dad," I sigh on his chest.

"How's my girl? Missed the hell out of you, you know that?"

"I know—and I'm good. Just glad to be here, seeing you guys."

"We're happy to have you." I pull away and Dad looks all around. "Where's Kyle?"

"I think he's outside taking a call. Should be back in a minute."

"Oh, okay. Well, your room is all set up for you. Changed the bedding last night."

"Thank you."

He sits on a chair at the four-top table in the corner of the kitchen—the one they use more than the one in the dining room.

"You look good," he says, beaming.

"Doesn't she?" Mom chimes. "I told her I like her with a little meat on her bones!"

Dad chuckles and I sit in the chair beside him, fighting a smile. "How's everything with you?" I ask.

"Oh—same ol', same ol'."

"Is work okay?"

I notice him hesitate, but he continues a smile to cover it up. "Work is...work, I suppose." He pushes his glasses up the bridge of his hawkish nose. "Enough about me. How is that new house of yours? Hilton treating you well?"

I don't ignore the fact that he's changing the subject, but I've just gotten here. I have time to ask him what's up.

"The house is great! It's huge, though. Five bedrooms."

"Way too many!" Mamá says with a shake of her head.

"Unless you two plan on filling those rooms with babies, I don't understand why there are so many."

Everything is always about babies with my mom. My Aunt Carolina, her sister, is the same way about them. They figure as soon as a couple is married, they should be trying to get pregnant. I'm not exactly down with that. Not that I don't want kids, it's just not the right time to try yet.

"I have a puppy now," I offer, shifting the subject. I pull my phone out of my back pocket, go to my pictures app and click on one of Callie. "Her name is Callie," I inform Dad, handing the phone to him. "Like Cammie's sister. Remember?"

"Oh, yeah. I remember. That's a nice-looking puppy."

"Let me see." Mamá trots over after turning the soup off, taking my phone out of his hand and squinting at the screen. "Oh—she's adorable!"

"Thanks."

"Who has her right now?" she asks.

"My neighbor is keeping her for a couple days. I would have brought her with me if we hadn't flown here. She's a sweet dog."

"Did you get her yourself, or did Kyle?" Mom asks, going to the counter and pulling out one of the loaves of bread.

I avoid her eyes when she focuses on me again, but it doesn't stop my heart from drumming. Marcel comes to mind. The way he held Callie in my living room and stroked her, like he loved her. "No, I uh, I found her. She was hurt so I took her in."

"You *found* her?" Dad asks. "Well, did you try and ask around the neighborhood? See where she came from?"

"I did, but no one seemed to know."

"That's strange." He scans me with his eyes. It's almost like he can tell I'm lying. Fortunately, Kyle walks into the kitchen, saving me from the speculation.

"Apologies. I had to take that one," Kyle says, and Dad stands when he approaches. They shake hands. "How are you, Will?"

"Good, good. And you?"

"I'm great. Glad to be here. Thank you for letting us stay the weekend."

"Oh, it's no problem at all. You guys know you're always welcome here."

Kyle takes the seat next to mine and asks, "What smells so great?"

"Oh, it's soup! French onion! You'll love it," Mamá declares after topping off a few bowls and then adding the cheese. "Give me just a few minutes and then we can eat."

"Take your time, Ma."

"Loving your new home?" Dad asks Kyle.

"I am. We're still adjusting, but I'm getting used to the idea of living on the beach." He smiles at my dad.

Dad studies Kyle very briefly before putting his focus on mine. "And you, Gabby? Getting used to it?"

"Yeah. Every day spent there makes it feel like home." But not right now. Right now, I'm so glad to be far away. I can't take looking at that splintered leg at the dining table any longer, and only God knows when or if I'll ever make tacos again.

"Good." Dad steps away. "Kyle, want a beer?"

"Sure. That would be great."

When Dad is at the fridge, I look at Kyle and put on a warm smile for him.

I know he doesn't want to be here. I'm sure he'd much rather be at home, not dealing with my parents, but he took this trip for me. And at least there's good food coming out of it.

THIRTY-TWO

GABBY

AFTER EATING two bowls of the soup with several slices of French bread, I'm stuffed.

It's nearing 6:00 p.m., and Mamá has asked me to go to the store with her to grab a few last-minute things for tomorrow's dinner. On the way to the store, she's listening to a podcast about organizing a closet. It's insanely boring, so I scroll through Pinterest, looking at portraits and artwork from some of my favorite artists.

We finally make it to the store, and Mamá goes straight to the wine & beer aisle. "Going to need this to get through the weekend," she says, grabbing several bottles of her favorite red. She picks up a case of Dad's favorite beer, and it's always those little things that I find so cute. She loves him, no matter what, and is always thinking about him anywhere she goes.

"So, tell me what's really going on with you and Kyle,"

she says, picking up a couple of lemons and inspecting them.

I frown at her back, confused. "What are you talking about?"

"Really, Gabby? Don't think I don't see it. There's a—a distance or something between the two of you. Last time we saw you, you two were stuck together like glue!"

"Well, the last time you saw us was a week after our honeymoon, Mamá, so of course we were going to be that way."

She purses her lips, then stuffs the lemons in one of the plastic produce bags. "You can't fool me. I see right through all of your shit, okay?"

"Ma, I'm not kidding. We're fine!" I laugh, but it's forced and winded.

"You suck at lying," she mutters nonchalantly, pushing her shopping cart down the aisle. She picks up a few limes too, then heads over to the lettuce.

"I mean, the distance bothers me a little. He still works in New York, and I'm stuck at home without him. I guess I'm still trying to get used to it." Who am I kidding? There's a deeper reason, but I refuse to tell my mother that I cheated on my husband with the landscape architect. I'm not even sure how she would take it, but the last thing I want to do is disappoint her.

"That's no excuse." I meet up to her side as she stops in the middle of the aisle. "You can't let that get in the way of your relationship. Work is work, but he always comes back home to you. You think, when your dad travels, that I'm happy about it? No, but I know he's doing it for us. The same reason Kyle is doing it. For the two of you."

"I know that already! I've accepted it. Things are just different when he doesn't come home every day. At least Dad isn't gone for more than two days."

"Nah-uh. Sometimes he is. He goes to those little conferences for business-owners he's always invited to."

"Yeah, conferences that are, like, three times a year." Knowing I'm not going to win this argument with her, I sigh and let it roll off my shoulders.

"All I'm saying, Gabby, is to not let that get to your head. Don't let your mind wander and don't think about it too much. He's working to provide for you—to keep a roof over your head. Working so that *you* don't have to work so much anymore." She pushes my nose like it's a button, then continues down the aisle.

I wish I could tell my mom about what's really going on with me. Hell, I wish I could tell someone *period*, but I'm too afraid I'll be looked at differently. I know my family loves me and would accept me regardless, but to cheat on a man who does everything for me is wrong, and they'd know it. And even though they wouldn't say it straight to my face, they'd be ashamed of my behavior.

I've been tempted to tell Teagan, but for now I'm keeping it to myself. It was one time, and I was really drunk and not thinking straight. Kyle has done many stupid things while drunk, and I've always forgiven him. It's no excuse, but for the sake of my marriage, I need to move past it and focus on the future.

~

Easter dinner is just as expected. Chaotic. But it's a

comforting chaos, because there's family and love, and the smell of good food cooking.

The twins, Niyah and Nella, are running around the house, screaming their heads off, while their mom, my Aunt Carolina, is wobbling around with an eight-months-pregnant belly. She doesn't speak much English. She came here much later than my mom did, and is a lot younger, so when she's around she just smiles at us, or my mom translates for her. She's a sweet woman though. I don't know much Spanish, so I can't talk to her well, but she and my mom talk all the time. Her husband, my uncle-in-law, Tino, is on the couch watching a soccer game with a beer in hand.

Ricky is seated at the dining table with Violetta, but Violetta is scrolling through her phone while he talks right to her. It's like she isn't even listening, and he knows this, but he's still chatting away. It's sad.

As if she's bored, Violetta places her phone down and then places a fist beneath chin, her elbow on the table. They arrived last night, and I could sense some tension between them, but Ricky smiled it off. Violetta ate some soup and then went up to their room for the rest of the night.

I place some sliced fruit on the table, glancing at Ricky when he's done with his conversation about how he has to fly to Florida next weekend. Ricky is almost as tall as my dad—six feet and two inches. My dad is six feet and four inches. Ricky's the spitting image of Mamá, though, when it comes to his caramel eyes and skin complexion. His dark-brown hair is freshly trimmed, his jaw square and covered in stubble. He's lean, and he always credits his basketball playing days to that.

"You okay?" I mouth to him when he looks up.

He nods and winks at me, the thing he always does to assure me he's fine, but it doesn't work in his favor this time because the sadness in his eyes can't be masked. He may be fooling everyone else, but I know the eyes are the windows to any soul, and his are hauntingly sad.

"*Ay dios!*" Mamá comes to the table to place a bowl of roasted potatoes down. "This place is busy, busy, but I love it! Nothing better than family, huh?" I go back to the kitchen to help her bring more food to the table. "Oh, Gabby, will you do me a favor and go to my car to get the serving spoons?" she asks. "I bought some new ones a few days ago but forgot to take them out of the backseat."

"Sure." I leave the kitchen, walking down the hallway. I get to the door and Dad, Kyle, and Uncle Tino are in the living room. The TV is on, and Uncle Tino is sitting down, sucked into the television, but Kyle and Dad are standing, talking right to each other. If I'm not mistaken, Kyle seems upset.

"What's going on?" I ask, and they both stiffen before looking back at me. "You guys okay?"

"Yeah, we're fine, babe." Kyle puts on a smile, but it doesn't reach his eyes.

"Dinner almost ready?" Dad asks, shifting the subject.

"Yeah. Mom is setting up the table now."

"Good. Tino, let's get ready to eat!" Dad claps Kyle on the shoulder. "Come on, Kyle. Time for a good meal."

"Coming right after you," Kyle tells him. Dad and Uncle Tino leave the living room and go to the kitchen, but Kyle lingers, putting his eyes on mine.

"What's going on?" I demand softly.

"Nothing is going on, Gabs. Where are you headed?"

"To get the something from the car for my mom. Don't change the subject. You looked upset. What happened?"

"It's just…work related, is all. I was telling him about a few changes I want to make to the company, but that I am nervous. He was talking me through it, is all."

"Oh." I nod, but I'm still confused. Since when does Dad care about Kyle's business life? And since when would Kyle take advice from my father? He normally takes those issues up with his father. "Well, go get ready for dinner. I'll be right behind you."

"Okay." Kyle walks away. I watch him round the corner, and then I go outside, heading for Mom's Camry. I find the box of serving spoons in the backseat and take it out.

On my way to the door, though, my phone chimes. I pull it out, and there's a notification that I have an email.

I unlock the phone and go to the emails, entering my parents' house again, but when I see who the email is from I freeze, standing right in front of the door. My mouth goes dry, and my hands start shaking.

Miss Gabby,

I've been counting the days since our night over tacos and tequila. One week and two days, and I haven't heard from you. I used to think I knew exactly what I was doing to a woman's body. I mean, you came all over me, I felt it, but since I haven't heard a peep from you, I'm assuming all of that was just for show?

I don't expect you to respond, just want to let you know

I'm thinking about you. If you need me, you know where to find me.

Marcel Ward
 CEO of Ward Landscaping and Design

Oh. My. God. Is he serious right now? Why would he send this?

I read the email way too many times to count, my heart drumming in my chest. My fingers are slick with sweat, and I almost drop the box of serving spoons, but I clutch it to my chest, keeping it steady.

"Gabby!" Ricky yells, walking my way, and I nearly jump out of the light green jumper Teagan and I picked out during our mall trip. "What are you doing? We're waiting on you to get dinner started."

"Oh—yeah. Sorry. Got an email and had to check it."

He takes the box from me. "Everything okay?"

"I'm fine. Everything okay with you?" I ask as we go back to the kitchen.

"Never better, sis." I can tell he's lying. He could be better. He's miserable with Violetta, but that's none of my business. Just like me and my mother, Ricky has a temper too. If you piss him off, it takes him a while to calm down.

The table is crowded with chairs. Some are chairs we pulled up from the four-top table in the kitchen. While some are high-backed chairs, others are shorter, but it works for our family. We're so used to doing it this way but I'm sure to an outsider it would look very strange. There's a card table and folding chairs set up in the living room for a kids' table. Aunt Carolina brought it along for the twins.

I take the seat next to Kyle, who lightly squeezes my thigh as I sit. I look up, and he's smiling at me. "Took you a while."

"Couldn't figure out where she put the serving spoons. Had to search." *Geez. When will I get the chance to stop lying?*

Dinner is delicious, of course, but I can't quite enjoy it. For one, the email Marcel sent is seared into my brain. I swear my cellphone is burning a hole in my back pocket. I read it so many times in the span of a two minutes that I memorized the words.

And two, because Kyle touches my thigh every few seconds under the table, passing little hints at me. When he touches me like this, so close to what's only supposed to be his, it means he wants sex. We haven't done anything in several days, so I suppose I can't I blame him for his growing need. We're usually all over each other.

After we've had dessert and played a game of charades over wine, my Aunt Carolina and the twins are hugging and kissing us goodbye. Ricky and Violetta are in the living room now, watching a soccer game with my Dad. Kyle and I are helping Mamá clean off the table.

"Dinner was absolutely amazing, Mrs. Lewis," Kyle says, dumping scraps in the trash bin.

"I'm so glad you think so! I had lots of time to figure out what I would make tonight. It all came out better than I expected." She's rinsing the juice out of a cup. "You two should come more often. It's always so much fun when we're all together."

"That would be nice," I murmur. "You know, we're

actually planning a housewarming next month on Cinco de Mayo weekend. You and dad should come down if you're not too busy."

"Cinco de Mayo?" Ricky asks, coming into the kitchen with an empty beer bottle. He goes to the fridge, taking out a new bottle.

"Yeah. Cinco de Mayo is on a Sunday, but we'll most likely host it that Saturday before. You should come. Bring Violetta." When my last sentence comes out, he shakes his head. "Gotta think about that one."

"Trouble in paradise?" Mamá asks lowly, giving him an *I told you* so glare and cocking an arched brow.

"No, Mamá. We're fine."

"Ricky, you're just as bad of a liar as Gabby."

I swear I swallow my tongue when she says that.

"What has Gabby lied about?" Kyle asks, a curious spark in his eyes.

Mamá looks at Kyle, then swings her eyes over to me. "I don't mean an actual liar," she responds hurriedly. "I just mean she's good at making things up. She's been like that her whole life—since she was a little girl."

"Has she?" Kyle's face is serious now. I don't know what he's thinking, but I don't like it.

"When she was a little girl, she'd tell me bedtime stories of her own. I always thought they were adorable, but I knew I was going to be in for trouble, because she could make them up so easily."

Kyle huffs a laugh, but nothing more. Great, now my husband thinks I'm a natural-born liar. *Way to go, Ma!*

I fight a groan, going back to the table to collect more empty dishes.

"Well, Gabby is right," Kyle goes on, and I'm glad his voice is relaxed. "It would be nice to have you all down for the housewarming. There will be plenty to eat and drink, and it'll give you a chance to see the home for yourselves. The images we showed you doesn't do it justice. Not only that, but we've had the patio redesigned. I'll be happy to book flights for you—shouldn't cost too much."

"Oh, really?" Mamá is happy to hear that. She loves when trips are free. "Well if you're serious about those flights, we will definitely be there."

"We have a wet bar and a hot tub now, so bring bathing suits. Hopefully weather is good that weekend." I smile at her.

"Shit, that sounds fun," Ricky says. "Email me the invite so I can put it on the calendar. I don't want to forget."

"I will."

Ricky starts to turn, but he halts, looking back at me. "What time are you leaving tomorrow?"

"Around five? Why, what's up?"

"Let's go out to Lake Anna, get a boat, like old times. Just you and me?"

I'm surprised to hear this. For one, Ricky hated being on a boat. I used to rock it, and he'd get so freaked out. Mamá would always snap at me for scaring him.

"A boat? Really?" I ask, walking back to the dining room. I collect the forks and he nods, chugging down some of his beer.

"Yeah, why not?"

"I just remember you not loving the boats so much."

"Yeah, well, things change."

He drops his eyes for a brief second. Something is wrong

with my brother. He's not being his usual self. My brother is usually a jokester, but he seems more serious now.

"Sure. We can go. I'd like that."

"Yeah?" His eyes are brighter. Happier.

"Yeah, I don't see why not. As long as we go early, it'll give us plenty of time."

"Okay, then. Sounds good."

He turns, leaving the dining room. I watch him go, and Mamá does the same. She then looks at me with a slight frown. I shrug, and she goes back to washing dishes. I glance over and Kyle is looking at me now. He beelines his way to me, picking up the knives from the table.

"My wife, the liar," he says in a joking manner.

"I'm not a liar," I mutter.

"But you're a damn good storyteller, so I've heard."

"I'm an artist, Kyle. Artists tend to have very vivid imaginations."

"Yeah. Clearly." He looks me over once, then meets my eyes again. "Is something wrong?"

"What do you mean?"

"I mean…well, you just haven't been yourself lately."

"Everything is fine." Lying. Straight through my teeth. Mamá was right. I'm not that great of a liar.

He walks around the table to get to me, setting the knives down and causing the blades of them to rattle. "It seems like you don't want me around right now."

I look away. "I think it's just that time of the month about to happen. You know how I am around this time."

"Your period isn't due for another two weeks." I frown, whipping my head up to look at him. *How the hell does he know that?* As if he senses my curiosity, he quickly adds, "I just remember you telling me when your last one was. We didn't have sex that week at all. I always count the weeks. Three in between, right?"

"It's weird you know when my period will come." I huff a laugh, walking to the kitchen with the spoons. Mamá has left. She's in the living room screaming her head off at the soccer game now. Apparently, a big score has happened because all I hear is the commentator yelling "GOALLL-LL!" and my parents and Ricky screaming their heads off.

Dishes are still in the sink, so I start washing a few.

"How is that weird?" Kyle asks, resting his lower back against the counter. "You're my wife. I like to know when things can happen and when they can't."

"Okay, Kyle. Sure."

He's quiet a moment. I avoid his eyes. "You've been acting so strange lately. I don't know what I did, but I hope you decide to get over whatever mood this is very soon. I came here for *you*, Gabby. The least you can do is appreciate that."

He pushes off the counter and walks away, leaving the kitchen. I peer over my shoulder for a while, listening to the stairs creak as he walks up them, then I get back to the dishes, but of course his comment remains stuck in my head.

I swear, everything is so fucked right now.

THIRTY-THREE

MARCEL

I DO REALLY stupid shit when I'm drunk. Honestly, it's fuckin' embarrassing.

I groan as I roll over, once again reading Gabby's response to the email I sent last night. I had a little too much whiskey, and I got bold.

I miss her, no lie. I've been thinking about her nonstop —not just about the sex, but her personality overall. I don't know when I started caring so much about what she's doing, how she's doing, or any of that shit. All I know is I need to see her again and find out for myself, but I no longer have an excuse to come around. We're done with her yard. I've been paid. In the past, life would have gone on. Things are different now.

It's all fucked up, and I blame myself for it. Maybe if I hadn't fucked her, I could have kept up my blasé charade.

But since I've had a taste, she seems to be all I want. All I think about. It's all wrong.

Mr. Ward,

I'm going to pretend you didn't say any of that. It's Easter weekend, and I'm here with family, so I have to make my response quick. I have been thinking about it too. How can I not? But I'm trying to consider it a one-time act and move on. Maybe you should too? It was something in our systems that clearly needed to be unleashed.

On the flip side, I'll be having a house-warming on Cinco de Mayo weekend to show off the new patio and hot tub. Kyle insists that I invite you, since you designed it for us, and it turned out so nice, and I'm sure our guests would like to know who the man is behind the layout, so I'm extending an invite to you.

Saturday, May 4th at 6:00 p.m. My back-yard. I understand if you can't make it, but if you do, let's pretend that what we did never happened, okay?

Best,

Gabrielle Moore

Her whole email pisses me off. She's formal, no longer using the nickname I gave her as a sign off. It's clear to me that the main thing she got from our encounter is a lot of guilt.

Can I blame her, really? I have no reason to feel guilty—I can't stand her husband and I'm single—but apparently, she loves him, and she doesn't want to ruin whatever it is they have.

It's best that I don't go to the housewarming. The last thing I want to do around her is pretend, and the last thing I want to see is that asshole husband of hers with his hands on her, touching her when I'm unable to.

I won't be able to handle it, so I guess I'll stay away.

For now.

THIRTY-FOUR

GABBY

WHEN NO REPLY comes within ten minutes of me sending an email back to Marcel, I stuff my phone into my back pocket and pick up the lunch Mamá packed for me off the counter. I stuff it into a tote bag she let me borrow and leave the kitchen.

Ricky and I are about to head out to the lake, and for once I'm glad I get to share some one-on-one time with my big brother.

"Be safe," she says, kissing both our cheeks.

"We will." Ricky hikes his backpack over his shoulder, then turns for the door. I follow after him, and a chill wraps around me. I'm so used to the heat in Hilton Head now that this low morning temperature takes me by total surprise.

"Shit, it's cold," I hiss.

"It'll warm up soon," Ricky says over his shoulder. "Sun has barely come up."

I march to the car Kyle rented and take out the jacket I brought that's lying stretched out on the backseat.

"Forgot what it's like here in the mornings?" Ricky laughs, unlocking his car doors. He heads for the trunk and tosses his bag inside.

"I brought a jacket just in case, but, yeah, I'm used to the heat down there now. I can literally take Callie outside with shorts and a tank on every morning. Feels so good there."

I give him my bag, and he places it inside the trunk before closing it. As we climb into the car, I hear a knock on a door. I peer up and Kyle is standing behind the screened door. He smiles with a mug of coffee in hand. I return the smile.

Last night wasn't any better for us. We didn't get too intimate, but Kyle did apologize over my shoulder for what he'd said to me in the kitchen. I apologized for acting so *strange*, as he'd called it. I told him I just hadn't been feeling like myself lately, to which he replied, "Well, hopefully you'll get over this low mood of yours soon." Not the kind of comment I wanted to hear, but I let it go and went to sleep. After all, Easter had been a long day. It wasn't hard to drift off, but I swear he could be a dick sometimes.

He waves to me and I wave back before getting inside the car. Ricky brings the engine to life and pulls out of the driveway. Kyle is still standing behind the door, watching us go.

"Piece of shit," Ricky grumbles, turning the wheel and driving away from the house.

"Oh my gosh! Ricky!" I gasp, focusing on him. "Why did you just say that?"

"Because it's true. Your husband is a piece of shit."

"Wow." I'm stunned, sitting back in my seat. I shouldn't be smiling about it, but I can't help it. "You know, you've never liked him."

"He thinks he owns people. Acts like everyone around him is inadequate because we don't own a million-dollar company. Piece of shit, like I said."

"He makes you feel inadequate?"

He looks sideways. "Dad, too."

"Oh, so you two have talked about this before?"

Ricky glances over with bright brown eyes. His are just like Mamá's. I got Dad's olive-green. "Let's not get into it." He sighs, looking through the windshield again. "How is everything with him?"

"Fine, I guess."

"You guess?"

"Yeah." I shrug. I don't feel like elaborating.

Ricky reaches for the radio, turning the volume up and letting a song by Bruno Mars play. We nod our heads to the beat, jamming to it. I sing the hook, and then we jam to another song by J. Cole. I used to love riding with Ricky. We have similar tastes in music, and just like me, he sings every lyric if he can.

My brother and I have gotten into a lot of fights before, but music was always the one thing that could calm us down and bring us together. He used to come into my room after we got into a brawl or argument. He'd have his iPod with him, one earphone plugged into his ear. He'd give the other one to me. I'd be stubborn at first, but then I'd stuff the earphone in my ear and lightly nod to the music with him.

It was his form of apology. He'd never been very good at

saying sorry—neither of us had, really. I'm sure we get it from our dad, a man who carries way too much pride.

When we get to the reservoir, Ricky goes to Dad's shed to grab one of the boats and a few paddles. He drags the boat close to shore, and I toss my bag in before climbing into it. Ricky pushes the boat even closer to shore and as it starts to bob on the water, he sloshes through, then steps into it, sitting opposite of me. We paddle until we're close to the middle of the lake, and I ask, "Why didn't we just ask to borrow dad's big boat? That way we don't have to paddle?"

"Because I need some exercise after all the food Mamá made yesterday," he chuckles, and I laugh with him.

"Ah, yeah. Makes total sense."

When we're in a good enough spot to enjoy the view, we put our paddles through the metal rings. Ricky takes out his portable speaker next, starting up a song by Khalid.

"I love Khalid," I sigh.

"Yeah. He's got a gift."

I look at the line of trees to my right as the wind brushes over the pines. "I missed this."

He looks at me. "Being home?"

"Yeah."

"Homesick?" he laughs.

"Yeah. I missed you guys!" I sigh. "So, what's going on with you?"

"With me?" His eyebrows shoot up. "I think I should be asking you that question."

"Nothing's going on with me," I tell him, still smiling.

"Seems like there's trouble in paradise." He reaches for his bag, taking an orange out of the front pocket.

"There's no trouble, Ricky." I watch him start to peel the orange.

"Good because if there is, I'll beat his ass."

I giggle. "Yeah, yeah. You're trying to steer the topic. I asked about you. Tell me about Violetta."

I notice his shoulders tense when I say her name, but he relaxes them almost immediately. Avoiding my eyes, he says, "What's there to tell? She's my wife. I love her."

"Do you really?"

He meets my eyes, giving me a stern look. "Yes."

"So why do you seem so sad when you're around her?"

"I don't," he mutters.

"Come on, Ricky. You didn't bring me out here just for the hell of it. You wanted to talk about something, now spill it."

He frowns, looking toward the line of trees. I wait for him to say something. I know he wants to, but I won't force it out of him. Instead, I pick up my bag up and take out a pear, biting right into it after cleaning it off.

"She fucked her boss," Ricky says, and I damn near choke on the skin of my fruit.

"What?" I gasp.

"Yeah. She fucked him. Only once, so she claims. She had this part-time gig at a furniture store. I saw the way he looked at her whenever I'd stop by and pick her up for lunch, but I thought nothing of it. One day I had to go back there because she forgot her name tag in the passenger seat and didn't realize it. I went inside and saw them through his office window. He had her on top of his desk, touching her everywhere." He pops a slice of orange in his mouth, chewing.

"Oh my God, Ricky. I'm so sorry!"

"Don't be."

"Well, I am. That's fucked up of her! How do you know it was only one time?"

"I don't know for sure, but she apologized—plus we were having a rough patch. We'd split up, and she was staying with her mom for about a month, but I still took her to work because she needed rides." He huffs. "I let it go. She told me I could have a pass, fuck anyone I wanted to. I told her no. I'm not that kind of person."

It's quiet a beat. He's so hurt; I see it deep in his eyes. God, is this how Kyle would look if he found out about Marcel? The last thing I want is to see him upset, especially over something I did.

"Anyway, I told her if it happened again with anyone, I would divorce her. She quit the job the next day, so she stays at home now." He looks up at me warily.

"What?"

"Does it sound crazy that I can track her by her phone now?" he asks.

"You can?"

"Yeah, there's an app out. Lets me know where someone has been for the whole day. I don't trust her, so I check it once a day."

"So why stay with her if you don't trust her? Tracking someone seems too time consuming."

Ricky gives me a cold stare. "The same reason you stick with Kyle, even though he clearly doesn't make you happy. The same reason Ma sticks with Dad."

I frown at his statement about me and Kyle, but I can't argue when it comes to my parents. My dad cheated on my mom—only once. My mom forgave him eventually, but I think it's only because she actually *needed* him. To this day, she still needs him. He's the reason she can stay in the U.S. He'd petitioned for her to become a permanent resident. Fortunately, she's in the final stages and will test for citizenship soon.

They'd split up for two days after what he did. I remember because Momma didn't come home for those two days. She said she was going to spend time with Aunt Carolina.

I recall them arguing and Dad telling her he was drunk. It hurt my mom, but not as much as it should have. She didn't fully love him, and he felt it...I think that's why he sought comfort elsewhere—to see if what he felt for my mom, he could feel in someone else.

I'm assuming he didn't, so he came out and told her the mistake he'd made. This was before they truly fell for each other. Ricky and I were young, and they were on shaky grounds as it was. Still, it's no excuse for what he did. I can't help thinking now that maybe I cheated because my parents made it seem like that sort of thing happening was nothing in comparison to their love...

"Anyway, I haven't forgotten it one bit. But I love her, so I stay," Ricky goes on.

"But how can you trust that she won't do it again?"

"I can't trust it," he says, very blatantly. "But pretending I can trust her is way cheaper than getting a divorce."

"God, Ricky. I'm sorry."

He shrugs it off, eating another piece of orange. I bite into my pear again, looking down at my boots. "If I tell you something, you promise not to judge me?"

"Why would I?" I know he never would. Ricky is good at keeping secrets.

"Because it's kind of fucked up. You have to promise not to say anything to Mamá or Dad."

"I won't, Gabby. You know this. I haven't even told them what Violetta did."

My brows dip. "I'm the first to know?"

"Yep. I know you'll keep it to yourself, plus Ma already gives me enough shit about being with her. If I tell her that, she'll never shut up about it."

"Well, I will keep it to myself." I draw in a breath, then sigh through parted lips. I can't just flat out say what I have to say, so I pick at some of the skin on the pear. Ricky is waiting, but not pressuring me to speak. We're both quiet for a while as Bruno Mars sings about grenades. "I…cheated on Kyle," I finally mumble.

I glance up, and his eyes are rounder. Bigger. "What?"

"It wasn't supposed to happen."

"With who?" he demands, frowning. He's already judging me.

"My landscape designer."

"Holy shit."

"I know." I drop my head.

"How the hell did that even happen? Kyle is like a fucking hawk. He'd have seen it coming from a mile away." Ricky is flabbergasted. I'm not surprised. Anyone would think I'd be the last person to cheat.

"Well he works out of town a lot now, so I'm home alone most of the time. My landscape designer was at the house almost every day to work on the yard, checking in with me. He was nice and we connected…but then things got carried away." I drop my head, trying not to look at him. "I hate myself for it, but I can't seem to shake that guy for some reason. It wasn't just a sexual connection with him. It was deeper than that."

Ricky is quiet a moment. I can tell he's staring at me. "Well, don't beat yourself up about it."

I look up with a frown. "How can you say that?"

"Because I know Kyle...and I know *you*. You wouldn't have done it unless you had a valid reason."

"No, that's wrong. Even if I had a valid reason to do it—which there never is in these cases—it's wrong, Ricky. I'm *married* to Kyle—I made a vow to him. Don't you see that?"

He shrugs. "Maybe he had it coming."

I sigh. "You don't think it's fucked up?"

"Oh, it's very fucked up of you, but I'd choose my sister over that motherfucker—or any motherfucker—any day."

I want to smile. I appreciate the comment, but now isn't the time to be happy about any of this.

I could bring up an excuse—like how I saw Kyle with his assistant Joanna when I visited him at his job once. She was in his office and way too close to him. They didn't hear me enter, but I heard him say the words, "Nothing changes" to her while he caressed her shoulder. Or maybe he just placed a caring hand there, and I allowed my crazy mind to blow it out proportion.

It was right before we got married, so of course I had reason to be suspicious. Joanna is a beautiful brunette who'd clearly gotten a boob job. She was never rude to me, but she did stare at me often whenever Kyle would have gatherings or social events, which always made things awkward.

But those words, they gnawed at me constantly. That day in his office, they both moved away from each other like a fire had broken out between them when they saw me, then Kyle looked at me and put on one of his charming smiles. I didn't fall for it. Joanna scurried out of his office, greeting me warily along the way, and then sat at her desk outside the door.

I asked him what that was all about, and he told me that she was having a bad day and had heard he was moving in a few months. She thought she was going to be out of a job, so he was comforting her. He swore it wasn't what I thought it was, but ever since that altercation, my trust for him became thinner. Not that I've ever caught him doing anything suspicious other than that. I checked his phone once, when the questions had gotten the best of me, and didn't find anything, so I was relieved. I felt gross for checking his phone, but I had to ease my mind, and ever since then I don't check it anymore.

Even so, I have no excuse. What I did with Marcel was wrong, plain and simple.

"Life is fucked up." Ricky leans forward, resting his elbows on his thighs. "Marriages are hard, but we go into them thinking everything will be easy and all will be solved." His head shakes. "Marriage is a full-time job—one none of us will ever get paid for."

"We get paid with joy," I say hopefully, like that's going to settle the debate.

He scoffs. "There is no joy, Gabby." He looks me in the eyes. "Makes me wonder why I still bother sometimes—or why I even asked her to marry me in the first place."

I know the real reason why he asked Violetta—to move on from Christina—but I don't say that. Instead I say, "Because divorce is actually something you do have to pay for." I place my hand on top of his. "Everything will be okay, Ricky. But if you truly, truly aren't happy with her, then do what's right. Don't waste anymore of your time if she doesn't set your soul on fire."

"I suggest you take your own advice then."

I sit back, pulling my hand away.

"Don't waste time on someone who doesn't set your soul on fire, Gabby. You're young and beautiful. I always thought it was too soon for you to marry him, but didn't want to say the wrong thing to hurt you."

"I always figured you thought that. Even I think we got married too soon, but Dad encouraged it and of course Ma agreed, because all she's ever wanted is for me to get married and be taken care of."

Ricky straightens his back. "Let me ask you something."

"What?"

"You said it wasn't just sexual—your affair. That it was deeper. Does that mean you still think about him? Still want him?"

My heart catches speed at the mere thought of Marcel. Sheepishly, I say, "Everyday, Ricky." And that's my response to both questions.

"Damn. That's tough." He shakes his head. "You'll figure it out though, I'm sure." He digs out a bottle of water from his bag, but before he bothers opening it, he's studying me carefully. "You know I'm always here for you, right? No matter what?"

I smile, but my eyes are burning with emotion. I have no idea if I'll ever be able to figure it out. I feel stuck, and I hate this feeling.

But I blink the fire in my eyes away and say, "I'm here for you too, Ricky. Always."

THIRTY-FIVE

GABBY

K YLE and I are back home by eleven that night. We're beat, but I'm so happy to see my Callie when I jog across the street to get her from Meredith.

"Was she good?" I ask, holding her in my arms. She tries to climb higher on me, and I laugh as she tries to lick my face.

"Oh, she was a doll! So freaking precious! I was hoping you wouldn't come back so I could have a reason to keep her!"

I laugh. "I would never abandon this adorable little face!" I hold Callie up, and she licks at the tip of my nose. "Thank you for watching her. I'll make it up to you with brunch or lunch soon!"

"Don't even worry about it, honey. It was my pleasure." Meredith waves me goodbye as I walk across the street, Callie tucked under one arm and her supplies and dog bed under the other. I barely make it to the door, so I place her down and adjust the items. Before I walk up the stoop, though, I hear Kyle's voice. I frown, looking toward the backyard. The light is on.

I place Callie's stuff down and walk across the front lawn to get there. There's a short path that leads to our backyard. The path is surrounded by bushes, which would make it hard for us to see if anyone was coming through the path if we are in the back.

I don't show myself as I watch Kyle standing by the wet bar, a hand planted on his hip, his phone to his ear.

"I don't give a shit about any of that! You told me this would work out!" he hisses into the phone. "No. That's not what we agreed. You got what you wanted, and I've been working my ass off to make up for that investment. You're lucky I can't abandon you, or I would have done it a long time ago. Fix this immediately, Will. Do you understand?"

Will? My frown grows deeper. Callie is at my side, panting, looking up at me curiously. She's probably trying to figure out why the hell I'm spying on my husband.

"You told me about meeting there, and I made a way there every week. You dug yourself out of that one, but this is different. If it hadn't been for that—" he sighs, exasperated. What in the hell is he talking about?

"Let's just drop it. I want this fixed ASAP." He ends the call and as soon as he does, Callie barks.

"No!" I whisper hiss, but it's too late. Callie is dashing through the backyard, going straight for Kyle. She's trying to climb his leg and he's looking down at her, clearly confused as to where she came from.

I move away from the bush and walk down the path,

acting like I've just gotten back. "Hey. What are you doing out here?"

"Oh—uh, phone call." He holds his iPhone in the air, but doesn't smile.

"She's happy to see you," I note, pointing at Callie, who is still feigning for Kyle's attention. But he doesn't provide it. He looks down at her again and then moves his foot. Callie plops down on her paws as he walks to the door.

"I need to check a few emails. Will you be okay?"

I look him over once before nodding. He's distressed, eyes cloudy. What the hell is going on with him? "I'll be fine. Go ahead."

He leaves without a word, and I sigh as Callie dashes back to me. I pick her up and take her inside, going to the porch to grab her things and then giving her a fresh bowl of water. She laps it up, and I lean on the counter with my elbow, a fist propping my head up as I watch her.

I always wonder why Kyle isn't affectionate toward Callie. She's such a sweet dog, and so innocent. Everyone who crosses her path loves her, yet he barely tolerates her. I understand he's not much of a dog-owning person, but he flat-out ignores Callie half the time.

But Marcel on the other hand…

Shit. Speaking of, he emailed me back, but I was boarding the flight home and didn't want to check with Kyle over my shoulder. I walk upstairs, my puppy trailing behind me, and head to my studio. I shut the door to be safe, and then sit at the chair behind my desk, opening the laptop.

It's funny that we email, considering we have each other's numbers. Emailing feels much more…*exciting*…even if it's wrong.

I find his email at the top and read it.

Gabby,

You're out of your damn mind if you think I can pretend what we did never happened, but don't worry. I'm not the kind of man who would boast about it. What we did was our moment, and I'll be damned if I share the details of it with anyone else. What can I say? I'm a selfish man, and it was mine.

The housewarming I'll have to give some thought on. Not sure I'll be able to handle being around you and the man who's in my way all night. Don't be upset if I can't make it. Consider it a good thing. It'll save you from the freak outs.

Marcel Ward,
   CEO of Ward Landscaping & Design

I sigh, slouching back in my chair. I'm worked up. Why do his words always slay me? I can pretty much hear his voice with every word, that sultry, sexy, Southern timbre that makes me fuzzy all over.

Knowing Marcel, he won't show for the housewarming. He has too much pride to stand in a corner and watch me. Not only that, but he's right. It would be safer if he doesn't come at all—that way I don't have to pretend or hide my feelings for him, and he doesn't have to act like I'm just the client.

If there is just Kyle, then it'll be much easier to play wife, but what I can't do is play wife *and* act like the man standing across the room is a complete stranger to me. At this point, doing that with Marcel is pretty much impossible.

THIRTY-SIX

MARCEL

I HAVE no idea what the hell I'm doing here.

I'm seated behind the wheel of my truck, parked along the curb, looking right at the driveway of Gabby's house.

I'm clearly insane.

My windows are rolled down, and I hear people talking as they get out of their cars, going down the driveway to get to her front door.

I shouldn't have come here...but *not* coming would have made me look like a coward. She only extended the invite because her husband asked, but the more I thought about it, the more I realized that if she really didn't want me to show up, she never would have mentioned it in the first place, no matter how insistent her husband was about it.

I watch a woman in pink heels get out of an SUV. "Hurry up, honey! We're already late!" She's scurrying toward the driveway, hollering, "Oh my God! Would you look at this place? This house is beautiful!"

A tall man gets out the driver's side, rolling his shoulders back after shutting the door behind him. "Slow the hell down before you fall on your face in those damn heels, Mariana!" They disappear, voices still carrying.

I sigh, sitting back against the warm leather. I need to get my ass in there already. I'll stay for a short while, show my face, then leave. Can't hurt anyone, can it?

"Fuck it." I roll my windows up, then push out of the car, grabbing the brown paper bag that's covering a bottle of liquor. I make my way toward her driveway as the sound of music carries through the streets.

"The fuck am I doing?" I mumble, but I keep going to the front door. I've never felt my heart beat this fast.

I ring the doorbell when I'm close, and it takes a while for someone to get it, but I wait. I spot a shadow from the sidelight windows, and then the door swings open.

Gabby is standing on the other side of it, wearing a pinkish-looking dress that stops at her ankles. There's a slit in the dress that reveals one of her slim, tan thighs. She looks good in it.

She's smiling when she answers the door, but as soon as she sees me, it fades, and her eyes grow wider.

"Surprised?" I smirk.

She blinks rapidly. "Marcel! I…uh…I didn't think you'd make it!" She starts tucking her hair behind her ears, like she suddenly has to fix herself up for me.

"Gonna let me in or what?"

"Oh—yeah. Duh." She steps aside, and I walk through

the threshold. I peer around, and there are a few people sitting on the couches. Several more are in the kitchen.

"The landscaper made it!" I hear someone yell, and I look toward the staircase. Gabby's husband is walking our way with a beer in hand. "I'm surprised you came. Gabby told me you probably weren't going to make it."

"Wouldn't have missed it." I keep my voice even with him. I still don't like the bastard.

"Well, I'm glad you did, now everyone can meet you. Can you remind me of your name again?" he requests.

I want to punch him in his smug face. "Marcel."

"Ahh—yes, that's what it is! You can call me Kyle tonight. No need for formal names."

I nod, but I don't smile. Fuck him and his basic-ass name.

"Marcel, we've got beer and drinks in the kitchen. Any preference?" he asks over his shoulder.

I look him over in his expensive button-down shirt and high-water pants. Is that supposed to be the style now? Because he looks like a bitch.

"I'll take a beer."

Gabby shifts on her feet, following Kyle to the kitchen. I follow their lead, already hating the decision I made to come here.

"What do you have?" Gabby asks me when Kyle opens the cooler in the corner, shuffling through the ice. She's standing a good distance away, but even so, I can smell her. She smells like honey and sweet cream.

"Oh." I place the bag on the counter and pull out the bottle. Gabby's smile drops almost instantly. "Jose Cuervo Silver. Always reminds me of good times."

She looks from the bottle of tequila to my eyes. I'm testing her, and she knows it. I just want to see if she still wants me, is all. Then I can know whether I'm wasting my time or not.

She's not falling for it, though. Instead, she takes the bottle from me and carries it to the counter where other bottles of liquor are lined up.

"That was nice of you," she chimes. "Perfect for almost Cinco de Mayo."

"Here you go." Kyle hands me a beer. I take it, glad it's a twist off. He walks away to talk to other guests, but not before giving Gabby a kiss on the cheek and telling her he'll be back. I look away, sipping my beer.

"Who is this?" a shrill voice asks. I peer over my shoulder, toward the double doors. A girl with light-brown skin, dark hair, and gold hoop earrings walks inside with a plastic cup in hand. She's looking me up and down, her eyes wide, burning with curiosity.

"T, this is our landscape designer, Marcel. Marcel, this is my best friend, Teagan." Gabby introduces us formally, looking even more nervous.

I extend my arm, offering a hand to her friend. "Nice to meet you."

She takes my hand and shakes it. "Nice to meet you too, Mr. Landscape Designer."

"Didn't realize you had a best friend." I focus on Gabby.

She shrugs. "There's a lot about me you don't know."

Yeah. Clearly.

"Well, there's a lot I *do* know about *you*," her friend says to me. "Now I see, Gabby! Now I see!"

I fight a smile. "Pardon?"

"Teagan," Gabby hisses, and her face is turning a light shade of pink. "Stop it. You're drunk."

"Not quite. But close." Teagan grins at her best friend before focusing on me again. "You did a great job back there. The patio is amazing! Everyone loves it!"

"Appreciate that."

"Is this the designer?" A rich Spanish accent comes from across the room, and the woman I saw in the pink heels trots our way.

"Yes, Mamá. This is the designer," Gabby sighs. "Mamá, Marcel. Marcel, this is my mom."

"Nice to meet you," I say, and I see where Gabby gets her looks from. She's like her mother, almost the same body size, hair, height, and everything. They're petite women.

"Wowwww!" She's sing-songs the word, looking me up and down more than once. She looks at Gabby and says something in Spanish, which embarrasses Gabby even more.

"Okay—guys, you know what?" Gabby holds up her hands, as if calling for an intermission. "Let's give him some space. He just got here, so let him get comfortable."

"You can call me Mariana," her mom goes on, ignoring everything Gabby just said.

"Will do."

"Your accent is the coolest thing I've heard, honestly," Teagan informs me. "It's dope."

"Again, I appreciate that."

Gabby knows they aren't going to back off, so she goes to the counter, pouring herself a glass of wine. Kyle is back in the kitchen at her side, watching her make it. He says something to her. Again, I look away. If I look away, I won't get mad.

As Mariana and Teagan pepper me with questions about my company and how long I worked on Gabby's patio, I notice Gabby leave. She's following Kyle out the double doors. I'm not sure how much longer I can keep this shit up—watching her follow after him like some lost puppy.

For the majority of the night, I handle it, though. I'm introduced to a lot of her friends and family. I meet her brother and father, who seem like good guys.

Her father asks me how long I've had the company, how long I've been around, and other things. The brother is quiet, letting his dad do all the talking, but the way he stares at me is unnerving. Almost like he knows something about me that no one else does...or like he's onto me.

Gabby's father commends me on the patio work just like everyone else, and then I meet several people who work with Kyle. They're all assholes. Even Mrs. Aarons is here, the woman who lives across the street from Gabby. I did her home a few months ago, and she tells me how happy she is that she hired me, but not without running her hands up and down my chest and shoulders a dozen times. She's always been very *handsy*.

I'm surprised Kyle's parents aren't around, but I overheard him talking to Gabby's father about how they had to attend a charity event in Hong Kong.

Through it all though, I'm stealing glances of Gabby. I can't help it. For one, she looks fucking amazing in that dress. And every time she laughs, I feel the need to gravitate toward her. Too bad her husband is right on her ass, hardly letting her breathe.

A small bark sounds up and I hear light panting. I spot something white running around and then the white spot is right next to me. I laugh as Callie jumps up, her front paws on my leg.

"Ohh!" I laugh. "Look at you! Bigger since the last time I saw you!" I bend down and scratch behind her ears. "You been good? Huh?" She does another little bark, like she's trying to talk back.

"She never does that to me when I'm home," Kyle remarks, and I look up, spotting him and Gabby coming my way.

"She does, you just never pay attention to her. Isn't that right, pretty girl?" Gabby coos, and Callie runs to her. Gabby picks her up in her arms while Kyle shakes his head, then sips his beer.

"Not a fan of dogs?" I ask, even though I already know the answer.

"I like them, but I'm not keen on owning one. Shocked me to see Gabby had one when I arrived home."

"I sent you a picture," she tells him, like that settles the debate.

He laughs. "Yeah, which was also completely unexpected. I thought it was a picture of the neighbor's dog until I read your message."

She rolls her eyes, then places Callie down. Callie trots over to my foot, and lays right on my boot, panting away. I smile, but when I look up and see Kyle glaring at Callie, my smile fades. His eyes shift up to mine, a spark of confusion within them, then he looks away, taking another swig of beer.

The song changes, and Teagan is doing her own dance by the wet bar.

"I really appreciate what you did out here." Kyle is looking at me again. "Everyone loves it."

"It was no problem."

"No, seriously. Worth every penny. I was skeptical at first, but you proved me wrong."

I try so hard not to narrow my eyes at him. He really has the nerve to act like that email he sent me never happened? This guy is a joke.

"Like I said, it was no problem at all. Just did my job." *And fucked your wife while I was at it.*

Kyle nods, then flips his wrist to check the time. "Getting late, huh?"

Gabby shrugs.

"Let's start cleaning the kitchen up a bit."

Kyle wraps an arm around her waist, reeling her closer to him. He turns with her, and she glances back at me before going to the door with him. Her eyes tell it all. She hates this just as much as I do—the position I'm in, anyway. My chest is tight as I watch them go, and I literally hate everything about it.

I take a seat in the built-ins, and from where I am, I can see clearly into the kitchen. They left the doors open—I'm assuming to keep the party atmosphere flowing. I wish they'd shut it.

My grip tightens around the neck of my beer bottle as I watch Kyle run a hand over her ass. My jaw clenches when he kisses the back of her neck, then moves around to kiss her cheek, his body flush to hers. He turns her to face him, interrupting her collection of the plastic cups on the counter, and she sighs as he cups her face in his hands and kisses her roughly. It's clear to me that she's fucked him recently, and I have no idea what I expected. I'm an idiot for thinking she'd quit sleeping with her own damn spouse.

Anger brews inside me. I snatch my eyes away, looking to the right, but my eyes meet a pair of familiar caramel-colored ones. Gabby's brother, Ricky, is looking right at me, brows bunched together. I jerk my eyes away from him too. Why the fuck does he keep staring at me?

I need to go. *Now.*

I head to the kitchen, glad Kyle is in the living room picking up trash.

"I think I'm gonna head out," I say to Gabby.

"Really? Already?" She's disappointed.

"Yeah. I just…I need to."

She locks her gaze on mine. She has no idea how badly I want to be right next to her, feel her smooth skin under my palm. She also has no idea how badly I want to rip Kyle in half for touching her. I sound like a fucking fool. He had her first—he *married* her, for Christ's sake.

"Let me walk you out," she offers.

I almost start to say that's not such a great idea, considering how I'm feeling right now, but then again, I would like a moment alone with her, even if it's only for a second.

Kyle goes back outside, yelling for Ricky to change the song to a better one. He starts picking up trash out there too. I breathe a sigh of relief.

Gabby dries her hands off on a paper towel and then walks around the counter, going past me. I'm glad Kyle went back outside. Don't feel like faking farewells with that motherfucker.

We head out the door, walking up the cobblestone driveway quietly. She's right beside me, taking slow strides, barely looking at me. The streetlights hit us as we walk across the street to get to my truck that's parked under a tree.

"Did you have fun?" She finally breaks the ice, looking up at me as we reach the driver's side. I'm parked between streetlights, and we're mostly in the dark.

"It was all right."

"Just all right?" She's biting a smile.

"Yep, just that."

She lets out a short sigh. "You didn't have to come. I would have understood if you hadn't."

"Needed to."

"Why?" Her head tilts.

"You already fuckin' know why, Gabby. Don't play games with me right now."

She shakes her head and rolls her eyes. I'm so tired of her rolling her damn eyes. I grab her upper arms, bringing her to the door and lightly pinning her back against my truck.

"You're jealous," she pants after studying my face.

"Damn right."

My chest is on hers, and I slide my hands down the insides of her arms, gripping her wrists and bringing them up, pinning them to the truck, too. She sighs then, barely putting up a fight, almost like she's been waiting for this to happen, or maybe she's had a little too much to drink. I don't care either way.

"He shouldn't get to touch you more than I do," I grumble.

"I married him, Marcel." It's a fact. I know it, but I can't stand the thought of it.

"You think I give a fuck about that? He doesn't make you feel the way I make you feel."

She doesn't say anything; she doesn't have to. She knows it's true.

"He had his hands all over you, and I just had to sit back and watch while he got to do it in front of everyone. It's bullshit."

"Well what do you expect after what we did, Marcel? I can't just flirt around with you and act like I'm not taken. I made a vow to him."

"Yeah, and I'm sure you've broken several of those vows with me. Shit, you're breakin' one right now."

"Ugh." She tries to find a way out. I hold her wrists tighter, gluing my groin to hers. A frown forms on her face. "I can't do this with you right now."

"Why the hell not? No one's lookin'."

"Marcel, I have to get back—"

"Meet me at a villa when he goes out of town for work again."

She stops putting up a fight. "W-what?"

"You heard me."

"Why would I do that?" she asks, voice hoarse.

"Because I know you've been thinkin' about me. About what it would be like to do it again."

Her head is shaking. "No. That's insane. This is not an affair—"

"I'm not lettin' him have you all to himself," I snap. "Fuck that."

She shuts her mouth, sweeping her eyes all over my face. "Wow! You're not just jealous. You're *crazy*-jealous!"

"You made me this way."

She scoffs.

I smirk.

"Meet at a villa like some cheap hooker? Do you realize how that sounds?" she mutters.

I run the tip of my nose up the crook of her neck, breathing her in. "You always smell so good."

"I can't go to a villa with you. It's too obvious."

"I could eat your pussy right here in my truck."

Her breath catches. "Oh my God."

"Make you mine all over again."

"Who said I was yours in the first place?"

"You did, the moment I put my mouth on yours, and you didn't pull away."

She shudders a breath. "You're making this so hard."

"It's not that hard to think about. Come to a villa on the beach with me and ride my cock with the ocean view behind you. Simple."

"I need to get back."

I nip at the area just below her chin with my teeth. She breathes even harder, and my cock twitches in my jeans.

She lowers her gaze, her lashes touching her cheekbones. "I'll think about it. Now let me get back before someone notices I've been gone for too long."

She tries to pull away. I don't budge. "Marcel," she snaps, annoyed. I don't care.

"Do you want me again? Answer it, honestly."

She looks away, clearly exasperated. "Why do you always have to make me state the obvious?"

"So, you *do* want me again?" I can't fight my smirk.

She gives me a serious once over.

"I want to hear it come out of your mouth." She challenges my stare, but I'm not having it. I need to hear her say it. Maybe that makes me some desperate, sad fuck. If so, I don't give a damn. I need to know that I'm not wasting my time.

I don't care that she's married. I don't expect this to last forever, but I want her again. And I want to know if she wants the same.

"Fine—yes! I want you again. I've been thinking about what we did nonstop ever since it happened, even while lying in the same bed as *him*! Does that make you happy to hear?"

I release her wrists, planting my hands on the truck, on either side of her head. She's looking up at me, trying to carry on her defiant charade.

She can't resist me.

I can't resist her.

We're fucking impossible.

"Kiss me and you can go." My voice is low, husky.

"I'm not kissing you out here! Are you crazy?" She looks all around, but there's no one out. We can still hear her guests in her backyard, drunk and laughing.

"No one's around, Gabby, and I'm parked in the shadows, away from the streetlights. You've got no excuse."

"Other than the fact that I'm *not* yours. You're ridiculous."

"You think I give a shit about any of that? The fact that you're married doesn't intimidate me, just so you know. If Kyle had a little respect, maybe I would feel a little guilty, but he doesn't, so I don't give a fuck. Now kiss me, and I'll let you get back to hostin' your party."

Her throat bobs as she focuses on my mouth. "You're going to ruin me."

I grin, probably a little too proudly. "I hope I ruin you for him, then maybe you'll come runnin' to me more often. Now shut up and kiss me already."

"Gah!" She pushes on her toes and leans into me, her mouth latching onto mine. One of her hands is on my chest, the other draping around the back of my neck. She kisses me deep and slow, then parts her lips, running her tongue over mine.

I groan in response, tasting the wine on her tongue, and my cock comes to life, hardening like a fucking rock for her. She drops a hand to palm my dick, rubbing the print of it, working me up.

Fuck. She is *everything*.

She pulls away, way too quickly for my liking, and then dips beneath my arm.

"There," she says, walking backward as she crosses the street. "You got what you wanted. I'll talk to you later."

I huff a laugh, using the pad of my thumb to wipe the corner of my mouth. "Hold on—before you go. Why was your brother starin' at me every time I saw him?"

She frowns and stops walking, eyes wide. Then she shrugs and says, "I trust him. That's all you need to know."

So, he knows what we did? *Shit.* That must have been embarrassing for Gabby, but the fact that she told her own brother makes it clear to me that what we share is so much more than I thought. I'm not crazy thinking it. She feels something too.

"Think about my offer," I yell after her, watching her turn and trot back to her driveway."

"Goodnight, Marcel!" She yells back, and I shake my head and laugh, climbing into my truck, cranking it up, and leaving with a cock that's way too anxious. If I had the chance, I would have fucked her right on the door of my truck, but a quickie wouldn't have sufficed. I need way more than that.

She had it wrong when she said I would be her ruin.

If anything, I'm almost certain she will become mine.

THIRTY-SEVEN

GABBY

"I CAN'T STOP THINKING about him."

There. I said it.

Plain and clear, out loud, for my only real friend to hear.

Teagan looks over at me, and I can tell she's frowning behind her sunglasses. "What are you talking about?" She's utterly clueless. Not that I expect her to know what I'm talking about.

I've been thinking about Marcel all morning, even more so after what happened last night by his truck, but of course, I've kept that tiny little detail to myself.

I slept on it. *Cherished* it. I'm terrible.

Teagan decided to stay another day since she didn't have to work Sunday. I figure this the perfect opportunity to tell Teagan everything.

Kyle is in the house relaxing before he has to go back to

work tomorrow. He's nowhere near me, and I need to get this off my chest before I explode.

We're on the beach, colorful towels spread out beneath us. The water is rushing to shore and seagulls are cawing a short distance away. It's a beautiful day, the sun bold and high in the sky.

Callie is running back and forth from my towel to the shoreline. She's nervous about the water, but she's a brave little thing, challenging the small waves and then barking when they rush away. I keep a close eye on her. I'd hate to see her get swept away by a rogue wave.

I'm sporting a bathing suit I bought last year when Kyle took me to Miami. Dark blue, but with extra cups in the top to make my boobs look fuller. Surprisingly, it's very comfortable.

"My landscape designer," I say without looking at Teagan. I'm still focused on Callie, grateful for the distraction. "I can't stop thinking about him."

I look over, and Teagan has sat upright to lower her glasses. She's staring right at me. "What do you mean *you can't stop thinking about him*? Like about his body and that sexy-as-hell face? Like I told you, I get why you find him so attractive. The man is fine."

"No, T…like…in a *deeper* way."

She frowns then. "I don't get what you mean…"

I sigh and sit forward, crossing my legs. I'm obviously quiet for too long because Teagan snaps her fingers in my face, pulling me out of my trance.

"Hello? Gabby, you can't just say stuff like that without explanation! What's going on with you?" She's leaning toward me now, fully concerned.

I feel tears creep to my eyes, but she can't see them behind my sunglasses and I'm glad. But sure enough, as I speak, she can hear the emotion thickening in my voice. "I slept with him," I confess.

And she's quiet.

So damn quiet.

All I hear are crashing waves and Callie barking at them.

"You...wait...with the *designer*?"

"Yes." I push my sunglasses up to the top of my head, then clear my eyes with my fingers. "It all happened so fast that night. I made tacos, we were drinking...things got carried away in the kitchen."

"Wow...G." It's all she can say.

I meet her eyes, and she's shocked, but not the kind of shock that comes with disapproval. She's shocked, like she always knew this would happen but can't believe it did.

"Is that why the table is broken?" She asks it softly, but there's still burning curiosity in her voice. She starts to crack a smile, and I can't help it, I laugh at her.

"I swear I can't stand you!" I half-laugh, half-sob.

"What? I'm just wondering! I saw it was broken and then you said things got carried away in the kitchen! I'm only putting two and two together!"

I swipe a tear away, then bring my knees to my chest, resting my chin on my kneecaps. "Kyle is supposed to get it fixed soon." Callie is back, and she sits at the end of my towel, panting like she just ran a marathon. "I feel so damn guilty about it. I mean, most people cheat when things have gone wrong or when the couple isn't interested in one another anymore, but it's not really like that with Kyle."

"So why do you think you did it?"

"I don't know. I've had time to think about it, and the main reason I can come up with is I was lonely. Kyle is hardly home. But even so, it's no excuse, because he always comes back."

Teagan clears her throat before saying, "That's your main reason?"

"Yes—things have been fine."

"Yeah, *now* they have. I recall a time not too long ago when shit hit the fan and you came crying to me about it."

I shake my head. "It's not like that anymore."

"People don't change overnight, Gabby. You put too much trust in Kyle."

"He's my husband, Teagan. I have to trust him."

"Yeah, and you do, for all the wrong reasons." I frown and she straightens her back. "Look, I get it. Kyle is safe. He makes great money, he's nice-looking, gives you whatever you want. But that's all mediocre shit, you know? It's conventional, material, but it makes sense for you to be with him, considering the struggles you've had before. But this landscape guy? Marcel? I saw the way he looked at you last night, Gabby. Every time I looked at him, he was watching you. At one point I swear he was going to crush his beer bottle with his hand when he watched you and Kyle together. By that alone, I could tell it was deeper for the two of you, but didn't want to say anything about it because I figured it must have just been him feeling something. I could tell things were more emotional for him than physical, you know? You don't have that with Kyle—you've never had it —so having it with someone else doesn't shock me."

"But it's wrong to feel this way about him," I argue.

"Yeah, but it's not like you're out here killing people,

Gabby! You're so good to Kyle that breaking a vow is driving you crazy!"

"Teagan, I *fucked* Marcel on the table Kyle got from his *mom*! Of course it's going to drive me crazy! I feel bad that I even did it!"

"But do you want him again?"

I blink quickly. "What?"

"Do you want Marcel again?" she asks, voice firm.

I swallow hard, snatching my eyes away from hers. My heart is racing just thinking about being with him again.

"I take that as a yes," she mumbles arrogantly.

I draw in a deep breath and then exhale. "He asked me to meet him at a villa when Kyle leaves. I hate that I'm even considering it."

She tosses her hands in the air. "I'm not even going to touch that subject. Last thing I want to do is put my friend in a sticky situation…but if I were you, I'd have fucked that man ten times by now. Married or not." She breaks out in a laugh and I groan, raking my fingers through my hair.

"God, you're nuts."

"Look, I can't tell you what to do, Gabby. It's your life, and you make your own decisions, but just know that even if you do or don't, we all have our secrets. Every single last human on this planet does…including Kyle. He's not perfect, and neither are you. Just…do what you feel is right. That's all I'll say about it."

She puts her sunglasses back on and lays flat on her back, soaking up some sun again. I pull my eyes away, focusing on the ocean.

Here I am seeking the green light from my own best friend. I wanted her to tell me it was fine—that what I did wasn't that wrong, and that I had a reason. But I don't. She knows what I did will change things forever, but she also knows that whether she tells me to stay away from Marcel or not, I'm going to do what I want.

After a while we leave the beach to shower and catch some lunch in town, depositing Callie in the kitchen while we're gone. Kyle is seated on the sofa, his laptop on his lap, and when we return, he's still there.

Callie comes rushing out of the kitchen, yapping at me, like I've been gone for so long, when it's literally only been an hour.

Kyle looks up at me with a smile, and I return it as Teagan walks around me to head upstairs.

"I'm so tired. I'm going to get a nap in," Teagan yawns.

I nod at her. "Okay."

"How was lunch?" Kyle asks, looking me over.

"It was good. Had chicken tortilla soup with extra avocado."

"Ah. I know how much you love your avocados," he chuckles, then sits forward. "While you're up, do you think you can do me a favor?"

"Sure." I place my keys on the coffee table.

"Can you go to my office and grab the black folder in the bottom drawer of my desk for me? It has a few papers I need to look over."

I walk behind him, rubbing his shoulder. "Yeah, I'll get it."

I head upstairs with Callie trailing behind me, going into his office and shuffling through the drawers until I find the black folder. As I take it out, my eyes shift up to the papers on his desk. There's a pale pink sheet that catches my eye beneath a white one. I wouldn't care about it, if the words *Lewis Docks & Rentals* weren't on it.

I frown as I shut the drawer, glancing at the door before picking the pink paper up. I scan the numbers, and then read over the fine print at the bottom of the page.

The sole proprietor of this company, William Lewis, hereby consents to selling *Lewis Dock & Rentals* to *Moore Investment Banking Company*. With this consent, the sole proprietor will herein receive one-hundred thousand dollars and fifteen percent of monthly fees accrued from *Lewis Docks & Rentals*.

What the hell? I frown, reading the fine print over and over again. Dad sold his company to Kyle? Judging by the date, March of 2019, this deal is fresh.

"Gabs? Everything alright?" Kyle calls, and I rush to put the paper back where it belongs. I tuck the folder under my arm and whisper, "Let's go," to Callie. When I'm downstairs again, I hand the folder to him.

"Took you a while," he notes, smiling.

"Sorry." It's all I can say. He opens the folder right away, and I walk to the kitchen, taking out a bottle of pressed juice. My mind is reeling, though. I never thought in a million years Dad would sell his docking company. He worked hard to open it.

Is he losing money? Is that why he and Kyle were whispering with each other when Easter dinner happened? And that phone call Kyle had when we got back from Virginia. He said my dad's name. Was he talking to him?

I want answers, but this is Kyle's business, and he hates when I snoop…but this is my family, too. Why wouldn't Dad mention selling the company? It doesn't make any sense.

When I fall asleep, I dream that I'm bleeding. Blood is dripping off my face and onto my hands, and I have no idea why, but I'm afraid. *Terrified*, actually.

I'm being chased, screaming for the person to let me go —to leave me alone.

I gasp when I wake up, wiping my face as if it's really bleeding. There's no sign of any blood. I look over at Kyle, who groans in his sleep and rolls my way. He peels an eye open with a frown and then sits up on his elbow.

"Gabs?" he croaks. "What's wrong?"

"N—nothing. Was just a bad dream."

Sighing, he wraps an arm around me, and I turn over, my back to him. "You need to relax. You've been too worked up lately."

I look at the window. With the house so quiet I can hear the ocean.

"Kyle?"

"Yeah?"

"How do you feel about our marriage?"

He's quite a moment, then he sits up. I can tell he's looking at the side of my face. "What do you mean?"

"I mean…are you happy?"

"As happy as I can be."

I frown and sit up, rolling over to face him. "What is that supposed to mean?"

"Just means we could be doing better." He rolls over, turning his back to me. "Doesn't matter. We'll get through this just like we have gotten through everything else. We'll get used to the changes."

I don't know why, but his statement leaves a bad taste in my mouth. I watch him for a moment before turning over, but it's hard to fall asleep again. How could he say something like that?

I slide out of bed quietly and walk to my office to get to my desk. I stare at my laptop for quite some time, and then I say, "Fuck it," and open it. I write up an email that I'm pretty sure I'll regret, then I hit send before I can think twice about it.

Kyle leaves to catch his flight the next morning around eight, but when he kisses my cheek, I feel no surge of emotion. I don't wish he could stay a little longer like I used to.

His mouth connects to mine, and I don't feel like I *can't* breathe without him. If anything, it's a *relief* when he walks out the door, especially after what he said to me last night. What kind of wife thinks this way? A terrible wife, that's who.

After finding that pink sheet on his desk, I keep wondering why he hasn't told me about it, or why my dad hasn't even mentioned it. Does Mamá know? Ricky? Not only that, but he's as happy as he'll get? Is he trying to blame me for what we're going through?

I don't know, but I can't think too much about it right now. As badly as I want answers, I want to be somewhere else more.

I drop Teagan off at the airport shortly after he goes, but not without a big hug. After our conversation on the beach, she spoke nothing of it again. Didn't even hint at it. I was grateful for that.

When I'm back home, I send Meredith a text message. She responds right away, and I'm pleased with her response. I then pack a bag—enough clothes for three days—then pack up Callie's things. An hour later, I'm carrying Callie across the street, tucked under my arm, as I make my way to Meredith's house.

A man answers the door, burly with a bushy brown beard. He's got a button nose and a slightly bald head. He reminds me of a gnome. He's almost adorable.

"Hey there!" he greets me, and from the pictures I saw on Meredith's walls, minus having the beard now, I know he's her husband, Bill Aarons. "Meredith is upstairs in the shower, but she told me you were bringing the pup!"

"Is it okay to leave her now or should I wait?"

"Naw, she can come on in. Meredith should be out in a minute."

"Thank you." I walk past him. It's nice to finally meet you, by the way! I'm Gabby."

"Oh—yes! I apologize for my lack of manners. I'm Bill. Nice to finally meet you, Gabby. Meredith's told me all about you, so I feel like I already know who you are." He chuckles.

"Trust me, I get it. Meredith talks about you a lot." I place Callie's stuff down in a corner with a laugh. She's still tucked under my arm, and I lift her up in the air, looking into her puppy-dog eyes. "You be good, okay?"

She licks the tip of my nose. I smile and place her down, and she goes straight for the back door, dying to go outside. The Aarons have a lovely backyard—fountains and grass and plenty of bushes and palm trees, courtesy of Ward Landscaping & Design, of course. They have plenty for Callie to pee and poo on. She adores it.

"Thank you guys so much again for watching her! I'll be back soon!"

"No problem at all." Bill is going to the back door, opening it up for Callie. I walk out, shutting the front door behind me.

On the way back to my house, my heart is pounding. I don't even go back inside, for fear that I may change my mind the second I think about how fucked up all of this is. I left my bags on the porch, along with my morals, so I snatch them up, then head to the open garage where Lady Monster is parked.

I check my phone, and there's a text from Marcel.

Room 310. Knock when you get here

I try and calm my breaths, but it's impossible. I'm shuddering each breath, my mind racing. I sent him an email this morning, while Kyle and Teagan were still sleeping. I let Callie out afterwards, and my mind was still reeling from what Kyle said, and after thinking about all we'd been through, I realized Teagan was right. I put too much trust in

Kyle. I also have a habit of making him seem like the perfect man when really, he's far from it.

As I stood on the patio, letting soft gusts of salty wind run over my skin while watching the morning waves crash to shore, all I could really think about was Marcel.

Maybe it was a mistake to email him and let him know I was in, but I think it would be an even bigger mistake to suppress whatever this is I feel for him, even if, in the end, it destroys my marriage.

Sometimes I wonder if my marriage even deserves to be saved anymore.

THIRTY-EIGHT

GABBY

I'VE ARRIVED...AND I'm freaking the hell out.

I stare ahead at the towering villa, made of white stucco with a thick blue design bordering the edges of the building.

Several people walk in and out of the building, most pulling up to valet. I have no idea what kind of place Marcel has booked, but judging by the flashy attire of some of the guests arriving and departing, as well as their expensive cars pulling up to valet, it's safe to assume this is some elite resort that not many can afford.

"You're already here," I murmur to myself. "Too late to back out now." *Or is it?*

I sit back in the seat, running a hand over my face. I know if I sit here any longer, I'll jet, and the last thing I want to do is stand him up. It astounds me that I even care this much, to the point I don't want to disappoint him. I've done it way too many times before, and he's been patient with me. I can't do it now, or he'll never talk to me again.

With that in mind, I get out of my car and open the back door, taking my overnight bag out. I sling it over my shoulder, then pick up my tote bag as well.

Calming jazz music pours out of hidden speakers as I walk to the entrance of the building. A man greets me at the door, standing in a gray vest and dress pants. I force a smile at him but keep going, making my way to the elevator.

When I'm aboard, I can literally hear my pulse thumping in my ears. I watch the digital blue numbers above climb, gripping the handle of my overnight bag anxiously.

When the doors split apart, I draw in a breath and walk out, exhaling as I make my way down the hall. This hall has tall, white columns and a shiny, marble floor. It's beautiful.

Room 310 is directly ahead of me. The banging in my chest is even heavier now. My pace slows as I approach.

And then I knock.

I hear some shuffling around, and then the door swings open. Marcel stands on the other side of it, shirtless, wearing only a pair of black basketball shorts that hang low on his hips, revealing two sharp dips below his abdomen.

By the shimmer in his ocean eyes, he looks relieved, and I'm glad to know he's happy to see I've made it.

"Thought you'd bail," he says, stepping back. "Come in."

I force a smile as I walk past him, stopping before I pass the kitchen on the left. It's a small kitchen tucked into a corner, but it has an oven with a stove, microwave, fridge, and a sink. Good enough for three days.

My eyes shift over to the furniture. Brown wood surrounds the ivory cushions of the L-shaped sofa, and there's a glass coffee table in the middle. Just beyond the furniture are sliding glass doors. Through the glass, I spot the ocean and lots of sand. It's all so beautiful.

I take it all in, and my nerves really become a mess. He planned all this for us. For *me*. Did he really want this to happen that badly? This is clearly his way of making an impression, and I truly am impressed…but he'll have expectations. God, I'm a nervous wreck.

I take my bag to a table in the corner, placing it on top of it. I unzip it and pull out the bottle of silver tequila—the bottle he brought to our housewarming. He watches me unscrew the lid and drink straight from the bottle.

"Gabby," he says, exasperated.

But I take another drink. And then another, turning to look at the ocean, my back to him.

He marches around me, grabbing my arm as I start to bring the bottle to my lips again. "Gonna drink the whole damn bottle?" He's frowning as he looks me in the eye. "Slow down." He reaches for the tequila in my hand, taking it from me and placing it on the table. "You're here, and everything's fine. Relax."

"It's too perfect," I blurt out, breaths ragged.

"What's too perfect?"

"This! It's too romantic! Too perfect!"

"Well, I was hopin' to make you comfortable. Figured that was what you would have wanted."

"I love it," I admit. "It *is* what I wanted. I just…I came in, expecting to be disappointed. Hoping to find any excuse to leave."

332

I walk past him, going to the sliding doors that reveal the beach. I expect to see a crowded beach, but there aren't many people around.

"This villa is located on a private part of the beach… just in case you're wonderin' where everyone's at. Only the people who are in this villa can set up out there. Most are either gone during the day on business or at the pool."

"Booking a room here must have cost you a fortune."

"Price doesn't matter."

I sigh, feeling the heat of his body behind me.

"You realize this isn't just…whatever you think it is, right?" his voice is lower.

I turn to face him. "What do you mean?"

"I mean…we can do things other than have sex. Walk the beach. Lay on towels like beach bums. Grab some food and drinks. Whatever you wanna do."

I notice the way his shoulders hunch a bit, and his eyes avert to the left. "You're nervous too," I point out.

"Nah. Just want you to feel good here. That's all." He'll never admit that he's nervous, but I see it all over him. He didn't think I would show. My presence alone has surprised him.

I take a step closer to him, my heart beating rapidly. "This place is great, Marcel. You did good."

He puts on a soft smile. I reach down to grab his hand, bringing the palm of it up and pressing it to my cheek. He looks at me oddly, confused, but I close my eyes and let out a relaxed breath.

My nerves are starting to settle, and I don't know if it's those swigs of tequila that's done this, or just the fact that he's right here in front of me. Whatever it is, I accept it.

"You're in good hands, Miss Gabby." His voice holds a mixture of serenity and playfulness.

"I know I am." I smile up at him, and he drops his hand, entwining his fingers with mine. His chest touches mine, and he's looking right into my eyes.

"Then don't be nervous. Be yourself. Just 'cause we're here, doesn't mean shit has changed."

I nod, dropping my eyes. "Kay."

He brings his other hand up, tilting my chin. "Don't do that."

"Do what?"

"Look away like you don't have a say-so. Is bein' yourself too much to ask for?"

"Sort of."

"How?"

"I don't know."

He drops his hand, but his other is still connected with my other.

"Can I be honest with you?" My chest feels like it's on fire. I need to tell him how I feel, unleash the heat that's burning me up inside.

"Sure."

"It feels wrong being here. Not that I don't want to be here. I just feel so guilty."

"Well, how can I make it right?" He doesn't hesitate with that question. It's almost like he saw it coming.

"I don't know." I shrug one shoulder.

Marcel studies me briefly, then he pulls his hand out of mine. My heart plummets, and I think I've just ruined this entire thing for him, until he opens both arms and wraps them around me. Surprised, I bring my arms up, locking them around the back of his neck. He's so much taller, so I'm standing really high on the tips of my sandals, but he's holding me close, keeping me steady enough that it doesn't hurt.

"I've got you," he mumbles in my ear. "No games and no bullshit for the next three days. No thinkin' about what's back at home, no guilt gettin' in the way. I'm huggin' you now 'cause I'm about to give you a choice." He pulls back, his large hands holding me just below the ribs to keep me in place. "You walk out that door right now and leave, and I won't blame you. Hell, I won't even be mad. Disappointed, yeah, but I'll live. But if you stay, I promise you the next three days will be nothin' short of amazin'. Why? Because I've decided to dedicate the next three days to *you*." He looks me over. "Choice is yours, Gabby. You go, and you won't have to live with the regret that comes afterward."

We stare into each other's eyes, his ocean blue boring into mine. How does he do that? How does he always make the choice seem so easy, yet so difficult all the same?

I back out of his grasp and watch his head fall. He's no longer looking at me. Walking around him, I grab my tote bag and go straight for the door. I swing it open, gripping the handle, and looking back.

"Well? What are you waiting for?"

He turns to face me, confused.

"You said we could do whatever I wanted, and I'm starving right now, so let's find something to eat."

He cracks a smile—probably one of the biggest, most handsome smiles I've ever seen on him. "You're a little jokester, huh?" He's still smiling, going for a duffle bag in the corner and pulling out a T-shirt to put on. I can't stop the smile that sweeps over my lips.

"You really thought I'd walk out on you like that?"

"Shit, wouldn't have surprised me. You're wishy-washy sometimes."

"Like I said…all with good reason."

"Yeah, yeah." He slides into the black Nike running shoes in the corner next, and I bite a grin. I love when we tease and bicker. Doing it with him feels natural, like we're supposed to do it. "All right then." He's at the door, towering over me. "Let's grab the princess somethin' to eat."

"Princess?" I giggle, watching him close the door behind him.

"Yeah, 'cause that's what you're actin' like. A damn princess, demandin' food and toyin' with my emotions like that."

I bust out laughing, bumping into his arm. He lightly bumps me back before we reach the elevator.

The doors peel apart several seconds after he hits the button and the cart is empty. The doors seal shut, and Marcel is standing right beside me, his fingertips in his front pockets.

He looks down at me. "You and those damn dresses."

I look down at my pink dress with yellow polka dots. It reminds me of lemonade. "What's wrong with my dresses, sir?"

"They make me want to rip 'em off."

"Oh really?" I drawl, battling a grin. "Then why don't you?"

"Oh, trust me. I will. Just not right now." He scratches the tip of his nose, turning to face me. "But there is one thing I need to do." He brings his body directly in front of mine, caging me between his arms. His mouth crashes down on mine and he groans, dropping a hand to cup my hip, and burying his groin into mine.

The kiss is powerful and deep. Passionate and hungry.

I moan behind the kiss, reaching up to tangle my fingers in his hair. Another groan builds in his throat, both of his hands coming up to cradle my face.

He's wanted to do this since I walked into the room, and I can't blame him, because I wanted the same thing, despite how nervous I was.

This fire.

This forbidden power.

The ache that only he can create and take away.

When the elevator comes to a stop and then chimes, Marcel has to force himself to pull away and stand beside me again. He reaches down to grab my hand with a grin, lips swollen and pink.

"Damn girl," he breathes, running a hand through his hair with his free hand. "Made me lose myself there for a second." He has this wide smile on his face, and I can't stand how sexy it is on him. The doors open and he leads the way out of the elevator, still holding my hand, and I blush from his words, avoiding eye contact with the people who have been waiting for the elevator to come down.

They probably see my face and know we were fucking around in there. He's insane! That's something Kyle never would have done, especially not on an elevator. Too much of a risk, and it breaks all of his polite, well-mannered rules, but Marcel? He doesn't give a damn about breaking rules. That was clear to me from the moment I met him.

I swear he's going to kill me by the time this trip is over. I just hope he does it softly.

THIRTY-NINE

MARCEL

WE CATCH lunch at a restaurant that supposedly sells the best piña coladas around. Gabby found it on an app on her phone and the rating was decent, so I drove there.

Gabby has had two piña coladas so far. She sips from her blue straw before diving into the sweet potato fries she ordered.

"That's all you're gonna eat?" I ask, pointing at her meal of salad and sweet potato fries with one of my *real* fries.

"Yes. Why?" she asks, meeting my eyes.

"That's fuckin' rabbit food," I laugh.

"Not! It's healthy, unlike your greasy burger and fries over there!" She gives me a smug smile, popping another orange fry into her mouth. "So, if I'm going to be spending the whole weekend with you, I'd like some facts. Tell me about you, Mr. Ward."

"Not much to know about me."

"I'm sure there's plenty." She takes another sip of her drink. Goddamn her lips. Pouty. Pink. Full. I'm wondering what they'll be like wrapped around my dick—anxious to find out, honestly. There's no doubt I'll find out tonight.

"What do you wanna know?" I place my elbows on the table, putting one hand on top of the other.

"You already told me where you're from. I don't know much about your love life, other than the fact that you haven't been in a relationship for longer than a month."

"I'm single—have been for a couple years now. Why are you always so curious about my love life?"

"I'm just wondering! It just seems like there would be some woman around."

"Well, there isn't. And that's the truth."

"Mm-hmm. And are you happy with that?"

"Yep."

She narrows her eyes. "I don't believe that."

"Why not?"

"Because you're here with me. You're obviously lonely if you booked a villa just so you could be with a married woman."

"It's lonely sometimes, but workin' makes up for that."

"Well what about family? Do they visit you?"

I lower my gaze to her plate. "No. Don't have much family that can visit."

"No siblings?"

"I had a sister." I don't know why I say it so blatantly. I don't like talking about Shayla with anyone.

She stops chewing, looking at me carefully. "Had?"

"Yeah, had. She passed about eight years ago."

"Oh my God. I'm so sorry, Marcel. I didn't mean to—"

I wave a dismissive hand. "It happened, and I've grieved. All there is to it."

She swallows the bite of salad in her mouth, still staring at me. I can tell she wants to ask me a thousand questions—I see them in her eyes—but I'm glad she doesn't. She changes the subject instead.

"Well, let's not get into family today. What made you want to get into landscape designing?"

I shrug. "I don't know. I've always been good with my hands. Good at buildin' and creatin' things. A few months after my sister passed, I enrolled in a community college, got my degree in landscape design, and started up the business. I got lucky one day. The governor reached out to me and said he needed his yard repaired after a bad storm hit. I told him I'd do it at a discounted rate. I guess I did a good job, because he recommended me to everyone he knew afterward."

"That's so good!"

"You could say say that."

"Are you really thinking about stopping residential work?"

"Not completely, but I'll most likely take less jobs when it comes to residential. More money in commercial, plus it's way less complicated. My residential clients can be a pain in the ass…including the client sittin' across from me."

She giggles and throws a fry at me. "Ha! Shut up!"

"Now tell me about you." I lean forward, smirking.

She's still laughing as she asks, "What about me, exactly?"

"What college you graduated from, favorite color —whatever."

"Okay…um, I graduated from Colgate University—it's a college in New York. And I have two favorite colors, pink and yellow."

"Colgate. Interestin'. I'm honestly curious how Kyle even met you. You're only twenty-five. Seems like you got married straight outta college, but he's older, right? How'd that happen?"

"I told you, he used to come to a restaurant I worked at a lot."

"Was it near the campus?"

"About a ten-minute walk from school."

"Where there was probably nothing but college students around. That's not weird at all, a grown man going to a place where college students hang out."

"He used to have meetings up the street from the café I worked at," she says defensively.

"Hey, I'm just sayin'. You wouldn't have caught me in an environment like that."

"Here you go, being a dick," she mutters with an eye roll.

"I'm not bein' a dick. I'm just sayin' that shit sounds sketchy from his end. Fuckin' predator," I laugh, and she rolls her eyes again, sitting back against her chair and folding her arms. "Come on, I'm teasin' you." I can't help laughing though.

She huffs, picking up her drink and sipping from the straw until she's finished the piña colada. The waiter comes to our table with the bill, and I pull out some cash and enough for a tip, leaving it on the center of the table.

"You're gonna be with me for the next three days, little thing." I stand with a grunt, extending my arm and offering my hand. "Might as well get used to the hell I give you."

She looks at my hand, then sucks her teeth, but accepts it. I pull her out of her chair, gripping her hand and leading the way out of the restaurant.

It's close to six in the evening. The sun is setting, and I hear Gabby sigh beside me. As we walk to my truck, she asks, "It doesn't feel weird being with me? Holding a married woman's hand?"

"Nope, and I wish you'd stop bringing up the fact that you're married. It's gettin' old, and it isn't like I don't already know that." I open the passenger door and she climbs inside. She's staring at me as I close her door.

"Why doesn't that bother you?" she asks when I get into the truck and buckle in.

"I've already told you," I say as I turn the ignition. "I don't think of you as his. When you're around me, you're mine." Our eyes connect and hers become misty. She runs her tongue over her lips before sitting back in the seat. "Buckle up."

I take off, rolling the sunroof back. Gabby's curly hair flies all over the place, but she tucks most of it behind her ears, then rolls her window down, letting more air in. She rests the back of her head against the headrest, smiling faintly.

I smile each time I steal a glance of her. My satellite radio plays a song by some singer named Billie Eilish—the name it says on my radio screen, anyway—and she starts tapping her fingers to the beat of it.

I don't know if it's just me, but I don't think she realizes just how beautiful she really is. Her olive eyes sparkle from the sunset rays, her skin a dewy caramel due to the glow. She's gotten a tan recently. It's a surprise I don't wreck from trying to look at her so much.

When we're back at the villa, we head up the elevator and to the room, but as soon as we're inside and I see that same sunset painting the whole room orange, something comes over me. I can't even help the feeling, nor can I fight it. As soon as her bag is down, I'm right in front of her, holding her face, kissing her feverishly.

She moans in surprise, but her arms tangle around the back of my neck and her body is flush to mine. I bump her forward and she stumbles backward, but I hold onto her until the back of her legs hit the couch and she drops down.

I'm on top of her in a millisecond, pushing the lower half of my body between her thighs. She looks up at me beneath hooded eyelids, the sun on her skin again, just like a fucking angel. I can't help the grind that takes over me, building both of us up. She's panting beneath me, grabbing for the hem of my shirt. I lift up so she can pull it over my head.

"You have such a nice body," she murmurs.

"Appreciate that," I murmur, then go back to kissing her. Her hands are all over my back, reeling me close. She sucks on my bottom lip, and I swear my cock is about to rip right through my jeans—I'm that fucking hard.

"Damn," I groan. But I can't say more. Every part of me is lit on fire, including the organ in my chest, but I ignore the emotions coursing through me. I consider it lust and nothing more.

I push her dress up, and she leans forward so I can take it off. Her panties and bra match—red lace.

"Undo my pants."

She sits up as I rest my knees on the edge of the couch. Her face directly in front of the bulge between my thighs. She unbuttons my jeans, biting into her bottom lip. When she's done, she looks up at me while pushing them down. I stand to step out of them, then I'm between her legs on the couch again, perched on my knees. She's staring now, not blinking.

"I've been thinkin' about what your lips would look like around my cock for so long. I'm sick of waitin'." I push my boxers down, letting my cock fall out. Her breath hitches as she studies me—all of me. "Come here," I command softly, pressing a hand to the back of her head and bringing her face forward.

She leans forward willingly, scooting across the couch to get closer.

"I need to see you with my cock in your mouth, Gabby."

"Kay," she breathes, and I feel her breath run over the throbbing head of my dick. Her tongue runs over her lips, then she licks the tip, making me throb even harder. She takes note of my reaction and does it again.

"Fuck," I groan. She runs her tongue along the head of my dick then brings it into her mouth, sucking lightly on it. "Oh shit." My hand is still palming the back of her head. "That's not enough." I push my hips forward and bring her mouth further around my cock. I'm being greedy, but I'm too eager to give a fuck. When her mouth is more than halfway around me and she looks up with big, gorgeous green eyes, I sigh, pulsing in her mouth. She takes me in inch by inch, holding my gaze. When I'm fully down her throat, I don't even know what the fuck to do with myself.

"Oh, fuck. Yeah. That's good." I stroke her hair back. "You look so goddamn beautiful with my cock in your mouth." She moans around me, sending a vibration down the insides of my thighs. My finger caresses her cheek, then runs over her hair again. I grab a fistful of her hair, groaning as I pull her head away. The absence fucking kills me.

"Have you ever had your mouth fucked before?" My voice is raw, gruff.

"No," she replies.

"Do you think you'd enjoy it?"

"I don't know. But I'm willing to try."

I smile down at her, stroking her chin with my other hand. "Good 'cause I really want to fuck your mouth right now." The hand with a fistful of her hair brings her head forward again, slowly. Carefully. What can I say? I love the torture.

She gags when the head of my cock is touching the back of her throat. I pull her back, and she sucks in a breath. "Apparently, you've gagged before, though. You know exactly what to do."

She smirks.

"Open up," I growl, and she does, taking my soaked, solid cock back into her mouth again. This time, I don't hold back. I can't, for the life of me. I keep her hair fisted in my hand and thrust forward, hitting the back of her throat repeatedly. She gags again, pressing her palms to my thighs, a weak attempt to try and pull back. I pull back, she sucks in a breath, and then I do it again. "Fuck, that feels good," I groan. Her eyes are on mine again, watery and wide, but she's taking it like a pro.

Gripping both sides of her head, I stroke into her mouth over and over again. Her wet tongue is soaking my dick up. She gasps with each stroke, but I don't stop. I'm so close, and as if she senses it, she drops her arms, letting me take full control. Tears are running down the sides of her face, but they're beautiful, exciting tears—tears that were created because she decided to try this with me.

It's her first time, and I want to leave my mark. I groan louder, slowing my thrusts, keeping her head in my hands.

"Oh, fuck. I'm about to cum." I can't keep my eyes open any longer. I toss my head back and slam my hips forward, making sure I'm fully in her mouth. She moans loudly, making a choking noise that I love, and I finally let go, my cock throbbing as hot cum pours down her throat.

"Oh, fuck, Gabby. Goddamn, baby, that's good."

She groans, but damn, she swallows it all, not letting a drop go to waste. I lower my head again, releasing hers, and she pulls back, licking a ring around the head of my cock before moving away completely.

"I can't believe I liked that so much," she says with a laugh, wiping her mouth with the back of her arm.

"I can't believe you swallowed my shit."

She blushes and looks away. She starts to draw her legs to her chest, but I shake my head.

"What the hell do you think you're doin'?"

"Nothing—you're satisfied."

"But you're not."

"It's fine. I can wait until you're ready again."

I frown. "Get the fuck out of here with that."

She frowns up at me in return, then yelps as I pick her

347

up off the couch and carry her to the bedroom. I toss her on the bed, not even hesitating to take her panties off.

"Marcel—"

She doesn't even know what to say, and I don't wait for her to try and summon the right words. I bring her to the edge of the bed and lower to my knees, tilting her hips up and studying her freshly shaved pussy. "Shaved for me?" I look up to meet her eyes.

She's breathing raggedly. "I got a wax a few days ago. Lasts longer."

"Mmm." I kiss the valley that leads to her pussy and her legs shake. "Your husband seriously has no idea what he's missing out on by not eating your pussy," I grumble, and then I seal my mouth on her pussy, assaulting her clit with my tongue. I dig down with my hands, cupping her ass, and she screams—literally fucking *screams*—as I eat her pussy like it's my dessert.

"Oh—God! Marcel, wait!" she cries, thighs already shaking. She's not pushing me away though. Her hands are in my hair, clutching tight. I don't even think she realizes she's pulling me in deeper, not pushing me away, so I keep going, lapping up the sweet taste of her pussy with my tongue.

Her reactions are beautiful, her moans music to my ears. She looks down at me, and I challenge her stare. She realizes the challenge and keeps watching me. I flatten my tongue and tighten my grip on her ass. She's spread wide open for me, tasting like dessert.

With her lips parted, she's moaning louder and louder. This is a challenge. She's trying not to come too soon, but I'm pure savage, eating viciously until she finally caves, tosses her head back, and thrusts her pussy closer to my face. I bury my tongue into it, and she cries out again. She moans my name next, gripping my hair even tighter.

Watching her come has to be the most beautiful sight I've ever seen. The way she sings my name, the way her belly tightens and her nipples bud beneath her bra. I should have taken it off so I could see them, but I have time.

When her body dies down, I drop her legs and stand between them. She falls onto her back, staring up at the ceiling. My cock is hard all over again.

"I would fuck you right now, but I've got three days with you. I don't want it all to happen so quickly." I plant my palms on the bed, outside her head. Lowering my face, I drop a kiss on her mouth, and she whimpers like she wants more. "Taste that? That's you. Sweet." Another kiss. "Delicious."

She's smiling, head shaking. "You are so not like any man I've ever met."

I chuckle, locking eyes with her. "I'll take that as a compliment, Miss Gabby."

FORTY

GABBY

I KNOW I may seem like a bad wife. Honestly, I know for sure that I am. I shouldn't be sitting between another man's legs on a pool chair, laughing about how he's afraid of cats because one scratched him really bad when he was eight, and now he has a scar on his wrist for life as a reminder.

I shouldn't be this happy to have his body near mine while wearing a bathing suit I snuck out to buy the day after the housewarming, just for this trip with him.

Truth is, I'm not a great wife. My husband is away, working so he can provide for me, and I'm here. The worst part of it is that I thought I wouldn't be able to shake that feeling, but the longer I'm around Marcel, the more I almost *forget* about Kyle. What kind of wife thinks this way? What kind of wife forgets that she's *married*, even if it's only for an hour or two? I think I'm losing my mind, losing touch with reality, and this other man is doing it to me.

I watch him in the pool as I lay on a floaty, sunglasses covering my eyes. He's remarkable. A breath of fresh air. He's a serious person, yet he knows when to let go and not to take everything so seriously. Kyle isn't like that. He takes everything seriously.

I watch Marcel get out of the pool, and water drips down the sharp cuts and creases of his body. He's a work of art, and I don't even think he realizes it. I sigh as he dries off with a towel, then I swim to the steps to get out.

I grab a towel, drying off too.

"You're quiet," he murmurs.

I shrug it off. I don't want to talk about it.

As if he knows that I don't, he tosses his towel on the chair. "Let's head back up."

"Sure." I smile as I take his hand, grab my bag, and we go inside. When we're back in our villa, he goes to the fridge and takes out a beer. "I'm going to hit the shower," I tell him.

He nods and I go before he can sense my crumbling mood. I don't want to ruin this trip for him. He's having a great time. I go for my bag and take out a blue maxi dress, then head for the bathroom to start up the shower. As I strip out of my damp top and bottoms, the door creaks open behind me.

"Mind if I join?"

I glance over my shoulder, and Marcel's eyes fall to my waist and hips, then down to my legs.

"I was hoping you would."

He comes in, shutting the door behind him. I go to the shower, pulling the glass door open by the silver handle and stepping beneath the stream. The water is warm and feels so good.

I stand under the shower, rinsing the chlorine out of my hair. The shower door opens again, and Marcel steps inside, looking down at me. My breath catches in my lungs when our eyes connect.

Smashing my lips together, I move aside so he can get under the water too. He rinses the chlorine away, the water making his hair darker, slicker. He then takes a step forward, peering down at me through wet lashes. He lowers his eyes even more and reaches for my left hand. He holds it up, then uses his thumb and forefinger to pull my wedding band and engagement ring off my ring finger.

"Marcel—"

"You're mine right now," he reminds me.

I sigh. This is the first time I've ever taken my rings off. I don't even take them off when I paint or sculpt. Weird, I know, but I love my rings. I don't argue as he places the rings on the soap holder. He puts his focus on me again, and no words are spoken as he holds me by the waist, and then picks me up to press my back against the wall. I wrap my legs around his waist, and he sighs, kissing the bend of my neck.

"Fuck. Him," Marcel growls, and I sigh again, squeezing my eyes shut. I feel him straining against me. One stroke and he'll be inside me. "You're here with me."

"I know."

"So, fuck him. I only have these three days with you. He gets you for the rest of his life." He kisses my neck again, then drags his lips up to my cheek. "Would you leave him for me?"

"Marcel…don't. I don't want to talk about that."

"You'll have to answer it eventually." He cups my ass in his hands. "I'll worry about that later, though. For now, I need to be inside you." He tightens his grip on me and thrusts upward, thrusting right into me.

I let out a shrill yelp as he unleashes a deep groan. "Fuck," he rumbles. I open my eyes and he places his mouth on mine. He kisses me hard, building up his thrusts. Each one brings me closer and closer to a climax I didn't even realize was within reach.

Picking me up off the wall, he lifts me up and down along the length of him. I have no idea why I love this position so much. The way he holds me always gets me going. It's primal and fierce. I feel protected and empowered all the same.

Water runs over the back of his head, some of it splashing on my face. I drop my head to plant my lips on his, coaxing a deep, guttural groan out of him. He doesn't stop lifting me up and down the length of him, and with each drop, I feel him growing harder. He's going to come soon.

I tighten my pussy around his cock, and he groans again. "Fuck, Gabby," he breathes when our lips part. "Your fuckin' pussy. It's everything."

I hold on tight to him, my arms locked around the back of his neck and my legs still snaked around his waist. His strong arms bring me up, then drop me back down. His cock fills me every single time.

He sucks on my neck, the skin above my collarbone, and then my bottom lip, like he can't get enough of me—will *never* get enough.

I moan as he lowers me again, completely burying himself inside me. He throbs hard, groaning heavily, and I can't help what comes next. I squeeze him tight, coming all over him.

"Oh my God," I breathe.

He presses my back to the wall, and I drop my legs, but he keeps me hoisted up, thrusting three more times. His mouth is on mine, both our lips parted. Pleasure takes over every single one of his features, his blue eyes turning into liquid as he finishes inside me with one more powerful stroke.

"Goddamn," he groans, dropping his forehead on my shoulder. He twitches when I clench around him. "Shit, don't do that, or you'll make me cum again."

I laugh softly, and he drops my legs so I can stand, but he doesn't move away. He cups my face in his hands—something he does that always makes me melt—and kisses me wholly. His tongue parts my lips to play with mine. I moan as he pulls back, sucking my bottom lip into his mouth, before giving me one more all-consuming kiss.

He is so perfect—everything I've always wanted in a man.

Too bad he can never be mine.

FORTY-ONE

GABBY

I HAVE no idea when I fall asleep. We had several shots of tequila (our favorite drink when we're around each other, apparently) at the bar downstairs after catching dinner.

Marcel had to carry me to the room by the end of the night because I'd had one too many. I'm not a big drinker of hard liquor, so whenever I do drink it, it always hits me hard. He, on the other hand, drinks it like a pro.

When I wake up, sunlight is spilling through the curtains. I look up and see the cream upholstered headboard above me, pinned with silver beads. Then I look over, taking in the view of Marcel.

He's still asleep, resting on his back. I roll over to watch him. He's adorable, with lashes feathered across his cheekbones. There are very faint freckles on his face, mostly above his cheekbones and lightly sprinkled on his nose. They seem like the kind of freckles that come out when he's been in the sun for a bit too long.

I run a hand over his chest, which isn't completely hairless, but not too hairy either, then slide my palm over his firm stomach. He groans and moves his head, but I continue down, not sure what's gotten a hold of me. I swear I'm a different woman around Marcel. I want to do *everything* with him.

I'm below his pelvis, running my palm over the ridge of his hard cock, which is rock solid. I push his boxers down a bit, taking his hot erection in my hand. He groans in his sleep, moving his head again. I start to stroke him slowly, and his breathing becomes quicker, heavier. He's harder than ever before, and I get way too excited about it. I stop, expecting him to wake up. He doesn't, so I move down, my face hovering over the head of his cock. I pull the boxers down some more, then run my tongue along his balls. That's what pulls him out of slumber.

"Oh, shit, Gabby. What are you—"

He looks down, but I shush him, planting a hand on his chest when he's about to sit up. He cooperates, but frowns down at me like this is the last thing he was expecting. I'm glad I can surprise him. I run the tip of my tongue up the length of his cock and he shudders. "Fuck, Gabby. You serious?"

"Why wouldn't I be?" I do it again. He grips the sheets, as I kneel over, taking the head of his cock into my mouth.

He curses beneath his breath as I slide my tongue back down again. His fingers snake in my hair, but I keep licking him. Only licking him. I make sure not to suck too much. I want to get him so worked up he can't stand it. He's still so hard, and I grip him in hand again. He throbs in my palm as I lick him all over for several more seconds. He applies pressure to the hand in my hair when I roll my tongue over the tip of his cock, but I resist. He wants me to take him all in. He's *dying* for it. Stiff as hell and impatient now.

"Gabby," he grunts. "I'm hard as fuck. Stop teasin'."

I smile behind his thickness, sucking on his head once more, tasting a dribble of pre-cum. Then I climb up the bed just as he sits up, and push him against the headboard.

"What should I do now?" I ask with a sultry voice. My knees are outside his thighs. I'm barely straddling him, but I'm close enough that all it would take is one word and my pussy would swallow him whole.

He knows I'm challenging him. There's a dip in his brow, and without any warning or hesitation, he grips my waist on either side with his hands, and drops me down, burying his hard cock completely inside me.

"Oh, fuck!" I moan way too loudly, and he puts on an arrogant smile, cocking a brow as he keeps me in place.

"Ride my dick," he demands, and I grip the top of the headboard, sighing as I begin riding him. In this position, he feels massive. With every grind, twist, and circle of my hips, I can feel him so deep inside me that it tips me right over the edge.

I don't know what it is about this moment. It could be the way the sun is hitting us, shining a light on every single one of our actions. Or maybe it's the way he's staring up at me as I work my pussy around his cock. He watches me with fiery, hungry eyes. I grip the top of the headboard even tighter, then get into a squat. I slide up and down the length of him, moaning each time he fills me up.

"Oh, fuck." That gets him going for sure. "Your pussy is grippin' the hell out of my dick, baby. Don't stop." And I don't. I keep going up and down, up and down, driving him crazy.

He holds my waist, keeping me steady. His eyes flicker back up to mine very briefly before focusing on where our bodies are connected again.

Up and down.

Up and down.

He's different from Kyle.

Kyle likes keeping control in the bedroom, but Marcel stays put, letting me do the work. He's not afraid to hand over control—to let me do things my way—and I like that about him. I like it a lot.

I'm panting now because I can't take it anymore either. Marcel thrusts upward as I pull up and I gasp as he wraps both arms around me and pulls me down so that my chest is flush to his. We move in unison, our lips connecting. The sound of skin slapping and deep grunts are all I hear as I ride him faster. Faster.

And before I know it, he's calling out my name. Literally yelling it as he comes. "Shit, Gabby!" I've never heard him get so loud, but I love it. I love it so much because I made him do that.

He holds me down, twitching, sighing, and pulsing as he comes. He curses again, and I whimper when he pulls out. He holds me close though, looking up into my eyes. Using a hand to push my hair back, he studies my face. "You're fuckin' amazing. You know that?"

I blush. I can't help it. I just rode him like I had no common decency. I was that hungry for him. "You're not so bad yourself."

He brings his mouth forward to kiss me, and just as he does, he flips me onto my back. I yelp as he leans over me, using a knee to spread my legs apart.

"What are you doing?" I ask through a ragged breath.

He doesn't respond. Instead he brings a hand down, trailing it across my thigh. His fingers spread the lips of my pussy apart, and he uses the pad of one of his fingers to massage my clit. I tremble as he looks me right in the eyes. The sun is shining brighter, making his eyes appear more intense.

Lowering his head, he kisses me again, this time ever-so-deeply. I sigh and groan as he continues massaging my clit. He pauses for a moment, his lips still on mine, then his finger is back on my clit again, but two fingers are inside me now. He's still using his hand to create magic, working me up.

My legs are shaking now, but I lean up to cup his face and kiss him harder. Heat sweeps through my body, blood rushing between my legs.

I feel Marcel getting hard again, his erection on my thigh. "Your turn," he mumbles, and then pulls his hand away. He's between my legs and inside me in no time, and my back arches as he fills me with his hard cock. He reaches down, holding the back of my neck, forcing me to look at him.

"You love me being inside you." It's a statement, far from a question, and one he already knows is the truth.

He's stroking torturously slow, but I'm so close and it feels so good. "Please," I beg.

"Please what?"

"I'm close," I tell him.

"I know you are."

He pulls his hand away and sits up higher between my legs. Gripping my ass and tilting my hips up, he uses my pussy to grind along his dick. Like I'm his own personal fuck-toy, he drops my hips then brings them back up, swelling inside me. He does it over and over again, and it drives me crazy. My back isn't on the bed, just the back of my head. I can't see him, but I feel *everything*, and he keeps going, groaning and sighing while clutching my ass in his hands.

"I feel you getting tighter," he rasps. "You're about to come all over my dick, baby. Go ahead. Give it to me. I'm ready to feel how wet your pussy can get."

His words? Orgasmic. His voice is deep, still thick with sleep, but he sounds so good, and he feels like nothing I've ever felt before. He grinds my pussy all over his dick, thrusting as he holds me hostage.

And then it comes.

I come.

I cry out like never before, and Marcel's voice thickens as he tells me how beautiful I am. I can hear him straining, slowing his thrusts. He stills and then falls forward, and I'm crushed beneath the weight of his strong body. His cheek is on mine as he pants heavily.

"You are too much for words," he says in my ear. "I don't know how I'm goin' to let you go."

I stroke his hair, but I don't respond. I can't. I don't want him to have any hopes that this can continue, because it can't. He has me for these three days, and that's it.

Even though it was never discussed, he knew that's how it would be once this was over.

It was a silent agreement we'd made when I arrived, and the mere thought of it depresses me.

I'm surprised Marcel makes breakfast for me. Blueberry pancakes and scrambled eggs to be exact.

"When did you even have time to go shopping?" I ask, popping a blueberry into my mouth.

"Went last night after you passed out."

"It was so late, though!" I exclaim. I can't believe he did that. "I can't believe I got that drunk. Did we do anything?"

"No, we didn't do anything," he chuckles. "And it was worth goin' out for. I wanted to make you somethin'." He smiles at me, flipping the final pancake. "Go sit. I'll bring you a plate."

I bite a smile, walking out of the kitchen and sitting at the table where my phone is. I check it, and there's a text from Teagan.

T: Did you bite the bullet??

Me: Yes...does that make me a bad person?

T: We're all bad people. Enjoy it while it lasts.

I sigh, shutting the screen off and sliding the phone to

the middle of the table as Marcel makes his way to me with a plate in hand, a bottle of maple syrup in the other. He places it all down in front of me on the table, and I grin up at him.

"Thanks, *chef*."

He smirks. "Don't hate on my cookin'."

"I'm not. I think it's cool that you like to cook."

He's back in the kitchen as I pour syrup on my pancakes. "Shithead doesn't cook for you?"

"No. He didn't need to. His family had a personal chef for him."

"Wow. Spoiled prick. No wonder he's such an asshole."

I shake my head, cutting my pancakes in triangles and ignoring his remark. "How did you start cooking?"

"My mom. She used to let me help her."

"Aww, that's nice."

He's quiet a moment. I take a bite of pancake. "She died when I was twenty-one." He doesn't look back. I'm not surprised. He doesn't like talking about his family for some reason. If both his mom and sister have died, though...that couldn't have been easy on him. I wonder what happened to his dad, but I don't want to ask. At least, not right now.

Marcel sits across from me at the table and digs right into his food. As I take a bite of my bacon, my phone rings and I freeze as my eyes shift over. Marcel looks too, and his frown doesn't go unnoticed.

I reach for the phone, looking over the set image of me and Kyle as the caller ID. The same image where Kyle is holding me from behind while we take a picture in our new bathroom.

Shit. I should have put my phone on Do Not Disturb

mode. I ignore the call, sending it straight to voicemail, then I go back to eating. Marcel never stopped, but I can tell he's pissed. That frown hasn't left his face, and his jaw is clenching.

He finishes his food much faster than anticipated, then pushes out of his chair, carrying his empty plate to the sink.

"We should go to the beach today," I suggest, hoping to warm him back up.

He doesn't buy into it. He rinses off his dish, then pulls his cell phone out. I don't know what he's doing but I think he's only scrolling through it so he doesn't have to look at me.

When I finish my food, I take my plate to the sink, walking past him. He slides away, sighing as he tucks his phone in his pocket again. I hate the silence. He knew this would happen.

"Why are you so mad about a phone call?" I demand, and I'm really annoyed now.

"I'm not," he mutters.

"Clearly you are, Marcel. I'm sure you knew he would call eventually. He *is* my husband!"

He glares down at me, his upper lip twitching. I'm certain I've said the wrong thing because in an instant he's picking me up by the waist and placing my ass right down on the countertop.

He points a finger in my face, still staring at me. "Shove that into my face one more fuckin' time, Gabby, and I swear to God I'm goin' to lose my shit." He's seething, blind with rage. I think he's already lost his shit.

"It's true, Marcel! Why pretend it isn't the truth?"

"Because I don't like thinkin' about that shit! How do you not get that by now?"

I swallow thickly as he pulls his hand away, raking both hands through his full head of hair. "I can't stand the thought of you going back to him. I was thinkin' about it last night, after you passed out. Every time I did, it pissed me off more and more." He sweeps his eyes all over me, then brings his gaze back to my face. "I want you all to my fuckin' self, Gabby, but I know you'll never leave him. You could, but you won't. Not for someone like me."

My breathing falters as he moves closer. He brings me to the edge of the counter by the waist and starts to undo the tie of my satin pink robe. His hand moves down the lapel of the robe before peeling it open. It falls halfway down my arms, and he locks his eyes on my exposed breasts, sighing.

"I can't stand the thought of it," he mumbles, bringing his mouth to the curve of my neck.

"I know, but I can't just leave him," I moan, holding the back of his head.

"You can. You're just too afraid to."

"We've just met, Marcel. You and me." I sigh as he drops his head and sucks my nipple into his mouth.

"Don't give a fuck. Feels like I've known you for years."

A breath shudders out of me. I can't argue with him. He'll always have something to say to back himself up.

"I want you to myself," he mumbles again, and then reaches into his shorts to pull his cock out. An arm wraps around my waist and he brings me as close as he can to the edge of the counter, just enough so that I don't fall.

I moan as he pushes into me, no resistance and no hesitation. His mouth is on my cheek, his arm tightening around me. He's holding me so close, like he never wants to let go, all while his cock fills me up.

"You have me right now," I tell him through a moan.

"I don't just want right now. I want you *forever*." He thrusts harder. "I know how I make you feel. I know you'd never feel it with him, no matter how hard you tried to make it happen. I've already ruined you for him."

He's right. He's so right, but I can't admit to that.

Another thrust.

Another moan.

A deeper groan.

"You're everything I never knew I wanted." He shudders a breath, pressing his forehead to mine. Our eyes connect. "It's just my luck that the woman I really want is already taken by someone else."

His words are heartbreaking, but they only fuel his desire. I don't want to think about it anymore. I don't want to think about the fact that after I leave here, we won't be alone anymore, so I cup his face in my hands and kiss him, and as if my kiss is all he needs, he picks me up off the counter, slowly gliding my pussy up, and then back down his shaft. He does it repeatedly while our lips are still connected, hungry and primal.

He stiffens only seconds later, pulling his mouth away, and a breathy groan spills out of him. Rigidly, he lifts me up and down, filling me up all over again. Our favorite position. Primal and feral, like animals.

"You have me," I breathe when he pulls out and places me on the counter again. I'm still holding his face. Our foreheads are touching.

"But only for now," he mumbles. "It's bullshit."

I close my eyes. "Don't do this, Marcel. Please."

"Do what?"

"Make this harder for me. At least I came to you. I chose you over him right now."

"Is it only going to be *right now* that you choose me over him?"

"No, it won't be." *That's a lie.*

He pulls back, pressing his lips. Then he exhales, gripping my chin and pressing a kiss to my lips. "Let's go to the beach."

I nod, glad he's decided to let this go. "Okay. I'm gonna clean myself up really quick. Be right back."

He watches me go. I can feel his heavy gaze on my back. I head into the bathroom to clean up, then I look into the mirror. My eyes are red, burning with too much emotion, but I blink it all away and shake my head, leaving the guilt behind.

As we get dressed, he in his swimming trunks and me in the same purple bathing suit I bought, he talks about how he's going to be slammed with work after taking three days off, but that it'll be worth it because of me.

When we're dressed and have a bag packed, he wraps me up in his arms and plants a kiss on my forehead before we walk out of the villa. I can't help feeling an ache in my chest when he does it, knowing that these hugs and kisses are limited for him.

It hurts because I know that after this trip, I may not see Marcel again. I told myself I would give him these three days—give *myself* these three days—and be done for good. I'd go back to the regular life I lived and act like it never even happened. Put the cheating and lying behind me and bury it forever.

But the more I'm around him, the more I realize that my life may not ever be the same again.

I'm starting to fall for this man—a man I know I can't have.

FORTY-TWO

GABBY

WE SPEND an ample amount of time at the beach and it's exactly what I need. I love how the sun hits me, wrapping me up in its warmth after I step out of the cool, salty water.

What I love even more though, is watching Marcel go into the waves with his dark-blue swimming trunks on. Every time he walks back out, he pushes his slick hair back and hikes his pants up his waist just enough, but never too much to hide that delicious V below his abdomen.

I swear he's like a god, powering out of the water, showing off abs that I want to lick. Droplets of water sparkle on his body like tiny gems. He's so damn breathtaking that I literally hold my breath as he walks to his towel that's spread out beside mine.

"What are you thinkin' about?" he asks, dropping down beside me.

I smile way too hard. "Nothing," I lie.

He smirks, like he knows something I don't. "Saw you starin'. Like what you see?"

"Who wouldn't?" I laugh.

He grins before taking a big gulp from his water bottle.

"I keeping thinking about something..." I pause, debating whether I should get into the topic in mind.

"Go on..." Water is dripping from his wet hair, falling over his eyelashes.

"Well, it's about what you said earlier. About us only being together for these three days. After spending all this time with you, I keep wondering how I'm supposed to move on from the idea of you."

He thinks on that for a moment, then sighs, looking at the ocean. "I don't want you to move on from the idea of me. That was the whole point of this trip." He's joking but dead serious all the same.

"But why, Marcel? Wanting me only makes your life more complicated."

He chuckles at that, then shakes his head. "A friend of mine once told me that I'm attracted to things I know I can't have. Apparently, she thinks it gives me a thrill—being with someone I know I can't keep."

"She?" It's all I can hear. I don't even have the right to be jealous but I'm curious who this *she* is.

He looks at me full-on, then his eyes stretch wide. "You didn't hear a damn thing I just said, did you? All you heard was *she,* and you got those panties in a twist." He clearly finds this humorous because he tips his head back to bellow a laugh.

I tuck my damp hair behind my ears. "I'm just wondering."

He clears his throat. "A woman I used to hang out with. Her name was Lucy."

"Wow. Lucy? She sounds easy."

"She was. It was kind of a part of her job."

I frown then. "Her job? What are you talking about?"

"She was a paid escort."

I blink rapidly, stunned. I did not expect to hear that come out of his mouth. "So, you paid her to *fuck* you?"

"Somethin' like that." He says it so nonchalantly that I want to cringe. "It was a premium agency. Expensive. All of the women who work there are clean, and the clients, like me, are always tested to make sure we are, too."

"That sounds complicated and pricey. Why not just try and find a girlfriend instead?"

"Because girlfriends are ten times more complicated and even more expensive. At least with Lucy, I didn't have to buy her things to make her happy."

I roll my eyes, leaning back on my palms. "Well, I think Lucy is right. You like things you know you can't have. And I think deep down you like it because of something that happened in your past, maybe. Deep down you know people like me and Lucy won't stick around forever, which will only cause you to end up alone." I narrow my eyes at him, hoping that's enough to get him to open up.

"What can I say? I'm a lone wolf."

"Being lonely isn't always a good thing. What if you grow old and have no one to take care of you?"

"I'll check myself into a good retirement home. I could

make friends there, all of us showin' denture smiles while playin' bingo and eatin' sugar-free rice puddin'."

I bust out laughing. "You are ridiculous!"

He smirks, then sweeps his eyes all over me. "Come here." His face is serious now, eyes mellowing. I crawl his way and he reels me forward so I'm sitting on his lap. "You fit on top of me perfectly, you know that?"

I feel a blush creep up from my neck to my cheeks.

"When this little trip is over, will you stay in touch with me?" he asks.

I blink quickly when he airs his question. My expression alone is probably enough to reveal the truth. My jaw goes slack, and I lower my head, inhaling deeply before exhaling. "I don't know."

"You don't know?"

"No. I don't know."

"Would you want to see me again?"

I shrug.

"Look at me."

I slide my eyes up to his.

"Would you want to see me again?" he repeats.

I press my lips and lightly bob my head. "I know I will… and that's what's going to kill me."

"Why let it kill you? Why not just make a trip to see me again? No one would know but us."

"Because it's wrong, Marcel. I can't live with that guilt."

"Even if the man you're married to treats you like you're a fuckin' object?"

His face is even, but when he narrows his eyes, searching my face for answers, I can tell he's annoyed. I start to move off his lap. I'm not in the mood to be interrogated. He's been upset about my marital status ever since this morning. I knew he wasn't going to let it go that easily, but having the conversation here is upsetting.

He doesn't let me go, though. He holds tight, forcing me to stay in place. "Let me go, Marcel," I mutter.

"Fuck no. I never want to let you go."

I can't lie, my belly flutters from those words, but I remain strong. "You'll have to eventually, and you know it. I don't know why you keep trying to avoid the reality of our situation."

"Reality is torture, Gabby. Torture that I don't want to go through again."

I frown at his statement, forgetting about my fight. "What do you mean *again?*"

His head shakes, and his eyes fall for the first time. "Nothin'. It's nothin'."

We sit for a moment, breathing. I watch him carefully, but he avoids my eyes, looking over my shoulder at the water again. "What happened to you?" I ask softly, and his eyes finally swing up to mine. They're damp now, full of a pain I don't understand.

"You're deflectin'," he mumbles and then places me down beside him. He stands up and walks to the shore again.

I follow him. "No, you're deflecting, Marcel. Something happened to you, and I can tell you never talk about it."

"Nothin' happened to me."

I don't want to push too much. I want him to be comfortable telling me his truth—his past—but we can't do it out here. Sighing, I grab his hand and he looks down as I entwine our fingers. "Come on. Let's go back."

He nods in agreement, turning with me. We pick up our towels and I grab my bag, trudging through the warm sand to get back to the villas.

Once we're back in our room, I notice Marcel is still quiet. We shower together, but we don't have sex this time. He smiles as I brush by him with soap on my body, and even kisses me after washing his hair. He smirks when I rinse off, but he's so damn quiet that it's maddening. He's never been this quiet around me. I must have really struck a nerve.

He orders a pepperoni pizza for us, and we eat it while watching a movie on the couch. He still doesn't talk much. I ask him questions about what his favorite color is, which is blue, and what his favorite music is, to which he replies, "I can listen to a little bit of everything. Don't have many favorites."

Around midnight, I can barely keep my eyes open. The sun and beach completely drained me.

"Let's get you in the bed," he murmurs after watching me yawn. He's off the couch, and I follow after him. We curl up beneath the blankets after changing into pajamas. Marcel is on his back, and my head is on his chest. I listen to his heart beat steadily in one ear, the distant ocean sounds in the other.

"Please tell me what happened," I finally whisper. I can't take it anymore. He seems so…*sad* now.

"Nothin' happened, Gabby."

I sit up to look at him. "Yes, it did. You can tell me. I swear I would never judge you."

He's quiet again for several seconds, then he says, "I

know you wouldn't, but I've never talked about it with anyone."

"Well try to now. Maybe it'll make you feel better."

He glances down at me, and I think he's going to open up, but instead he shakes his head and pushes me away to sit up against the headboard. "This is our last night, and you want to know about somethin' that doesn't matter right now." He scoffs.

"Don't scoff at me. I know you're covering something up, and if it's bothering you so much, then clearly it matters to you all the time. I'm not letting it go until you tell me."

"Jesus Christ, Gabby!" He pushes out of bed and storms out of the bedroom. I waste no time climbing off the bed and chasing right after him.

"You know more about me than I do about you, Marcel!" He's standing in front of the patio door, running a hand through his hair. "You play this role of a good guy who acts like he doesn't have any worries, but there's always this cloud of sadness that surrounds you. It's like you will never be able to escape it and you know it." My voice breaks as I study his back. He refuses to look at me, and I hate being ignored so I rush across the living room, past the coffee table and sofa, to get to him. I grab his arm and twist him around, and though it requires me to use all my strength, I'm able to.

He's facing me, breathing hard through his nostrils like an angry bull. "Drop. It. Gabby." He's angry, the rage broiling in his eyes. Why is he so upset? What could possibly be so bad that it's made him this way?

"Please," I plead with him, then I push his arms away to wrap mine around his large torso. He freezes up, holding his arms out at his side. A breath shudders out of him and, finally, he closes me in his warm arms. I keep my cheek to his chest, holding him tight. I refuse to let go until he understands that I'm here for him. I want to know his truth. Hell, I want to know everything about him.

He's quiet for so long. I hear the ocean roaring outside the patio doors. It's a soothing sound. His body is no longer tense, breaths no longer ragged.

"I don't like talkin' about it," he mumbles.

"You can trust me," I whisper.

The ocean sounds swallow the silence again. My heart is beating rapidly. I'm so worried for him, afraid he'll do something crazy if he doesn't let it out.

"It was my fault," he says brokenly. "All of it."

"What was?" I pull back to look up at him. His eyes are wet and red now, like he's trying to fight tears but is losing the battle.

Silence again.

"Marcel," I beg, focused on his eyes. "You can trust me."

His Adam's apple bobs, and he finally lowers his gaze to look at me. We watch each other's eyes for just a moment, then he drops his hand to grab mine, leading the way back to the bedroom.

He's quiet as he lies back down and pats the spot beside him. I climb on the bed and rest my cheek on his chest again, sighing. Waiting.

"My sister died because of me," he mumbles after what feels like an eternity.

I don't move. I'm afraid that if I do, he'll think I'm judging him or ready to demand answers, so I remain perfectly still and meekly ask, "How?"

"She needed me to pick her up one night. She was in trouble—always gettin' in trouble. We got into an argument on the road, and I wasn't payin' attention. I lost control, and my truck veered off the road. Slammed right into a tree." He sucks in a sharp breath. His body is tense all over. I finally make a move by looking up at him, and his eyes are squeezed tight. I feel his fist clenching between us so I sit up to look at him. "There was...*blood* everywhere. I kept callin' her name, wantin' her to answer me. She never did. I was so mad at her when I picked her up, complaining about how she wasn't doing anything with her life and hangin' with the wrong people. If I could, I would take that whole argument back if it meant she could be here right now. She was all I had left, and now she's gone because of a mistake I made."

"Oh my God, Marcel. I am so, so sorry." I have no words. I wasn't expecting this truth at all. "I'm sure it was just an accident. You can't blame yourself for—"

"No, it wasn't a damn accident, Gabby! *I* was drivin'! I was supposed to take her home! I wasn't supposed to be yellin' at her about somethin' that didn't even fuckin' matter!"

His voice booms, and when his eyes open, I see the corners are filled with tears. Literal tears. *Oh my God*, I can't take it. My heart hurts over and over and over again for him. I feel my eyes getting prickly hot so I look away, before he can notice the tears and feel worse about himself.

"It was cold that night, and I didn't realize it then, but there was a lot of black ice on the road we were on. We were arguin' and she kept tellin' me she wanted out the car. I told her I should let her ass out and freeze to death. It was one of the last things I said to her, right to her face. Didn't even get the chance to tell her I loved her. She got on my nerves so damn much, but I loved my sister. Still love her." He swallows hard, still fighting the tears. "We became closer after our mom died, but she started hangin' out with the wrong crowd soon after. It annoyed me because I knew she was better than all of the shit she was putting herself through."

"Is that how you got this scar?" I ask, running my fingers along the raised scar below his left rib.

He nods, swiping at the tear that runs down his cheek. Another one falls, but before he can get to it, I'm reaching forward to wipe it away with the pad of my thumb. I climb on top of him, holding his face in both my hands. "Marcel, look at me."

But he doesn't. Of course, he doesn't. If I thought he was stubborn when he was just his regular self, his stubbornness is ten times worse when he's reliving grief.

I force his eyes on mine and he breathes raggedly. "That wasn't your fault. You didn't know it would happen."

"But it did, and I was behind the wheel. I was a few points shy of gettin' a DUI that night. It was my fuckin' fault."

I sigh, closing my eyes. "You can't blame yourself for that."

"She would have been better off walkin' home, not ridin' with me." His throat bobs as he swallows the pain. "When I lost Shayla, I lost myself. I had nobody else—no friends or family. We lost our mother to a car crash six years before that. She died instantly, and even though I had grieved, I found myself lucky to still have someone to protect and love. My father died when I was nine. Cancer ate him alive, and by the time he went to be diagnosed, it was too late. He had a lot of pride…it's probably where I get it from." He sucks in another breath. "I'm a fuckin' disease, Gabby. That's why I want things I know I can't have. Because I know they can't stay forever. If anyone else stays for too long, there's a fair chance I'll lose them sooner rather than later, and it's always fuckin' tragic. I know it. So, it's better to be prepared in advance, or better to keep a distance."

"So, you want whatever this is between us to be temporary?" I ask.

"No…but I know it has to be that way. I know you'll never leave him, and even if you did, I wouldn't deserve you."

I drop my eyes, pulling my hands away. "Your past is your past, Marcel. I can't blame or judge you for any of it. Whatever is meant to happen, happens. That's life. I mean, I can't imagine losing my brother, so I can only imagine what you must feel, but blaming yourself for it instead of forgiving it will only have you running in circles. You have to forgive yourself."

"I'm not ready to."

"It takes time, I'm sure."

He lets out a shaky breath, then hauls me forward. My face is between the crook his neck, my arms going around him as best as I can in this position.

"I've never told anyone what really happened to Shayla. I've been tryin' to run away from what I did…"

"Well you don't have to run anymore."

He pushes me back to look me in the eyes. His mouth is

close to mine, the tips of our noses touching. "I'm afraid you'll end up hurt too," he murmurs. "Because of me."

"I'll be fine."

"Maybe it's best you go back to him. Forget about me."

"I would never be able to forget about you."

He presses his lips together, and I move to the side, cuddling between his arm and the side of his body. Holding me close, he kisses my forehead twice, his warm breath running over the bare skin of my shoulder.

"If I tell you somethin', you promise not to freak out."

I look up at him, meeting mellow blue eyes. "Depends on what it is…"

"I know I'm not supposed to, but I think I'm fallin' for you."

My heart thumps in my chest. I don't have the words. I don't want him to feel this way—things will only be harder tomorrow—but the truth is I've fallen for him too. Hard and fast, without any restraints or limits.

I blink quickly, putting my head back on his shoulder.

"It's alright." He sighs. "I don't expect you to say anything. Just thought you should know."

He sounds defeated, and I feel an ache in my chest. Tomorrow will be our last day, and I'm not glad about it. I know I'll be back to reality soon, but reality will be a bore compared to this.

The two days I've spent with Marcel so far have been a dream. Even though my time spent with him is illicit, it feels so right. Deep down I'm glad I took the chance of coming here. Had I not, I would have regretted it and wondered about what could have happened here for years.

Time ticks on, and eventually we fall asleep. I'm sure I

fall asleep first. Marcel always stays up longer. He holds me all night, though, and I hold him just as tight, knowing he needs the comfort.

I want him to know he has someone he can trust. Even if things are never the same again, he can trust me. I would never tell a soul about his past, and he knows it.

I'm here for him, just like he's here for me.

FORTY-THREE

GABBY

WHEN I WAKE UP, Marcel is no longer in my arms.

I sit up, rubbing the sleep out of my eyes as I look toward the window, where the ocean is. The waves are gentle, sunlight slowly creeping over the horizon.

I rub his side of the bed, and it's cold. Panic sets in as I look at the corner where his duffle bag was last night. It's no longer there.

Scrambling to get out of bed, I rush out of the room in my gown. There's no sign of him in the kitchen. It's cleared out, no food or drinks on the counter. *Did he leave without saying goodbye?*

I already want to curse him out, but then I see his bag by the coffee table, and then I see *him*. He's sitting on a chair on the patio, focused on the ocean. I think he's watching the sun rise.

Relief swirls in my veins as I watch him for a moment,

and then sigh. His arms are on the arms of the cushioned chair, and he's at an angle, so I can see the left half of his face. Something seems to be bothering him.

I hear a buzzing in the room and go back to check my phone on the nightstand. It's a text from Kyle. I sigh as I read it.

Kyle: What's going on? You didn't answer yesterday. Feeling okay?

Me: I'm fine. I was napping when you called.

Kyle: Okay. See you soon

I shut the screen off, placing the phone back down.

"I'm a terrible person," I whisper to myself. My eyes shift over to the wedding band and cushion-cut diamond ring beside it. I pick my rings up, running the platinum bands between my fingers.

I have no idea what I'm doing, or what tomorrow brings. When I walk out of that door today, I don't know if I'll want Marcel more, or wish that I'd never met him.

I place the rings back down, and they clink as they hit the wood. As I leave the room, I rub my bare ring finger, a reminder that these are my last few hours with Marcel.

I walk back out of the room and go to the already open patio door. I'm swept up by a salty breeze as I walk out, the same breeze that's toying with Marcel's hair. He looks up at me, and whatever was bothering him before is quickly replaced with a smile.

"Hey." He greets me with a faint smile.

"Hey."

He pats a spot on his lap, and I walk over with a grin, curling up sideways on his lap. "Did I wake you?" he asks on the shell of my ear.

"No. I was worried for a second. I thought you'd left."

"Why would I leave?" He sounds truly curious, like that thought never even crossed his mind.

"Your side of the bed was cold, and I didn't see your bag."

"I was pickin' up some of my stuff I laid around. That's all." He kisses the side of my face.

"What are you out here thinking about?"

"You," he replies honestly.

I look up and study his shimmering blue eyes. The light from the sunrise reveals the darker flecks inside them. "What about me?"

"Hatin' that this will be our last mornin' together."

I drop my head, avoiding his eyes.

He grabs my legs, spreads them apart with ease, and positions me so that I'm straddling his lap. He then slides to the edge of the chair.

Running his palms up my thighs, he says, "I'm gonna ask you again…would you leave him for me?"

I shake my head. *Not this again.* "I'm not answering that."

"Fine. Stand up for me," he commands.

I stand and he reaches down to lower his shorts. Right after, he's going under my gown, sliding my panties down to my ankles. I step out of them willingly, and he grips my hips, bringing me back on top of his lap. I'm positioned right above his cock, and he slides me down, our mouths parting wider with every inch.

"It's our last day," he growls on my lips. "Since you won't answer it, *ride me* like you mean it."

And I do. I ride him in front of the sunrise, not giving a damn if anyone can see. He cups my ass, assisting me as I roll my hips forward and backward. His teeth nip at the bend of my neck as I breathe raggedly, and then he licks that same spot.

"Would you leave him for me?" he asks again, this time with a voice that's drenched with pleasure.

I sigh, holding him around the back of his neck, my fingers getting tangled in his bed hair. I kiss him to shut him up, and he kisses me back, but only briefly. In a flash, he's standing up, carrying me into the villa. My back lands on the couch, and he's on top of me, between my legs like he knows that's where he belongs, but he doesn't press fully inside me. He only gives me the tip, and I ache for more.

He yanks on the top of my gown, revealing my breasts. Sucking one of my tan nipples into his mouth, he groans around it, and I feel his cock twitch with the action.

He's close.

I'm close.

Fuck.

He snatches his mouth away from my nipple. "I won't make you come if you don't tell me the truth."

"Please," I beg. "I need it."

"Then tell me the truth. I wanna hear you say it."

He looks me over, eyes filled with hunger, lust, and something else that I can't quite figure out. In only a second, he's fully inside me again, and my back arches as I gasp, but he lifts me back up.

"Tell me," he commands. "Would you leave him for me? I have to know."

He buries himself completely, balls deep. "Marcel—I'm close. Please." I'm pleading with him.

"Would you leave him for me?"

"Ugh—yes! Yes, I would leave him for you!" We lock eyes, both of us breathing raggedly. "But I can't."

"Fuck that," he grumbles, and he hammers his hips, giving me exactly what I wanted. "You know you belong to me. *Fuck him.*"

He's angry-fucking me but I don't make him stop. It feels too good, and deep down maybe I deserve this angry-fuck. I led him on, made him want more. I caved this week, and had I not, maybe he would be better off. He would have gotten over me eventually, but no. I had to come here and make him fall even harder for me.

He fucks me until I come, screaming his name and dragging my nails over his forearms, and then he leans forward, stealing kisses from me, parting my lips with his tongue and sucking mine until he comes too.

"Damn, Gabby," he groans as he comes with his mouth on my neck. "It's too soon. You can't go. Stay with me."

His words...*oh, God.* They hurt me. They cut me deep. I hear the brokenness in his voice, how much he wants this to continue.

Tears creep to the corners of my eyes. He's still on top of me, trapping me beneath his weight. I try and push him off, and when he finally moves, I slide from beneath him to stand.

Angry tears have come out of nowhere, running down my cheeks. I'm *fuming*.

I hate the situation we're in.

I hate my temper.

I hate that he fell for *me*!

"You knew I would have to go back, Marcel!" I scream at him. "You knew this couldn't go on forever! You can't say shit like that to me and expect everything to be okay in the end!"

"Well it's fuckin' true, Gabby!" he barks back, pushing to a stand too. "I fuckin' want you! I want you more than the air I'm fuckin' breathin' right now! Sorry if that shit offends you, but I'm a fuckin' man, and I'm not about to lie to you or myself about how I feel! Life is too short for that shit!"

I shake my head, turning away from him. "This was a mistake." I rush to the bedroom and grab my bag, picking up loose pieces of my clothes off the floor and stuffing them inside it.

He's trailing right behind me. "A mistake?" he asks, like he can't believe I've just said that.

"Yes, it was a mistake! All of this! I never should have come here!"

"But you did, Gabby, and we fucked the whole time, and you loved it! You loved when I made you laugh! You loved when I put my hands all over you! You loved every fuckin' moment of it, so don't pretend this was a mistake!"

I'm blinded by tears, but I don't stop packing. I go to the bathroom to get my toothbrush and other toiletries, but after I stuff them in the bag, Marcel is right beside me, grabbing my arms before I can go anywhere else.

"Let me go!"

"No. Not until you calm the hell down!"

"Don't tell me to calm down!" I'm so frustrated, and he sees it, but he doesn't let me go. I try beating on his chest, but they're weak attempts. He doesn't flinch, just holds me tighter. "We can't be together! I'm married! You knew that when you met me!"

He doesn't say anything. Just stands there, letting me sound stupid, which pisses me off even more.

"Why did you have to come around, huh? My life was perfectly fine before you showed up!"

"*You* hired *me*, Gabby!"

"Yeah, but I didn't think you'd come in like *this*! I was happily married, living a great life!"

"That's bullshit, and you know it! You were miserable and lonely as hell! You married him for comfort and convenience, but there's no fuckin' passion with him! None! But for us? That shit seeps out of our pores and drips through the goddamn walls, Gabby. You burn for me, so much more than you ever would for that motherfucker, and you know it. You fucking know it." He reels me in to his chest, swallowing me with his arms. "Why stay? Why waste your time with him when that's not what you want?"

"I can't leave!"

He grips my shoulders and pushes me back to look me in the face. "Why the hell not? What does he have on you?"

"He doesn't have anything on me!"

"You act like you're afraid of him."

"I'm not afraid of him." I'm panicking all over again. I breathe rapidly, and when his grip grows limp, I snatch away and take out a dress from my bag. I pull off the nightgown and slide into the dress.

"What does he have on you, Gabby?" His voice is demanding. He's no longer trying to convince me to stay. He knows I'm hiding something now, but I'm not about to tell him.

"I don't know what you're talking about."

He grabs me again. I try and yank away, but he's twice my size and too damn strong. "You're wastin' your time with him."

"I'm leaving."

"Gabby—"

"Let me go, Marcel! I need to get back home!"

He blinks down at me. "If you call that a home, you really are delusional. You have more of a home in this villa than you do there."

I ignore him, picking up my rings and walking out of the bedroom with my bag. As I slide into my sandals hurriedly, stuffing the rings into the pocket of my dress, I say, "It was fun, but this is reality, so just deal with it." I hike my bag on top of my shoulder then pick up my tote and go to the door.

He chases after me with a hopeless frown. "You told me you'd leave him for me. When?"

I look into his misty eyes long and hard. I see the anguish. I'm hurting him. Not only that, but he's afraid to be alone again. After what I know about him and his past, I can't blame him for that. But I can't stay. I just...I can't.

I wish I could be selfish and give him everything, but this was wrong from the start. From the moment I hired him, and our eyes connected, I knew he would be trouble, but I let him stick around anyway.

"If my circumstances were different, and leaving was simple, I would leave him for you, Marcel, but unfortunately, they're not." Another tear skids down my cheek as I step toward him. I reach up to cup a hand around the back of his neck, bringing his head down to kiss his cheek. Then I kiss his lips, and he kisses me back, but this isn't like the other kisses that filled me with hope and pleasure.

This one fills me with nothing but dread, because I know that once our lips part and I walk out that door, I won't see him again. I can't. Kyle is...he would...*ugh*.

Our lips part, and I step back, pressing my lips before turning for the door. I grab the handle and open it, but before I go, I say, "You told me last night that you were falling for me." He stares at me, confused. Broken. All because of me. "Well, I've fallen for you too, Marcel. I really, really like you." I huff and shrug, blinded by tears now. "I wish things were different for us. I really do."

"Gabby," he calls again, reaching for my hand. I look down at his tan hand in mine. I love how masculine they are. They're not too rough, not too soft. I squeeze his hand. My eyes shift up to his again, and he sighs, defeated.

He knows this has to happen, whether we want it to or not. I can't stay here forever, and we've only just met. Yes, it seems like we've known each other for a lifetime, but that's not the reality of this situation. I've known Kyle for years, and Marcel for only three months. I'm glad he's not fighting me on it anymore.

"Take care of Callie," he murmurs.

"I will." I squeeze his hand again. He squeezes it back.

We linger.

Breathe.

More tears threaten to escape me. He steps forward to

cradle the back of my head, reeling me back in for another kiss.

Our final, *final* kiss.

This one brings way too many emotions out of me. There isn't just the sadness and hopelessness I felt before, but a fleeting spark of joy and relief.

He's a dream come true, Marcel. He's not perfect, but after spending these days with him, I realize how romantic he can be without even trying. How selfless he is, despite his rough background. He's exactly the kind of man who would have stolen my heart, and had I not met Kyle, I would have let him take it.

But had I not met Kyle, I never would have moved to Hilton Head. Never would have been in that house with a yard that Marcel landscaped. I never would have even met Marcel. I don't know if he's a life lesson, a stumbling block, or something much more...but I know we're not meant to last.

So, I finally pull away. Completely away.

"Take care of yourself, Marcel," I murmur, stepping back.

He doesn't say anything. With lips pink and swollen and eyes as wet and blue as the ocean behind him, he watches me go.

I would love for him to walk me to my car, but that will only make this situation harder. Right now, we must part ways...even if the act alone crushes both of us to pieces. But damn, walking away is one of the hardest things I've ever had to do in my life.

FORTY-FOUR

MARCEL

I saw my sister die right in front of my eyes, and that nearly destroyed me.

When the cops knocked on the door of my momma's house and told me my mother had died, I felt like I couldn't breathe.

When my mother told me my father was no longer with us, I didn't know how to take it, nor did I know how to handle seeing his frail body and bald head on his sick bed.

With Gabby going, there is that same grief, almost similar to when I lost my mother, sister, and even my father. I can't explain it, but it lingers, and I'm left wondering why I'm the one who has to deal with this kind of pain.

I constantly ask myself, *"whose sins am I paying for?"* Yes, I've done a lot of fucked up things, but deep down I know I'm a good man. I work hard. I'm respectful. I'm dedicated...

But you fell for a married woman.

Perhaps that's why I'm being punished.

Gabby is on the elevator now, and as she boards. I hope she'll look up to find me still watching by the door of the villa we shared.

She peers up beneath her damp eyelashes, but she doesn't smile. She just swipes the tears away and presses a button on the inside, and the doors close instantly.

She's gone, and my heartbeat shifts to a slower rhythm. I go back into the room, slamming the door behind me. I'm standing near the kitchen, staring at the porcelain figurines on the counter above the sink, my chest heaving as I breathe raggedly. The longer I stare at them, the angrier I get.

"Goddamn it!" I shout as I knock them down, sending pieces cascading across the floor. I grab one of the chairs at the dining table and shove it forward, nearly cracking the spine of it as it hits the wooden table.

They'll charge me for the damage. I don't give a fuck. I head for the bedroom and sit on the edge of the mattress, dropping my face in my palms, fighting whatever the fuck this is I feel for her.

I have no right to want her to stay. She's married, and she made a vow to another man, but damn how I wish that man was me.

As I pack, I can't get her out of my head.

Her smile.

Her giggle that's so damn cute it's contagious.

Her body and how perfectly she wraps around me.

Check-out is in an hour, but I decide to head out earlier. As I do one final sweep, and make sure to pick up the pieces of that damn figurine, I spot something shiny on the night-stand in the room. It's her wedding band.

As I hold it between my fingers, I start to think she left it on purpose, as a means for me to come see her again, but she wouldn't do that. She most likely didn't grab both when she went for them, as upset as she was.

I pick it up and tuck it into my pocket, then look around the room again. Nothing's left here. Without her, this place isn't the same.

When I'm inside my truck, driving home, the truth really sets in for me.

I swore I wouldn't let anything get to me—not her touch, her need, or her body. But it did. All of it did, and I'll never be able to let it go. I didn't just fall for Gabrielle Moore this weekend.

I *fell in love* with her, and that truth cracks me open, leaving me vulnerable and raw with nothing but need.

For the first time in my life, I've fallen in love—in love with a woman that I most likely wouldn't deserve, even if she weren't already taken.

How can any man survive knowing that sad truth?

That he fell in love with a woman he can't even have?

FORTY-FIVE

GABBY

My music is blasting on the drive home.

I'm doing whatever it takes *not* to think about Marcel, but even as Kings of Leon spill through my car speakers, there's no escaping the thought of him. He's been inside me, wrapped all around me. I can still smell his soap. It's like his hands have left invisible prints on my body, as well as his cock. Not even time will help me escape the reminder of him.

Months ago, I remember thinking something was missing in my life. Well, I no longer think it's some*thing*. It was some*one*. It was him all along.

"God," I groan, as a single tear slides down my cheek. I swipe it away as I pull into Venice Heights and park in front of Meredith's house first so I can pick Callie up.

On the way up, I dig into my pocket and notice that I only grabbed my engagement ring and not my wedding band. "Damn it!" I hiss before getting to Meredith's door. The last thing I want to see is the look on Marcel's face after he watched me walk away. I won't be able to bear that guilt, but I'll need my ring eventually, before Kyle notices that it's gone.

"Hey!" Meredith squeals when she sees me. Callie is right on her heels, and she starts yapping, rushing to my feet.

"Hey!" I chime, picking Callie up. "Was she good?"

"Oh, she was fine! You know I love having her!"

"Good!"

"Let me go grab her stuff for you." It takes no time for Meredith to return with Callie's things.

"Did you enjoy your getaway?" she asks, walking by my side to get to the car.

I nod and force a smile, putting Callie on the passenger seat and then closing the door. "I did. Thanks for asking." I help her put the stuff in my trunk and then close it.

"That's great. It's always good to have that me-time. You know, I was going to see if Kyle wanted Callie at the house with him since he was back, but then I remembered you saying he wasn't a fan of having her around, so I changed my mind." She laughs but my heart drops to my stomach.

What the hell did she just say? "W-what?"

She looks at me and is hesitant to respond this time. "Well, I saw Kyle was home, so I was thinking about asking if he'd wanted her with him. I saw him pulling into his driveway last night when I was giving Callie a walk...but I figured if he wanted her he would have come for her, right?" *No, he wouldn't have, because he has no idea I even left her with you!*

Oh my God. No. No, no, no! He can't be back already!

395

"Are you okay, honey?" She puts a hand on my shoulder, brows dipping with concern. "You don't look so well."

"I—I'm fine. Just didn't realize he'd be back so soon." I pat her hand and then walk around my car to open my door. "Thank you for watching her! Please let me know if there's anything I can do for you."

"Oh, it was my pleasure!" She waves and tells me she'll see me later, and I jump behind the wheel, putting the car in reverse and then turning into my driveway. Sure enough, Kyle's BMW is parked right out in the open, like it always is when he's home.

My heart is beating so hard I swear it's going to rip right out of my chest. With shaky hands, I push out of the car, trying to think of a million excuses I can tell him as to why I wasn't home last night—or even the nights before.

If he was home, what was with the text he sent this morning? If he's been home, why would he send that? Was he testing me? What if Meredith only saw him last night but he's been home for *days*?

Oh, God. I'm going to be sick.

As I take Callie out, she barks, looking ahead, toward our porch. I look with her and Kyle is standing in front of the door, head tilted, and one brow cocked.

"Hey!" I try to say with way too much enthusiasm and curiosity. "What are you doing here? I thought you weren't coming back until tomorrow night!"

"Conferences ended early." His tone is dry. Casual. I can't read it.

He looks me over with narrowed eyes. I ignore his scrutinizing gaze. He knows something, but I won't feed into it, so

I carry Callie up the stoop so we can get inside. He blocks the door.

"What are you doing?" I laugh nervously.

He looks down at me, his face tighter, a grimace in full form. Then he digs into his back pocket, holding up a business card. As he switches it between his fingers, I spot the name **Marcel Ward** in big, bold print. This time, I really do think my heart is going to jump out of my body somehow.

I can't think.

Can't move.

"Why do you have that card—"

"Shut the fuck up and get in the house, Gabby." When he speaks in my face, it's then that I smell the alcohol on his breath. He reeks of it. It's too early to drink, but I don't say that because his tone catches me completely off guard.

He steps to the side, glaring at me, waiting for me to go. I walk in, placing Callie down. She scampers off, sniffing around, glad to be home. *At least someone is.*

I watch her rush to the double doors in the kitchen, already wanting to go outside, then I turn and start to ask Kyle what's going on, but the door slams behind him and then his hand is locking around my throat. I claw at his arm and try to yell, but I can't. I can hardly breathe—he's crushing my windpipe. He backs me all the way up until my back slams into the nearest wall.

"You must think I'm an idiot!" he snarls, that familiar, angry vein popping up on his forehead. "Did you think I wouldn't find out? You haven't fucked me in *days*, but you're more than happy to sneak off and fuck *him*?"

"Kyle, I—" I still can't speak. He's squeezing harder, and I claw at his hand even more.

He sniffs the air, then flares his nostrils. His eyes are like pits of fire. I've seen him angry, but not like this. "You smell like him. You're fucking disgusting." He finally releases my throat, and I suck in a breath, collapsing to my knees. Callie is whining and cowering at my side now. "You better end whatever the hell it is you have going on with him, or I swear you will regret it, Gabs," he growls through clenched teeth.

"Kyle, I swear, I didn't mean for it to happen!"

"But it did!" He barks back. "I saw the way he looked at you every time he was around! And you know what's worse? I found his fucking business card under the table that morning I got home early—the night you were sleeping on the couch, which you never fucking do! You told me you hated that couch! He must've worn you out, huh? At first, I thought, surely my wife isn't stupid enough to bring another man into my house while I'm away. I figured maybe the card was just a coincidence, considering the fact that he had been working on our yard recently, but then you disappear for days *behind my back*! And to top it off, I see the neighbor with your fucking dog! Did you think I wouldn't find that unusual? You were good at hiding it for a while, but then I saw the emails. Ohh, the emails, Gabs. I was in total shock when I saw those." He crouches down, grabbing my face between his fingers way too roughly.

"Stop!" I beg. "Please, stop! It's over!"

"Of course it's over! You knew I wouldn't tolerate this shit! *You can't have him*—you can't have anyone but *me*!" He releases my face and looks down at me as I sob. For a while he just watches me, looking down as if I'm the dirt on the bottom of his shoe.

But then he does something that I don't see coming, not even from a mile away.

He kicks me.

Right in the face.

Kicks me.

I gasp and crumple over from the blow, and my tears come to a sudden halt. I'm dazed, unable to grasp what just happened.

"You're fucking worthless, Gabby," he spits out as he grabs a fistful of my hair, and blood slithers down my throat as I pull in air to scream. "Your father was wrong about you. You're no trophy. You're *garbage*."

He releases me, and blood pours from my nose and mouth, but all I can see are black spots. I hear his voice taunting me, yelling about how he has given me everything, and I've betrayed him. He's right, I have, but it's for this very reason that I did it.

I knew he would hit me again. I knew that his grabbing and bruising on my arms and upper thighs would turn into something so much worse. He's always been good at hurting me in places I could hide behind long-sleeved shirts and sweatpants.

I knew he could get aggressive when we were out, making sure I was always at his side, keeping me close so I couldn't socialize too much with anyone else—including my friends—but I always thought it was cute and that he couldn't handle being away from me for too long. I felt like his air.

Little did I know, his intentions weren't pure. All along,

he considered me his. In his fucked up mind, he *literally* thinks he *owns* me and, unfortunately, I didn't figure that out until it was too late.

Kyle was the first man I took seriously.

He was my all. I loved him to the core. I knew he could take care of me and my family, but as soon as we got married, he'd changed. *Everything* changed...or maybe I just hadn't paid attention to the signs.

You only see what's on the surface, and so does Marcel. Throughout, it may have seemed like I was the unfaithful wife—the ungrateful woman who couldn't appreciate the good surrounding her—but when you live in fear and under so much scrutiny, waiting for the day your husband decides to crack open a bottle of liquor, flip his switch, and dehumanize you, how can you appreciate such beauty?

Many times, since the first time he laid his hands on me, I've wanted to back out of this marriage—and maybe that feeling is why I migrated to Marcel in the first place—but unfortunately, I can't. Why? Because I have no doubt in my mind that Kyle would do something drastic to harm me. He's stated it many, many times before. In fact, I have no doubt that if it came down to it, he would *kill* me.

What I did was wrong, yes, but what Kyle does to me is pure evil. Of course, I decided to be selfish for once in my life and get a taste of what a *real* man could treat me like—a *good* man. But when I got that taste of him, it became impossible to stay away. How could I, when being a part of something with Marcel is so much better than what I have right now?

With Marcel it's real and positive and *healthy*. He isn't the man I can't have. He's the man I've *always needed*.

Kyle? He's the one I should have stayed away from.

Kyle's yelling becomes a dull hum. Callie is still barking, and he's shouting at her, telling her to shut the hell up.

I can't fight anymore.

I'm losing this battle.

The dark spots blurring my vision double in size. Breathing turns into wheezing. My fingers are damp with my own blood.

Before I slip into darkness, and allow it to become my safe place, I hear one name spill from my lips.

It's the only name I need in order to get through this— the kind of name that makes me feel protected, even when he's not around.

"Marcellus."

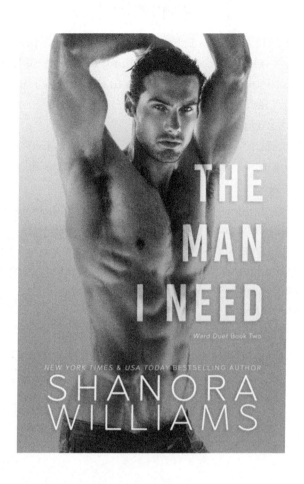

THAT CLIFFY THO!

gasps

Fortunately, you don't have long to wait for the conclusion to
Gabby & Marcel's story!

The follow up book, *The Man I Need*, will be releasing on
June 13th, 2019!

Sign Up For My Newsletter to stay updated on the

release for book 2 by visiting this link:
http://eepurl.com/dKXt-Y

If you feel the need to vent, rage, scream or chat with other readers who have read *The Man I Can't Have*, please join **TMICH SPOILER ROOM** on Facebook! :-)

FOLLOW SHANORA

Feel free to follow me on Instagram under the username @reallyshanora! I am always eager to chat with my readers there!

Join my Facebook Fan group! Just search for **Shanora's Naughty Sweethearts**!

Join My Newsletter for exclusive updates at this link: http://eepurl.com/dKXt-Y

Visit www.shanorawilliams.com for more book information and details.

WHAT TO READ NEXT?

I have plenty of books that I could share with you, but to make your life easier, I'm going to give you a few books of mine that are reader favorites and books that I loved writing. These will definitely hold you over until the release of *The Man I Need* and you can find them all on my website at www.shanorawilliams.com

If you love forbidden romances with age gaps, check out *Wanting Mr. Cane*, a juicy love story about a girl who falls for her dad's best friend.

Another juicy one is Dear Mr. Black, where a girl falls for her best friend's dad! Both are reader favorites and favorites of mine.

Trust me, the plots may seem scandalous, but I can guarantee you my forbidden romances are always full of emotion and angst.

If you love dark romances, then I have the perfect treat for you. My *Venom Trilogy* will cure any dark lover's craving!

Need something quick and hot to bide your time? Check

out my *Nora Heat Collection!* All of the Nora Heat stories are quick, easy, blazing hot reads!

The rest of my standalones are filled with angst and lots of emotions and you can find them on my website at shanorawilliams.com!

Made in the USA
Middletown, DE
14 February 2025

71306522R00226